Pr

MW00831604

(Reserved page)
Praise for D. Manning Richards's
Destiny in Sydney

Destiny in Sydney

An epic novel of convicts, Aborigines, and Chinese
embroiled in the birth of Sydney, Australia

D. MANNING RICHARDS

ARIES
BOOKS

ARIES BOOKS - Fiction
2619 Fort Scott Drive
Arlington, VA 22202
www.AriesBooks.com

ISBN 978-0-9845410-0-3

for Judy

My wife, who shares my love for Sydney and Australia, researched with me, wrote early narratives, and provided salient review comments throughout numerous drafts.

CONTENTS

	Author's Note	*ix*
	Family Tree	*xii*
	Maps	*xiii*

1.	**New Horizons**	1
2.	**Arduous Voyage**	28
3.	**Starvation**	82
4.	**Rum Corps Gentry**	147
5.	**Mutiny Against Bligh (of the *Bounty*)**	213
6.	**Mockery of Macquarie**	238
7.	**Emancipists Prevail**	281
8.	**Antipodean El Dorado**	324
9.	**Boom Times**	371
10.	**Who Are We?**	402
11.	**A New British Nation**	430

	Epilogue	*453*
	Historical Note	*455*
	Acknowledgments and Sources	*465*
	About the Author	*471*

AUTHOR'S NOTE

This novel is the result of a longtime interest in Australia and, in particular, the wonderful City of Sydney. My interest was initially stimulated by the fun-loving and likeable Australians whom my wife and I met while backpacking for six months through Europe. I was fascinated to learn back then that Sydney began as a British penal colony; so far from Britain?—it made no sense to me. But Sydney looked attractive in the travel brochures with its alluring beaches, healthy tanned people, sail-filled harbor, and dramatic Sydney Opera House under construction. So in 1973, my wife and I immigrated to Australia and worked in Sydney for two years.

I came to appreciate many traits of Australia's unique and appealing society: egalitarianism with a desire to cut down "tall poppies," unpretentiousness, mateship, a healthy balance between work and play, a religious ambivalence compared to the USA, a general disdain for authority, and a certain playful irreverence. Were these vestiges of their convict past? I wondered.

The years 1973-75 were an exciting time of unprecedented reforms by Prime Minister Gough Whitlam, including giving the Gurindji people title ownership to part of their ancestral lands, which began the process of returning traditional Aboriginal land. But how could it be that there were no Aboriginal-owned tribal lands when there were hundreds of Native American-owned reservations? In Chinatown, I was told that the Chinese had constituted a much larger percentage of the population during the gold-rush years. Evidently, the White Australian Policy, recently repudiated, had successfully kept Australia predominantly white and the huge population of nearby Asia, principally the Chinese, at bay. I felt this exclusionary policy was inherently wrong, but then thought, didn't the USA do the same thing? Just how did this country of Stone Age Aborigines, white British convicts, and Chinese deal with their differences to form the Australia I liked?

These questions and others like them, combined with Sydney's colorful past, have motivated me to research and write two historical novels covering the history of Sydney: *Destiny in Sydney* and *A Gift of Sydney*. Because Sydney is the birthplace of Australia and its largest city, the novels also include much about Australia's history.

Destiny in Sydney begins the multigenerational, multicultural, family saga in 1787, when the First Fleet of convicts left England on a perilous voyage of fifteen thousand miles to establish a penal colony in New South Wales, and ends in 1902 with women gaining the right to vote following the federation of Australia. *A Gift of Sydney* continues the story of the imaginary Armstrongs and Fongs, adds the Hudson Aboriginal family, and ends in the year 2000 during the Summer Olympic Games held in Sydney.

The families in *Destiny in Sydney* are invented, including all of the members of the Armstrong and Fong families. A Family Tree chart follows that shows the lines of descent of these families. Any resemblance of these fictional characters to actual people, living or dead, is entirely coincidental.

The principal Aborigines in the story: Arabanoo, Bennelong, Colebee, and Pemulwuy actually lived. Their stories in the early part of the novel are drawn from writings of the time and historians' accounts. The Aboriginal clans in the Sydney region were decimated by epidemics, battles, murder, and the taking of their land for white settlements and farms. By 1850 few Aborigines remained in the Sydney region. The Armstrongs and Fongs dominate the novel from 1850 to 1900, until the Aboriginal girl Baranga is introduced. She starts the imaginary Aboriginal family followed in the second novel.

The history in *Destiny in Sydney* is largely accurate. I have taken every opportunity to include historical action-adventures, and misadventures, to enhance the excitement, drama, and pace of the novel. My fictional characters often take part in actual incidents and interact with the real personages who were involved. Captain James Cook, Governor Arthur Phillip, Aborigine Bennelong, Captain Bligh (of the *Bounty*), Charles Darwin, and Mark Twain are just a few of the real people included in the novel. The portrayal of these notables and other historical figures, and the events that made them famous, are based on recorded history. Their dialogues are often taken directly from their letters, diaries, journals, memoirs, and other documents of the time.

With a commitment to accuracy, I have consulted well over two hundred sources; nevertheless, no work of such scope can be entirely free of error or controversy, especially when historians' accounts disagree. In such instances, the historical interpretations are mine alone. For readers who would like to learn more about the facts of history underpinning the story, I have appended my primary sources in Acknowledgments and Sources. In an attempt to anticipate readers' questions regarding fact or fiction, I have provided answers by chapter in a Historical Note following the novel. My website www.DManningRichards.com may be visited for additional information.

Four maps provide the locations of most of the incidents in the novel. The maps "Sydney (late 1800s)" and "Sydney Region" show places that can be visited today. One of my joys of reading historical novels is to learn the history of sights worth seeing. *Destiny in Sydney* and *A Gift of Sydney* can help prepare a tourist for his or her trip to Sydney and bring the novels alive when the sights are visited.

A Gift of Sydney will be available in 2012.

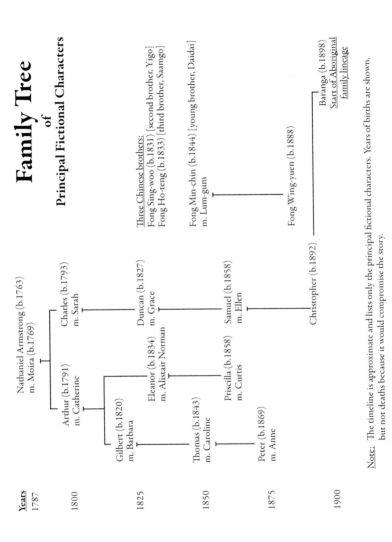

Family Tree
of
Principal Fictional Characters

Years
1787

Nathaniel Armstrong (b.1763)
m. Moira (b.1769)

Three Chinese brothers:
Fong Sing-woo (b.1831) [second brother, Yigo]
Fong Ho-teng (b.1833) [third brother, Saamgo]

Charles (b.1793)
m. Sarah

1800

Arthur (b.1791)
m. Catherine

Fong Min-chin (b.1844) [young brother, Daidai]
m. Lum-gum

1825

Duncan (b.1827)
m. Grace

Eleanor (b.1834)
m. Alistair Norman

Gilbert (b.1820)
m. Barbara

1850

Samuel (b.1858)
m. Ellen

Priscilla (b.1858)
m. Curtis

Thomas (b.1843)
m. Caroline

Fong Wing-yuen (b.1888)

1875

Peter (b.1869)
m. Anne

1900

Christopher (b.1892)

Baranga (b.1898)
Start of Aboriginal
family lineage

Note: The timeline is approximate and lists only the principal fictional characters. Years of births are shown, but not deaths because it would compromise the story.

xii

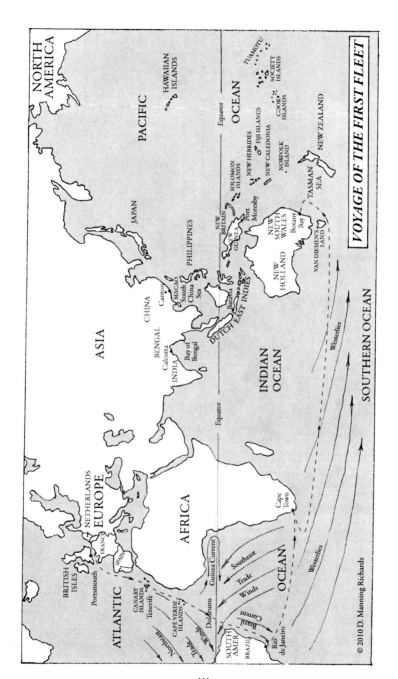

VOYAGE OF THE FIRST FLEET

© 2010 D. Manning Richards

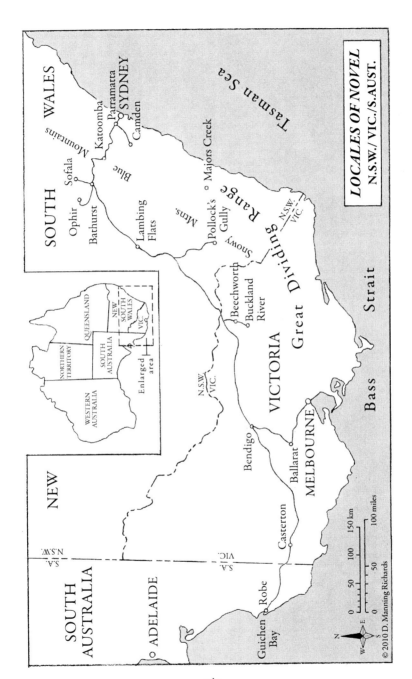

LOCALES OF NOVEL
N.S.W./VIC./S.AUST.

SOUTH WALES

SYDNEY
Parramatta
Katoomba
Camden
Blue Mountains
Sofala
Ophir
Bathurst
Lambing Flats
Majors Creek
Pollock's Gully
Snowy Mtns.
Great Dividing Range

Tasman Sea

SOUTH

NEW

QUEENSLAND
NORTHERN TERRITORY
SOUTH AUSTRALIA
WESTERN AUSTRALIA
NEW SOUTH WALES
VIC.
Enlarged area

N.S.W.
VIC.

Beechworth
Buckland River

VICTORIA

N.S.W.
VIC.

Bendigo
Ballarat
MELBOURNE

Casterton

SOUTH AUSTRALIA

S.A.
N.S.W.

S.A.
VIC.

ADELAIDE

Robe
Guichen Bay

Bass Strait

N
W   E
S

0   50   100   150 km
0   50   100 miles

© 2010 D. Manning Richards

xiv

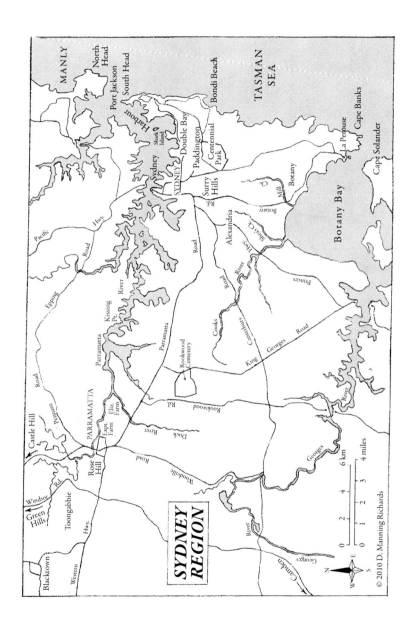

SYDNEY REGION

MANLY

North Head

Port Jackson

South Head

Harbour

Shark Island

Sydney

SYDNEY

Double Bay

Paddington

Surry Hills

Centennial Park

Bondi Beach

TASMAN SEA

La Perouse

Cape Banks

Cape Solander

Mill Ck.

Botany

Botany Rd.

Alexandria

Shea's Ck.

Rd.

Botany Bay

Pacific Hwy.

Road

Epping

River

Kissing Pt.

Parramatta

Parramatta River

Parramatta

Road

Cooks River

Princes Hwy.

Canterbury Rd.

Georges Road

King

Rookwood Cemetery

Castle Hill

Road

Pennant

PARRAMATTA

Eliz. Farm

Expt. Farm

Rose Hill

Windsor Rd.

Green Hills

Toongabbie

Western Hwy.

Blacktown

Duck River

Rookwood Rd.

Woodville Road

Georges River

Georges

Camden

River

0   2   4   6 km

0   1   2   3   4 miles

N
W   E
S

© 2010 D. Manning Richards

xv

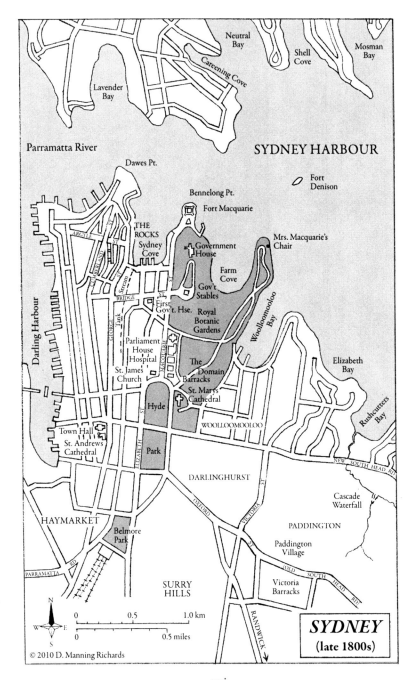

Neutral Bay

Shell Cove

Mosman Bay

Careening Cove

Lavender Bay

Parramatta River

SYDNEY HARBOUR

Dawes Pt.

Fort Denison

Bennelong Pt.

Fort Macquarie

Mrs. Macquarie's Chair

THE ROCKS

Sydney Cove

Government House

Farm Cove

ARGYLE ST

CUMBERLAND ST

Stream

BRIDGE ST

Gov't Stables

First Gov't. Hse.

Royal Botanic Gardens

Woolloomooloo Bay

Darling Harbour

GEORGE ST

Tank

MACQUARIE ST

Parliament House

Hospital

St. James Church

The Domain

Elizabeth Bay

Barracks

St. Marys Cathedral

Rushcutters Bay

Hyde

WOOLLOOMOOLOO

Town Hall

St. Andrews Cathedral

ELIZABETH ST

Park

NEW SOUTH HEAD RD

DARLINGHURST

Cascade Waterfall

HAYMARKET

OXFORD ST

PADDINGTON

VICTORIA ST

Belmore Park

Paddington Village

PARRAMATTA RD

OLD SOUTH HEAD RD

SURRY HILLS

Victoria Barracks

RANDWICK

N
W E
S

0   0.5   1.0 km

0   0.5 miles

SYDNEY
(late 1800s)

© 2010 D. Manning Richards

xvi

Destiny in Sydney

Man can will nothing unless he has first understood
that he must count on no one but himself; that he is alone,
abandoned on earth in the midst of his infinite responsibilities,
without help, with no other aim than the one he sets himself,
with no other destiny than the one he forges for himself on this earth.

—Jean-Paul Sartre
L'Être et le Néant (*Being and Nothingness*)

Chapter 1

New Horizons

Pain . . . Rolling over onto my good side, away from the ache, I try to put disturbing thoughts of death out of my half-awake mind. Gradually falling back to sleep, I'm drawn through a haze by a beckoning, distant figure . . . myself . . . standing on a gunwale. I point my cutlass down at enraged, screaming men in a smaller ship. Grappling hooks thrown and set. Cannon booming. Acrid smoke from exploding gunpowder fills my nostrils. In mortal fear, I'm screaming too, but can't hear the sound of my own voice.

The captain gives the command to board. Calum jumps, and I follow, landing on others bunched up along the rail. Losing balance . . . teetering . . . grasp a shroud to keep from falling. An American seaman misses with a pike thrust; I grab the shaft and swing my cutlass, gashing the side of his head. He drops, and I jump onto the deck. A rebel shoots me. *Ahhh-God!* Falling. A sword slashes my face. Somebody collapses against me. There's a lot of blood— *Calum's blood!*—gushing from a neck wound. I press my hand on his neck to try to stop the blood—

Marine Lieutenant Nathaniel Armstrong jolted awake. Groggily, he moved his legs to the edge of the bed, pushed himself up, and sat there rubbing his eyes. He rose unsteadily, walked to the washstand, lowered his head over the basin and poured a pitcher of water over it, supporting himself on a bent arm. Water dripped from his long hair into the basin.

Damme, why did I dream that again? he asked himself. . . . my first battle and the slow, agonizing death of Calum . . . just eighteen. It must be because I'm home.

The dawn flamed through the narrow opening between the drawn curtains and cast a long shaft of sunlight across the floor and up the wall. Nathaniel dried his face and hair in a towel and collected his thoughts. After putting on his breeches and a shirt, he walked barefooted from the bedroom, down the hall, and into the parlor, dimly lit by slivers of morning light, to a closed coffin sitting on the dining room table. Opening the lid, he looked at the corpse of his aunt, his surrogate mother, who had raised him from the age of eight. She appeared at peace with a slight smile; even in death at age fifty-nine, her fine-featured face was handsome.

He had rushed home from London on New Year's Day 1787, upon receiving a letter that she was gravely ill, but arrived too late—the final evening of her wake. An old friend, Mr. Fiddes, invited him to stay overnight with his family, but Nathaniel declined, wanting to spend a last night in his boyhood home. His aunt's body held no fear for him, nor ghosts; he had made peace with death's specter.

It's ironic, Nathaniel thought as he looked at his aunt, she'd been worried *I'd* die first. She tried to keep me from joining my father's regiment because of the war and her fear that I'd be killed—and I was afraid I was goin' to miss it! Who would have believed back then that the war with our American colonies would go on for years longer?

He recalled that she had said, "I told you courageous stories about your father and gave you adventure novels because you were being raised without a father, *not* to encourage you to follow in his footsteps. You have too much to offer to throw it all away in the marines."

But her concerns had had no effect on him, an ungrateful youth, who at sixteen joined the marines with his best mate Calum, leaving behind the only person who had stepped forward to raise him. Later, he realized that she wanted him to be around into her old age. A widow without children, she had no one else.

Feeling guilty, Nathaniel patted her cold hands resting on her Bible. Remembering how she loved poetry and appreciated his poor efforts at writing it, he opened the curtains of the window to let the sun stream in and sat down at her writing table. He would write an elegiac poem for her alone; he would not make a copy. It would express his sorrow and hope that he would see her again to make amends for his selfishness. Writing quickly, he allowed his feelings to flow:

> Death is not the end, but the beginning,
> For one whose goodness has shone.
> The sorrows of this world receding,
> You begin the journey alone.
>
> So pure of heart, you have nothing to fear,
> For no pain or suffering should you bear.
> Having lived a life of righteousness,
> A just Lord will surely provide happiness.
>
> A place where cares are relieved;
> Life's mistakes are atoned;
> Family and friends are rejoined—
> No longer alone.

He withdrew the Bible from beneath her folded hands, placed the poem between the cover and first page, and returned it to beneath her hands.

Not knowing when the undertaker would arrive to take her body to the morning funeral service, he decided to dress quickly. While shaving, it came to him that he had lost the opportunity to learn more about his relatives. He wondered why he had never drawn out his mother's older sister about their English family.

Their family name was Brooks, he knew, and they had been raised in a town near Oxford; the name of Abingdon came to mind. Both sisters had been well educated before marrying Scots, which enabled his aunt to teach school after the death of her husband. She never discussed her English family with him. He had a vague memory of a visit once by an Englishman relative, but could not remember any other visits by her family members during the nearly eight years he had lived with her.

Finished dressing, he went through a large box of items his aunt had kept for him. On the top was a tarnished silver plaque engraved with the Armstrong coat of arms: a raised, muscular arm with a clenched fist and the motto *Invictus maneo*, I remain unvanquished. Unvanquished? . . . not quite, Nathaniel thought, but a proud and valiant history, nevertheless. He held up his father's moth-eaten tartan kilt to look at the Armstrong clan colors: a plaid field of green and blue overlaid by a squared pattern of thin red lines.

His English aunt had taught him to be proud of his Scots heritage, to give him a sense of who he was and where he had come from. His great-great-grandfather was Hamish Armstrong, one of the few Armstrong leaders to live through the bloody Anglo-Scots border wars. He refused to escape to Ireland, as many of his clan had, and instead moved north ahead of the pursuing English. Although he tried farming, herding, and other endeavors, he never regained the wealth and standing lost in the wars. His displaced, hard life had dispersed the family and left Nathaniel with no close family members on his father's side.

From the bottom of the box, he picked up a creased and yellowed copy of the farewell ballad "Armstrong's Last Good Night" that his aunt had given him. She had told him the story of one of the last great Armstrong warlords, Johnie Armstrong of Gilnockie, captured by the English in 1530. Supposedly, he had written the ballad the night before the English hanged him. Nathaniel read his favorite stanzas:

> This night is my departing night;
> For here nae longer must I stay;
> There's neither friend nor foe o' mine,
> But wishes me away.

> Adieu, the lily and the rose,
> The primrose fair to see;
> Adieu, my lady, and only joy!
> For I may not stay with thee.

The undertaker and his helper arrived. Nathaniel rode with them to his aunt's church, the Church of Scotland, situated on a hill at the edge of the village. He had received his religious education there. She was to be buried on the rise behind the church.

Nathaniel sat with Mr. Fiddes and his wife during the service. After five years at the parish school, learning reading, writing, arithmetic, and the catechism, he worked for Mr. Fiddes to farm his croft and keep his animals. Nathaniel enjoyed working in the outdoors to plant, reap, milk cows, raise chickens, and slaughter pigs. By the age of sixteen, he was a strong and proficient plowman.

Mr. Fiddes had three daughters. Without a son, he took an interest in Nathaniel and treated him well. A hunter, Mr. Fiddes taught Nathaniel how to shoot. They enjoyed many outings together hunting hares on the moors.

A cold January wind whipped through the mourners gathered around the open grave. Nathaniel stood to the pastor's right, nearest the coffin. A marine for seven years, he was proud of his first lieutenant's rank and wore his full-dress uniform to honor his aunt. At five feet ten inches, muscularly lean, straight-backed, and square-shouldered, he was an imposing figure.

"Men shou'd *tremble* afore God, who foon' wickedness on the Earth an' warned *He* shall jeedge the richteous an' the *wicked"*—

Annoyed, Nathaniel stopped listening; the pastor shouldn't be using fire and brimstone at my aunt's burial, he thought, to make sinners fear Judgment Day. He scanned the mourners for familiar faces: my aunt's closest longtime friend Mrs. Stockbridge, the schoolmaster Mr. Nisbet from the school where she had taught, the butcher McCulloch, fat Corky Coutts the baker, and Constable Macdonald. The other thirty or so must be members of the church or from my aunt's school.

The pastor paused. He eyed the mourners dubiously, then continued his preaching. "Suffer nae thy mouth tae cause thy flesh tae *sin"*—

Nathaniel was elated to see Mysie, the youngest daughter of Mr. Fiddes, walking up the path. She had not been at the church service, which disappointed him. He had been looking forward to seeing her; she was his first romantic interest. Holding a baby, she stopped at the edge of the gathering, with her husband and their two young children, and made eye contact with him to convey her condolences. He nodded, acknowledging her sympathy.

Mysie was two years older than he and had been like a sister until he entered puberty. He then became so enamored of her that he was tongue-tied in her presence. Her developing figure, the sound of her voice, and the way she moved entranced him. Too afraid to express his feelings, he had admired her from a distance until she announced that she would marry soon. She was seventeen and he fifteen. Summoning all of his courage, he asked her to wait until he was old enough to marry her. She had laughed at him and said "Ye're so sweet," not taking him seriously.

Even after three children, she was still beautiful. Noticing the angry stare of her husband, he turned his eyes away from her and listened to the pastor drone on.

—"dust return tae the earth as it was, an' the speerit shall return unto God"—

Nathaniel looked at the coffin. He yearned to take one last look at his dear aunt before she was placed in the ground. She was his last link to family; he could not picture any other relatives. His mother had died while giving birth to his still-born sister when he was eight. A year later, pirates killed his father Angus Armstrong in a battle in the Bay of Bengal. He was buried at sea.

He felt his aunt had raised him well. There had been little money, but he never felt deprived. There was always enough to eat. They lived in the same rented cottage she died in. Although there had not been enough money to continue his schooling, he went on learning through his aunt's efforts. Being a teacher, she borrowed books for him on literature, art, philosophy, and government and patiently answered his questions. He read everything she brought home, including his favorite reading: adventure stories by Defoe, Smollett, Swift, Shakespeare, and others. She encouraged his interest in poetry and demanded that he use proper English grammar and pronunciation around her. To fit in with his friends, he hid this ability and spoke the Scots dialect.

—"accept ye into the kingdom o' heiven. Amen." The pastor closed his Bible.

Nathaniel and five other men solemnly stepped forward, picked up the ropes passing beneath the coffin and, after the cross supports were removed, lowered it into the grave. The others stepped back to allow Nathaniel to shovel the first scoop of earth onto the coffin. It began to snow as the mourners walked down the muddy path toward the church and their carriages.

◉

Mr. Fiddes drove Nathaniel in his buggy to meet a London-bound packet boat. They rode most of the way without talking. Approaching the harbor town, Nathaniel said, "I'm most grateful to you, Mr. Fiddes, for helping my aunt all these years when she needed a man's assistance."

"Ach, whit are neibours fir? 'Tis jist a wee bit doon the lane."

"I feel terrible that I've been away so much and wasn't here for my aunt at the end. She was a good woman and mother to me."

"Aye, that she was, a fine, guid wumman."

They rode through the town in silence.

"Where will they sen' ye next, laddie?" Fiddes asked as they entered the port.

"I don't know, Mr. Fiddes."

"D'ye think ye'll micht come back hame, after the marines, mebbe tae farm?"

"I'm landless and don't have the money to start farming. I don't know what I'm going to do, really."

Nathaniel thought of the young woman, whom he had been courting for a year, and her merchant father's request that he stop calling on her. With his aunt's death, he had now lost both women who were important to him.

The packet in sight, they completed the journey consumed in their own thoughts. Fiddes tied the horse to a post while Nathaniel removed his bags from the back of the buggy.

When they came together, Fiddes said, "Weel, ye've got yer military rank an' pay, Nathaniel."

"That's right, Mr. Fiddes, but these aren't the best of times for a

Scots military man, with no connections in England. I'm struggling on reservist's half pay and have no savings. I'm doing rather poorly right now and have to think about my future."

"Ye'll be fine, laddie, if ye don't mind me sayin' so. I've watched ye from a bairn, an' wondered how ye'd turn oot. Ye returned tae us a bonnie-lookin', strapplin', upstandin' yoong mon—an' an officer at that! Ye got yer whole life in front o' ye. Look on the guid side, Nathaniel. Ye can do whitever ye wint. Set new horizons. Don't be afraid, that's whit I say. I wish I was a yoong mon again an' in yer shoes."

"Ye're right; I shouldn't be so gloomy." Nathaniel smiled, not wanting to leave with a frown on his face, and put out his hand. "I'm going to miss you, Mr. Fiddes, more than anyone else."

The old man took his hand in both of his and shook it vigorously. "Guid luck an' Godspeed, ma laddie . . . Nathaniel."

"Thank you, Mr. Fiddes. You've always been good to me. I'll continue to write from time to time, to let you know how I'm getting on."

"An' I thenk ye fir that. Me an' the guidwife always enjoy yer letters."

"Keep yourself safe, and say goodbye for me to your wife. Goodbye, Mr. Fiddes."

Nathaniel turned and walked up the gangway to the packet boat and through its passenger cabin to the seating outside where he could see the Scottish coastline, perhaps for the last time, as the boat sailed south. He sat down and rested his head against the cabin wall.

Old Mr. Fiddes is all I have left here, he reflected. Calum's family has moved away. The truth is . . . I've never fitted in well here . . . half English and half Scots. Maybe that's why I wanted to leave so badly. I wanted something more . . . excitement? . . . to prove myself? Now's the time to make something of myself . . . but I need land—what good's a man without land?

Whoooosh. The sound of the sails, billowing on a fresh wind, caught his attention. He looked up and gazed at the majesty and power of the sails that drove the ship.

Need to focus on the future, find a place to settle, start my own family . . . but where? Not in Scotland . . . England? If I stay in the marines, maybe. Still, England has many problems . . . and heavy war debt . . . and, for some reason, I don't feel entirely comfortable there. (He could not admit to himself that he often heard conde- scension in Englishmen's voices when they talked to Scotsmen.) The Americas? Not the United States, couldn't live with rebels. Their future's poor now, having stupidly cut their ties to Britain. Canada? . . . hmm . . . perhaps. A gust of wind ran a shiver through him—no, it's too cold there, like Scotland.

Refocusing on the coastline, he saw a bank of fog rolling in and went inside.

◉

Returning to London and his marine regiment lifted Nathaniel's spirits. In the early morning of his first day back, he spent an hour meticulously polishing his uniform's silver buttons, gorget, sword, scabbard, and clasp on the white leather strap that crossed his chest and held his sword. He buffed his knee-high black leather boots to a high gloss.

While dressing, he tied a red silk sash around his waist, en- suring that the ends of the knot hung at an equal length. He placed his officer's gorget around his neck and centered it at his throat. Gathering his long, unpowdered, auburn hair together at the back of his head, he brushed it down, and then folded it up twice and tied it with a black ribbon.

Looking at himself in the mirror, he admired how his scarlet jacket with its white facing and collar contrasted with his white breeches and waistcoat. He flicked dust from the cockade decorat- ing his black cocked hat before placing it athwart on his head. Satis- fied that his uniform was fully presentable, he left to report for duty.

There was an unusual buzz of activity in the air as he walked into the officers' mess hall.

"Nate!" Second Lieutenant Tom Nichol called out, "you're back, m'lad." He walked toward Nathaniel with his arms outspread; but instead of embracing, he placed his left hand on his shoulder while shaking hands with his right. Obviously glad to see each other, they exchanged greetings as they walked over to a group of officers seated around a table eating breakfast.

"Hullo, Lieutenant," Captain George Evans said as he stood and shook hands, "how are you?"

"Fine, Captain Evans."

"Welcome hame, Nathaniel, how was yer trip?" Captain Dugald McArdle asked as he offered his hand. "An' yer aunt?"

Nathaniel shook hands around the table and told of his aunt's passing. The condolences of the officers moved him. *This* is home, he told himself.

Excusing himself, Nathaniel walked away to obtain some breakfast. While filling his plate, he noticed several officers having an animated conversation in front of the noticeboard. Sitting down to eat with his friends, he asked, "What's all the commotion about, Tom?"

"A new recruitment notice, went up two days ago, for Botany Bay in New South Wales. It's that island, er, uh, continent?—yes, unknown continent—on the other side of the world."

"That's *Terra Australis Incognita*, Tom, Latin fir 'unknown soothern land,' " Captain McArdle said. "But yer won't wint tae go there, Nathaniel, *nasty* business—convicts."

"Speak for yourself, *Dugald*," Captain Evans said, using McArdle's given name when he knew he preferred "Doug." "Should be a great adventure, Lieutenant. I've volunteered. Captain Cook explored the east coast of it in '70, claimed it for King George, and gave it the name of New South Wales. The Dutch have claimed the western part of it and call it *New* Holland, but haven't established a colony there yet."

"Ye volunteered fir the *money*, eh, George?" McArdle chided, knowing that Evans had been placed on reserve and was receiving half pay during the peace that followed the American Revolutionary War.

"That's right," Evans said. "It's good pay, Doug. I've got a wife and three-year-old son to support." He looked over at Tom who was married with two young children. "You're going to volunteer too, aren't you, Lieutenant?"

"Still thinking about it, Captain. I'd like the money but not guarding convicts."

"Officers won't have much to do with the felons, I'll wager," Evans said. "Jailers will be sent from the hulks to deal with them."

Hulks were decommissioned and demasted troop transports and warships, anchored in the Thames River and southern naval ports, used to imprison convicts overflowing from English jails since convicts could no longer be transported to America. Britain was half-bankrupted from the war with America and its allies (France, Netherlands, and Spain) that had ended in 1783. Since then, the British Parliament had been ineffective in improving the ailing economy or relieving the high unemployment that was driving desperate people into crime.

"The Hame Office is under pressure tae ship the convicts aff tae someplace," McArdle said, "so I reckon New Sooth Wales is it."

"You're not married, Lieutenant Armstrong, you should consider volunteering," Evans said. "It's only for three years. After that, you could stay on and become rich. Land will be there for the taking or cost very little. Military officers got *rich* in the Americas."

Nathaniel started to answer with "I'd—" but was cut off by McArdle.

"*That* was different, George," McArdle said. "America didnae start as a *penal* colony. It started wi' the likes o' settlers, planters, and tradesmen. Convicts were transported later, as indentured servants, tae work on plantations in Virginia, Maryland, an' other places; however, they wur never a big part of the population. Botany Bay will have naethin'—*nae* towns, *nae* plantations, *nae* businesses, *naething*—jist convicts an' Indians."

Evans persisted. "Well, there were only Indians when the first planters went to the Americas. The main thing is to get there *first* to acquire land. You can't get that in any other posting—not India, the West Indies, or Canada; it's all been taken."

Nathaniel thought of the large plantations in Virginia and the South. This could be his chance for land and a new start. Rising from his seat, he said, "I think I'll take a look at the noticeboard." He walked over and read the recruitment notice: " . . . no fewer than

200 marines, all ranks up to and including captain, to be formed into companies . . . a penal colony at Botany Bay in New South Wales . . . approximately 800 convicts, of which 200 will be women . . . guard the convicts on ship . . . form a military establishment upon arrival to protect the settlement from the natives . . . preservation of good order. . . ."

He walked back to his friends. "Who's going to lead the marines?"

"Major Robert Ross, a hard but able *Scot*," McArdle replied. "Captain Arthur Phillip is the naval commander. Dinnae know of him."

Nathaniel had heard that Major Ross was a stern leader with a reputation for looking after his men.

"Phillip's a relative unknown," Evans said. "No victories that I know of. Served in the East Indies. Evidently, the Admiralty chose him because he's transported convicts before, to Rio or somewhere in South America. Not very impressive, I daresay."

"D'ye know whether many officers have volunteered yet?" Nathaniel asked Evans.

"Don't know exactly," Evans replied. "I know Dawes put his name in . . . wants to work on his astronomy there. Captain Watkin Tench is talking about keeping a diary to write an account of the expedition."

"You seem interested in the expedition, mate," Tom said. "The regimental office has a good map of the south seas and Cook's and others' accounts of the voyage of discovery there. It's fascinating reading."

After breakfast, Nathaniel excused himself to go to the regimental office as Tom had suggested. Before he left, Tom offered to buy dinner at a public house of Nathaniel's choosing to celebrate his return. He chose The Rose and Crown, hoping to see Mary, a waitress there.

Tom knew that Nathaniel was sleeping with Mary since his courting of an attractive, young, English woman from a prosperous merchant family had fallen apart. He understood that her parents disapproved of him because he had no family and his prospects were poor. Nathaniel had told him that he was disappointed but little beyond that.

Tom had initially wooed Mary, but she preferred Nathaniel. He couldn't understand why; Nathaniel was no more handsome than himself and not nearly as entertaining. Some women must like the quiet sort, he reasoned, though Mary didn't seem the type. Regardless, he envied Nathaniel; Mary was a bit rough but very sexy. Also, she had her own room above the pub, which made everything easier.

When Tom walked through the door of The Rose and Crown, Mary threw him a kiss from behind the bar and asked him what he wanted to drink. He joined Nathaniel, who was already seated at one of Mary's tables with a drink in his hand. She delivered Tom's beer and sat down with them to chat for a few minutes. During dinner, she kept up a lively banter with Tom. Although Nathaniel ordinarily did not engage much in small talk, which was fine with Tom because he enjoyed talking, he noticed that Nathaniel had been particularly quiet throughout the evening.

"What's wrong, m'lad?" Tom asked, using one of his favorite expressions "my lad," even though he was only two years older than Nathaniel. "You seem even more mum than usual?"

Nathaniel was still upset about the death of his aunt and had considered discussing it with Tom, but decided to maintain a manly facade with him. He would discuss it with Mary instead.

"I've been thinking about my aunt. I didn't arrive in time to say goodbye to her."

"That's a pity. The same thing happened to me. I was in Charleston when my father died. It's hard."

"I found where New South Wales is," Nathaniel said to change the subject to something he wanted to discuss. "You were right when you said it's on the other side of the world. It's east of New Holland."

"What do you think of it?"

"I read some of Cook's log and Joseph Banks's papers. Banks was his botanist and described Botany Bay. Their accounts make it sound like an untouched paradise. Its location on the thirty-fourth parallel in the southern hemisphere should give it an ideal climate similar to the American Carolinas in the northern hemisphere.

They wrote that the climate's salubrious, the soil's fertile, and the Indians few and cowardly. The bay is full of fish. You've read my favorite book by Defoe, *The Adventures of Robinson Crusoe*. Doesn't it sound like that?"

"I don't know . . . How can you compare the two? Crusoe was on an island by himself, shipwrecked."

"I mean a lush island, starting fresh, a new land—the adventure of it all."

"You're *goin'* to volunteer, aren't you?" Tom asked with a grin.

Nathaniel smiled and mischievously took a long sip of his wine, keeping Tom waiting.

"Aye!"

"Me *too,* we'll go together!"

"What about your family?"

"Well, er . . . frankly, m'lad, leaving them behind probably would be a blessing. I'm not that good with children, actually. And Emma . . . you know how she spends . . . As for me, well, I don't have to tell you about my excesses." He took a swallow of his beer. "The thing is . . . we're hopelessly in debt."

Nathaniel knew that Tom and Emma competed at wasting money, but did not know their family was in jeopardy.

Tom sensed his concern. "Not to worry though. My father-in-law is well off and knows our problem, quite well, actually. He's kindly offered to take in the family until I return. I'll be earning a jolly salary and have nowhere to spend it—perfect!"

"I'd like full pay again too, to start saving."

"Always the responsible one," Tom said. Affecting an air of seriousness, he continued: "But I have an even bigger problem, which is . . . How can I say this? . . . I don't know whether I could"—he paused for effect—"put up with *you* in close quarters for *three— long—years!*"

"*Me?* what about *you!*"

Both laughed heartily.

"Well, mate, shall we agree to put up with each other and volunteer together?" Nathaniel asked as he raised his glass.

"I'd like nothing better, Nate." Tom clinked his mug against

Nathaniel's glass to seal their pact.

After Tom went home, Nathaniel ordered another claret, the favorite wine of Scotsmen. Mary served it and asked, "Wot's troublin' yer, daarlin'?" She placed her hand on his. "Yer look like the weight o' the world's on yer."

Before Nathaniel could answer, a customer called her away.

When Mary's dinner shift was over, they went to her room. Without pretense, they undressed and slipped under the covers of her bed.

"What's botherin' yer, luv?" Mary asked again.

"My only remaining family member, my aunt, who raised me and was like a mother to me, died unexpectedly. That's where I've been. I was too late to say goodbye to her and feel terrible about it."

"Did she suffer much?"

"No, it went quickly."

"How old wos she?"

"Fifty-nine."

"Ah then, she lived abaht as long as a body c'n expect these days. Even so, she wos the one 'oo raised yer, so that's a sad loss, ain't it?"

"It's just that I didn't expect it. I've been thinking about it. I feel more alone now than ever before in my life. I should have appreciated her more when she was alive."

"Ye're the thoughtful one, dearie. I like that in yer."

To console him, she drew his head to her breasts and stroked his long, auburn hair. She had a soft place in her heart for sensitive, handsome men.

◉

Ten days after Nathaniel and Tom volunteered for the New South Wales expedition, interviews were arranged with Major Robert Ross. Nathaniel reported ten minutes early to Ross's office and was directed by his secretary to wait in the anteroom. Twenty minutes later, he was shown into Ross's office. Ross was standing behind his desk going through stacks of papers. Nathaniel came to attention and saluted. Ross returned his salute and motioned him to sit in front of his desk and then returned to searching through the papers until he found the one he wanted.

"Ah, yes, Lieutenant Armstrong." Still standing, the major said, "Armstrongs... border clan... guid fighters. Had tae keep the peace between the Scots and English, eh?"

"Aye, sir," Nathaniel agreed with a slight smile.

The major walked about in the space behind his desk as he read. "I see ye have battle experience . . . um, woonded . . ." He glanced at the scar down Nathaniel's cheek. ". . . commendation fir valor . . . two years in the American insurrection." The major's head nodded. "I mysel' foucht the American rebels . . . first at Bunker Hill, a most decisive early victory. His Majesty's Marines proved their worth as a versatile force in that war. The newspapers said the marines were most coorageous, better than the army or navy." He looked for Nathaniel's response.

"Aye, sir."

"*Bloody* stupid thing we lost the war. Blasted politicians!" Ross sat down at his desk and laid down the paper. "Weel, Lieutenant, I tak' it ye understan' the nature of the assignment? Three years— ye've read the recruitment notice. Durin' the voyage, we'll protect the fleet and maintain the discipline. In Botany Bay, defend the settlement and gen'ally preserve the guid order. 'Tis a war post with guid pay. Commissioned officers cannae tak' their wives."

"I have no wife, sir."

"Guid." Ross leaned back in his chair. "I notice ye spe'k wi' an English accent."

"Yes, sir, my mother was English."

"Ye're makin' a wise decision tae volunteer, Lieutenant. I've been appointed second in command of the new colony—the *lieutenant governor* of New Sooth Wales—which can only mean one thing: His Majesty has great plans for the Marine Forces. Nae doubt, we'll soon be made the *Royal* Marine Forces."

"That's *very* good news, sir. Allow me to offer my congratulations."

"Aye. Thenk ye," Ross said perfunctorily. "Yer papers seem in order, Lieutenant," he said in a tone indicating the interview was over. "Ye'll receive yer commission when ye report tae Portsmouth, Monday next."

"Aye, sir." Nathaniel stood and saluted smartly. "Thank you, sir."

Walking away, Nathaniel was disappointed that Ross had not given him an opportunity to ask questions about specific duties, long-term plans for the colony, and when free settlers would be allowed to come.

Tom was also accepted. They traveled together to the Portsmouth docks and reported for duty. The second morning, they filled out a battery of forms. When the duty officer read that Nathaniel had suffered a gunshot wound in 1781, he ordered him to the infirmary for a medical examination. After the doctor had poked around the scar on the left side of his back and asked a few questions (Nathaniel did not tell him that the old wound pained him occasionally), he signed a medical fitness form. Nathaniel returned to the headquarters where the duty officer told him to report to the fleet's flagship HMS *Sirius*.

Nathaniel walked along the docks hoping the *Sirius* would be a line-of-battle warship. When he saw the three-masted ship, he could not believe his eyes.

This is the flagship? Nathaniel asked himself as he walked up to her. The *largest ship* of the fleet?—she's *small*. He walked alongside her, stepping off her length ... only one hundred and ten feet. Can't be much over five hundred tons. One gun deck with ten ports ... twenty guns ... hardly even a sixth-rate frigate.

He was looking for other armaments when Major Ross appeared on deck and motioned him to come aboard. Ross introduced him to his aide Captain George Evans, not caring that they already knew each other, and then went below.

"Congratulations on your selection as the major's aide, Captain," Nathaniel said. Trying to be positive, he added: "The *Sirius* looks to be a fine ship for passage."

He thinks he's been assigned to the *Sirius*, Evans thought. "You've been given command of thirty-three marines on board the convict transport *Scarborough*." Evans paused to give him a chance to digest his assignment.

Nathaniel was taken aback—a *convict* transport! "Thank you, sir. I'll do my best."

"She's the second largest transport, Lieutenant. You'll be guarding only men, some two hundred felons. You should feel fortunate . . . women convicts are sure to be more of a problem with their thirteen or so bastard children sailing with them. I've assigned Second Lieutenant Tom Nichol as your second in command."

"Thank you, sir."

"Major Ross and I will be on the *Sirius*, which will lead six merchant transports and three storeships. The other naval ship, armed with eight guns, is the tender HMS *Supply*." He pointed at a ship moored nearby.

Nathaniel saw why she was a tender and named the *Supply*. She was a two-masted, brig-rigged sloop designed to sail swiftly among the other ships of the fleet to provide communications and supplies. But at approximately seventy feet long and two hundred tons, she appeared too small for the open sea.

"Both naval ships have been completely overhauled," Evans said, "and will carry the naval contingent and some of the marine families. Around thirty of the enlisted marines have their wives with them and fifteen to twenty children. It's hoped that most of these families will choose to remain in Botany Bay as the first free settlers. The sergeant and several other marines on the *Scarborough* have their families traveling with them.

"The *Scarborough* is a chartered commercial vessel with its own master and merchant seamen. A private contractor has provisioned the ships. It shall be your job to make sure the cooks don't shortchange the convicts' and marines' daily allotment of food. You're to watch over their general health with the ship's surgeon. Your primary responsibility is to guard the convicts and establish order and regularity, which means, maintain watches, post sentinels as needed, and discipline the convicts. At night, you'll want to maintain a wat—"

"Ye two, come wi' me," Ross said, emerging in a huff from a companionway. He set a brisk pace as he strode down the gangplank, past moored ships, and wove his way around wagons and dockworkers unloading sacks and rolling barrels along the ground. Nathaniel and Evans hurried to keep up. Two large wagons rumbled by carrying male convicts, chained together and under guard. Most of them were mangy and poorly clothed. Nathaniel's look was met by mostly downcast eyes, but a few stared defiantly back at him. Ahead, he saw two naval officers walking toward them.

"That's Captain Arthur Phillip," Evans said to Nathaniel out of the corner of his mouth. "He'll be governor of the new settlement . . . speaks *five* foreign languages. Lieutenant Philip Gidley King is his adjutant."

As Captain Phillip neared the marine officers, he smiled.

"Good day to you, Major Ross."

"Guid day, Captain," Major Ross replied and gave a brusque salute. Nathaniel and Evans also saluted.

Nathaniel's first impression of Phillip, the leader of the expedition, was not favorable. His bearing was that of an unassuming, fifty-year-old schoolmaster. Shorter than average height, narrow-shouldered and slight of build, his stature did not command respect. Framed by a white powdered wig, his thin face was pinched toward the center by close-set eyes, a long nose, and a pointed chin. As he spoke, Nathaniel noticed that he was missing a front tooth.

"I've only a short time to inspect a few of the ships before I must return to London," Phillip said, "so I'd be obliged if you could tell me the status of your preparations, my dear Major."

"Aye, sir, certainly. I've chosen all of my officers an' assigned them tae their ships." Then he began spewing a litany of problems: "There's an ootbreak of ship fever among the felons on the *Alexander*. Five have died, and I'm concerned it'll spread tae my marines. The contractors, over whom I have *nae* control, are makin' slow progress on the cabin modifications, and the cabins of my commanding officers are *inferior* tae those of the civilian officers. Munitions have *nae* arrived. The victualer, obviously tae save money, is substitutin' rice fir flour, which *winnae* provide the antiscorbutics needed tae fight scurvy." Finished, he looked askance at Phillip.

"Thank you, Major, for your diligence. I shall include your concerns in my discussions with Lord Sydney at the Home Office and with the Admiralty." He turned to Lieutenant King, who was writing in a journal. "Lieutenant, note that rice is *unacceptable*, determine the status of munitions, and ask Surgeon General White to remove transportees with fever."

Seeing that Ross was impatient, Phillip said, "Major, I don't wish to hold you any longer, though I would like you to assign one of your officers"—indicating with a nod either Evans or Nathaniel—"to accompany me on my inspection so that he may report back to you."

Ross turned and ordered: "Lieutenant Armstrong, accompany Captain Phillip, keep guid notes, an' report back tae me." With that, the men exchanged salutes and Ross and Evans walked away toward the transport *Prince of Wales*.

"Shall we start with the flagship *Sirius*, Mr. King?" Captain Phillip asked in a genial tone to his aide.

Phillip moved quickly through the ship directing modifications to be made. He counted the number of guns and carronades and asked King to determine when the last three of ten extra six-pounder guns he had ordered would arrive. In his own cabin, he noted there were no wine glasses and that he needed a map holder near his desk. Nathaniel was impressed by Phillip's command of details, and the way he worked pleasantly with his aide.

They next inspected the *Supply*, and then partway through inspecting the transport *Alexander*, Phillip said "We are running out of time, Mr. King" and looked down the line of ships along the wharf. "Is the *Lady Penrhyn* docked nearby?" he asked the master of the *Alexander*.

"She's the third ship down, sir," the master replied, pointing.

On the way there, Phillip said, "She's to carry most of the women. I want to ensure they are not ill treated."

Phillip, King, and Nathaniel followed the civilian master of the *Lady Penrhyn* below deck. The women's prison was cold and damp; some women were wrapped in blankets to stave off the winter chill while others shivered in filthy rags.

Phillip asked a woman: "When were you last above deck for fresh air and sunlight?"

"Not since I've bin put in this hole ova ten days ago, Guv'nor."

Returning to the upper deck, Phillip asked, "Master Sever, why have the women been confined below deck?"

"We *can't* let 'em on deck, sir. They'd distract my crew an' the dockworkers."

"My dear fellow, you know as well as I, that kept below many of these women shan't survive the journey, and the others will arrive sickly. We must improve their health *before* the voyage begins."

The master looked pained. He wanted to deal with the women convicts as little as possible. Finally, he said, "Beg pardon, sir, but the felons are *not* the navy's responsibility."

"Am I to understand that you refuse to honor my request, Master?"

"No sir. I'll bring 'em up from time t'time, when *I see* fit."

"You are on a month-to-month contract, are you not?"

"Well, not exactly . . . my understandin' is that we've won the contract to Botany Bay."

"No, you are incorrect, sir. You've won a *month-to-month* contract that hired your transport at a rate of ten shillings per ton per month—*at my pleasure*. I'm meeting tomorrow with Lord Sydney, His Majesty's secretary of state for the Home Department." In his most imperious tone, Phillip asked, "Shall I take up your recalcitrance with Lord Sydney?"

The master crossed his arms and rocked back and forth, eyes down, as he made up his mind. "That won't be necessary. I'll start bringin' the *doxies* up, in shifts, straight away . . . *sir*."

Phillip turned to the *Lady Penrhyn*'s commanding marine officer. "Lieutenant, *assist* the good master and provide security when the women transportees are brought to the upper deck."

"Yes, sir," the lieutenant said as he saluted.

To Nathaniel, Phillip said, "Lieutenant, make a note to ask Major Ross to order his marines to assist *all* civilian captains to bring their transportees up once a day for fresh air and exercise. The marines are to ensure that the women on the transports are not abused by any of the men."

"Aye, sir," Nathaniel said.

"Thank you, Master Sever, for obliging me," Phillip said. "While the transportees are your responsibility en route, they are mine once we arrive. I need them in good health to establish the colony at Botany Bay. This is but the first of many fleets, mind you. The East India Company expects you to assist in its *long-term* profitability through convicts to Botany Bay and tea from China. Do we understand each other?"

"Yes sir," murmured Master Sever.

Phillip bade him goodbye and walked down the gangplank.

Following Phillip and King, Nathaniel heard Phillip say, "The master thinks this is a scheme simply to rid England of felons. If that were so, the Beauchamp Committee would have decided on West Africa to transport the convicts. It's much closer and would be less costly. I wish I could share with him the strategic importance of Botany Bay."

"To establish a foothold in the new continent before the Netherlands and France do," King said.

"Yes, Mr. King. They are our adversaries in the contest to gain dominance over trade in the East Indies. Our economic destiny depends on trade with India, Malaya, and China, now more than ever, since the loss of America.

"Our Botany Bay settlement may play a pivotal role in this inevitable struggle. According to Captain Cook's log, there are tall, straight pines for masts, spars, and ship's timber on Norfolk Island and flax ideal for sail cloth and clothing. I expect this is why I recently received orders to colonize Norfolk Island as well as Botany Bay. The region's raw materials may prove invaluable to our East Indies' fleet. In the not too distant future, Botany Bay may well serve as a safe haven for refitting our ships during war with the Dutch or French."

This strategic information captivated Nathaniel's imagination. The expedition suddenly took on a national importance far beyond anything he had previously imagined.

"What of the list I've requested of each transportee's conviction, term of sentence, and skills, Mr. King, and other essential information?"

"It's a very disorderly and confusing situation, sir. The provost marshal told me the convicts' papers are to be delivered to the transport captains at the same time that the convicts are delivered. But this hasn't been done, for the most part, or the ship captains don't know where the papers are. Perhaps the contracting agent has them. I intend to get to the bottom of this."

"You won't have time, my dear boy," Phillip said. "Impress the provost marshal that this is *his* responsibility. We need to know the terms of their sentences and skills *before* we sail. I intend to assign them work en route to keep them out of trouble and to be useful upon arrival. The thought of arriving with eight hundred people in varying conditions of ill health without any idea of their capabilities is frightful."

Nathaniel decided to take a chance. "Captain Phillip, sir, if I may make a suggestion?" He stood at ramrod attention, eyes straight ahead, expecting Phillip's censure for speaking when not spoken to. To his surprise, Phillip nodded for him to proceed.

"As there is a commanding marine officer on every transport, perhaps we could determine what information the civilian captains have and supplement it with interviews of the convicts."

"Splendid idea, Lieutenant, splendid!" Phillip said. "If the provost marshal provides the information as well, we'll have a cross-check. Capital idea. Your name again is Lieutenant . . . ?"

"Armstrong, sir."

"Lieutenant *Armstrong*, I appreciate clear thinking *and* initiative. Pray add 'interviews' to your list of directives for Major Ross." Phillip resumed walking and issuing orders. "Mr. King, add venereal and infectious diseases to your list. Have the surgeon general remove any diseased transportees already on board and ask *again* that diseased convicts not be sent to us for transport."

When Nathaniel returned to the *Sirius* and gave his report to Major Ross, he mentioned his suggestion that the marine commanding officers could assist Captain Phillip by interviewing the convicts.

" 'Tis Captain Phillip's problem—*nae* oors!" the major said. "Ye'd do weel tae tend tae yer *own* business, Lieutenant."

It was dusk when Nathaniel left the *Sirius* looking for his assigned ship, the *Scarborough*. The port naval officer told him she was anchored offshore and arranged a boat to take him to her. Still smarting from Ross's rebuke, Nathaniel consoled himself that the *Scarborough* was one of the largest ships in the fleet.

Scarborough's boatswain piped him aboard. Nathaniel saluted aft toward the captain's quarterdeck.

"Welcome aboard, sir," Tom said, grinning as he saluted. "Congratulations on your command."

Returning Tom's salute, Nathaniel said, "Thank you, Lieutenant Nichol."

As they walked away from the watch, Tom said, "Someone did us a favor, Nate, by putting us together."

"It was George Evans. He's Ross's aide. I thanked him."

"Good for him. But where have you been all day? I was afraid you got a medical discharge. Ha ha."

Nathaniel told of his chance meeting with Captain Phillip and gave a glowing account of him and his aide King.

"I'm pretty well settled," Tom said. "Seems a solid ship." He added in a low voice: "Bad luck to be assigned to one of the *convict* ships, eh?"

Nathaniel commiserated in an equally hushed voice: "Aye, I'm not happy about it, but there are only two naval ships out of eleven."

"I've been through most of the ship. The ship's master and surgeon are quite agreeable lads. Let me show you around, starting with your quarters."

Nathaniel was pleased with his small cabin fitted out in the stern of the upper deck beneath the quarterdeck. It had wood partition walls and a hinged, lockable door.

"My *suite* is next to yours," Tom said. As Nathaniel stepped out of his cabin, Tom pulled aside a canvas sheet to reveal a seven- by six-foot space defined by two canvas sheets, Nathaniel's wall, and the curving hull of the ship. "The usual," Tom said. "I've already selected a private to serve as our orderly. I assumed we'd share, however, if you'd rather have your own . . ." Nathaniel shook his head. Good, thought Tom, pleased that their difference in rank continued to present no awkwardness between them.

At the morning muster, Tom introduced Sergeant Westover to Nathaniel. It took only a few answers from the short, stocky, gruff marine for Nathaniel to be pleased that he had been assigned an experienced, no-nonsense sergeant. From the quarterdeck, Nathaniel told his marines, standing at attention, exactly what he expected of them and then inspected each man's uniform and weaponry. The sergeant ordered the marines to retire to their quarters and prepare for Nathaniel's inspection.

The marines' quarters were in the stern of the middle deck. The convicts' prison occupied most of the remainder of the deck, except for the bow where firewood, sails, ropes, and extra clothing were stored. Thick bulkheads, filled with nails, sealed both ends of the prison.

After Nathaniel inspected the marines' quarters, Tom suggested he look through the bulkhead separating the marines from the convicts. Spaced every five feet, loopholes through the bulkheads provided a place for surveillance and to fire through in the event of a riot. Nathaniel swiveled aside the cover over a loophole and looked into the prison. He could barely make out the convicts in their murky space.

Stepping over a hatch next to the bulkhead, Nathaniel thought to visit the cargo hold below. A lantern was lit, and Westover led the way down the ladder. They walked along a central aisle, between high stacks of cargo, until they were beneath the prison.

The foul smell of fetid bilge water nauseated Nathaniel. He pointed up at a sliver of light coming through the planking above.

"I don't much like that. You'll have to inspect the planking daily, Sergeant, especially in the corners, to ensure the convicts haven't pried up any planks to gain access to the supplies. Lieutenant Nichol, make the cargo hold a watch station, so a marine will be down here at all times. Let's visit the convicts' prison now."

A secured hatchway through the upper deck provided the only access into and out of the prison. A vile smell rose from below as a marine private opened the solid iron hatch. Westover led the way down the ladder followed by two armed privates, Tom, and then Nathaniel. The repulsive smell of body odor and excrement sickened Nathaniel. Part way down the stairs, his stomach churning, he heard Westover's gravelly voice:

"Stand back from the ladder yer stinkin', scurvy rogues."

Nathaniel stopped at the landing and lowered his head to look into the dimness of the prison. There were no portholes. Filtered light entered through two hatches in the upper deck, secured by bolted-down iron gratings. The convicts were quiet; they had stopped talking when the marines came down the rungs. His eyes adjusting to the gloom, Nathaniel made out several groups of men standing nearby, looking at him. Other men were lying in two tiers of stacked shelves, braced between the decks, running continuously along both sides of the hull. The shelves were divided into seven- by six-foot bunks to sleep four transportees each. Still more men sat at two, long, parallel tables, nailed to the floor, that ran the length of the central area.

The convicts, in chains, were staring at Nathaniel, not knowing what to expect. He choose not to proceed further into the prison, unwilling to bow his head to the convicts at each overhead crossbeam.

"Go wan, yer lot, we're jus' inspectin' the brig," Sergeant Westover told the gawking convicts.

Nathaniel smelled an overwhelming stench near him. Looking down, he saw several slop buckets grouped together at the side of the ladder to be emptied overboard. Deciding he had seen and smelled quite enough, he quickly climbed the ladder fighting a strong urge to vomit. Exiting the hatchway, he gulped in great breaths of fresh air and repeatedly swallowed to settle his queasy stomach.

Over the next week, Nathaniel established procedures for *Scarborough*'s marines: four-hour watches, morning exercises, inspections, drills, and manning a rowboat to circle the ship at night to discourage escape. He made a schedule for the marines to bring up sixteen convicts at a time, from four bunks, to exercise for thirty minutes each day on the upper deck before bringing up the next group.

On March 16 the *Scarborough* sailed from Portsmouth Harbour to join other ships of the fleet assembling at the Motherbank, an anchorage off the northeast coast of the Isle of Wight. The Home Office wanted the fleet to depart in April, but Phillip refused to sail until the ships were fully provisioned. During the wait, the surgeon general, John White, arranged for two pest-infested ships to return to Portsmouth to be fumigated. Rumors circulated among the fleet that the delay was giving the Dutch time to form a squadron of warships to oppose the establishment of the colony at Botany Bay.

A swallow-tailed pennant was hoisted up *Sirius's* mizzenmast on May 7 signaling that Captain Phillip, now the commodore of the fleet, was on board. Expectations were high that they would soon set sail, although still short of certain essential stores and munitions and replacement clothes for the women convicts.

On Sunday morning, May 13, Phillip ordered *Sirius's* flagman to hoist the signal flag directing the fleet to weigh anchor. It took hours for the ships to make final preparations, unfurl the sails, and maneuver into position for. In the afternoon, under cloudy skies, with a fresh breeze and a leading wind, the fleet left the Motherbank astern.

Nathaniel looked fore and aft at the ships of the fleet. He was enthused by the pure audacity of their expedition. The naval warships HMS *Sirius* and HMS *Supply* led the way; followed by the convict transports *Alexander, Scarborough, Prince of Wales, Charlotte, Friendship,* and *Lady Penrhyn*; and bringing up the rear, the storeships *Borrowdale, Fishburn* and *Golden Grove.* All sailed one after another around the Needles, high pointed chalk formations at the westernmost tip of the Isle of Wight, and out into the English Channel.

We must be transporting the largest number of people over the longest distance ever, he marveled. My fellow officers are a congenial lot, and Captain Arthur Phillip seems a compassionate and able commander. The fleet is ready, more or less. And the convicts haven't caused any serious problems—yet.

Looking over at Tom, Nathaniel saw that he was holding his wife's embroidered shawl that she had given him on impulse at the last moment of their parting. He was staring dolefully at the distant shore. Nathaniel walked over and placed an arm around his friend's shoulders.

"Well, mate, we're off on our *grand* adventure!"

Tom relaxed. He smiled and offered his hand. "Here's to easy, clear sailing, m'lad."

Nathaniel shook his hand. "Aye, Tom, calm seas and a bonnie wind."

Chapter 2

Arduous Voyage

Nathaniel stood on the quarterdeck of the *Scarborough* observing the ships of the fleet forming a line to receive orders from the officers on the *Sirius*. He counted nine ships, including the *Sirius*. After four days at sea, the two ladies, the *Lady Penrhyn* and the *Charlotte,* had established themselves as the slowest ships. They would be the last in the succession of ships to pass within hailing distance of the *Sirius*'s stern. As the *Scarborough* approached the *Sirius*, Nathaniel, Tom, and Sergeant Westover saluted Major Ross, Lieutenant King, and Captain Evans, who returned their salutes from the quarterdeck of the *Sirius*.

"GOOD MORNING, LIEUTENANT ARMSTRONG," King called out through a speaking trumpet. "REPORT."

Nathaniel returned his greeting through a trumpet and reported:

"ALL PRESENT AND ACCOUNTED FOR. NO PROBLEMS, SIR."

Evans took over the trumpet from King to convey the orders of the day.

"FIRST, COMMODORE PHILLIP HAS ORDERED THAT THE IRONS MAY BE REMOVED FROM WELL-BEHAVED CONVICTS—TO MAKE THEM MORE COMFORTABLE. SECOND, HE ORDERS THAT THE CONVICTS ARE TO BE INTERVIEWED, AS PREVIOUSLY

DISCUSSED. DO YOU UNDERSTAND?"

"AYE. I UNDERSTAND, SIR," Nathaniel called back and saluted.

As the *Scarborough* sailed away from the *Sirius*, Nathaniel said, "Sergeant, I want you to rely on your corporals to choose whose irons may be safely removed. Tell them that I want the irons left on anyone who seems to be the *least bit* threatening. I don't want any problems. This should be a reward for good behavior, not a right."

"Most of them are so seasick, they can't cause much trouble," Tom said.

"Probably, but as a precaution, double the watch, at least for the next few days." Nathaniel looked up at patches of blue sky showing between the clouds. "Sergeant, have a table and chair brought on deck at midday for the interviews. Bring the felons up to me individually, I want to interview them in private."

"Yus, sir." Sergeant Westover saluted.

On the fourth and last day of interviewing, Nathaniel talked to a diffident, soft-spoken convict with a worried look on his thin, drawn face. The man gave his name as Robert Fox and said he was a farmer. Sensing that the man was concerned about something, Nathaniel asked, "Do you have something you want to tell me?"

Apprehensively, Fox looked around to see if anyone was listening. "No, sir."

Nathaniel engaged him in conversation and told him that his knowledge of farming would make him a valuable man in the new colony. Nearing the end of the interview, Nathaniel said, "If you have something useful to tell me, you'll be rewarded."

"I'm jus' a simple farmer an' don't want no trouble, Lieutenant."

"Is there trouble I should know about?"

Fox shrugged. "I dunno."

Nathaniel considered how to coax the information from him.

"You don't want to be drawn into something that could get *you* into trouble. Is that it, Fox?"

"That's right, sir."

"Ah . . . well . . . now that you've told me that, I'll know you weren't part of anything that might happen."

"Thank you, sir."

"Of course, you could be forced by the others to pick sides, whether you like it or not. You don't want that to happen, do you?"

"No sir, Lieutenant."

"You know my name is Lieutenant Armstrong?"

"Yes sir."

"Well, I can help you, Fox. You're going to be under my care for many months. I can solve this problem for you and make your life easier. Give me some idea of what I should be concerned about."

"I can't say nothin', Lieutenant Armstrong, or I'll be in trouble if they 'ear."

Nathaniel lowered his voice and confidentially said, "Anything you tell me shall be kept secret between you and me. I'll look into it in a day or two myself, without telling anyone that I heard it from you or anyone else. No one else shall know. If there's anything to it, I'll reward you in private. Now that's fair enough, isn't it?"

"I don't know, sir. I jus' 'eard some things. Maybe you can ask some of the others, now that you know somethin's brewin'."

Speaking quietly, so as not to alarm him, Nathaniel pressed him.

"You've raised it, Fox. You have to give me some idea of what to look into. You can trust me, man."

"There's daft talk of tryin' to tike ova the ship," Fox whispered.

"Who's talking?"

"I don't know, sir. Like I said, I jus' 'eard things."

"Come on, my good man . . . in for a penny, in for a pound. *Tell* me their names. I want to help you, Fox, if you'll let me." Seeing he was frightening him, Nathaniel reassured him. "I gave you my word, as a gentleman, that I'll keep this a secret between us. *Don't* you trust me?"

"I'll be *killed* if they or any of their mates fin' out I tol' you, Lieutenant Armstrong. Y'can't tell Capt'n Marshall or nobody."

"Agreed. Who's been talking?"

Fox's answer was barely audible: "Grafise an' Farrell." Fear made his eyes tear. "Please, sir, don't tell no one I tol' you. I'll be killed in me sleep, I will."

"Don't worry, Fox. I gave you my word."

Nathaniel remembered seeing Grafise and Farrell talking surreptitiously on deck during exercise periods. Philip Farrell was an unremarkable man who said he had been a boatswain's mate, but Thomas Grafise was a different matter. He was a proud, haughty, former master of a French privateer who was quite capable of sailing the ship to France, which lay to the east.

The next day, Nathaniel asked Sergeant Westover to question the marine guards whether any convicts had been seen furtively talking together. When the sergeant reported back that Grafise and Farrell had been seen suspiciously huddling and whispering, Nathaniel had them shackled and chained together.

The sea was calm the following morning when Nathaniel and Sergeant Westover climbed into a waiting longboat where Grafise and Farrell were already seated, guarded by marines. They were rowed to the *Sirius*, as ordered by Major Ross. The two accused convicts were brought before Captain Phillip and Major Ross, acting as judges. Nathaniel presented the charges against them supported by testimony from a corporal and private. Grafise and Farrell denied all charges.

Captain Phillip summarized the charges. "So the evidence against these men is that they've been seen by the corporal and private, as well as yourself, Lieutenant, talking together in a suspicious way, although no one has actually heard them conspiring to take over the *Scarborough*. Am I correct?"

"May I speak to you and Major Ross in private, sir?" Nathaniel asked.

After the room was emptied, Nathaniel said, "Inasmuch as Grafise and Farrell have denied the charges, I must tell you that during my interviews, one of the convicts told me that he had *heard* them making plans to take over the *Scarborough*."

"Whit's his name?" Major Ross asked.

"I had to pry the information out of him," Nathaniel said, trying to avoid answering Ross's direct question. "He looked worried about something, so I asked him if—"

"*Whit's* his name, Lieutenant," Ross interrupted, "an' *why* isn't he here givin' testimony?"

"I told him that I wouldn't divulge his name, sir, and that I would try to reward him in some—"

"This is *preposterous!*" Ross said. "We dinnae make *deals* wi' *convicts*, Lieutenant! Whit's his name? I wint him here tae testify!"

"He'll be killed for snitching, Major Ross. I gave him my word! His skills will be most importan—"

"*Ach*, that's *quite enoogh!*" Major Ross said. "*I'm orde—*"

"*Just* a moment, pray, Major," interrupted Captain Phillip, before Ross could order Nathaniel to divulge the convict's name. "How did you obtain this information again, Lieutenant Armstrong?"

Without using Robert Fox's name, Nathaniel explained that he had sensed that the convict had something to tell him, how he had complimented his skills and asked about his family to gain his confidence, and then had offered to reward him in some way if the information was valuable.

Ross interrupted Nathaniel's explanation. "If ye promised tae *reward* him tae obtain the information, then it has nae value whitsoever."

"Although you would agree, would you not, Major, that there appears to be reason for *some* concern?" Phillip asked.

"Weel . . . yes sir, seein' how the two o' them have been seen actin' suspiciously . . . an' Grafise is capable of sailin' the ship."

"I think we should leave it at that then. Find them guilty of conspiring, limit their lashes to two dozen each for mutinous behavior, and move them from the *Scarborough* to different ships to separate them. What do you say, my good Major?"

Ross put a hand to his chin. "Hmmm . . . I agree, sir."

After the trial concluded, Nathaniel handed Phillip his report from interviewing the *Scarborough* transportees.

"Your report is the first I've received, Lieutenant Armstrong. Since we're all here, I'd like you to summarize your findings for us. Mr. King and Captain Evans, pray move your chairs over here by us."

Nathaniel decided to keep his impromptu presentation short.

"I compared the partial information Master Marshall had with what I learned from the interviews. Most of the convicts on the *Scarborough* are common thieves from cities and towns. Only a few have committed violent crimes. While many claim to have been caught in their first or second thievery, I daresay that many appear to have devoted their lives to criminality. As to age, most are in their mid-twenties, but range from ten years old to sixty-six. Few are able to read and write." He paused to see if anyone had questions so far.

"What of their trades and occupations, Lieutenant?" Phillip asked.

"Regrettably, sir, well over half said they were common laborers, often unemployed. The trades and occupations of the others are mostly useless to us, such as a ragman, street peddler, and seaman. The ten year old was a chimney sweep. I separately listed in my report those artificers possessing the most useful skills." He paused again.

"Can you recall the kinds of artificers, especially those trades necessary to start our new colony?" Lieutenant King asked.

"From memory, Lieutenant King, I listed over 30 convicts out of the 205 as having useful skills. I recall two carpenters and a cabinet-maker, a cooper, a bricklayer, stonecutter . . . fisherman, fishmonger, and a waterman . . . a baker, two butchers, a cobbler, tailor, barber, blacksmith . . . a domestic and a gardener . . . and a watchmaker—oh, and a farmer. There are others that I've forgotten." He paused for the third time.

"Thank you, for the summation of your findings, Mr. Armstrong," Phillip said.

"Aye, thank ye, Lieutenant," Major Ross said, pleased with the brief presentation.

◉

The morning of the twenty-first day at sea, Nathaniel saw a dark triangular form piercing the flat southern horizon. Enjoying the balmy weather, he walked over to the gunwale, leaned on it, and stared at the new shape on the horizon.

Activity on the nearby *Alexander* caught his attention. A white form was thrown overboard that splashed into the sea. He knew it was a body sewn into its bedsheet or hammock and thanked goodness that he had been assigned to a healthy ship.

Master John Marshall emerged from his cabin. "Mornin', Nathaniel," he said as he approached him, "that peak be our first port of call."

To encourage a friendly working relationship, Nathaniel had asked the master to call him by his first name when they were alone. Marshall had reciprocated by asking Nathaniel to call him John. A cordial relationship had developed, and the master often invited Nathaniel and Tom to his table for dinner and conversation.

"Good morning, John, nice to see land again. Will we reach port today?"

"More like tomorrow evening, if this nor'easter holds. That be the volcanic mountain of Pico del Teide, over twelve thousand feet high, occupying most of the island of Tenerife in the Spanish Canaries. We'll anchor beneath her snowcapped top in the port of Santa Cruz."

Silhouetted against the clear azure sky, the conical peak seemed to grow out of the sea with each passing hour. It reached its magnificent zenith when they dropped anchor opposite the town of Santa Cruz on June 3. The slow *Charlotte* was the last to arrive, just before dark.

Up close, the conical, volcanic mountain appeared barren and inhospitable to Nathaniel. The close hills were harshly jagged, dark brown, and treeless. An uninviting, black sand beach sat in front of the town, which was unremarkable, except for its white appearance that contrasted favorably with the bleakness of the surrounding scenery. The temperature was a comfortable seventy-two degrees and the sky clear blue.

The broad bay, sheltered by high hills, held a large number of ships, many of them slavers, displaying flags from ten or more countries. The busy harbor attested to the fact that the Canary Islands were well positioned in the Atlantic sea lanes to provide convenient anchorage and provisions.

The Marquis de Branceforte, governor of the Canary Islands, invited Commodore Phillip to dinner at Government House. He had heard that Phillip spoke fluent Spanish and was anxious to learn more about his voyage. Nathaniel was not among the officers Phillip chose to attend the affair.

In compliance with Phillip's directive, Nathaniel oversaw the shackling of the transportees while in port. He increased the number of guards during exercise periods to discourage any thoughts of escape or mutiny. After the daily routine was established, Nathaniel left Tom in command while he and three marines accompanied Master Marshall into Santa Cruz to purchase needed provisions for the ship.

The next day, the ship's surgeon invited Nathaniel to join him to see the sights of the town. As they approached the docks, Nathaniel noticed the surgeon's money pouch hanging from his sash. So not to offend him, he casually said, "When I was on the docks yesterday, we had to fight our way through a mob of pickpockets, aggressive street prostitutes, and grabbing beggars." Appreciating the discreet warning, the surgeon smiled and made a show of placing the money pouch into an inside, buttoned coat pocket.

While walking through the town, they came on a slave auction in front of the fort Castillo de San Juan. The spectacle of miserable black men, women, and children being sold disgusted Nathaniel. Seeing Englishmen bidding, he said:

"I thought Parliament outlawed slavery in Britain."

"It did, over ten years ago, but not in the colonies," the surgeon said. "These wretches are most likely going to the British West Indies where slavery is still permitted."

Just before sunrise on the fifth day at anchorage, Nathaniel was awakened by a general alarm from the nearby *Alexander*. The commanding marine officer of the *Alexander* yelled across to him that a convict named John Prescott had escaped during the night on the ship's jolly-boat. He asked Nathaniel to launch a search party.

A half an hour later, a detachment of marines sat in a longboat bobbing beside the *Scarborough*. About to descend on the ship's ladder, Nathaniel shouted down to Sergeant Westover:

"D'ye have anyone down there, Sergeant, who speaks Spanish? I want to look in the slums where the fugitive Prescott may have sought refuge."

"Corporal Pettingale, 'ere, says 'e speaks some Spanish, sir."

Nathaniel was turning to descend when Master Marshall called to him from the quarterdeck: "Lieutenant Armstrong, a word, if you please." They met on the stairs to the quarterdeck.

"I don't want to interfere, Nate," the master said quietly, "but do you want some advice?"

"Of course, John, anything."

"You won't be findin' him in town, in my opinion, or anywhere east or north of us. During the night, the tide was goin' out, the current was southerly, and there was an eight-knot north wind. If he be as weak as most of these convicts, he couldn't make land for two to four miles lee of us. There be only a few southern coves down there where he could put in. I'd look in each one for his boat. He shouldn't be too far away, after his hard row."

"Thanks, John. That's splendid advice. That's where I'll look."

"Here, this might help." Marshall held out his brass telescope.

"Thank you, I'll take good care of it."

Tom was left in command. Nathaniel asked him to tell Ross where he was going to search.

Shortly after Nathaniel and his search party had rowed away, Major Ross and a detachment of marines rowed over to the *Alexander*. As Tom was rowed to the *Alexander* to meet Ross, he heard the major loudly reprimanding its commanding marine officer and replace him. Ross then led three longboats into Santa Cruz, where he told the Spanish governor of the escape and gained the aid of the police to search the town.

At the entrance to the second cove, Nathaniel saw through the telescope what appeared to be the stern of a rowboat deep within the rocky cove surrounded by steep cliffs.

"That could be him. I want the fore and aft oarsmen to take us in, very quietly." Nathaniel pointing at the four men in the middle of the boat. "You men stow your oars. No talking from here on in. Stay by the boat when we land. I'll discipline anyone who makes unnecessary noise. The sergeant and I will go in to see if it's him. Join us only if you hear shots."

Nathaniel and Westover were landed on a small sand beach just inside the mouth of the cove. The sergeant carried a short-barreled, marine sea service musket loaded with small shot. Nathaniel held a pistol. Bending low and moving quickly, they made their way over the rocks and walked silently along the face of the cliff. They were apprehensive; *Alexander's* marine officer had said Prescott could be armed.

It was *Alexander's* jolly-boat, all right, partially hidden behind a boulder. They followed a single pair of fresh footprints from the boat into a ravine of scrubby small trees, waist-high bushes, and grasses. Losing the tracks in the dense undergrowth, they searched about until Westover found footprints along the side of a streamlet. The footprints led them to a gap in the cliff's face.

The gap ran to the top of the cliff, more than a hundred feet above. It was steep, overgrown, and strewn with large boulders, but climbable. The sergeant looked at Nathaniel, who nodded up, meaning only one thing: Let's start climbing. They climbed quietly through the jumble of weeds, prickly vines, and small bushes, boulder to boulder.

Ting.

The faint sound of metal against metal. Westover was slightly ahead and signaled stop with his hand. Nathaniel had heard the metallic sound too. Both men listened.

A man's head suddenly popped up above bushes fifty feet above and looked down at them. In the instant that Nathaniel's eyes made contact with the convict's, he saw a look of surprise and great disappointment. The convict dropped to all fours to conceal himself and moved quickly up the slope through the bushes and rocks.

Westover raised his musket and aimed at the movement.

"*Don't shoot!*" Nathaniel yelled as he stepped forward and reached to deflect Westover's musket. The sergeant was lowering it when Nathaniel's hand reached the barrel. Cupping his hands into the shape of a trumpet, Nathaniel shouted:

"*DON'T* MAKE US CHASE YOU, JOHN PRESCOTT! YOU *CAN'T* GET AWAY. IT WILL ONLY GO WORSE FOR YOU, MAN."

The scurrying noise stopped, and Prescott rose above the

vegetation again. This time, his hands were up in the air. His manacles hung from a wrist.

"GOOD! *Now come down—carefully.*" Nathaniel said.

At four o'clock in the afternoon, Phillip sent a message to Ross, who was in town, that Lieutenant Armstrong had captured the escaped convict and delivered him to the *Sirius.*

The next morning, Nathaniel stood with Prescott before Phillip and Ross.

"So you come before us once again, Lieutenant Armstrong," Captain Phillip said, smiling. "How did you find the escapee?"

"I took the advice of Master Marshall, sir. He advised me to look in the coves south of the *Alexander*, because of the tide, winds, and current."

"Sound advice," Phillip said, "by Jove."

"He had pulled the jolly-boat behind a boulder in an attempt to hide it and hid himself in a steep break in a cliff's face. He told us he was sleeping when he heard us approaching." Turning toward Prescott, Nathaniel said, "I should add that the escapee gave up peacefully."

"Weel dune, Lieutenant," Major Ross said with a dour look. "I wou'd appreciate, however, if ye wou'd await my orders afore chargin' aff."

"Yes sir, of course, I'll await your orders next time—my mistake, sir."

"Nae at all," Ross said, satisfied. "As I said, guid work."

Under questioning, Prescott said, "No one else wos in on it. I wos one of the helpers bringin' water onboard an' hid under a tarp. When it got dark, I let meself dahn the anchor line an' swam over to the jolly-boat, untied the rope, and let her drift a bit before usin' the oars."

Prescott's punishment was one hundred lashes. After receiving the flogging, he was sent back to the *Alexander* and placed in heavy irons.

While making final preparations to leave Tenerife, Nathaniel was ordered to transfer to the *Sirius* to replace a first lieutenant, who had been seriously ill for two weeks and was hospitalized in Santa

Cruz. Tom helped Nathaniel pack and carry his things to the ship's waist rail.

"Well, we had it good for a while, m'lad," Tom said with a sad expression. "I bet you're being rewarded for capturing Prescott, you lucky sod."

"I hope so, Tom, but I wonder what my new assignment will be."

They shook hands and wished each other well.

A longboat crew rowed Nathaniel across to the *Sirius*. A sergeant met him with two sailors to help carry his belongings. The sergeant led the way down the hatchway one level to the gun deck. He placed a hand against the overhead beam and cautioned him:

"Mind yer head, sir."

Nathaniel lowered his head in the five-foot-four-inch height to the underside of the crossbeams. A line of cubicles ran along both sides of the deck defined by hanging sheets of canvas that could easily be removed before battle. A few high-ranking officers had wood cabins near Phillip's cabin, which occupied the stern of the gun deck.

"This be it, sir, a seven by six," the sergeant said, holding the front sheet of canvas aside so Nathaniel could enter. "This be a guid one, ye dinnae have tae share it wi' a cannon." The sailors carried in his sea chest.

"Would there be anythin' else, sir?" the sergeant asked.

"No, Sergeant, carry on."

◉

In the late afternoon of June 10, an hour after the fleet had set sail for Rio de Janeiro, Nathaniel was summoned to Major Ross's cabin. Ross sat at his small desk, but did not invite Nathaniel to sit. Without any introductory remarks, except a joyless "Guid afternoon, Lieutenant Armstrong," he picked up a piece of paper and looked at it as he spoke.

"Ye're tae serve as a liaison officer, regardin' certain matters o' interest tae the commodore an' myself. In this capacity, ye'll work closely wi' oor aides: Captain George Evans, who spe'ks weel o' ye, an' Lieutenant King." Ross did not seem pleased. "Yer first project will be tae report tae Lieutenant King tae compile an' analyze the survey of the convicts." He looked up and pointedly said, "But ye'll remain under my command." His eyes returned to the sheet of paper. "That's all, dismissed."

Nathaniel sensed that saying thank you would be inappropriate; he saluted and turned smartly. Walking away, he could easily have exclaimed an ecstatic *hallelujah!* He had not slept well wondering what Ross had in store for him—but this! Phillip had to be behind it. I've caught his eye, he gleefully concluded. And I also like Philip Gidley King quite a lot. This is better than I had hoped for. Now to find Lieutenant King.

King said that he and Captain Evans were overloaded with work and had come up with the idea of a special projects liaison. To Nathaniel's disappointment, he did not mention Phillip's involvement. King handed Nathaniel a stack of surveys from the six transports. Nathaniel leafed through them as King continued to talk. He asked him to compile and analyze the surveys with particular application to convict work assignments, both during the voyage and in the new settlement.

As King spoke, Nathaniel found himself liking the sincerity and intelligence of the man, who he estimated at thirty or so, seven years older than himself. Nathaniel had high regard for naval officers, believing as did many other marine officers, that naval officers advanced in rank through intelligence, marines on their fighting skills, and army officers on how much they paid for their commissions.

"Phillip shall also want a verbal report, mind you," King said. With a playful smile, he suggested, "Perhaps you could be a bit more loquacious than you were in your last *brief* presentation."

"I'll try, sir," Nathaniel said, smiling.

At the end of their meeting, King passed along Phillip's invitation to join other officers for drinks in the captain's cabin after dinner.

That evening, while walking from his cubicle to Phillip's cabin, Nathaniel playfully counted to himself the nineteen crossbeams he had to duck his head beneath. He could stand erect only between the crossbeams.

When he entered the commodore's cabin, he was impressed by its spaciousness and by the amount of light coming in. The cabin was a "roundhouse," where the windows wrapped around the stern of the ship. After paying his respects to Major Ross, he accepted a glass of wine from the captain's servant. Seeing Captain Phillip talking to Lieutenant King, he worked his way over to them. As he walked up, Phillip was in mid-sentence:

—"two crimes that would merit death are murder and sodomy." Phillip nodded at Nathaniel to acknowledge his presence and completed his point. "For either of these crimes, I would wish to drop the criminal off on the island of New Zealand where the cannibals can *eat* him," he said, laughing. "The dread of this would operate much stronger than the fear of death, I daresay."

King chuckled, and then he and Phillip turned to Nathaniel.

"Thank you, Commodore, for inviting me," Nathaniel said.

"You are quite welcome, my dear Lieutenant. Thank you for your conscientious work with the convicts."

"It's my pleasure, sir—to assist Lieutenant King and Captain Evans," Nathaniel said while giving a courteous bow of his head to excuse himself. He did not wish to intrude. Seeing an empty seat next to Captain Evans, he went over to thank him for his new assignment.

Captain Evans was involved in conversation with naval Captain John Hunter, yet he acknowledged Nathaniel as he sat down. "Good evening, Lieutenant, have you met Captain Hunter?"

They had not met. Fifty-year-old Hunter was second-in-command of the naval contingent and the captain of the *Sirius* in Phillip's absence. After introductions, Nathaniel thanked Captain Evans for selecting him as his special projects liaison.

Evans accepted Nathaniel's thanks and said, "Captain Hunter was just answering my question: Why are we crossing the Atlantic twice instead of sailing directly south to Cape Town?"

"I was curious about that myself," Nathaniel said and looked expectantly at Hunter.

"The short answer is that it takes advantage of prevailing trade winds and favorable ocean currents for a smoother sail. If you are curious beyond that, it becomes more complex." Hunter was a hand-some man with dark, piercing eyes that looked at them for encouragement to continue.

"I'd like to hear the longer answer," Evans said. Nathaniel nodded that he would too.

"Very well," Hunter said, pleased. "We are presently running nicely before the northeast trade winds boosted by the Canary Current flowing southwestward. The decision of the course to Cape Town has to be made south of Cape Verde, depending somewhat on the season, but more importantly on the objectives of the captain. Sailing directly south past the rump of Africa can be faster than twice across the Atlantic but is a more difficult sail. There's the convergence of the northeast and southeast trade winds to deal with, the doldrums where these winds meet at or near the Equator, and the fickle Guinea Counter Current. You see, south of the equator the ocean currents rotate counterclockwise between South America and Africa, so one is beating into the southeast trade winds, or tacking, all the way to Cape Town while working against the current flowing northward. The commodore chose to avoid this kind of rough sailing for the sake of the convicts. Crossing the Atlantic twice is an easier sail and allows the fleet to reprovision in Rio de Janeiro.

"The course to Rio has only the equatorial doldrums to deal with. If we are fortunate, the northeast trade winds will be stronger at this time of year than those from the southeast, which will allow us to squeak across the equator in the mid-Atlantic without becoming unduly becalmed. Then we pick up the favorable southbound Brazil Current and the southeast trades, which we can sail close-hauled to Rio. Leaving Rio, the prevailing westerlies provide a fast and easy downwind run eastward across the Atlantic assisted by the counterclockwise current to Cape Town. So the decision to sail to Rio is as much a matter of avoiding the rough direct southward route to Cape Town as it is choosing the accommodating winds and currents twice across the Atlantic."

The sound of music drew their attention.

"That's *Sirius's* surgeon, George Worgan, playing his pianoforte," Hunter said. "He plays quite well, wouldn't you say?"

Evans and Nathaniel concurred.

Conversation quieted as most of the officers politely listened. Later in the evening, Hunter played the pianoforte even better than Worgan had.

During the eight days of sailing to reach the windward islands of the archipelago of Cape Verde, Nathaniel worked on the convict survey. While sailing through the archipelago, he met with King, Evans, Hunter, White, and Ross regarding convict work assignments.

A pleased Phillip issued orders along the lines of Nathaniel's recommendations. The convicts were ordered to pump out the bilges, apply oil of tar twice a week to destroy insects and purify the air, mend their own clothes with assigned needles and thread, and carry their bedding and linens topside every third day to dry in the sun. He put Nathaniel in charge of selecting convicts to learn carpentry from the ship carpenters. Transportees who willingly participated were given more time on the upper deck to enjoy the fresh air while repairing sails, tarring ropes, unraveling old rope to make oakum, and performing other duties.

When the fleet passed over the tenth degree north line of latitude, they entered the Atlantic equatorial doldrums. The wind became inconsistent and the weather grew hotter and more humid with each passing day. At times, when there was not a breath of wind, the sails hung limply, and the glassy sea reflected mirror images of the ships.

The hatches had to be battened down to keep out the sudden, drenching, tropical downpours that occurred at least twice a day. The convicts, confined below, were not able to exercise on the upper deck for days in a row. Their holds turned into festering, steaming ovens. The putrid smell below deck became unbearable; rats, cockroaches, fleas, and other vermin moved up from the bilges to the higher decks for relief, tormenting the convicts and inflicting illnesses. The transportees started to die in greater numbers.

The fleet slowly reached the prevailing southeast trade winds that propelled them into the Brazil Current flowing southward. With the improved weather, the convicts were permitted back onto the upper deck. It had taken four weeks to sail through the doldrums.

Three days from Rio de Janeiro, Phillip asked Surgeon General White to share his report with other senior officers around the meeting table. White turned to the summary page of his report.

"Sixteen convicts have died thus far on the voyage," White began. "There have been five births; three of the newborns are still alive. Sickness is rife throughout the fleet. Ninety-five convicts are seriously ill. Two marines, a marine's wife, and two children are also seriously ill.

"The convicts' clothing are lice infested and should be replaced in Rio de Janeiro before it spreads to everyone on board the transports. The women's clothing, which was not replaced in Portsmouth before sailing, is now in tatters and has contributed to lustfulness on their ships. In the stifling heat below deck, some of the women have exposed themselves to their guards. Civilian crewmen in two of the ships broke through the bulkheads into the women's prisons, and female convicts were found in the sailors' quarters. Three sailors are confined awaiting trial for their involvement. They gave the women rum in exchange for their favors—"

"Yes, a deplorable breakdown in conduct," Phillip interrupted. "Thank you for your report, Mr. White."

"I was leading to a recommendation, Commodore," White said.

"Excuse me, if I interrupted you, Mr. White, pray continue."

"The drunkenness of the women has become a problem I have to deal with far too often, sir. Some of the women are shameless and incorrigible. They have no regard for authority and are impossible to deal with. Disciplining them with thumbscrews, shaving their heads, and placing them in irons has not worked well. I recommend that the worst of them be flogged to put the fear of authority into them."

"You are not alone in making such a recommendation," Phillip replied. "I shall consider such harsh punishment if their misbehavior continues."

◎

Twenty miles from Rio de Janeiro, Captain Phillip ordered the quartermaster to set the course one point large on a distinctive mountain piercing the distant coastline. "That's Sugar Loaf Mountain, Pao de Acucar in Portuguese, over 1,300 feet high," he said to Lieutenant King and Nathaniel, "a stone monolith standing like a sentinel at the entrance to the harbor." That evening, August 5, the fleet anchored within a group of ocean islands opposite the entrance to the harbor.

At dawn the next morning, Phillip sent King ashore to request permission from the Portuguese viceroy of Brazil, Don Luis de Vasconcellos, for the fleet to enter the harbor. King returned at noon with a harbor master and a pilot. Before a gentle sea breeze, the fleet approached the entrance. The day was sunny with a clear sky and a balmy temperature of seventy-seven degrees.

Passing by Sugar Loaf Mountain off the larboard side, Nathaniel marveled at the solid granite mountain, devoid of vegetation except for the jungle at its base. Beyond the mountain, on the same side, Fort Lozia commanded the top of a hill. Across the entrance on the starboard side, Fort Santa Cruz jutted out on a rocky peninsula. Phillip ordered a salute of thirteen guns, which Fort Santa Cruz answered with an equal number.

Pristine, white sand beaches and tropical forested slopes bracketed their approach to the town. The mountains were an amazing assortment of disordered shapes, tilted and heaped together in mad confusion. Screeching loudly, flocks of brightly colored birds flew overhead. Three miles beyond the forts, the channel opened into Guanabara Bay, a large estuary, dotted with eighty or more lush islands. The fleet entered a road with many moored ships near Fort Cobras, a fortified island protecting the town. When the *Sirius* dropped anchor, it had been nearly two months since leaving the Canary Islands.

As each ship of the fleet found anchorage in the road, one or more local boats, rowed by black slaves, came alongside. White boys climbed up the sides of the ships selling a variety of luscious fruits and breads.

Overwhelmed by the beauty of the place, Nathaniel said, "This lives up to my expectations, Captain Evans—an exotic, tropical town of fabled gold and diamond mines."

"Yes, a stunning setting, Lieutenant Armstrong," Evans replied. "An excellent port protected from storms . . . with ample anchorage right in front of the town."

Nathaniel's attention was drawn to Corporal McLean, who shepherded his wife and young daughter to the gunwale.

"Beautiful view, isn't it, Corporal . . . and missus?" Nathaniel said, tipping his hat to the lady. She smiled and turned her attention to her daughter.

" 'Tis like naethin' I've ever seen afore, sir," Corporal McLean replied.

In the two months that Nathaniel had been on the *Sirius*, he had seen the attractive Mrs. McLean only a few times during families' allotted periods on the upper deck. He knew there were wives with children behind a bow bulkhead on the lower deck, but seldom saw them. He concluded that they spent most of their time terribly cooped up.

A skiff with a gaily striped canopy glided by the *Sirius*. It was propelled by two muscular slaves whose ebony skin glistened in the bright sunlight. A large turtle surfaced and swam between the boat and the *Sirius*. Lounging in the skiff were a well-dressed lady and a gentleman. He poked his head out from under the canopy and waved and greeted them enthusiastically in Portuguese, English, Spanish, and French: "*Boas-vindas, welcome, bienvenida, bienvenue!*"

Nathaniel returned his greeting with a wave and shouted down "*Good afternoon!*"

Evan said, "It's certainly much larger and more beautiful than volcanic, barren Tenerife. Forty thousand people live here, Captain Hunter told me, not counting the Indians and nigger slaves." Looking over the town, he observed: "There certainly are a lot of churches."

A hundred or more church spires punctuated the plane of two- and three-story buildings. The town spread up several hills. A large citadel sat on the central hill overlooking the town. The northern end of the town terminated on yet another hill dominated by a group of prominent buildings, which Nathaniel later learned was a Benedictine convent.

The second day in port, Phillip and his officers were invited by the viceroy to attend a welcoming ceremony at his imperial palace. Nathaniel was pleased that he was one of those chosen by Phillip to attend.

At the city wharf, Phillip's entourage was met by the captain of the imperial guard, several soldiers, and a friar, who led them to a large square. The white palace of the viceroy sat at the far end. It was an unremarkable, three-story building with few embellishments. The friar pointed out the buildings around the square: a richly decorated church dedicated to the Virgin Mary, an opera house, the mint, and a prison. A large marketplace along the wall of the prison bustled with activity.

They were taken into an unadorned chamber of the palace where many government officials and military officers were waiting. Minutes later, His Excellency the viceroy entered and greeted Phillip as though he was a long-lost friend. Phillip, speaking fluid Portuguese, introduced each of his officers to Don Luis de Vasconcellos, who then took Phillip up onto a small platform. An interpreter translated the viceroy's words for all to hear.

He told how Commodore Phillip had retired from the British Navy to his farm estate for a number of years before obtaining permission from the British Admiralty to join the Portuguese navy, Britain's ally, in its war with Spain. After several years of dauntless service as captain of a Portuguese man-of-war, Phillip had resigned out of patriotism to rejoin the British Royal Navy in its war with America and France.

"The commodore's meritorious service will never be forgotten by the grateful people of Portugal and Brazil," the viceroy said. "Now that Senhor Phillip is to become the governor of New South Wales, I hereby order the palace guards and soldiers to pay *His Excellency* Phillip the same honors as they pay myself as the representative of the Crown of Portugal."

Phillip graciously tried to decline the honor, but the viceroy would hear none of it. Moreover, he directed that Phillip's officers would be permitted to visit all parts of the city and travel as far as five miles into the countryside unattended by military escorts.

Nathaniel assumed this had to be an unusual honor for a colony that jealousy guarded its gold and diamond mines.

They were then led into another chamber where a variety of drinks and hors d'oeuvres were set on long tables. After a round of toasting and conversation, the reception concluded. On the way back to the ships, the officers exchanged positive comments about the friendliness of their Brazilian hosts that boded well for a pleasant visit.

As in Tenerife, Phillip provided the fleet with meat, fresh vegetables, and fruits to improve the general health of all and to fight scurvy, which had sickened some of the convicts during the latter weeks of the Atlantic crossing. After two weeks on the healthy diet, the number of sick convicts was reduced to thirty.

Tom and Nathaniel visited the marketplace one morning and then leisurely strolled along the town's main commercial street, Strait Street, hoping to meet young women. They were frustrated in their pursuit because white people were carried in enclosed sedan chairs by their black slaves directly to the stores they wished to visit. Within the stores, young white women were chaperoned and wore dark veils that obscured their faces.

In the afternoon, they wandered down neighborhood streets. The first floors of most houses were slave quarters without windows. Their white owners lived above and viewed the street through the privacy of latticed wood balconies, which felt unfriendly to Tom and Nathaniel. At many a street corner, there was an altar with an image of the Virgin Mary or some other saint, decorated with items such as garlands, curtains, and strings of prayer beads. Passengers often halted their sedan chairs by these altars, emerged, and fell to their knees. Bringing their hands together, they prayed or sang loudly to declare their religious devotion.

"Disgusting papist zealots!" Tom spat out, after watching one such display. "More showy fervor than *real* devotion." He looked at Nathaniel for agreement.

Nathaniel looked back with a noncommittal expression. He did not feel the need to criticize these emotional Catholics, even though their exhibitions of piousness were too public and fervent for his liking.

As part of the departure preparations, Nathaniel accompanied Phillip and Ross on their inspection of the convict transports. Phillip took the opportunity to lecture the convicts. His message was simple and direct: Those convicts who maintained good conduct would be treated fairly; those who did not, would receive swift punishment. When told that six women on the *Charlotte* had taken lovers, he exchanged them for six well-behaved women from the more disciplined *Friendship*.

Marines were also disciplined by Phillip and Ross. Private Cornelius Connell suffered one hundred lashes for being caught in the act of intercourse with a female convict. Private James Baker received two hundred lashes for trying to purchase goods in town using forged coins made by convict Thomas Barrett from old buckles and pewter spoons. A third private, Thomas Jones, who had tried to bribe a sentinel to enter the women's hold, was sentenced three hundred lashes. The following day, thinking the sentence was perhaps excessive, Phillip recommended clemency to Jones's commanding officer, who reduced his punishment to hard duty.

Tom told Nathaniel that he had located a first-class bawdyhouse with good-looking women, whites and blacks, although he assumed that some of the blacks were slaves. Phillip had warned his officers that the local police were very strict, and he would not come between the law and any wrongdoer. Nevertheless, Nathaniel decided to chance it with Tom, hoping it wouldn't cost too much.

On a warm, humid evening, Tom led Nathaniel along the town's main street and then up a dark, steep, side street. Rounding a corner, they saw flickering lights ahead and heard an eerie, mournful chanting.

At the cross street, they were stopped by a religious procession. There were hundreds of people, of all ages, dressed in a variety of costumes, many wearing masks and carrying lighted candles. A swaying statue of a bloodied saint was carried on the shoulders of robed and hooded men. Lanterns swung to and fro from the ends of poles. Monks were chanting in Latin and the procession was moaning in unison with them. Tom wanted to push through, but Nathaniel asked him to wait; the mysterious and exotic aura captivated him:

the mesmerizing lights . . . dancing shadows on the buildings . . . chanting . . . church bells pealing in the distance . . . the spirituality of it all.

After the procession passed, Tom led the way a block further and knocked on a nondescript door. It was opened by a large swarthy man who smiled and welcomed him in. Upon entering, Nathaniel scanned the large room. A screen separated a narrow bar from a salon. There were several men and women at the bar. In the salon, two couples sat apart from a group of five women who were talking and drinking together. A thin, white woman, not older than seventeen or eighteen, left the group of women and sauntered seductively over to Tom. He embraced her and kissed her on the neck. She laughed and said something to him in broken English.

Two other women from the group stood up simultaneously and, verbally sparring in Portuguese, walked over to Nathaniel. One grabbed his right arm and the other his left. They continued speaking rudely to each other.

Tom laughed loudly. "Looks like you've attracted trouble, Nate—take them both!"

To quickly resolve the matter, Nathaniel said, "You" nodding in the direction of the dark-haired, sultry-looking women on his left arm. The other women let out an "Ugh" and abruptly withdrew her arm with a disdainful look.

Tom and Nathaniel sat down on a sofa with their two women. A black male server walked up with four drinks.

Nathaniel looked suspiciously at the server. "What's this?" he asked Tom.

"They make you buy at least one grog for the girl and one for yourself. It's watered-down, cheap rum and costs too fucken much—devil take them."

Nathaniel took two glasses and gave one to his woman. He smelled the drink and took a sip. She drank most of hers.

"Good, good," she said to him, encouraging him to drink.

He looked over at Tom and his woman. Their drinks were sitting untouched on the table. Tom was kissing her and had his hand on her bosom.

Nathaniel took another sip of his drink. He looked at his woman while thinking of something to say. "Your red dress looks nice on you." Instantly, he thought, *damn!* what a barmy thing to say. He was saved from embarrassment when she shook her head that she did not understand him. "Tom, break it up for a moment, mate. This lassie can't spe—"

"Bugger it, Nate, not now!" Tom said without looking at him. "Take her to a room and give her your blanket hornpipe."

Nathaniel's woman said something to him in incomprehensible English. When he indicated he did not understand, she ran her forefinger down the scar on his cheek while giving him a pouting look of concern and sympathy. Nathaniel placed his drink on the table and acted out swordplay resulting in his scar. She shook her head sorrowfully and rose up and kissed the scar on his cheek. Not knowing quite how to react, he smiled at her and said, "Thank you." He appreciated her creative attempt at communicating.

Taking another swallow of his drink, Nathaniel wondered what he should do or say next. Sensing his indecision, she suggestively slid her tongue along the lip of her glass as she looked seductively at him and ran her hand up the inside of his thigh, electrifying him. She gestured toward the open door at the rear of the salon. Nathaniel nodded, and they both rose. A heavyset man, seated by the door, stood to tell Nathaniel the cost of the two drinks and the woman. Nathaniel haggled for a moment, realized it was pointless, and paid the requested amount.

His heart pounding, Nathaniel followed her down a narrow hallway and into a small room furnished with a bed, chest of drawers, and a large mirror on the wall opposite the bed. A flickering lantern lit the room. She closed the door. He took off his coat, boots, and shirt while she undid his belt and helped him out of his breeches. As he was taking off the last of his underclothes, she stepped back.

Standing there in front of him, she spread the shoulders of her dress and let it drop to her feet. She was wearing nothing under her dress. Her tanned, glistening body looked beautiful to him. Smiling, appreciating his stare, she leisurely let out her long, black hair that fell down to the small of her back.

Nathaniel sat down on the edge of the bed. She stepped between his legs and pressed her breasts into his face. Placing his hands on her thin waist, he picked her up and rotated her by him onto her back. Before he could turn and lie on top of her, she rolled off the bed laughing and directed him to lie on his back. She stroked him affectionately and then mounted him. Moving up and down, she rubbed his broad hairy chest with her hands and looked at his handsome face. He couldn't wait. Grabbing her waist again, he rolled over on top of her in one smooth motion and quickly satiated himself.

◉

The day before departure from Rio, Nathaniel was part of the official party that visited the viceroy to say farewell. This time he saw a part of the palace that impressed him. Their party was taken through a private entrance that connected to a colonnade festooned on either side with sweet-smelling flowers. A walled, linear garden ran alongside the colonnade, filled with blooming tropical plants, espalier flowering shrubs, and bubbling fountains. Hanging from fruit trees were caged, colorful birds singing melodiously. Nathaniel was enchanted.

At the end of the colonnade was the viceroy's spacious private office complex. Don Luis de Vasconcellos warmly greeted them in a richly decorated anteroom and led them into a large room, where they were asked to sit. After drinks were served, Phillip toasted His Excellency for satisfying the fleet's every need and for being a gracious host. The viceroy reciprocated with toasts of praise for the commodore and his British officers. While this was going on, Nathaniel took in the well-appointed, luxurious room.

A beautiful ceiling fresco featured Brazil's exotic tropical birds, fruits, and vegetables. Large oil paintings of dignitaries, ships, battles, and religious scenes covered every wall. Weapons of war hung from the walls and occupied the corners along with suits of armor. The heavy wood chairs, tables, and a large desk in the room were all carved in intricate, exquisite designs. The mosaic tile floor was no less beautiful than the rest of the room.

As they were leaving by way of the colonnade, Nathaniel yearned to spend a few minutes alone in the garden to fully appreciate its delights. He promised himself—someday—he would have a private garden as marvelous as the viceroy's.

At dawn on September 4, the *Sirius* signaled the fleet to weigh anchor. While the fleet sailed by Fort Santa Cruz, it saluted with twenty-one guns, which was answered by the *Sirius* in the same number. A land breeze carried the fleet swiftly through the ocean islands, lying opposite the entrance to the harbor, and out into the Atlantic. After several miles, the wind gradually died and remained low throughout the remainder of the day and into the night. The next day the fleet made little headway. In the afternoon of the third day, a favorable breeze from the west came up to push the fleet eastward. The sun was setting when they finally lost sight of Sugar Loaf Mountain and the South American coast.

The steady west breeze turned into a gale with dark clouds, squalls of rain, thunder and lightning, and heavy seas. The hatches had to be battened down to keep out the rain. The rough weather continued for a week. All but seasoned sailors became seasick. The ship reeked of vomit. On September 14 the weather cleared sufficiently to allow people onto the upper decks to recuperate and wash clothes.

Nathaniel and Captain Evans walked to the bow of the ship where several orderlies were washing clothes in basins. Evans was carrying his extra uniform jacket.

"I found it on the goddamned floor *floating* in puke and God knows what else," Evans complained to Nathaniel. "I'd throw it away, if I could replace it." He handed the jacket to his orderly. "This still reeks of vomit."

"I washed it twice already, sir," the orderly said looking up in despair. "The smell won't come out."

"Well wash it again, dammit!"

"Tie it to the rigging and let the wind blow the smell out," Nathaniel suggested as he leaned back against the foremast and raised his face to enjoy the warming rays of the sun.

"Good idea," Evans said and walked away toward the bowsprit.

A couple of minutes later, Nathaniel heard Evans's desperate scream "*HELP!*"

Nathaniel ran toward a group of people who were gathering at the starboard gunwale. As he pushed his way into the group, a man came out saying, "I'll get a rope!" Nathaniel looked down and saw Evans holding with both hands onto a bowsprit shroud that ran from the bowsprit to the side of the ship. As the ship pitched into a trough, Evans was hit hard by a wave.

Nathaniel realized that the rope was going to be too late, and Evans would not be able to grab it anyway. He saw the anchor cable hanging near Evans. The anchor was in an upside-down position for open sea sailing. Its curved double-hooked arms were lashed to the cathead with its metal shank and wood stock hanging freely below. The thick anchor cable dipped down near Evans and then curved back up into a bow port.

Without comment, Nathaniel jumped over the gunwale and sat himself on the cathead. Scooting out over the anchor as the bow rose, he hung from the cathead and wrapped his legs around the anchor shank. Unable to let himself down gradually, he let go and slid down the wet metal shank. The crash of the bow into a wave threw him off balance. His feet slipped off the wet wood stock. Falling to one side, he held onto the shank with one hand and slid down to the stock. Hanging there for a moment, he wrapped his legs around the anchor cable and looked down to see how Evans was doing. His pained, desperate expression told Nathaniel he had to move quickly.

A rope suddenly dangled from above. Nathaniel grabbed hold of it and put it between his teeth. He let go of the wood stock and slid down the slippery thick cable. Reaching down, he grabbed hold of Evans. Together they were drenched by a wave. He passed the rope quickly around Evans's torso and tied a knot, just as the next wave hit them both forcefully. Flung up and back against the ship, Nathaniel was washed into the anchor shank. He grabbed hold of it, gasping for breath, as another wave passed beneath him.

Nathaniel looked down at Evans. *He was gone!* Looking up, he saw two legs disappear over the gunwale. Thank God, he's saved! Nathaniel rejoiced.

The rope appeared again. Nathaniel grabbed it, tied it around himself, and was pulled to safety. Four willing men carried him quickly to sickbay and placed him in a hammock next to Evans. The ship's surgeon piled blankets on Nathaniel and gave him a pannikin of rum to drink. Evans opened his eyes and whispered "Thanks, Nate" before falling into an exhausted deep sleep. Nathaniel finished his rum, closed his eyes, and also fell asleep.

◉

One inky night, Nathaniel stood near the helm on his watch, marveling at the brilliance of the stars. Halfway across the Atlantic, the weather had cleared. Captain Hunter was standing nearby taking celestial sightings. Nathaniel waited until Hunter had rested his sextant on a rail before addressing him.

"Sir, may I ask a question?"

"Certainly, Lieutenant Armstrong."

"I'm curious, sir, where's the Southern Cross? I know it's several stars in the form of a cross, but I haven't been able to find it." He knew the constellation served the same navigational purpose in the southern hemisphere as Polaris, the North Star, did in the northern hemisphere.

Hunter pointed at the southern horizon. "There . . ." He made a cross with his index fingers. "It's quite low this time of year . . . that's why you couldn't find it."

"Ah . . . there it is. I see it now."

Nathaniel wondered why Hunter was making celestial observations when the *Sirius* carried Captain Cook's chronometer set to Greenwich, England time to calculate the ship's longitude.

"May I ask why sightings are necessary, sir, when we're carrying Captain Cook's chronometer?"

"Indeed. I want to compare my calculations of longitude with the chronometer's. By the time we arrive at Cape Town, I'll know whether adjustments are necessary to apply to our Southern Ocean passage."

"Thank you, sir," Nathaniel said. They stood silently looking at the heavens together for a minute or two, before Hunter lifted his sextant and resumed his work.

Eight bells signaled the change of watch. Shortly thereafter, Nathaniel's replacement walked up.

"Good night and thank you, sir," Nathaniel said to Hunter.

"Good night, Mr. Armstrong," Hunter said.

Nathaniel went below, yawning.

The weather turned stormy again on September 23. The hatches were battened down to keep out the sea breaking over the ship. Seasickness returned as the *Sirius* pitched and rolled. Coping with the wet, uncomfortable conditions below deck kept the convicts busy and out of trouble. However, after several days of moderate weather, on October 6, Nathaniel formed up with other military personnel on the deck of the *Sirius* to witness the flogging of John Prescott, again.

A convict on the *Alexander* had told a marine guard that several men, led by Prescott, were planning an escape when the ship reached Cape Town. A crowbar, hammer, and screwdriver had been found in the sleeping bunk occupied by Prescott and his bunk mates.

At his trial on the *Sirius*, Prescott admitted his intention to escape and refused to implicate his bunk mates. He said he alone was to blame. Found guilty, he was taken to the upper deck to receive his punishment.

The drummer beat out the Rogue's March as Prescott was led to the flogging triangle. His shirt was removed. He did not resist when two marine privates trussed his wrists to the top of the wood triangle and spread his legs apart to lash his ankles to the base of the triangle. The surgeon placed a folded piece of leather between his teeth to prevent him from inadvertently biting into his tongue.

He should be hung by his neck instead, Nathaniel thought, as an example to the other convicts that if you try to escape twice, you'll be executed. Why should Prescott receive only 150 lashes when Private Baker received 200 for *just trying* to pass a forged coin in Rio? It's unfair and demoralizing; they're sterner with the marines than with the convicts.

The cat-of-nine-tails began to fly. The boatswain set the cadence

by counting out the number of lashes loudly. Nathaniel never enjoyed watching a flogging. After several minutes, he wanted to turn
his head from the sickening view of the cat clawing into Prescott's
back.

He's a courageous bloke . . . not cryin' out—I'll give him that.
He took responsibility, just as he did when I captured him . . . told
the commodore and Ross he wanted his freedom. Straightforward.
Gawd, blood's saturating his trousers and pooling at his feet already.

A lieutenant, standing behind the flogger, ordered his marine
unit to step back three paces to avoid being splattered with Prescott's
blood from the flailing cat-of-nine tails. A fresh cat was brought out.

I rather like the man, actually, Nathaniel admitted to himself.
That's probably why Phillip didn't hang him. He's a likable bastard.

Prescott fainted after 103 lashes. He was startled back to consciousness by a bucket of saltwater thrown onto his lacerated back.

Nathaniel occupied his mind with speculation: his back opened
up rather quickly . . . never completely healed from the last flogging,
I reckon. Poor devil, I can see his backbone and shoulder blades glistening. Ach, he's fainted again.

Prescott was revived by another bucket of seawater, screaming
out horribly this time. Fifteen lashes later, he fainted away again. A
bucket of saltwater did not revive him.

I'm happy they can't revive him, Nathaniel thought . . . otherwise, he'd never make it through 150 lashes. The flogger's layin' it
on a bit hard. *Fancy that!* . . . I'm feelin' sorry for the poor bugger's
suffering! He'd be free if it wasn't for me.

Prescott's lashes were stopped at 136 by Surgeon Worgan, because of the convict's "soft back" and delicate, passed-out condition.
He was sent back to the *Alexander* in heavy irons and strapped face
down to the deck for twenty-four hours, so any convicts still considering escape could fully consider his shredded back.

◉

The morning of the fortieth day at sea, King, Evans, and Nathaniel
were meeting below deck when they heard that the African coast

had been sighted. As others went above, King suggested that they finish their meeting.

"There won't be much to see until the morning haze burns off."

They were finalizing a list of supplies to buy upon arrival in Cape Town, where the fleet would remain for several weeks to reprovision and recuperate prior to the last and most grueling leg of the voyage, crossing the Southern Ocean to New South Wales.

"Cape Town's climate and latitude are similar to Botany Bay's, so we'll purchase plants and livestock here for the new colony," King said. "Cook reported seeing *no* domesticated animals in New South Wales. Odd that."

"Do you expect the Dutch will be willing to provide everything we need, sir?" Nathaniel asked.

"How so?" King asked back.

"I mean . . . they were allied with France and America against us four years ago, and Commodore Johnstone tried to capture Cape Town. I expect they won't be too happy to learn that we intend to start a colony near their East Indies possessions and New Holland."

"Very perceptive, Mr. Armstrong, however, I don't wish to speculate. I'm sure the commodore is prepared for any reluctance on their part to help us."

When the three men finally went above deck, they were greeted with a picturesque landform, unlike anything Nathaniel had seen before. Ten or so miles away, sitting alone, was an unusual arrangement of three mountains.

"The center mountain looks like a long table to me, and the mountains to either side look like end chairs," Nathaniel said.

"You've got a vivid imagination, Nate," Evans said teasingly.

Nathaniel noticed that Captain Evans used the familiar "Nate" again. It was obvious that since saving his life, Evans had become friendlier toward him. Nathaniel reciprocated by calling him "George" but only after Evans called him "Nate" first.

King, who had been to Cape Town previously, said, "That's Table Mountain with Devil's Head on the left and Lion's Head on the right. Table Mountain is the highest, approximately 3,500 feet. Cape Town sits at its base."

"Does it have a good harbor?" Evans asked.

"It's called Table Bay. We'll sail directly into it. It's not a safe harbor, because it's unprotected. Westerly winter storms, from May to August, can drive ships to shore. In summer, the southeast gales that sweep down from the summit of Table Mountain are strong enough to drive anchored ships out to sea. We've arrived at a good time though; their spring generally doesn't have violent winds."

"How large is the town, Lieutenant King?" Nathaniel asked.

"In population, I wouldn't hazard a guess. There are more slaves, mostly from India and the Dutch East Indies, than there are Dutch. It's not a very pleasant place, because they have to work hard at controlling their slaves, and it's not the tropical paradise of Rio. In physical size, it's a small town . . . perhaps one-fifth the size of Rio. One thing you'll enjoy is the Dutch East India Company's produce garden, which has a menagerie at one end with some interesting African beasts."

The next morning was cloudy and gray when Nathaniel and George Evans were rowed into town to make a preliminary assessment of the availability and prices of supplies the fleet required. They noted that the *Sirius* and *Supply* were the only naval ships in the harbor. There were several Dutch East Indiamen, a Danish trader, and two French merchantmen.

On the way in, they discussed Cape Town. A large fort guarded the pier and the eastern end of town. The town appeared to be composed mostly of white, two-story buildings; only two church spirals projected above. Beyond the town, a second fort protected its flank and the entrance into the harbor from the south.

By the time their boat was rowed alongside the city pier, Nathaniel had decided he did not like the look of the arid, rocky, gray-green countryside. He wondered whether he was going to like Botany Bay any better, as it was at the same latitude.

"What do you think, Captain Evans? Up close, I don't like the lack of greenness of this place or the feel of Table Mountain, treeless and darkly brooding over the town."

"The mountain dominating the town doesn't bother me, Nate," Evans responded, not appreciating that Nathaniel's main point was the bleakness of the place.

They were going to the fort, named the Castle of Good Hope, where the stores of the Dutch East India Company were secured. Walking up to the main gate, they noticed a body hanging from a gibbet at the far end of the fort. With morbid curiosity, Evans said, "Let's take a look."

As they approached the gibbet and the male body hanging in chains from it, a Dutch soldier leaning against the fenced enclosure slowly stood to attention. In addition to the gibbet, there were a gallows, two crosses, a whipping post, and a wheel for breaking the bodies of felons.

"George . . . is that poor wretch *dead*?" Nathaniel asked, pointing at a man stretched across the top of the wheel.

"*Damn*, I *hope* so. He appears to be an Oriental, probably a slave. Yes, he's dead—see there." He pointed at a display board next to the wheel. "Those must be his hands nailed to that board."

Nathaniel was horrified to see the man's body was missing its hands. "*Beastly* . . . I wonder what the poor bastard did to deserve *that*?"

"Stealing or pick pocketing, I fancy, so they cut his hands off and displayed them as a warning."

While Evans spoke, Nathaniel noticed an implement of punishment set in the far corner of the enclosure. "By gad, that's *medieval*. See that post over there in the corner, George, with the sharpened spike sticking out the top of it? I think that's for impalements!"

"Disgusting business!" George said. "Not my preferred way to die—with a spike up my arse."

"Bugger this place," Nathaniel said. "Let's go."

After working hard for ten days, Nathaniel crossed paths with Tom in Cape Town. Tom suggested that they find a pub, but Nathaniel begged off saying he had too much to do.

"My life has become nothing but hard work, Tom. I started out as King's and George Evan's liaison, then Phillip's convict specialist, and now Surgeon General White has me going around ensuring that the convicts are gettin' their extra rations to build up their strength for the final passage."

"Humph! You asked for it, m'lad," Tom said dryly. "You like

being needed. You can't expect any rewards in the service of His Majesty. You should know that."

"Well, at least Ross leaves me alone. That's some kind of a reward."

"I try to stay away from that rotter," Tom said.

Phillip directed that a large number and variety of animals be purchased, including horses, cows, bulls, sheep, goats, hogs, and domestic fowl, for fresh meat during the voyage and to breed in Botany Bay. The execution of this endeavor fell to King, Evans, and Nathaniel. The job of overseeing the construction of the animal pens was assigned to Nathaniel. He worked with the ship carpenters and their convict apprentices. Many other convicts were assigned as laborers. Eight guns on the *Sirius* were dismounted to provide room on the gun deck for animal pens. The twenty women convicts on the *Friendship* were removed to other transports to make room for sheep pens. Horse pens were built on the *Lady Penrhyn*. A large proportion of the animals were put on the *Fishburn*.

I'm building Noah's Ark for goodness' sake, Nathaniel often chuckled to himself.

Nathaniel was not pleased that his work was increased by the large number of livestock bought by many of the officers for their private use. He purchased only three chickens, a rooster, and two pigs for himself, for he could not risk his limited funds on animals that might die during the voyage.

Four days before they were to sail from Cape Town, Nathaniel was able to take a day off. He and Tom went to relax in the Dutch East India Company's produce garden.

They sat under a shade tree next to Government House situated in the center of the garden. Tom wrote a letter to his wife while Nathaniel read.

Tom looked up from his letter and asked, "What are you reading?"

"Hume's philosophical thoughts in *An Enquiry Concerning Human Understanding.*"

"Not interested," Tom said with a smile. "What's the other book?"

"*Gulliver's Travels.* It's particularly appropriate for our voyage into the unknown. Have you read it?"

"It's a children's book, isn't it? about little people. My mother read parts to me as bedtime stories."

"You're referring to the Lilliputians, six-inch-tall humans, who Gulliver encounters on his first of four voyages. There are many fanciful accounts like that, enjoyable for all ages, but it's really an adult social and political satire about human vices and follies. Gulliver goes mostly to strange fictional lands, but he also goes to New Holland!"

"*New Holland?* What's written about that?"

"It's only a short passage. Gulliver is chased by naked savages who shoot poison arrows at him, wounding him in the leg, then he's saved by a Portuguese ship."

"I'd like to read it, or at least the part about New Holland."

"Here." Nathaniel handed the book to him. "Just try to keep it dry, Tom, won't you?"

"For sure, m'lad, thanks. How many books did you bring?"

"Fourteen. I've traded a few with others."

Tom returned to his writing. He had received a letter from his wife delivered by the *Ranger* on its way to India.

While Tom wrote, Nathaniel put down his book, closed his eyes, and sat thinking. He asked himself, what shall I do if Botany Bay is as arid and sea-bitten as Cape Town? I'd miss the greenness and beauty of England too much to stay. No use thinking negatively, I'll just have to wait to see whether I like Botany Bay.

"D'you want to hear what I wrote?" Tom asked, "that's not of a personal nature?"

"Yes," Nathaniel answered.

Tom began to read:

"Cape Town is nothing at all like Rio de Janeiro. First, they are Calvinists and Lutherans here and don't go through that mumbo jumbo I wrote you about that Catholics do in Rio. Second, the Dutch are level-headed like us and dress in English clothes. They are very orderly people in everything they do. The town is laid out in a grid pattern with the homes in neat rows on wide, tree-lined streets and everyone has a garden. Their stone houses are cemented and whitewashed and the front of their houses are flagstoned and kept very clean.

"The town is next to a high, flat mountain called Table Mountain and two other mountains. It's not as green and beautiful as Rio. The scenery is dry and brown.

"The Dutch governor said he could not fully provision us, because they had a famine, but there seems to be plenty of everything, so I think they did not want to help us settle near New Holland. Captain Phillip had to threaten them before they sold us everything we wanted, but at very high prices. Now we can leave soon. There isn't much to do here, so I've spent very little money.

"Everyone is healthy and ready for the longest part of our trip. Nate is good too. We have all been very busy making changes to the ships to take many animals and supplies with us.

"Nate and I are in a beautiful garden now with a menagerie of African wild animals at one end. It's the produce garden for the whole colony and has nice shaded walks under fruit trees. You would like it."

Tom finished reading. "I need an ending... something that will make Emma feel good about the last part of our trip."

"Well . . ." Nathaniel pondered for a moment. "You could say that we are sailing at a bonnie time of year, the end of spring into summer. Also the fleet couldn't be better prepared, and you are anxious to see what Botany Bay looks like."

"Good. I'll write that."

◉

After a month's stay in Cape Town, on November 13, Captain Phillip ordered the hoisting of the flag signaling weigh anchors. The fleet sailed northward on a southeast wind toward Robben Island, which Phillip intended to pass before changing course to sail close-hauled southwestward out of Table Bay and into the Atlantic.

The *Sirius* was leading the way when a large Dutch man-of-war entered Table Bay from the north, complicating the fleet's maneuvers. As the Dutch warship passed by the *Sirius*, she did not salute the flagship. Nathaniel looked up at a large number of troops looking down at him and felt uneasy. *Is their passing portentous? Are they simply reinforcements from Holland or something more ominous? Could they be headed to New Holland? or perhaps even to New South Wales to challenge us!*

By leaving on a southeast wind, Phillip was gambling that after a day or two of sailing on a southwestward course, he would reach the prevailing westerlies and the strong eastward current that together would drive the fleet toward New South Wales. His gamble did not pay off, when day after day, the wind incessantly blew from the southeast in concert with a great swell from that direction. Unable to sail eastward, the fleet was being forced west, in the wrong direction, further and further into the Atlantic Ocean. The sea grew larger, stressing the animals and the people alike. After six days of unfavorable southeast winds, the fleet was five hundred miles west of Cape Town and two hundred miles south.

Phillip decided he had had enough and called the naval and marine officers into his cabin. "Gentlemen, I know you are all frustrated by the contrary winds that plague the fleet but rest assured the prevailing westerlies cannot much longer forsake us. However, we are losing valuable time. In response, I've decided to split the fleet." There were murmurs of concern. "*But only* after the westerlies have graced us, and we've sailed one hundred leagues" (three hundred miles), "to the east of Cape Town. Then, I shall sail ahead in the *Supply* with the three fastest transports, *Alexander, Scarborough,* and *Friendship*. My intention is to reach Botany Bay a fortnight or so ahead of the rest of the fleet to select and prepare a site for our new colony. The six slower ships shall follow the *Sirius* under your command, Captain Hunter."

"Yes, sir," Hunter said.

"Major Ross, you shall transfer to the *Scarborough*. As lieutenant governor, you and I should be on different ships in these heavy seas."

Ross understood Phillip's concern and acknowledged his order with a nod. Nathaniel wondered whether Phillip had found a tactful way to rid himself of the disagreeable Ross.

"Lieutenants King and Armstrong shall accompany me." Looking at Nathaniel, Phillip said, "I want you to ensure that the convict carpenters, farmers, blacksmiths, and other useful artificers, and their tools, are transferred to the three transports accompanying us."

"Aye, sir," Nathaniel said.

The morning of November 20 greeted them with a light breeze from the northeast that allowed the fleet to steer southeast. Over the morning hours, the breeze grew in strength, gradually shifting counterclockwise to north and then north-northwest, until the long-sought westerlies were gained in the afternoon to drive the fleet in the desired eastward direction. On November 23 the fleet finally made its way back to Cape Town's longitude from which it had started ten days earlier, however, now 330 miles directly south. Two days later, they reached Phillip's objective of one hundred leagues east of the Cape Town. There were still 6,200 miles to sail across the Southern Ocean to Botany Bay.

The transfers of people, tools, and baggage were accomplished in a day and a half. In the late afternoon of November 26, *Supply* led the way before a fresh west breeze at a bearing of east-southeast. By nightfall, Phillip's squadron of four ships had sailed far ahead of Captain Hunter's seven-ship squadron. The morning found the two squadrons out of sight of each other.

The little *Supply* sailed worse than Nathaniel had expected in the large swells. She was no longer the swift sloop she had been in the moderate swells of the Atlantic. Sitting low in the deep troughs, her battened down topside was racked by crashing waves. Although the pumps were manned continuously, it was impossible to keep bilge water from intermittently raising through the floor planking of the lower deck.

As *Supply's* squadron forged on, the westerlies became stronger, the sea continued to build, and the air temperature dropped. Due to the worsening weather and sailing conditions, the convicts were brought above deck less frequently. Although inured, after seven months, to the miserable living conditions in the holds, they were terrified by the violent seas and sickened by the cold. Their miseries were occasionally lightened when they were brought up for short periods of exercise and observed the extraordinary sights of the Southern Ocean: pods of whales breaching and spouting, seals and penguins porpoising, and majestic long-winged albatrosses, gulls, and blue and black petrels flying about the ships.

In the second week of December, a cold west gale came up, temperatures plummeted, and ice formed on the deck, rigging, and sails, making an eerie crackling sound. The *Friendship* fell behind, and the *Scarborough* and *Alexander* waited for her. Phillip had placed Lieutenant Shortland in command of the three transports with orders to keep them together; the *Supply* would set the pace and sail on ahead whether or not the transports could keep up. Five days before Christmas, it sleeted with large hailstones that bounced off the deck and sent the crew scurrying for cover.

The gale did not spare Christmas Day. In spite of the foul weather, the marine wives strung festive garlands of intertwined green yarn and red ribbons and made Christmas pudding. The cook prepared a feast of sheep and hogs that had died from being knocked about their pens. Nevertheless, the holiday meal in the candlelit haze of the battened-down ship was somber. They were alone; the three transports had not been seen on the western horizon for more than a week.

The howling wind and heavy seas continued, day after day, without letup.

Twweeeet. Nathaniel heard the boatswain's pipe trill, and the call for the next watch. "All hands, morning watch! *Rouse* out there! Lively now!"

It was not Nathaniel's watch. In his swinging hammock, he pulled his wet blanket over his head. He was freezing and thought, Ach, if it's this cold in summer, how unbearably cold must it be winter?

Waves crashed onto the *Supply*. Water dripped through the deck above and sloshed across the floor as the ship pitched and rolled. The bow groaned as it plunged into yet another trough and slammed into the next wave. The ship's timbers creaked loudly; snapping sounds seemed to indicate she was breaking up. Nathaniel wondered how much longer their little ship could take this beating.

Ding-ding-ding-ding. Four bells rang, one for each half hour, signaling that two hours had passed since the start of the four-hour watch. Nathaniel was exhausted. He shifted his body and tried hard to sleep.

Twweeeet. His forenoon watch. It was eight in the morning. Nathaniel felt the ship pitching and yawing oddly and sensed something was wrong. Half-asleep, he rolled out of his hammock while holding on to it for balance. He was fully dressed but put on extra dry clothes from his sea chest: another pair of stockings, another pair of breeches, flannel waistcoat, a foul weather hat, and greatcoat, which he usually wore all day. Entering the hatch house, he was thrown against the wall. He opened the door and peeked out. The morning was gray and foggy. A furious storm had the ship in its grasp. A wave nearly ripped the door out of his hand; he slammed it closed with both hands.

As the ship leveled, Nathaniel quickly stepped out, slammed the door shut, and grabbed a lifeline rope. Three lifelines ran the length of the ship. Knee-deep, icy-cold, foaming water came rushing at him from out of the half-light of the murky morning and knocked him off his feet. Holding onto the rope with both hands he slid toward the bulwark until the rope grew taunt. He fought to regain his footing and staggered his way along the rope to report to the quarterdeck. The roar of the raging sea and wind shrieking through the cordage were enough to strike terror into the heart of the most seasoned seaman. Two men were fighting to control the wheel. Nathaniel took his position at the quarterdeck railing and looked aghast at the sea around him.

The ship was surrounded by mountains of water that turned into angry white, frothing cliffs before crashing onto the *Supply*. The waves seemed to be coming from all directions. Frightened and sure that the ship could not possibly survive the storm, Nathaniel suddenly retched. Then he saw what was causing the ship to act and sound oddly.

The fore topgallant mast had broken off, taking with it the topgallant yards, which were fouled in the main topsail yard. The ship was groaning in response to the partially unfurled sails among the broken rigging. Forty feet above, ten or more topmen were perched precariously, hacking away with hatchets at the broken, tangled mess.

The torn and loose sails whipped and snapped overhead making a *rap-rap-rap* sound. Nathaniel could almost feel the icy shrouds freezing the poor seamen's hands and stiff sails smacking against their bodies. Suddenly, two of them were wrenched from the topsail yard, one hung on, but the other fell screaming—"AAHHHHHH!"—loud enough for Nathaniel to hear above the deafening noise of the storm. The seaman hit the main yard, partially breaking his fall, before crashing onto the deck with a sickening *thud*.

Nathaniel grabbed the lifeline and started toward him but was washed off his feet by a wave crossing the deck. Holding onto the lifeline, he looked over his shoulder and saw the wave slam the seaman against the starboard bulwark. As the ship rolled, the seaman was washed back toward the center of the ship and grabbed hold of the center lifeline with one arm. The wave rushed over him, and he came up sputtering. Nathaniel moved quickly toward him. He was sure the man's right arm was badly broken; it flopped around as if loosely attached to his body.

When Nathaniel was within an arm length of the seaman, a huge wave crashed onto the deck that lifted them both up. Nathaniel had to hold onto the lifeline with both hands; his eyes met those of the terrified man the moment the wave ripped him from the rope and tossed him over the bulwark into the sea.

I should have grabbed him! Nathaniel screamed to himself.

Distressed, he was unprepared for the overpowering force of the next wall of foaming sea that tore him from the rope. Washed across the deck, Nathaniel hit the larboard bulwark on his left side, injuring his old gunshot wound; for a moment, the pain paralyzed him. His body rose on the surging water, and he felt himself being sucked into the black abyss. He grabbed hold of the gunwale and slide along it with the wave. The surge slowed. Kicking desperately, Nathaniel hooked one leg over the gunwale. The ship rolled to starboard, and he tumbled back onto the deck.

"*Hhh hhh hhh.*" Struggling to catch his breath, he reached for a lifeline. A larboard wave drove him into the rope, which he grasped with both hands. The wave washed over him.

Hold on . . . frozen, exhausted . . . my hands . . . numb. He willed himself to stand and forced his freezing hands along the icy rope as he staggered to the hatch house and entered to safety.

◉

"**The aurora australis**"—southern lights—"is especially bright tonight," Lieutenant King said. He was standing next to Nathaniel; both were looking in awe at a colorful, constantly changing, atmospheric phenomenon in the night sky over the southern horizon.

"The gods must be celebrating the end of 1787 and the start of the new year," Nathaniel said.

They were captivated by the spectacular display of undulating green-blue curtains of light, mixing and curling with brilliant white, yellow, and orange streamers, occasionally accented by dazzling arcs of purple, crimson, and pink.

"It's even more wondrous than the lights we saw on the water," King said, referring to an amazing phenomenon they had observed two nights earlier. The *Supply* had sailed through a vast sea of white lights that no one could explain. As far as they could see, the water glowed with lights seemingly floating on the water's surface. When the seamen scooped the lights into a bucket, they collected only dark sea water.

Anticipation was building that Van Diemen's Land would be sighted soon because increasing amounts of seaweed were floating by, a sure sign that land cannot be far away. Dutchman Abel Tasman had discovered the land in 1642 and named it after Van Diemen, a Dutch East India Company governor. On January 3 the lookout called from the mainmast crosstrees "LAND HO!" The southwest cape of Van Diemen's Land gradually came into view through a thick morning haze.

Jubilant congratulations were offered all around. Resisting the urge to steer in to take a better look, Phillip ordered the helmsman to hold his eastward course to make best use of the westerlies, which had been with them almost continually for a month and a half.

Too far from the shore to see much, Nathaniel anxiously awaited the telescope to be passed to him. Through it, he saw rugged, dark blue-gray mountains, running continuously from west to east, which appeared to be barren in some places. Disappointed that he could not see better, Nathaniel reasoned that the appearance of the land here was of little relevance to Botany Bay, some eight hundred miles further north.

At the eastern extent of Van Diemen's Land, the fleet was hit by a wind from the north and a strong current flowing southward that frustrated Phillip's desire to sail north. He ordered the crew to sail the *Supply* close-hauled to the wind on a northeast tack, losing sight of Van Diemen's Land on January 5.

For a week, north and northwest winds drove the *Supply* further into the Tasman Sea and away from New South Wales. When a favorable east wind came up, Phillip turned the bow west and made for land. On January 13 they sighted New South Wales from fifteen miles out and continued sailing to within eight miles of the coast. With the sun setting, Phillip decided to shorten sails and stand off until morning to make a safe approach to Botany Bay.

From eight miles away, Nathaniel thought the land looked flat and uninteresting except for a hill resembling the crown of a hat, which Captain Cook's map showed about seventy miles south of Botany Bay.

They were unable to sail the next day due to a lack of wind. When King determined their latitude by meridian angle at noon, he found the strong southbound current had taken the ship far south. The north winds pushed them further away from Botany Bay over the next three days.

During his night watch, Nathaniel saw many spots of light that he assumed were native campfires, just as he had seen along the coast of Van Diemen's Land. It was a comfortable night at sixty-six degrees. The temperature during the day, around eighty, had also suited him fine. He considered how he preferred these warmer temperatures to London's comparable mid-July temperatures, in the mid-fifties at night and about seventy during the day.

Near the end of his watch at midnight, Nathaniel and the quartermaster noticed that the wind had shifted around to the southwest. Phillip was notified of the favorable shift in wind direction. He immediately ordered the crew to make sail.

At ten o'clock in the morning, the *Supply* was forty miles from Botany Bay. Sailing three miles from shore, Nathaniel liked the varied landscape he saw: high chalk cliffs resisting the crash of the surf, yellow sand beaches, verdant woods, grassy slopes, and lowland marshes. But the vegetation was the same gray-green color that he had found unusual in Cape Town. Nearer to Botany Bay, the coastline became increasingly high headlands with half-moon beaches, one after another.

Nathaniel turned the telescope to the south and searched the horizon for Shortland's three transports. He was worried about Tom and George; their squadron had not been sighted for more than a month.

Using Captain Cook's charts, Phillip navigated the ship's slow approach toward the opening into Botany Bay. Cook had named the north headland at the bay's entrance Cape Banks and the south headland Cape Solander. At two in the afternoon of January 18, 1788, the *Supply* was about to complete a voyage of more than fifteen thousand miles in eight months and five days.

Nathaniel stood next to Lieutenant King, at the larboard gunwale, anxiously awaiting the first sight of the extraordinary bay he had read about in Cook's and Banks's accounts. It was a sunny and hot summer afternoon.

"INDIANS!—runnin' down that hill!" a seaman shouted, pointing at Cape Solander.

Another voice called out, "I see them!—*see 'em?*"

Others along the larboard side searched the hill.

"There's more comin' out!"

"They're black ... *and nude!*"

"What are they doin'?"

Men and women rushed from the starboard side of the ship and joined in the excited pointing and shouting, thrilled by the sight.

"They're yellin' sumpin.'"

Nathaniel saw a group of eight to ten natives running down the hill brandishing their weapons. More emerged from the woods at the bottom of the hill and joined the others in shouting, jumping about, swinging clubs, and jabbing their lances, or spears, at them. At the bay entrance, the *Supply* came within five hundred feet of them gathered along the shore. Nathaniel strained to hear what they were yelling. Across the unobstructed water, the words "*Warra! Warra! Warra!*" reached his ears, repeated again and again.

"Not an auspicious welcome, I daresay," King said drily to Nathaniel as he handed him the telescope.

Through the telescope, Nathaniel confirmed what he thought he had seen: black men, utterly naked, with wood spears, clubs, and shields. *Savages*, he dismissively concluded, not much of a threat.

Captain Phillip ordered: "Furl the main topsail, Boatswain. Lieutenant Ball, make for the northern side of the bay, so we can be seen by Captain Shortland coming up the coast."

As the *Supply* angled north, four natives in two canoes urgently paddled for the northern shore.

Nathaniel scanned the large bay, perhaps four-miles wide. The land was mostly low and undulating with a few small hills here and there. Alluring sand beaches, golden in the bright sunlight, were interspersed with indefinite shores of tall grasses and reed marshes. The higher ground was well treed. After months of breathing salt air, he luxuriated in the refreshing breeze blowing down from the hills. A great variety of seabirds, disturbed by the ship entering their fishing grounds, flew up to scream their protest at them. Nathaniel peered down through the crystal clear water and was delighted by the large number of fish darting about.

"It's a large, beautiful bay," King said to himself as much as to Nathaniel.

Pleased and relieved, Nathaniel's first impression of Botany Bay was positive. "It's everything I'd hoped it'd be," he said, perhaps too fervently, because it drew a curious look from King.

"Sound out your depths *loudly!*" ordered Lieutenant Ball to the two seamen dropping lead sounding lines to determine the water's depths.

Nathaniel noticed that the four Indians had pulled their canoes onto the beach and sat down, evidently, to watch the approach of the ship.

The anchor was dropped in five fathoms a third of a mile from the beach. Within minutes of anchoring, Phillip commanded, "Hoist the longboat. I want to have a look around." While the boat was being removed from the deck and put overboard, Phillip took King and Nathaniel aside.

"You've both read about Cook's landing here eight years ago. It was opposed by two Indians whom Cook felt obliged to fire on to force their withdrawal. I do not intend to repeat that most unfortunate first contact. We are here to establish a colony and must, from the start, win the trust of the native people. I intend to approach them alone and unarmed with signs of friendship to win their confidence. When I am making my advance, I expect you two to maintain order. Nothing less than absolute necessity shall require you to fire on them. Do you both understand?"

King and Nathaniel said simultaneously "Yes, sir."

Nathaniel assembled his men. "You three, load shot. You two, powder only." The powder only loads would be used to warn and scare the natives.

Phillip did not head for the four native men sitting peacefully on the northern shore as Nathaniel had expected. Instead, he ordered the coxswain to row the boat some distance west before landing. He and King walked across the beach and up onto a grassy dune and briefly discussed whether the grass there was suitable for the animals on board the ship. Reboarding the longboat, Phillip directed it further west before ordering their return to the *Supply*.

Nathaniel was confused—were they going to make contact with the natives? Nearing the ship, Phillip finally ordered the coxswain to land the boat twenty feet west of the four natives, who were still sitting quietly on the beach. I see now, Nathaniel told himself, the commodore wants the Indians to see we mean them no harm before rowing toward them.

As the longboat approached the landing spot, the native men stood and warned them away by threatening with their eight- to twelve-foot spears. Phillip stood at the bow of the boat offering brightly colored bead necklaces and ribbons of red cloth. He spoke in a soothing tone.

"We come in peace. You have nothing to fear from us."

Nathaniel assessed the danger to Phillip. Although agitated, the savages did not look enraged enough to throw their spears, some tipped with jagged fish or animal bones held in place by a gummy-looking substance. Most of their spears were simply sharpened to a point. Each native held a hooked stick, about three feet long, which did not appear to be much of a weapon. One also held a small shield made of wood bark.

They were thin, straight, rough-looking, black men, around five and a half feet tall, with tangled black hair and bushy beards. All four were naked. Their chests and arms were ornamented with lines of raised scars. Two wore a white bone or stick, fixed crossways, through the septum of the nose.

Even though Phillip had told him his intentions, Nathaniel considered it unwise when the commodore ordered everyone to stay in the longboat except the coxswain who would land the boat. Discreetly, Nathaniel cocked a hidden pistol.

Speaking in a calm voice and offering the trinkets in outstretched arms, Phillip walked alone toward the four native men. The men backed away as he approached, leaving their canoes. Keeping his eyes on them, Phillip said:

"Coxswain come here and attach these gifts to their canoes."

While the coxswain did as ordered, Phillip asked the natives, through sign language, where drinking water could be found. They pointed east, down the beach. Thanking the natives, Phillip turned his back to them and walked calmly back to the longboat. While Phillip climbed into the longboat, the four men walked back to their canoes and excitedly divided the necklaces and ribbons among themselves.

Obviously curious, the four natives walked along the beach opposite the longboat as it was rowed eastward. After walking a hundred or so yards, they pointed into the woods and backed away when the boat was landed. Taking Nathaniel and two privates with him, Phillip found a small pond of fresh water two hundred feet from the beach.

To express his gratitude, Phillip again approached the four with different trinkets, but they would not come close enough to receive them. The oldest-looking man pointed down indicating that Phillip should lay the gifts on the sand. He did so and backed away. The old man came forward and, as he picked up them up, exclaimed "*Ah!*" when he saw his reflection in a small mirror gift. Laughing ecstatically, he ran back to show the others.

Phillip was pleased with this first contact. He bid the natives goodbye and returned to the *Supply*.

The next morning at nine, everyone on the *Sirius* was surprised and relieved to hear a shout from the mainmast crosstrees "AHOY! *the three transports are comin'!*" By ten, Shortland's three ships were anchored near the *Supply*.

Ross was the first officer to board the *Supply*. He was in an cantankerous mood and, instead of greeting Phillip, said, "Have the Indians been a problem, sir? We saw a great number o' them on Point Solander shoutin' at us an' threatenin' us wi' their weapons!"

"Welcome aboard, Major Ross," Phillip said as though he had not heard his rant. "We arrived ourselves only late yesterday afternoon. Shortly after, we had a very satisfying parley with four armed natives on the northern shore. They pointed out a pond of fresh water for us. They were quite friendly, I'm pleased to tell you. We shall further explore the northern side of the bay today. Perhaps you'll join us?"

"Of coorse, sir, it wou'd be my pleasure," Ross responded coolly.

The two men moved aside to allow Shortland, George, Tom, and other officers to step onto the deck of the *Supply*. Tom and Nathaniel, beaming, vigorously shook hands and then spontaneously embraced. Aware of their unmilitary behavior, they quickly separated and beat each other on the back. George walked up and shook hands enthusiastically with Nathaniel. Everyone was celebrating and dispersing into groups to share their stories.

"How—" Tom and Nathaniel both asked at once. They laughed, and Tom went first.

"How was it on the little *Supply*? I was worried about you in the large seas we had."

Tom, George, and Nathaniel talked for thirty minutes until the coxswain's pipe announced that the two explorer longboats were ready. Tom returned to the *Scarborough* as the marine commanding officer of the day. George and Nathaniel joined the explorers.

Captain Shortland commanded the longboat that Nathaniel was assigned to. Shortland was ordered by Phillip to explore the most northerly extent of the bay. The party rowed up a river for four miles in search of solid ground on which to establish the colony. The land was mostly boggy along both side of the river. Leaving the boat at several promising locations, they did not find any fresh water.

Phillip's party headed for a large river entering the bay on its southwestern side. They explored its many tidal coves, leaving the boat several times. At one possible settlement site, they found a freshwater streamlet and three deserted native shelters, which were small and crudely made of mounded branches covered with leaves and bark. The land looked fertile but was hemmed in by marshes. When the lateness of the day forced their return to the ships, Phillip was disappointed that they had not found a site for the colony.

At eight the next morning, a seaman on watch called out that a ship was approaching from the south. It was the *Sirius*, not expected for a week or two! She proceeded into Botany Bay followed, one after another, by the six ships of her squadron: *Prince of Wales, Borrowdale, Fishburn, Lady Penrhyn, Charlotte,* and the *Golden Grove.* As greetings were shouted, Phillip waved to Captain Hunter with a big smile. When Hunter came aboard the *Supply*, Phillip greeted him grandly.

"Upon my soul, my dear Captain, how in heaven's name did you get here so quickly with all your slow ships in tow?"

Hunter beamed. "I took the squadron further south after your four ships disappeared over the horizon, Commodore. We had strong westerlies all the way. We're completely out of wood and coal and hay for the animals. Some of the ships are riding low in the water . . . but we're all here, sir."

Phillip was thinking, damme, I haven't found a site for our settlement yet! What am I going to do with all these people? "We arrived ourselves only two days ago, Captain. I regret to say that we have not found a suitable site for our colony on the northern and western sides of the bay. I am sending out three boats this morning to explore the southern side. I would like you to take soundings using Cook's maps to identify possible anchorages close to shore."

King and Nathaniel were sent to a promising cove on the southern shore. After exploring the cove from the boat, King led Nathaniel and four marines up a hill where he hoped to find a freshwater stream. When they reached the top, a large, reddish dog came out of the undergrowth, snarling and growling.

"*Don't shoot him, men!*" Nathaniel ordered. "He doesn't look wild; it could be an Indian's dog."

No sooner had Nathaniel said these words than a large group of native men suddenly appeared with their long spears. They angrily shouted and made motions with their hands for them to leave.

"Everyone remain calm," King said in a voice of quiet authority, while he unbuckled his sword and let it fall to the ground.

Nathaniel did not like the odds: There were eleven Indians and just six of them; only two of his marines carried muskets loaded with shot.

King offered beaded necklaces and ribbons, while speaking reassuringly as Phillip had done. The native men held their ground and let him know to come no further. He laid the gifts on a log and backed away. Three of the men came forward and took the trinkets back to the others. Laughing and jostling one another, they put the necklaces around their necks and tied the ribbons around their heads, necks, and arms.

A native suddenly stepped back and threw his spear wide of King's group to show the distance it would go. Nathaniel saw that the short hooked stick was not a weapon but a throwing stick for a spear. The thrower ran after his spear, some forty yards away, and made a great show of exertion pulling it out of ground.

Less hostile now, the natives returned to shooing King's group away while saying, "Warra! Warra!"

"Back away slowly," King said, "they mean us no harm." At the brow of the hill, King halted and offered them more trinkets. The men refused. King, Nathaniel, and the four marines slowly backed down the hill.

The natives followed them until they occupied the top of the hill. They started to yell and jump about in a way that Nathaniel could not interpret. Are they furiously warning us off or celebrating victory? He did not trust the natives and kept his eyes on them as he continued to back down the slope. Seeing one of them step back and arch his body, he realized the Indian was about to throw his spear. In horror, he saw the spear heading for the marine nearest him, who did not see it coming.

Shouting *"Look out!"* Nathaniel hit the marine with his body and spun with him behind a tree. The spear whistled by and stuck in the ground below them.

King had also seen the native throw the spear and ordered:

"Powder only—*fire at them!*"

BANG, BANG.

The two musket shots echoed through the woods and the natives disappeared from the top of the hill.

Rowing out of the cove, King's group saw Phillip's longboat coming toward them. Phillip had hurriedly left Point Solander when he heard the shots.

"What was that firing we heard?" Phillip asked testily.

After King related the encounter, Phillip ordered a return to the hill.

As their two boats approached the shore, the same group of warriors appeared on the slope yelling and making threatening gestures with their weapons. Phillip ordered King to stay back, while his boat went forward and landed. He then repeated his solitary approach that had been successful the first day and reestablished peace with the natives.

Feeling reproached, King whispered to Nathaniel, "I fear for the commodore's safety if he continues to put himself at such risk as this."

Nathaniel said, "They may respect him for his old age and perceive him as less of a threat than someone younger, such as yourself, sir."

After all of the boats had returned in the late afternoon, Phillip called a meeting in his wardroom to assess the findings of the explorers. The leaders of the reconnaissance boats reported disappointing explorations.

In a concerned tone, Phillip said, "I'm afraid we face a very serious situation, gentlemen. None of the reconnaissance boats has found an adequate source of fresh water to sustain the colony. The soil is generally poor for farming here, either a thin layer of loam with sand beneath or boggy." Looking at Hunter, he asked, "Captain, what do you think of the anchorage?"

"I couldn't find any anchorage of four or more fathoms close to shore, sir. All anchorage is beyond the reach of piers."

"It appeared so on Cook's maps," Phillip said.

"Lighters would have to be used to ferry cargo to and from the shore," Hunter continued. "I'm also concerned that the bay is open and unprotected, Commodore."

"I am as well," Phillip agreed. "A greater concern is that I've found no site with the physical aspects for settlement that I'm looking for."

"Whit are ye lookin' fir, Commodore?" Ross asked.

"Ideally, Major, I'd hoped to find a raised site divided by a bridgeable freshwater stream running into a protected harbor, where ships could moor to a short pier. The soil along either side of the stream should be good for crops. I'd put the convicts on one side of the stream and everyone else on the other side. I've found nothing close to that around Botany Bay.

"Tomorrow, I shall take a cutter and two longboats north to explore Port Jackson and, if necessary, Broken Bay. Captain Cook sailed by both inlets and gave them their names but did not enter either. If I do not find a better site, we'll have to settle here. The site on Cape Solander looks the best to me." Turning to Ross, he said,

"Major, pray begin clearing land near the small stream we found there. Mr. King, I want you to continue exploring the bay, in case we've missed a better site. Captain Hunter, you shall accompany me. Lieutenant Armstrong, I want you to bring along two of your convict farmers.

"Now, before we adjourn, I would like Surgeon General White to report on his count of the number who have died on the voyage here."

"Since embarkation, we have lost thirty-six convict men, four women, and five of their children," White said. "We have also lost one marine, one marine's wife, and one of their children. A total of forty-eight in all. God save their souls. This is a sad, but I think, a very reasonable number, Commodore Phillip."

"Thank you, Mr. White, and all of you, gentlemen, for your diligence in keeping this number a low one."

Leaving the meeting, George invited Nathaniel to sup with him and Tom in the *Scarborough*. Tom and George had become close friends on the *Scarborough* during their voyage together across the Southern Ocean. After supper, the three of them sat in George's cozy cabin imbibing his Constantia wine from Cape Town.

Nathaniel told them about the spear-throwing incident that morning, and they discussed the perils of Phillip's policy of placing himself at risk to make peace with the Indians.

"We had another encounter with them in the afternoon," Nathaniel said. "Although this time, it was funny and rather bizarre. As we continued west, we rowed up a cove to its head where there was a small village and a group of friendly men and boys. They came over to the boat, and we gave them gifts. Through sign language, King was able to engage them in confused conversation. A grisly old man, stinking from some kind of oily substance smeared all over his body, asked a question by pointing at King's crotch and then his own hanging cock."

"We broke out laughing when we finally understood that the old chief was askin' King what *sex* he was. I think they thought we were women because we don't have beards as they do. Anyway, King ordered seaman Farnley to"—recalling the scene, Nathaniel laughed—"to drop his breeches! Farnley, bein' the clown he is, obliged, and there was this great *whoop* of surprise from them . . . or maybe admiration—Farnley had his back to me." Chuckling, Nathaniel paused for a drink of wine.

"By now most of us are out of the boat. The old black yells something and, lo and behold, out of the woods pops ten or so women and girls all in their *au naturel.* They come prancin' over for gifts, and the chief *offers them to us!*"

Tom said, "No!—*for sex?*"

"Aye."

"Eh, what!" George said. "Pray, why would he do that?"

"I don't know, George, but 'pon my word, he did." Regaining his comical face, Nathaniel continued. "King says 'No thank ye very kindly, old fellow' and takes a handkerchief out and covers his own crotch with it and points. . . ha ha . . . *at a woman's bush!* tellin' her to *cover up!*"

Tom guffawed and George chuckled.

"I'm not . . . ha ha ha . . . kiddin.' She walks right up to him— *stark naked*—and King holds his handkerchief in front of her most private part. She's laughin'—*we all are!* She doesn't know what the hell he's doing . . . so she takes his handkerchief and *ties it around her neck!*"

Chapter 3

Starvation

"Port Jackson is an unbelievably beautiful harbor with many large bays, sandy beaches, snug coves, and scattered islands. You'll be amazed when you see it."

After two days of exploring the waters of the port, as a member of Phillip's party, Nathaniel enthusiastically described what he had seen to Tom and George.

"It's a sheltered, good-feeling harbor, not broad and exposed like Botany Bay. It's entered through two, high, rugged heads about a mile apart. Phillip said it's one of the finest harbors in the world, in which a thousand ships of the line might ride in perfect safety."

"How far north is it?" Tom asked.

"Twelve miles or so, a short sail. Once through the heads, the port branches off into several arms where the land is generally high and covered with trees except for occasional sand hills and grassy slopes. The shores are picturesque with the most interesting, sculptured rock cliffs I've ever seen."

"It sounds extraordinary," said George with impatience in his voice. "But did the commodore find a better place for our settlement? *That's* what I care about."

"Yes. The second day, about five miles in, we arrived at a protected cove that he liked. It has a good depth of water to accept the entire fleet and anchorage close to shore. The land slopes down to the water and a stream of fresh water runs down the center of it. There's an abundance of fish in the cove; the American seaman, Nagle, dropped a line in and caught a large one for our dinner. Convict Fox, a farmer, told me the soil looks good for crops, not boggy as at Botany Bay. Phillip was quite pleased and named it Sydney Cove in honor of Lord Sydney."

Tom asked, "Did you see many Indians?"

"We saw them often in small groups along the water's edge and fishing from their canoes. A large group of them waded out unarmed and unafraid to receive the baubles the commodore was holding out to them. He told us to land, and we ate there with them sitting around staring at us. Their faces and bodies were smeared with a disgusting white clay. Phillip was impressed by their *manly* behavior and named the place Manly Cove. I didn't see anything manly about them myself, more like children, I'd say."

"So we'll be moving again," Tom said. "All the work we've done here is for nothing."

"I don't mind, Tom," George said, "if we have a better place to settle. We can get the livestock and everyone back on board tomorrow and leave the next day."

At dawn the next morning, as Nathaniel was dressing, he heard somebody yell down the hatchway that a large warship was approaching. Thinking it was a joke, he laughed with others around him until they heard the shrill sound of the boatswain's pipe calling all hands to their assigned stations. Nathaniel rushed up the ladder to the upper deck and, as he set foot on it, was astonished to hear the cry "*A second man-of-war!*"

The Dutch have followed us to Botany Bay! was Nathaniel's first anxious thought—or it could be the French!—*are we at war again?* He ran to the quarterdeck and stood next to Lieutenant Ball, who was looking through a telescope at the two ships.

"They're too far off to make out their flags," Ball said.

Both warships were much larger than the *Sirius*. A northwest wind blowing out from the bay was working against their approach. Captain Phillip came up to the quarterdeck. Ball handed him the telescope. The commodore loudly ordered "QUIET!" to stop the excited chatter. *Supply's* flagman stood near Phillip, awaiting orders to signal the *Sirius* and the other ships of the fleet.

"What do you see?" Phillip asked the quartermaster, who was looking through a telescope and reputedly had the best eyesight on the *Supply*.

"Can't tell, Capt'n, their flag looks white—French—but I can't be sure, sir."

Next to the flagman, a marine drummer stood ready to beat "Hearts of Oak" that would send the ship's company and marines to their battle stations.

"Beat to quarters, Commodore?" Ball asked.

"Yes, Mr. Ball," Phillip said, but immediately changed his mind. "No, belay that!" He watched the two ships tack into the wind again. They were being driven south with every tack. Their captain had not adequately compensated for the strong southbound current, which in combination with the northwest wind would drive them by Botany Bay and further south.

"They will not be able to manuever into Botany Bay in this wind." Phillip handed the telescope back to Ball. "Signal the other ships, no change of orders."

The unknown ships were soon out of sight. Later in the morning, Phillip recalled that in late 1785 two French ships under the command of Comte de La Pérouse had set out on a voyage of discovery around the world. He concluded these had to be La Pérouse's two ships.

At daybreak the next morning, the unconfirmed ships were nowhere in sight. The fleet was ready to sail; the wind, however, had shifted around strongly from the southeast making it impossible for eleven ships to maneuver safely out of the bay.

Phillip met with Hunter. "On this wind, I expect the two ships we saw yesterday will be able to make their way into the bay. I believe they're La Pérouse's expedition. Whether they are or not, I've decided to attempt to sail the *Supply* out of the bay to prepare Sydney Cove for the arrival of the entire fleet. Lieutenant Armstrong is transferring all of his convict artificers to the *Supply* as we speak. You are to follow with the fleet as soon as conditions permit."

"Yes sir, Commodore," Hunter said as he wondered what he would do if the two warships turned out to be hostile.

Phillip continued. "My Home Office instructions are to abstain from intercourse with foreign powers, for obvious security reasons, until our settlement is well established. Therefore, if La Pérouse enters the bay before you leave, you are to tell the Frenchman, simply, that the fleet is leaving to find a better location for settlement. Under no circumstances are you to mention Port Jackson or allow La Pérouse to accompany you."

The *Supply* arrived in Sydney Cove that evening. In the morning, the convicts were put to work clearing the land. A flagstaff was erected and the British Union Jack displayed. By late afternoon, there was still no sight of Hunter and the fleet. Phillip was concerned that the fleet might arrive with La Pérouse, compromising Britain's claim of sovereignty with French ships in Port Jackson. He gathered the officers around the flagpole to claim Sydney Cove, the site of the new colony, for king and country. Phillip's declaration was followed by three volleys from the marines and three cheers from the men on land and on the *Supply*.

When the fleet finally arrived at sunset, Hunter went ashore and reported to Phillip. "It was La Pérouse as you presumed, Commodore. He entered the bay as we were attempting to leave. Through an officer I sent to greet him, I was able to advise him as you instructed. We left him in Botany Bay."

Phillip was pleased and invited Hunter and other officers, who had come ashore, to join him at the flagstaff for a second ceremony. The commodore toasted His Majesty, and they all drank to the success of the new colony. The date was January 26, 1788, celebrated years later as Australia Day; the day that Britain took possession of Australia.

Early the next day, the male convicts were organized into work details to prepare Sydney Cove for settlement. The women convicts were left on the transports, so they would not distract the men from their work.

Phillip had prepared a rough village plan with the surveyor general and walked around with his officers pointing out where various camps and facilities were to be located. The stream allowed Phillip to realize his hope of segregating the convicts from the rest of the settlement. He placed the men's and women's convict camps beside each other on the rocky west side of Sydney Cove and located "respectable" people on the east side. Because many of the convicts were ill, the hospital was sited on the west side near them. The marines were to establish their camp along the stream, at the head of the cove, to act as a buffer between the two groups.

A prefabricated "Government House," a wood-framed, five-room, white canvas tent, would be placed high in the center of the east side. Phillip pointed out locations for the lieutenant governor, judge advocate, provost marshal, surveyor general, commissary of stores, Chaplain and Mrs. Johnson, and other officials. To reward the male convicts who had been working well with Nathaniel, Phillip placed their camp on the east side. The commissary's storehouse would be built next to a future wharf and pier into the cove. The storehouse, normally a military food and supply depot, would serve everyone.

During an afternoon staff meeting concerning implementation of the village plan, Judge Advocate Collins said, "Commodore, I'm concerned that the men's and women's convict camps may be a source of mischief placed next to each other. Wouldn't it be prudent to separate them, perhaps by the marines' camp or the hospital?"

"I expect you're right, Mr. Collins," Phillip said with a knowing smile, "but what can we do, really? I fear that we must be harshly realistic and bow to the inevitability of the convicts' immorality. My main concern is to preserve the settlement from dangerous urges and gross irregularities between men. The convict men, after all, have been separated from women for a very long time."

As the meeting proceeded, Collins's concern gnawed at Phillip's conscience. There must be some women of moral character, he thought, who deserve to be protected. If I remove 30 women, I will still have more than 160 females to accommodate the 570 sex-starved male convicts and some 350 rowdy, discontented sailors until the ships leave. I expect the prostitutes among them will live quite well for a while.

Near the end of the meeting, Phillip said, "Mr. Collins, you made a good point earlier. Lieutenant Armstrong, I would like you to identify not more than thirty women who have been well-behaved on the voyage, and place them on the east side out of harm's way. The rest of the convict women, most of abandoned character, will serve nature's purposes, whether we like it or not."

After four days of work, a brewing conflict between Ross and Phillip came out into the open while the commodore was leading his staff on an inspection of the work underway. Approaching Second Lieutenant Freddy, who was in charge of the marines guarding a gang of convicts clearing an area for the convict camps, Phillip said, "I'm very disappointed, Lieutenant, that you've made so little progress since I was last here, two days ago."

The lieutenant, who had come to attention when the group of officers walked up, said, "Yes sir, sorry sir. These shirkers won't work hard, sir."

"Well then—prod them, man!" Phillip said sternly. "I want the women off the ships and into this area in a few days!"

The lieutenant looked at Major Ross with pleading eyes and said, "Yes sir."

"It's nae his responsibility tae *prod* the convicts, Commodore," Ross said flatly from behind Phillip.

Phillip turned angrily and glared at Ross for questioning his order.

Ross met Phillip's look with haughty disdain. "My orders are *quite* clear, sir. The marines have nae responsibility, whitsoever, to *oversee* the work o' convicts."

"Now is not the time to discuss this matter, Major. Since the Home Office neglected in their planning to provide us with overseers—"

Ross interrupted him. "*Plannin'*, ye didnae see fit tae include *me*, sir."

"—we must be flexible to accomplish our goals," Phillip completed his sentence. "Your marines need to do more than simply march the convicts to their work assignments and guard them. I simply ask that they *encourage* the convicts to do their work, that's all I ask."

"*Nae sir,*" Ross replied adamantly, "I winnae order them tae *encourage* or tae *oversee,* in any way, the convicts' work." Ross's jaw was set and his cheeks were reddish. He appeared rigidly committed to his position. "Those are nae traditional duties of His Majesty's Marines an' the Admiralty didnae assign them tae me."

"Then *how*, my good Major, are we to *cope*?" asked an exasperated Phillip.

Ross looked unconcerned and did not answer for several seconds, then with an insolent air, he said, "I suggest ye find anither way, Commodore."

Mockingly, Phillip said, "*You* do not have a suggestion, I assume?"

Ross did not respond. Angry, his lips were set tightly. Their confrontation grew tense as the two men stonily stared at each other.

Speaking quietly, Nathaniel asked the major, "May I make a suggestion, Major Ross?" Ross's reddened face swung around to him; surprisingly, he nodded. Nathaniel looked for permission from Phillip, who also nodded for him to proceed.

"May I suggest that we select convicts as overseers. Men with some degree of leadership or even harshness, to force the others to work. Of course, Commodore, you'll have to give them extra privileges or some kind of incentive to do so. Perhaps they should oversee in pairs, for safety. If the other convicts attack them, then, of course, the marines shall keep order."

"Do you think you can identify convicts willing to *turn* on their fellows?" Phillip asked, a bit too harshly, "because that's precisely how it shall be seen by the other convicts."

"I can try, sir," Nathaniel answered, "after we discuss the incentives you are willing to offer them."

"And what, pray, do you think of your lieutenant's suggestion, Major?" Phillip asked Ross.

"I see nothin' in conflict wi' my orders, Commodore."

"Very well," Phillip said. "Lieutenant Armstrong, you may proceed with your suggestion. Gentlemen, I'll see you in my quarters at fourteen hundred hours, but now I have several private matters to attend to. Excuse me." Obviously disheartened, Phillip turned and stomped away alone, his head down, toward the eastern side of the cove.

On February 6 longboats plied between the transports and shore all day until the last boatload of women was brought ashore by late afternoon. The transport captains celebrated the unloading of their last convict transportees by giving their sailors extra rations of grog. At dusk, a violent thunderstorm rained down on the settlement, forcing everyone into their tents to shelter from the storm.

As it drew dark and the storm raged on, the male convicts, singly and in small groups, moved into the women's camp. About the same time, many drunken sailors rowed ashore to make merry with the convict women. Pandemonium broke out when the two groups of men met in the women's camp: fistfights, women shouting for their sailor lovers, men soliciting women with rum, singing, dancing, and raping, all under the cover of darkness and the noise-dampening thunderstorm.

The next morning the marines went into the convict camps and separated the men and women and sent the sailors back to their ships. With drums and fifes playing, the marines herded the drunken convicts into a clearing and told them to sit on the ground in front of a table. The marines formed around them. A short while later, Phillip, Ross, Judge Advocate David Collins, Surgeon General John White, and Reverend Richard Johnson arrived and sat down at the table. Collins read a royal commission document appointing Arthur Phillip the captain general and governor in chief over the territory of New South Wales. His supreme powers in all matters were clearly enumerated.

The governor thanked the civil officials and naval and marine officers for their many sacrifices. He then named the members of the magistrates court.

"I hereby direct these magistrates to deal harshly with all offenders, who break the laws of a decent and fair society. From this day forward, public disturbances, such as the one last night, will not be tolerated. Any unauthorized men seen in the women's camp after nine o'clock in the evening shall be arrested. If they try to flee, the sentries may fire at them with ball or shot.

"Some of you are idlers and shirkers who refuse to do your share of the work. I assure you that if you do not work you shall not eat, for the industrious should not labor for the idle.

"Furthermore, stealing and killing any livestock for food will be a capital offense, punishable by hanging. These animals cannot be replaced. Be forewarned, there will be no mercy, because the survival of our colony is at stake."

Phillip went on to tell the convicts that by industry and good behavior they would regain the advantages that society has to offer them. He strongly recommended marriage and offered to assist those willing to conform to the laws of morality and religion. The governor finished by pledging that he would serve the colony to the best of his ability and would act in all matters for the public good.

To conclude the event, the naval band of drums and fifes played *God Save the King*, stopping between stanzas for three musket volleys. The convicts were conducted back to their camps by the marines, and Governor Phillip treated the officers and officials to lunch in a tent pitched for the occasion.

Over the next week, Chaplain Johnson married fourteen convict couples.

◎

I'm sorry you're leaving, sir," Nathaniel said to Lieutenant Philip Gidley King as they walked together toward the governor's five-room tent. Appointed by Phillip as the superintendent and commandant of Norfolk Island, King would be leaving soon to colonize the island.

"The governor is going to be lost without you. I fear I'll only disappoint him as his adjutant."

"Bosh, my good Lieutenant, you'll do fine," King said.

"I don't have nearly your experience. I was quite content with my previous position working for you and Captain Evans."

"You underestimate your abilities, Nathaniel. Don't think about it, just keep doing what you've been doing, and you'll serve him well."

"Believe me, sir, I'm not looking for compliments, but *what* have I been doing that Governor Phillip likes?—other than working with the convicts."

"You're rather strategic in your thinking. You see possibilities and solutions. Most people who are ambitious, and I count you as one and myself as another, think first of themselves; you don't. And then there's truthfulness. If you do nothing other than continue to advise His Excellency honestly, without guile, you'll serve him well. Mind you, the moment you start telling him what you *think* he wants to hear, you change from an advisor to a sycophant. In the end, though, you're just one of several advisors; the governor will weigh all the advice he receives and then do what he believes is best."

"I'll remember that, sir, thank you. However, I still don't understand why the governor has decided to send you off so quickly to settle Norfolk Island."

"Well, as you know, His Excellency dispatched me to meet with Monsieur de La Pérouse in Botany Bay." He winked. "Ostensibly to pay his respects and to offer assistance. . . . I learned that just before coming here, the Frenchman had sailed around Norfolk Island and tried to land. He was prevented by a heavy sea and violent surf. My impression is that he intends to return to the island.

"The Home Office and the Admiralty have both ordered the governor to colonize Norfolk Island for its timber and flax, *before* the French or some other foreign power can establish a conflicting claim. The governor wants me to establish our settlement and claim the island before La Pérouse arrives."

On February 14 King sailed out of Port Jackson on the *Supply* with provisions for six months, a small staff, six marines, and fifteen convicts (nine men and six women) to colonize the island, located a thousand miles northeast into the Pacific.

Three weeks later, La Pérouse sailed out of Botany Bay and vanished. In 1826 the wreckage of his two ships was found off the Solomon Islands.

Nathaniel walked to the government farm established in the next cove east, named appropriately Farm Cove, to see how Robert Fox, one of the convict overseers he had chosen, was doing in his new role. Six acres had been cleared and sown with wheat and barley.

Fox explained that the soil was not as good as they had initially thought. He called another farmer, James Ruse, over to support his assessment.

"He's right, Lieutenant; 'tis thin soil. Let me show you." Ruse scraped away leaves and debris with his spade. "The top layer is leaf mold an' un'er that there's only a thin layer o' loam." He bent down on one knee and dug through the loamy soil with his hand. "See below, 'tis mostly sand an' rocks—not very fertile." He dabbed a dirty finger onto his tongue. "An' it taste salty too. Withaht animal manure worked into it, an' we don't 'ave none, crops'll be poor."

Fox added a thought. "Better soil is prob'bly inland, away from ocean sand an' salty air."

"You ough'a be lookin' at the start of the port," Ruse said, "above where it's tidal, along freshwater streams."

"You're probably right, but we need crops here where the settlement can use them," Nathaniel said. "You'll just have to do the best you can until we have a chance to explore the port's headwaters. I'll talk to the governor about it."

Later that day, during a staff meeting with Phillip, Nathaniel detailed the farmers' negative opinion of the soil at Farm Cove and their suggestion that better soil might be found along the freshwater tributaries of the harbor. The governor grumbled:

"We were misled by Joseph Banks's glowing report of rich soil at Botany Bay and now we find Sydney Cove's is little better. The home secretary expects us to be self-sufficient when the second fleet of convicts arrives."

"When is the second fleet expected, sir?" George asked, thinking of his family.

"I don't know exactly, but well within two years of our arrival here. The Home Office will await my dispatch, I should think, before sending the second fleet. They, of course, haven't heard from us since Cape Town, so they don't know that all eleven ships arrived safely and the colony has been established. I've discharged the *Charlotte, Lady Penrhyn*, and *Scarborough* to proceed to China before returning to England. They'll carry my dispatches requesting overseers, skilled convicts, additional supplies, and more women to remedy the imbalance of the sexes." Phillip noticed the judge advocate's concerned look. "What's worrying you, Mr. Collins?"

"Does that mean we have to wait *two years* to be resupplied, Governor?"

"*Oh*, I'm sorry—*no*—not at all, my dear man. I expect to be resupplied by storeships later this year. We arrived with two years' provisions, and I was told that we would be reprovisioned by the end of the first year, so we would never be reduced to less than a year's provisions in store. Nevertheless, we need to produce greens to fight scurvy, so finding fertile soil is of the utmost importance. Mr. Armstrong, pray organize an expedition to Port Jackson's headwaters. We'll take provisions for a week.

"Now let's move on to another matter. Why are the natives staying away from the settlement?"

The seven men around the table looked at each other.

"Come now, gentlemen, no theories?" the governor asked. "How about you, Lieutenant Armstrong?"

"I don't know why, sir, but I think it's a blessing."

"Oh, I can't agree with that," Phillip said. "We need to understand them to ensure that they know we mean them no harm. Hostilities and wars often occur because of unfounded fears and misunderstandings."

"Sir, I think we have little tae fear from the blacks an' their primitive stone an' wood weapons," Ross said. "They're in a rude an' uncivilized state."

Phillip nodded toward Ross and looked around the table for further opinions.

"They are heathens and intimidated by us, Your Excellency," Reverend Johnson said. "They're ashamed of their nakedness. I imagine they are hoping that we leave soon."

Collins, sitting across from the reverend, said, "Chaplain, my concern is how they'll respond when they fully appreciate that we intend to stay."

There was a quiet moment.

"Sir," Nathaniel said to Phillip, "as our settlement expands, I feel that we're bound to come into conflict with them. That's why I said it's a blessing that they're leaving us alone now, when we're at our most vulnerable."

"You would agree, Lieutenant," Phillip asked, "that it would be helpful to know more about them? How many indigenes reside in the region, how they are organized, whether they have chiefs, or are unaffiliated family bands, as they appear?"

"From a military point of view, yes sir."

"Well . . . our orders are to treat them fairly, gentlemen, and to try to improve their lot," Phillip said, tired of the fruitless exchange. "It's a practical as well as a humane directive. There may be thousands of native warriors in the region against our two hundred. We do not want an Indian war on our hands, on top of everything else, now do we?"

That night, before falling asleep, Nathaniel pondered Phillip's often repeated directive that the Indians were to be treated with respect. He agreed but wished to heaven that they weren't here at all.

Nathaniel awoke the next morning to the raucous, laughing call of a kookaburra. Through the open flap of his tent, he could see the fiery morning sun rising clear in the bright blue eastern sky. Another glorious sunrise in Sydney Cove, he said to himself, so much better than the perpetually hazy gray mornings of London. Nathaniel dressed and walked over to Tom's tent where he found him dressing.

"Tom, how would you like to go exploring?" Nathaniel asked him enthusiastically. "The governor has directed me to organize an expedition to explore west for better soil to cultivate."

"I'd like to, Nate, but Ross has put me in charge of guarding the brickmakers at the clay site on Long Cove" (present day Darling Harbour). "I'll be there for a fortnight, at least. It's going to take me away from my new girlfriend, Isabella, who I haven't told you about yet."

Nathaniel held up his hand. "I don't want to hear about you having sex, you lusty rascal—just don't get caught. There's regulations against us going to Whores Lane."

"She's not one of those drunken, old hags! She's just a kid."

"Really, Tom, I don't want to hear it; it's *hard* enough without listening to you, mate."

"Nate, no one cares! Aren't you tired of whacking off? I can get you laid for a pannikin of rum or a half pound of flour, m'lad. It's only you and the governor who go without—and maybe Ross. When the convicts build my hut, I'm going to have her live with me."

Over the next two days, Nathaniel recruited George, Sergeant Westover, five privates, and Robert Fox. Phillip brought along Judge Advocate Collins, Lieutenant Ball, and Surgeon General White, who had requested to be included.

The expedition left the settlement early in the morning in two longboats rigged for sailing. After the two parties had sailed and rowed west about ten miles, the waterway split into two tidal branches. They got out of the boats to explore and shot several ducks and teal. Finding the lowland too sandy and marshy for cultivation, but the upland looking promising, Phillip sent the boats back with orders to return in a week. Tents were pitched for the night while the birds were picked, stuffed with salt beef, and roasted slowly over the campfire for a delicious dinner. It rained through the night.

The governor awoke in the morning complaining of an ache in his side and loins, which White thought was caused by the dampness and cold. Although in pain, Phillip led the way westward.

Most of the morning was spent fighting their way through an area of dense undergrowth. Frequent hatchet marks were made on trees to mark the route back. Coming out of the thicket at the northern branch of the harbor waterway, the explorers walked along it for two miles until the waterway narrowed and ran shallow over an area of large broad stones. Past the shallows the tide ceased and the water ran fresh. With the governor and some others feeling fatigued, camp was set up. Dinner was a kettle of soup made from two crows and a white cockatoo shot along the way. That night it rained again.

In the morning, the governor was still bothered by the pain in his side. When the surgeon general expressed concern, Phillip said, "We must go on, Mr. White, we haven't found the arable soil we seek."

The group struck uphill from the waterway and walked through gently rolling country where the trees were far apart with little underwood. Hopeful that the soil was fertile beneath patches of green grass, Phillip directed Robert Fox and three privates to dig a test pit.

Fox pointed at distinct layers of soil. "There's at least four inches of loam soil 'ere an' clay beneath, instead of sand like at Sydney Cove." He tasted the soil on his finger and spat it out. "It don't taste salty like at Sydney Cove, neither." A trick learned from Ruse, Nathaniel recollected. Pleased with the good soil, Phillip had Fox sow some seeds in several rows of turned earth beside the test pit.

Proceeding west, they investigated a grouping of three native shelters and concluded that they had been unoccupied for some time. A short distance beyond, a kangaroo was sighted drinking at a stagnant pond. George quickly fired a shot at it, but the kangaroo bounded off into thick cover. While organizing their camp for the evening, the tops of trees were filled repeatedly by flocks of vivid lorikeets chattering so loudly that the men had to yell to one another to be heard.

The next day, the party continued westward to the top of a rise that Phillip named Belle View. They saw a chain of high hills in the distance some twenty or so miles away, running in a north-south direction. The governor named the highest to the north Richmond Hill, a grouping of hills directly west Lansdown Hills, and several knolls to the south Carmarthen Hills. With the governor now unable to walk without an excruciating pain in his side and their provisions running low, they started back following the hatchet marks left on the sides of trees. While traversing a valley, the governor fell into a hole concealed by tall grass that further aggravated his aching side. The party rested at the test pit they had dug on the third day.

"Having found no better soil than here," Phillip said, "I name this area 'Rose Hill' after Sir George Rose, a past secretary of the treasury and a close friend and neighbor of mine. I intend to send a detachment to farm here, as soon as I can spare some people from the urgent work at Sydney Cove."

◉

On May 21 convict William Ayres staggered into Sydney Cove badly wounded by a spear. His companion, Peter Burns, had been dragged off by the natives. Ayres said they were picking wild "sweet tea" leaves when the Indians sneaked up on them and attacked for no reason. Captain George Evans led a detachment of marines that found Burns's bloody clothes but not his body, which was never found. Burns was the first white person murdered by the natives.

Convicts William Okey and Samuel Davis, nine days later, were found murdered in the fourth bay east of Sydney Cove. They were rushcutters who had been left in a camp there to cut rushes for the thatched roofs of the wattle and daub huts being built by the convicts in Sydney Cove. The natives left three spears in Okey's chest. Phillip himself led an unsuccessful search for their murderers as far south as Botany Bay.

On June 22 John Prescott and two other convicts escaped from the settlement. It was learned from other convicts that Prescott had talked about walking north to China, where the transports had gone, a distance he wrongly said was two hundred miles more or less. A unit of troops was sent in pursuit. They lost their way several times and returned five days later without success.

The three escapees had managed to steal a marine's musket, ammunition pouch, two knives, an iron pot, and provisions. When their food ran out, they intended to shoot game and pick berries to sustain themselves.

While exploring Broken Bay from a longboat, the surveyor general was hailed by two of the escapees. The convicts were starving and willingly surrendered their knives saying they were lost and had been walking in circles for days. They had been attacked, and Prescott was killed as he fired the musket at the Indians.

Over drinks with Tom and George, Nathaniel expressed his frustration with Phillip, who would not agree to strike back at the natives in retribution for the murder of the four convicts.

"The governor finds all kinds of reasons why the convicts have brought this on themselves. He points to the stealing of Indian canoes, spears, and shields to sell to the sailors for resale in England. Even if that's true, we can't allow them to kill us without retaliation. He wants to find the ones who did the killing, but that's impossible. I think we have to show them the superiority of our weapons before this gets out of hand."

"I agree," George said. "The blacks are tellin' us that we can't live in peace with them. They want a fight. So let's get on with it. I'd rather fight them now than later, when Martha and my son arrive."

"You've *already* sent them letters to come?" Tom asked.

"Yes, I've given a letter to each of the transport captains that have left and have four more letters going out on the *Alexander, Friendship, Prince of Wales,* and *Borrowdale.*"

I wouldn't want to stay, Tom told himself, and then recalled that George had wanted land from the start.

"I'm concerned for Phillip's safety," Nathaniel said. "He's going to get himself killed the way he places his trust in these savages. After the murder of the rushcutters, we marched to Botany Bay and unexpectedly came on a large group of them. He disarmed himself and walked right among them."

"The blacks know he is our chief and that there would be war if he were killed," George postulated. "Have you noticed that the governor is missing a front tooth like so many of them?"

"Tench thinks it's some kind of a manhood initiation rite," Tom said.

"That may have helped the governor initially to be seen as some kind of a father figure, but not anymore," Nathaniel said, "not after the murders and not after they know we intend to stay."

As Fox and Ruse had predicted, the first harvest in August and September of wheat and barley at Farm Cove was paltry. The private gardens of officers and officials were equally disappointing. There was speculation that the seed was old or had been damaged in the long passage. The few plants that vegetated were attacked by field mice and ants. Phillip ordered the picking of wild spinach, parsley, celery, figs, berries, and sweet tea under marine guard to supplement the few greens harvested.

The governor asked the commissary for his assessment of the amount of food left in the government store and was advised that, at full rations, there was enough for only a year. Grains (flour, rice, and barley) were in the lowest supply. The governor made two decisions: to cut the weekly ration of grain by a pound to seven pounds and to send the *Sirius* to Cape Town for grains, seed for planting, and salt. He left unchanged the weekly rations of six pounds of salted meat (beef and pork) and three pints of dried peas. Every adult male, whether convict, marine, or official, received the same rations. Women received two-thirds of the men's rations because they were generally smaller and did not do heavy work. Children received one-third of the men's rations.

When Nathaniel was entering his twelve- by twelve-foot hut with his weekly rations, Tom rushed up to him in a distraught state. With terrified eyes, he said in an accusatory tone:

"*Nate*, did you know my name is on the list for the voyage to Cape Town?"

"*It is?* I'm sorry, Tom, I haven't seen it."

"*Rot*, you *had* to see it!" he said.

"Phillip left it to Ross. *Ach! are you accusing me?* I wouldn't have put you on it. *Dammit*, Thomas, what the hell's *wrong* with you?"

Tom's anger yielded to bewilderment. "I don't know . . . we never spend any time together anymore. I thoug—"

"So you thought I put you on the list to get *rid* of you?—for God's sake, Tom!"

"I'm not thinkin' straight," he said apologetically, "uh . . . I'm desperate, Nate. I *can't* go through the hell of the Southern Ocean again—and I'll lose Isabella. I like her. If I'm gone for six months, she'll move in with another gent. You're the governor's favorite; make me your assistant or think up some way for me to get *out* of this!"

"I don't have any sway with Ross—you know that. He's called me an *opportunist* to my face. I hate to say it, Tom, but he may have put you on the roster to hurt me, by sending off my best mate."

The *Sirius* set sail on October 2, 1788, with Tom on board. As the weeks passed, Nathaniel missed Tom and began to blame himself for his absence. If he had asked Phillip for a favor, might he have granted it? He knew he wouldn't have, still he blamed himself for not having tried.

The poor harvest and impending food shortage obliged the governor to establish a new government farm on the better soil he had found at the head of the harbor. Henry Dodd, who had farmed before becoming Phillip's butler, was made superintendent of Rose Hill. On November 2, Captain George Evans led a marine detachment guarding one hundred convicts, including Fox and Ruse, up the river to the test pit dug six months earlier.

Phillip, Nathaniel, and the surveyor general followed a few days later and marked out the ground at Rose Hill for a public farm, a redoubt, barracks, and convict camp. When they returned, the *Golden Grove* was anchored in Sydney Cove, safely returned from taking supplies to Norfolk Island. Commandant Philip Gidley King's dispatch gave a glowing report of the fertility of the island and its healthful climate. Nathaniel heard from *Golden Grove*'s captain that King was well and had taken a convict mistress, who lived with him in Norfolk Island's Government House.

Nathaniel decided that he had been chaste long enough. The privates in their barracks regularly visited Whores Lane, and most of the officers had woman convicts living with them in their huts. Even Captain Collins, the respected judge advocate, had a convict mistress, Nancy Yates, sharing his hut. Nathaniel was sure that Phillip knew by now that the "housekeepers" provided casual sex in addition to cooking, cleaning, and sewing. Nathaniel felt lonely and knew that Flora Hanson, an attractive convict woman, was available.

Flora was not among the thirty well-behaved women Nathaniel had chosen to live on the east side of the cove, but she had been less trouble than most. She married another convict the first month in Sydney Cove. After her husband had been hung for stealing and butchering an officer's pig, she was forced from their hut to live in a one-person pup tent.

Nathaniel saw Flora sitting on a tree stump, mending a sock, next to her tent in the women's convict camp. She stood when she realized he was walking up to her.

"Good afternoon, Flora, why are you living alone in that wee tent?" Nathaniel asked.

She seemed embarrassed that he was talking to her. All the convict women knew the name of the good-looking, kind lieutenant who worked closely with many of the convicts.

"Yer know thet Ben Jackson, Lew'tenent Armstrong, 'e forced me aht of me hut. The soldiers wouldn't do nuffin' abaht it. Told me ter live in this little tent, they did."

"Ben Jackson married Hannah . . . I can't recall her last name, but they have a baby, don't they?"

"Thet don't give 'em no raight to tike me John's hut thet 'e built wi' 'is own 'ands! It ain't raight! says I."

"I agree it's not right—that a women *as beautiful as you* should live alone in a tent." He was pleased that his statement surprised her and made her look down. "Would you like me to find you better housing?"

When she raised her head she was grinning. She coquettishly lamented, "Thet I would, sir. Wi' John gone, I don't 'ave no strong, 'and*some* man ter protect me, Lew'tenent."

"I have duties to attend to now, Flora. Would you like to discuss what I can do for you over supper in my hut this evening?"

She flipped her skirt and saucily said, "Ye're too kind, sir. Wot time?"

"How's eight o'clock?"

"Gud, sir—Lew'tenent Armstrong."

Her gleeful attitude told him that his chaste days were over.

◉

In the early months of 1789, fishermen and hunters reported that a plague of some sort was killing off the Indians around Port Jackson in increasing numbers. Phillip decided to take a boat out to see for himself accompanied by Surgeon General White, Nathaniel, and Arabanoo, a native man kidnapped several months earlier.

Arabanoo's capture had been ordered by the governor after deciding that hostilities with the natives could be avoided only through peaceful communications. Phillip wanted to learn their language and teach Arabanoo English, so the native could act as his intermediary. Lieutenant William Dawes and Captain Watkin Tench, who had taken an interest in the Indians, were assisting Phillip. The governor showed his good intentions to Arabanoo by housing him in Government House, dressing him in fine clothes, and dining with him as often as possible. Arabanoo had accepted his captive state well and was learning English, while the three officers were learning the rudiments of Arabanoo's language.

Because the natives had deserted the southern coves of the harbor near Sydney Cove, Phillip directed the coxswain to row across the harbor and into Shell Cove. Rowing near the water's edge of the cove, they came upon an emaciated man lying beside a flickering fire, attended by a young boy no older than nine. The boy anxiously shook the man who turned his head toward the boat but appeared too weak to move. Behind them, at the entrance to the natives' shelter lay the bloated body of a dead women and, a few feet away, a more recently deceased female child. The natives' skin eruptions became evident as Phillip's party walked up to them.

"Bugger me, they've got the pox, don't they?" the coxswain declared and stepped back. The marines next to Nathaniel murmured something in horror and also shrunk back from the family of natives, dead and dying in front of their crude, mounded, leaf and bark shelter, called a *humpy* by Arabanoo. Nathaniel forced himself to hold his place next to the governor and White.

"What do you think, Mr. White?" Phillip asked. "I trust it's measles or chickenpox, rather than smallpox."

"Their numerous pustules are a clear indication of smallpox, Excellency," White replied. "I'll know better after I treat them, if that's your desire."

"Yes, of course . . . we have a responsibility to help them. What do you think, Nathaniel?"

"I don't know, Governor." Turning to White, Nathaniel asked, "Do you mean treat them here or in Sydney Cove, Surgeon White?"

"In a separate part of the hospital."

Nathaniel was repulsed by the pustules covering the man's body. "It's highly contagious, isn't it?"

"Yes, especially to those who have never been exposed to it. I think that's why it's killing so many Indians, if our reports are accurate."

"Then they shouldn't be brought into Sydney Cove, in my opinion, Governor, certainly not near the hospital where there are so many sick and dying." Seeing the look on Phillip's face, Nathaniel quickly added: "Although it's harsh, Your Excellency, I think we should leave them alone and order our people to stay away from them until this runs its course."

"We *can't* do that, Nathaniel—in all humanity!" Phillip said, aghast. "I'll have a tent erected on the far west side, Mr. White, away from the hospital, though close enough for you to treat them in isolation."

The boy told Arabanoo his name was Nanbaree and the others were his parents and sister. While the marines gingerly moved the sick man to the boat, Arabanoo started to dig a hole in the sand with a flat stick. Phillip talked to him and then ordered several of the boat crew to help him dig a grave. Nathaniel maintained a distance from the smallpox victims. Arabanoo lined the grave with grass and helped place the mother into it. He then tenderly placed the body of the young girl next to her mother. The crewmen helped him pull more grass to place over the corpses before covering them in a mound of sand. Phillip noticed that Arabanoo said nothing over the grave.

Nanbaree and his father were taken to Sydney Cove, and a tent was erected as the governor had directed. The native man died two days later. Nanbaree survived and was adopted by Surgeon General White.

Over the next two months, many natives were treated in the remote smallpox station, but only a few survived. One young survivor who did not have a family to return to, a native girl named Booroong, was taken into by Reverend and Mrs. Johnson. Arabanoo contracted the disease and died two weeks later. At his burial,

Phillip estimated that half of the fifteen hundred natives in the area had either died or fled into the interior to escape the disease.

Hearing this, Nathaniel reasoned, it's too bad for them, but that explains why we haven't had many Indian problems lately.

On May 6, 1789, after being away for seven months and six days, the *Sirius* sailed through the heads into Port Jackson. The governor, Nathaniel, and many officers eagerly took boats out to meet the ship. Captain Hunter looked haggard as he greeted Phillip. Nathaniel looked around for Tom and noticed that the ship was undermanned.

"I was able to purchase most of what you ordered, Governor," Hunter said. "I'm sorry to report that no storeships preceded us here from Cape Town, and there was no news of ships on their way from England."

Below deck, Nathaniel found Tom in a hammock. His eyes were closed, and his face was covered with reddish spots and blotches, which Nathaniel knew immediately was ship fever.

He shook him lightly. "Tom, it's Nate."

Tom stirred and mumbled in a weak voice, "No . . . *can't*. Emma, *please* . . . I'm not—"

"Tom, it's Nate; you're back in Sydney Cove."

Tom stared at him with delirious, bloodshot eyes. "Nate? . . . where?—Sydney! I don't believe it . . . didn't think I'd make it. Sick . . . terrible . . . sick."

Nathaniel shouted at two sailors, "You two, a stretcher over here, *now*! Let me help you up, Tom. I'm taking you to the hospital."

"Oh, *oh, ooooh,*" Tom moaned as Nathaniel forced his arms under him.

"I'm sorry, Tom." He lifted him up—he's so light!—and placed him on the stretcher. "Ye'll be fine, mate."

Sergeant Westover helped Nathaniel ferry Tom ashore and place him in the hospital where he underwent a bleeding. Nathaniel visited Tom twice a day, sometimes with George. Usually, Tom was asleep, but once he awoke and told of the voyage in a faltering, weak voice.

"Stupid . . . didn't know we were goin' *around* the world. The first part of the voyage wasn't bad. Later it was freezin' . . . bitter cold.

... *ice* islands off Cape Horn. ... lost two teeth to scurvy. Just gettin' better ... when we left Cape Town. Ship fever all the way back."

The afternoon of the fourth day, Tom looked terribly pale. When he opened his eyes and saw Nathaniel sitting beside his cot, he whispered, "God, Nate ... so tired. Didn't die ... hung on ... 'cause ... didn't want to be buried at sea ... in a sack."

Nathaniel patted his hand and then held it.

Tom asked, "Write who I was on a headstone ... won't you, m'lad?"

"Don't talk like that, Tom, you're improving," he lied, "your color looks much better today."

"Write Emma ... tell her ... I'm sorry."

"You can write her yourself, Tom," Nathaniel said, choking back tears. "When you feel better." He had seen the advance of ship fever many times before and thought that Tom didn't have much time left.

Tom closed his eyes and fell asleep.

That evening, when Nathaniel returned to his bedside, Tom's breathing was shallow with a rough gurgling noise, the start of a death rattle, that he had heard before. An hour later, with Nathaniel holding his hand, Tom drew his last breath. Although expecting his passing and hardened to death, Nathaniel surprised himself by shedding tears quietly for a few minutes before covering Tom's face and informing Surgeon General White.

That night in bed, Nathaniel told Flora: "My best mate, Tom, died this evening. I should have tried to remove his name from a roster of those who sailed to Cape Town."

"Ah, buck up, dear 'eart. Wot's done is done. 'E brought us food, an' fer thet I thank 'im. Thet bleedin' 'ospital don't 'elp no body. Everyone as goes in there dies. If I gits sick, I'll tike care o' meself before I goes in there, Gawd blind me if I don't. G'nite, luv."

Nathaniel could not believe her insensitivity. *Damme*, he swore to himself, for getting involved with this hard woman—all she cares about is herself! He rolled away from her.

◉

Governor Phillip sent Nathaniel to Rose Hill to assist Superintendent Henry Dodd in his preparation of a status report regarding
the building of shelters, clearing of land, and cultivation. While
inspecting the government farm with Dodd, Nathaniel had a conversation with Robert Fox and Fox's friend James Ruse. Ruse told
Nathaniel that he had served out his seven-year term and implored
him to ask the governor for his freedom.

When Nathaniel met next with Phillip, he said, "The convict
James Ruse, a farmer, said that he has served his seven-year term, sir.
I checked what he had said in the convict survey, and July 1789 was
the date he gave back then. I believe him; he's an honest and hard-
working man"

"Do we have his official records?"

"No, sir."

"Then we can't release him. He'll have to wait until his records
arrive."

"Could we give him a conditional release, sir?"

"What would that accomplish, dear boy? There's no ship for
him to sail away on. As a free man, he could refuse to work, and we
would still have to provide him government rations. Other convicts
could make bogus claims. I know that you would like to be fair, but
. . ." Seeing the disappointed look on Nathaniel's face, he said, "Let
me think about it."

Nathaniel told Phillip that forty acres at Rose Hill had been
cleared and planted with wheat, barley, corn, and oats. Dodd expected to harvest the crops by the end of the year.

The governor quickly calculated in his head that not more than
three hundred bushels of produce could be expected from forty
acres, enough to sustain the colony for only a month. He had been
expecting resupply from Britain for nine months and had recently
received bad news from the commissary that rats had burrowed under a corner of the storehouse and destroyed eight casks of flour
and several sacks of rice. A new inventory of the stores had determined that there remained not more than six months of provisions
for the colony. The government farm at Farm Cove was producing
only enough greens for the sick in the hospital, and private gardens

were being abandoned because of the unproductive sandy soil and persistent thievery of what little sprouted.

Having no way of knowing when they would be resupplied or whether Rose Hill's harvest would be bountiful, Governor Phillip decided to reduce the rations by one-third to five pounds of grain, four pounds of salted meat, and one quart of dried peas per week.

The next weekly rations day, Flora angrily entered the hut she shared with Nathaniel and dumped her rations on the table in front of him. "*Look 'ow little!* Yer gotta tell the guv'nor, a body can't live on this little food. It ain't poss'ble—that's wot I says. I'm goin' ter git sick!"

Tired of her constant whining, Nathaniel rose from the table. "Phillip has no choice. Work on our garden if you want more food."

"I'm *too* weak, from *lack o' food,* ter work in the hot sun."

Grabbing his hat from a peg set in the wall, he grumbled, "I'll bring home some extra tonight," and walked out the door to attend a staff meeting with the governor.

Phillip had come up with an idea. "I believe I have a solution for our James Ruse problem, Mr. Armstrong. I want to determine how long it takes for a settler, with some government assistance, to become self-supporting. Dodd agrees that this Ruse is an experienced farmer. I'm willing to give him a conditional warrant of emancipation and a grant of land, initially two cleared acres with a hut on it, and a guarantee of thirty if he succeeds. We shall call this Experiment Farm. In exchange, he must commit to settle in the colony and to work the land with the objective of going off the government store as quickly as possible. What do you think of that?"

"I've heard him say he likes it here, so committing to stay should not be a problem. I'm sure he will be very happy with the rest of the deal, Governor. I'll talk to him. Thank you for finding a solution, sir."

Seeing an opportunity, George asked, "Would you consider making land grants to officers and providing convicts to work the land, Your Excellency? I know I can get much better results than the convict overseers."

"No, Captain. The convicts should work on crown land only. If they are made to work on officers' land, it's sure to evolve into some degree of personal gain. All convict work should be done for the government store."

Phillip resumed his agenda. They discussed the recent increase in native murders of convicts and the killing of livestock. Phillip asked his advisors whether the attacks were random or organized.

"They're a cunnin' lot o' primitives," Ross said, "but I think they're totally disorganized an' only able tae attack in random small clan groups."

"I agree, Major," the governor said. "It's a shame Arabanoo died, he could have been our envoy to the natives. Lieutenant Armstrong, prepare an order for my signature to capture another male native . . . no, two men, so they'll have company."

"Sir, might not the kidnapping of two indigenes lead to greater conflict with them?" Judge Advocate Collins asked.

"I'm willing to take that chance, Mr. Collins. We need to communicate our desire to live in harmony with them, and, as much as we are able, to increase their comforts and well being. Their clans are the beginnings of a society that may not be as primitive as some may think. We've learned from Arabanoo that they have thoughts of where they came from and of a creator. Their careful attention to burying their dead indicates they believe in some kind of afterlife. They're afraid of spirits. We've seen them use plants and charms to produce cures. They show artistry in their crude rock carvings. I find them rather fascinating and worthy of our efforts. Wouldn't you agree, Mr. Collins?"

"I would, yes sir."

Worthy of our efforts! Nathaniel wanted Collins to tell Phillip his epithet for the natives: "children of ignorance." I wish Phillip would ask me, Nathaniel thought. I'd give him my honest opinion, even though I know he doesn't agree with me. I'm not interested in them and have no respect for them. They're lazy and can't even provide for themselves. They shiver in the cold for want of clothes. I'm repulsed by their nakedness, squalor, and stink of fish oil. They've been no help to us, only a hindrance. They beat the tar out of their women to keep them submissive. I agree with Ross: They're treacherous and can't be trusted. It's all very well for Phillip, Collins, Dawes, Tench, and others to be curious and open-minded about them; they'll be leaving; but if I stay, I'll have to deal with them. They'll never fit into our society.

A week later, Nathaniel traveled to Rose Hill and presented Phillip's proposal to James Ruse. Overjoyed, Ruse said the requirement that he settle in the colony was fine with him, because he never wanted to set foot on a ship again. On the way back to Sydney Cove, Nathaniel laughed inside at the irony: the first emancipated convict was about to become the first recipient of crown land, before any military officer or civil official.

When Nathaniel returned, Sergeant Westover reported that he had been unsuccessful in his assigned task of capturing two male Indians. Lieutenant Bradley suggested that Westover's unit should dress as fishermen and use fish to attract the natives. With that, Nathaniel invited Bradley to join him and Westover in a new attempt. Dressed as fishermen, Nathaniel, Bradley, Westover, and seven large marines rowed a longboat along the southern side of Port Jackson for a distance and then crossed the harbor to row back along the northern shore, as though returning from ocean fishing.

They saw two Indian men walking along a sandy beach. Bradley, who had learned a few words of their language, called out in a friendly voice. He and Nathaniel, standing on opposite sides of the boat, each held up a large fish. The natives motioned the longboat in. As the bow of the boat approached the beach, the two men laid down their spears and waded out, grinning, to accept the fish. Bradley gave his fish to the man who waded to his side of the boat, while engaging him in broken conversation. Nathaniel handed his fish to the taller of the two men, who accepted it cheerfully and turned to wade back to the beach.

Bradley jumped out of the boat while talking to the native; the prearranged signal that he was about to grab him. Nathaniel jumped from his side of the boat and grabbed the taller native from behind around the waist, swung him around, and pushed him toward the boat. Bradley grabbed the other native. Both natives dropped the fish they were holding, shouted out, and fought their attackers. From far down the beach, several men armed with spears came running from the woods.

The marines in the boat were having trouble pulling the wet naked men into the boat. Nathaniel knocked up the feet of the man he was holding, grabbed his legs, and heaved him up. He could hear shouts from approaching warriors and expected a spear in the back at any moment as he pulled himself back into the boat.

Four of the oarsmen rowed the boat away while the others subdued and bound their captives. Nathaniel raised his musket and pointed it at the warriors, who had their spears set in their throwing sticks. A number of women and children ran out from the woods wailing loudly and threw themselves onto the sand beach and rolled about in a great show of lamentation.

Some distance from the shore, Nathaniel ordered one leg of each of the captives to be lashed to the seat, prior to loosing the ropes around their wrists. Their terror lessened, but the man Nathaniel had forced into the boat eyed him balefully the entire way back to Sydney Cove, as if casting an evil spell.

The adopted native children, Nanbaree and Booroong, knew the men. They called the taller one, about five feet eight, Bennelong and the other Colebee. Both of their faces were deeply pockmarked, indicating they had survived smallpox. They became noticeably less anxious after the children told them that they would be well treated. Bennelong, about twenty-five years old, had a more robust body than most native men. He continued to eye Nathaniel with a look of malevolence and revenge.

The two native men were taken to Government House and warmly greeted by Phillip. An iron shackle with a long rope was attached to one ankle of each man. At the end of each rope was a large marine assigned to each native to prevent his escape.

◎

The harvest reaped at the end of 1789 was not abundant. Only twenty-five bushels of barley and fifteen bushels of wheat were gathered at Sydney Cove's government farm. The first crop harvested at Rose Hill's forty-acre public farm was much better: two hundred bushels of wheat, thirty-five bushels of barley, twenty bushels of corn, and a small quantity of oats. But it added little to the colony's food reserves, because most of it had to be reserved for seed to plant in February.

The colony's inhabitants had been subsisting on two-thirds rations for four months. The storehouse was down to a few months of provisions at present rations. All talk revolved around when the resupply storeships would arrive.

The governor made the decision to send Lieutenant Governor Ross, a detachment of marines, and more than two hundred convicts to Norfolk Island on the *Sirius* and the *Supply* to reduce the number of mouths to feed at Sydney Cove. Ross would replace Philip Gidley King as the commandant of Norfolk Island, so King could return to Sydney Cove. If a storeship had not arrived by the time of King's return, Phillip would send King to England as his envoy to plead for the immediate resupply of the colony.

The *Sirius* and the *Supply* left Sydney Cove on March 6 with orders to return quickly. The round-trip voyage to Norfolk Island was expected to take less than three weeks. When the ships had not returned by the end of the month, Phillip suspected a problem. On April 5 the signal flag on South Head was raised indicating one or more approaching ships.

Speculation was rife. Were they the returning *Sirius* and *Supply* or the long-overdue storeships? With little wind in Port Jackson, Phillip, Nathaniel, and Tench took a cutter out to see who was arriving. As their crew rowed them across Port Jackson, they saw Lieutenant Ball in a longboat rounding a headland coming toward them. It's the *Sirius* and *Supply,* Nathaniel thought. Phillip waved a hello, but Ball returned odd, incomprehensible gestures. Drawing nearer, they saw Ball's grim face.

"We should prepare ourselves for bad news, I fear," Tench said.

When the two boats came alongside, Ball said, "I regret to inform you, Your Excellency, that the *Sirius* was lost on a reef in Cascade Bay at Norfolk Island. All on board were saved, thank God.

Captain Hunter decided to stay to recover as much of the ship's stores as possible."

That evening, Phillip called a meeting to discuss the crisis. The governor decided to send Lieutenant Ball on the *Supply* to Batavia, in the Dutch East Indies, to buy supplies. Philip Gidley King would accompany Ball and obtain passage to England to appeal for resupply. Weekly rations would immediately be cut, for the third time, to four pounds of grain, two pounds of salted meat, and a pint of dried peas to every person over eighteen months old. The rations would be issued daily from the storehouse to prevent irresponsible convicts from eating their entire weekly ration in a few days.

The following day, the governor ordered that all fishermen and game hunters, who had previously been employed by officers and officials, would now hunt and fish only for the government store. He also sent additional convicts and marines to Rose Hill to clear more land for cultivation.

On April 17 the *Supply* sailed for Batavia. King carried a package containing Tom's personal items and a letter of condolence to his wife Emma written by Nathaniel. Watching the small *Supply* sail away, Nathaniel had a worried thought: There goes our lifeline; if she sinks and the resupply ships do not arrive, we shall slowly starve to death here.

Several days later, Nathaniel was invited with others to dine with Governor Phillip. In the grand sitting room, Nathaniel encountered Bennelong's scornful gaze over the shoulder of Captain Tench, who was trying to converse with him. Dressed in British clothes, Bennelong's scraggly beard had been shaved off and his hair cut. Nathaniel could see a rope running from a shackle, around one ankle, across the floor to a large marine seated unobtrusively in a corner. Although Colebee had escaped shortly after being captured, Bennelong appeared to accept his captivity and new surroundings.

Phillip greeted Nathaniel. "Good evening, Mr. Armstrong."

"Oh, good evening, Your Excellency. I'm sorry, I didn't see you, sir. I was just watching Bennelong. You've worked miracles with him, sir, he looks civilized . . . almost, ha ha."

Hearing his name and seeing Nathaniel chuckling, Bennelong eyed him suspiciously.

When the guests were seated at the dinner table, Nathaniel watched Bennelong, who seemed confused about his place setting. Bennelong looked up and saw Nathaniel staring at him.

That bastard soldier keeps watching me, Bennelong angrily thought. Waiting for me to do something to laugh at. I'll put the white cloth on my lap and smooth it out as everyone else is doing. It's so white . . . so soft . . . and clean. I wonder whether they wash them after every meal? Beenena is smiling at me . . . I guess I did the right thing.

Phillip and Bennelong had agreed on the native word "Beenena," meaning Father, for Phillip. The governor called Bennelong by his name or "Dooroow," native for Son.

The wine server was going from person to person filling wine glasses. Bennelong indicated he wanted some. Nathaniel had seen the Indians spit wine out before and was surprised when Bennelong sipped it and then swallowed a large gulp. He's developed a taste for wine, Nathaniel thought, although he hasn't learned to wait for everyone to be served before drinking. When the toast was made, Bennelong's glass was empty.

Food was placed on the table. Bennelong waited to see which utensils the others picked up before picking up his own. It's so much easier to eat with my hands, he said to himself, but I've got to use their clumsy tools, or Beenena will scold me like a child and the others will think of me as a *myall*, wild savage. While cutting his meat, his fork slipped away and fell beside his plate. There were titters. Bennelong glared . . . they better not be laughing at me!

It angered Nathaniel to see Bennelong eating better than most of the people in the colony, especially as he himself furtively placed a morsel of meat into a handkerchief for Flora.

After dinner, guests returned to the sitting room where the pianoforte was being played. Nathaniel and George joined a group of officers listening to Phillip.

"Bennelong's been a font of information about the local tribes, which appear to be independent family groups or clans only loosely connected by a common language called Darug. Bennelong's clan is called the Wangal, located between here and Rose Hill on the south side of the river. Sydney Cove is Cadigal territory running to the ocean and as far south as Botany Bay. The north side of Port Jackson is yet another group, the Cameragal. The Garigal occupy Broken Bay. All these groups living close to the water are 'fishing people,' who call their coastal area Eora."

The governor called Bennelong over to illustrate the words he had taught him. He pointed at various objects and waited for Bennelong to respond in English. If he could not remember, Phillip would quietly whisper the word and look expectantly at him until he answered correctly.

Like a circus animal, Nathaniel thought contemptuously. He was surprised when Bennelong, becoming frustrated, unexpectedly showed independence and personality by speaking a kind of fluid English gibberish that mimicked the sounds of the conversation around him. It drew stares, then chuckles. A grin formed on Bennelong's face.

Seeing he had everyone's attention, Bennelong started to dance to the music. He seemed to be enjoying himself. Amused, Nathaniel saw that Bennelong was an uninhibited, natural entertainer. By the end of the evening, he had charmed many in his audience, even Nathaniel liked him better.

Although Bennelong had been receiving more food than most in an effort to impress him and to conceal the food shortage, he still complained when he was not given food whenever he wanted it. After several days of acting dejected, he escaped during the night.

Sydney Cove was falling into a state of melancholy brought on by famine. People moved about lethargically, accomplishing little. Feeling pity for the convicts, Phillip reduced their work hours by a third.

While walking by the storehouse, Nathaniel saw a male convict fall to one side while waiting in the ration line. He knew the man and stopped to help, but the cadaverous convict just lay there looking up at him and died without a whimper.

Continuing his walk home, Nathaniel's thoughts turned morose. Only shirkers, cheaters, thieves, and whores are makin' it through this. The dead convict was a good worker who'd done his part, without complaining. Dammit! he swore quietly, there's not enough food for an honest convict to live on. . . . hell, I'm living with a shirker myself! Flora does precious little for me. She's lazy and slovenly and is always too tired to do much of anything. I put up with her just for sex. I'm sick of her complaining; she's draggin' me down. And she *steals* from me. When I bring home extra food for us, she eats her half quickly, and then picks at mine until it's nearly gone—then *lies* about it. It's intolerable!

Arriving home, Nathaniel went to the cupboard and opened a tin where he had stored some food for himself, expecting that most of it would be gone.

"What happened to the salted meat that was in here?" he asked Flora.

"I dunno," she replied from the bed.

"I bring home extra food for *both* of us, not just you!" he threw the tin against the wall. "That was my portion you ate!"

"*I did not!* Yer mus've eat it last night an' forgot."

"You lazy, bold-faced *liar!* I can't stand it anymore. I *want* you to leave. I've had it with your lying!"

Flora raised herself and sat on the edge of the bed. "I'm sorry, luv. Maybe sometimes I nibble a bit, but *I'm starvin'!*" She stood and put out her arms. "Look 'ow thin I is. Yer gits more food than me!"

"No I don't. We all get the same rations now, even the governor."

"*Oh rubbish!* Off'cers 'ave gardens an' animals. Yer eats wi' yer officer mates an' the animals they kill. 'Tisn't fair. We convicts don't 'ave *nuffin'*, but wot little the guv'ment store gives aht!"

"You shouldn't be hungry. You don't do *anything* around here or work in the garden. You're so goddamned lazy!"

"I mends yer clothes an' cooks yer meals!"

"In God's name," Nathaniel said, exasperated. "I can mend my own bloody clothes and cook my own bloomin' meals, which will be larger when you're *gone!*"

Flora sensed the finality of Nathaniel attitude and turned mean. "I 'ad ter put in wi' a officer too poor ter own a pig or a chicken. Other women 'ave fresh eggs an' meat ter eat every once an' a while. Their soldiers shoot wild animals, but yer only bring home *scraps* from the guv'nor's table! *Ugh!* a body'll die wi' yer!"

"If you don't like it—*leave!*"

I still 'ave me looks, yer know; there's plenty of men better off than yer who'll want me!" She began to cry.

"*Good*, just go! I'll help you get your things out the door, you can leave right now!"

"I'll go live wi' somebody 'oo knows 'ow to make love to a woman. I'm tired of bein' *raped—all yer needs is a sheep!*"

With that comment, Nathaniel threw her out, glad to be rid of her.

◎

"The flag has been hoisted by the lookout on South Head!" was yelled joyfully from person to person until Nathaniel heard it in his hut. Sydney Cove resounded with shouts of jubilation. It was June 3, 1790, too early for the return of the *Supply*, which wasn't expected until November. This had to be the resupply storeships!

Captain Tench used his pocket glass to confirm that the flag was indeed up. Nathaniel ran over to Government House while Tench and Surgeon General White took a boat out to meet the new arrivals. Only one ship entered through the heads. The welcoming party directed her into sheltered anchorage in Spring Cove, to avoid the strong west wind of an approaching storm.

Tench brought back news from the ship to the governor and his staff. "She's a lone convict transport, sir, the *Lady Juliana* carrying only females, 222 of them. Her stores are not extensive. The women are in excellent health though, thanks to their agent and the captain having made a leisurely ten-month passage. There were only five deaths along the way."

Collins exclaimed, "This is dreadful news, a cargo so unnecessary as 222 females with few provisions! They shall be a burden to the settlement, Excellency."

"Quite, Mr. Collins, we'll have to send most of them on to Norfolk Island, I fancy."

Tench continued. "The supply ship we've been expecting struck an iceberg and limped back to Cape Town, where it now lies derelict. Most of its supplies had to be thrown overboard to save the ship; however, the *Lady Juliana* has brought some of what was saved. They said one thousand convicts, mostly men, were to sail the latter part of last year. They've no information about other storeships."

"Any good news from the mother country?" Phillip asked.

"An army corps of foot, called the New South Wales Corps, has been raised to relieve us. The captain did not know when it will be sent. There's shocking news about France, sir. There's a peasant revolt against King Louis XVI. A mob stormed and captured the royal prison, the Bastille, in Paris. They said there's fighting in many cities across France."

That should keep the Frogs busy and discourage adventures against us, thought Nathaniel.

The *Lady Juliana* warped into Sydney Cove three days later. She was in need of careening for repairs. Nathaniel was dispatched by Phillip to arrange the disembarkation of the women convicts.

Climbing aboard, Nathaniel headed for the quarterdeck to find the captain. The upper deck was full of women convicts. He heard a woman's robust, joyous laugh. The infectious happiness of it drew him to look for her. He saw her across the way, from the side, the tallest of a group of women. Laughing, she was gesturing with her hands in a graceful, lively manner. Her shoulder-length, reddish blond hair gleamed brightly in the sunlight.

He moved further along to get a better look at her face and front. Although mid-winter and windy, her convict brown serge jacket was open except for a few buttons at the bottom, where the jacket formed around her small waist. The wind pressed her ankle-length, wool skirt against her hips and legs revealing a voluptuous figure. She was a full, shapely figure of vitality.

So that's what a happy, healthy woman looks like, he marveled, I'd almost forgotten. By gad . . . she's a corker.

Anxious to see her closer, Nathaniel walked over to the group not knowing yet what he was going to say. "Good day, ladies. Could you point out the captain?"

Her face was strikingly exquisite: high cheekbones, small nose, and a wide mouth with full reddish lips. She looked about twenty-five. Her pinkish cheeks radiated a healthy glow.

His eyes were drawn to her white, linen blouse and projecting bosom, appearing too large to allow her jacket to be fully buttoned. Looking up, Nathaniel met her vivid, blue eyes.

Oh darn, she groaned to herself; he's oglin' me.

She did not appreciate the lewd aggressiveness of this haggard, skinny, and disheveled scarecrow of a soldier. His uniform was patched and shabby, coat faded, white breeches yellowed and spotted, and leather boots deeply creased and cracked. He acted and looked roguish with a scar down his sunken cheek. And he was directing all of his attention toward her. She looked away apprehensively, turned, and walked for the nearest hatchway to the lower deck.

Nathaniel misread her reaction as meekness. It empowered him to act more aggressively than usual. She was stepping down when he took hold of her elbow.

"I'd like to speak to you for a moment," he said with a smile, letting go of her elbow when she turned to face him.

"Yis sir," she said with a concerned look on her face.

"My name is Lieutenant Nathaniel Armstrong, aide-de-camp to Governor Phillip. What is your name?"

"Why do . . . Moira."

"Moira what?"

"O'Keeffe, sorr."

"I'm here to discuss disembarkment with your captain. Housing is going to be a serious problem. We didn't expect so many women at one time. You are to be squeezed into the two women's camps and the overflow into leaky tents. I have need of a housekeeper. Would you like to fill this position?"

Bastard, she angrily thought, fill yer bed, y'mean. "I'm t'be married to First Officer Williams, sorr, as I've bin livin' wid him these ten months now." She spoke with an Irish brogue in a mellifluous, throaty, arousing voice.

"He'll be going to Careening Cove with the ship for repairs, which could take weeks."

"Shure then, I'll be goin' wid him," she said, trying her best to be pleasant and avoid trouble.

Nathaniel shook his head. "I'm afraid that won't be possible. You're our responsibility once you've arrived in port." He sensed his heart was beating fast. "You'll have to disembark with all the other convicts."

"Ah well then . . . I'll stay in the women's camp, till he returns. Mr. Williams wants t'settle here an' marry me," she said a second time.

"I doubt that will be possible, but it's not for me to decide. My housekeeping offer stands, for the time being, if you find you want better housing, food, and drink."

"Uh-huh," she murmured, not caring about his proposal but disconcerted by what he said about the unlikelihood of her marriage. "Er . . . can I go, sorr?" she asked, her beautiful face now marred by a worried look.

"Yes."

She turned, lifted her skirt enough to see her foot, and carefully stepped down to the first step of the steep stairs.

Nathaniel was upset that their conversation had gone so poorly. Pompous arse, he reproached himself. He watched her gracefully descend the steps, hoping she would glance back up at him at the foot of the hatchway. He was disappointed when she did not.

He found Captain Aitken. During their meeting, they were joined by First Officer Williams, who was a large, handsome Welshman over six feet tall with a barrel chest and huge biceps. Nathaniel felt puny next to him; having lost nearly forty pounds over the past two years, he knew his threadbare uniform hung ridiculously. He could see why convict O'Keeffe would prefer this colossus over himself. It hit him in the form of a realization: Quite simply, he was unattractive to a woman whom he found attractive.

Two days later, as the longboat carrying Moira approached the shore, she could not believe her eyes. The women of the *Lady*

Juliana were healthier and better dressed than the marines standing at attention along the wharf. Their uniforms were in tatters and many were barefooted. Most were appallingly gaunt with dark eyes hollowed from lack of food, and they were leering at them. Tears welled and panic seized her—*Jesus, Mary an' Joseph!*—what godforsaken place ha' they brought us to?

Nathaniel approached Moira before any of the other officers had a chance. "Hello, Moira, have you reconsidered my offer?"

" 'Tis as I said afore, sorr. First Officer Williams an' me will marry whin he returns from Careenin' Cove. He's goin' to arrange it wid the guv'nor."

Nathaniel forced himself to say, "I hope it works out for you, Moira." He assigned her group to the women's district on the east side of the cove, to keep her away from Whores Lane. She was marched away with the others.

Several days later, Surgeon General White told Nathaniel about an Irish beauty with a sexy voice who had been assigned to work in the hospital kitchen. When he described her striking appearance, Nathaniel was not surprised to hear her name was Moira O'Keeffe. She shared one of the huts near the hospital assigned to nurses, midwives, cooks, seamstresses, and washerwomen. Nathaniel made a point of stopping by the hospital kitchen to have a few words with her each time he visited sick friends in the hospital.

During his most recent visit, Moira asked, "Is it true, whin the *Lady Juliana* is fixed, we're all goin' t'be sent off to some small island in the middle of the ocean called Norfolk?"

Nathaniel answered truthfully. "Our stores are very low, Moira. Norfolk Island can take more people. You'll probably be sent there; a final decision, however, hasn't been made yet."

"If Guv'nor Phillip lets me marry Mr. Williams, can we stay here?"

Nathaniel shrugged. "I don't know."

Moira had already decided how to use his interest in her. "Will ye help me, Lieutenant Armstrong? y'ar' the guv'nor's assistant."

Nathaniel found her so beautiful and earnest that he found himself saying, "I'll ask the governor, but I can't—."

She let out a little squeal of delight. "Oh, praise the Lord!" and threw her arms around him and hugged him. "Thank ye, thank ye, Lieutinant!"

Nathaniel walked away confused and angry with himself.

Before he had a chance to talk to Phillip, the *Justinian* store-ship arrived. It had made an incredibly fast five-month voyage by sailing past both Rio de Janeiro and Cape Town. Her captain informed Phillip that three transports, sailing together and carrying one thousand convicts and two companies of army soldiers, would soon arrive. The soldiers were the first contingent of those who would eventually replace the marines. The stores of the *Justinian* were so extensive that Phillip reinstated full rations again.

A feeling of salvation sweep through Sydney Cove. During this period of rejoicing, Phillip decided that *Lady Juliana* crewmen could marry their convict mistresses, provided they remained in New South Wales with their new wives. Knowing that Moira would soon hear of Phillip's decision, Nathaniel told her the governor had approved her request to marry and stay in Sydney Cove. (He told her in a way that gave her the impression that he had arranged it.) He accepted her hug and kiss on the cheek, while he resigned himself to losing her.

One week later, three transports, the *Scarborough*, the *Neptune*, and the *Surprize*, came into Sydney Cove. This second fleet of transports carried two companies of the New South Wales Corps with their families, many of whom were very ill, but their 733 convicts were in much worse condition. During the voyage, 273 of the original 1,006 transportees had died and been heaved overboard. Phillip ordered everyone in Sydney Cove to pitch in to bring the sick ashore as quickly as possible.

The hospital was quickly filled with emaciated patients who were too sick to walk or feed themselves. Nathaniel worked with Moira and others to set beds on the ground around the hospital. The patients' filthy clothes, crawling with fleas and lice, were removed and burned. The patients were washed, covered in blankets, and given food and drink. Nathaniel was impressed by Moira's caring and diligence as they worked together long into the night by lantern light.

When Nathaniel did not see Moira around the hospital two days later, he asked one of her friends where he might find her. She told him that she was ill in her hut. Knocking on her door, he heard her crying and mumble something that he took for "Enter." She was lying face down on her bed, crying on her arm. Sitting on the edge of her bed, he asked her what was wrong.

Sobbing loudly, she told him that Williams was married with three children and had to return home. "He *lied* t'me!" she said, turning her head to look at him, tears streaming down her cheeks. "He said he *loved* me!" She returned her face to her arm. "*I just want t'die!*"

Nathaniel was elated but concealed his joy. While gently patting her shoulder, he consoled her. "I'm sorry, Moira. He's a lying scoundrel, but no one wants you to die because of it. The best thing for you is to get back to helping the sick and dying, who need you. Over one hundred have died already and many more will die without your help. Forget the bastard."

His words had no effect as she continued to cry. "I'll come back later with some tea, when you feel better."

The *Lady Juliana* sailed off on July 25 with first officer Williams bound for Canton. The governor announced that most of the women from the *Lady Juliana* would be sent to Norfolk Island on the *Surprize*, as soon as it could be stocked with supplies for the settlement there.

The women did not want to go. They preferred the known of Sydney Cove to the unknown of Norfolk Island and dreaded the thousand-mile voyage on yet another convict ship to a small island sitting by itself in the broad expanse of the Pacific Ocean.

Moira wanted to stay with her friends at the hospital and anxiously looked forward to Nathaniel's next visit; he cared for her and would help again. She would even become his housekeeper, which was preferable to the uncertainties of the voyage and Norfolk Island.

When he visited her later that day, Moira pleaded: "Pl'ase help me, Lieutenant. I can't bear the thought o' bein' at the mercy of the crew all the way there an' then goin' through the whole thing ag'in whin I reach the island. Can ye git my name removed? My friends are here, an' I like workin' in the hospital."

Nathaniel was prepared for her question. "All the women from the *Lady Juliana* who haven't been married or made attachments are being sent, Moira. If your name is removed, then other unattached women will want the same privilege. There's really nothing I can do." He knew what he wanted her to ask next.

"Would my name be removed if I wor yer housekeeper?"

Nathaniel wanted to convey a professional, blasé expression but found himself smiling.

She smiled back at him.

"I could ask the governor. He may do it for me as a personal favor."

"Could I keep workin' part of my time in the hospital?"

"Aye, Surgeon White told me you're a real help to him."

They agreed, and Nathaniel went off to see what he could do. Inasmuch as he had made up the list, it was no problem for him to remove her name.

After giving Moira the wonderful news that she could stay in Sydney Cove, Nathaniel helped her move her things from the hospital to his hut. In the afternoon, he went off to attend to other matters. That evening they had their first meal together that she had prepared. She had rigged a hanging sheet to define her own narrow space against a wall and made a bed for herself on the floor.

Cheeky minx! Nathaniel thought to himself, chuckling.

Before going to bed, she washed her hands, arms, and face in a bucket and said, "G'night." Stepping behind the sheet with a candle, she started to undress. Nathaniel stopped washing his face to watch her. She lifted her shift over her head and stood nude for a moment before decided to sleep clothed. He could see her alluring, shapely figure as a shadow on the hanging sheet. She put her shift back on, put out the candle, and scooted into bed.

Nathaniel had not had sex since Flora left; he was fully primed. He quickly dried his face, undressed, and blew out the candle. In the dark, he moved to the hanging sheet between them.

"You're the most beautiful woman I've ever seen, Moira, and a fine, caring woman as well. I want you more than I can bear."

He lifted the hanging sheet and picked her up, bed sheets and all, and carried her to his bed. He chuckled and asked "How do I get at you?" when he had difficulty removing the sheets from around her in the dark. He pushed her shift up past her breasts.

She said nothing and did not resist. Irate and disappointed, she had hoped that he would wait awhile. She had to go along, or he could send her on the ship to Norfolk Island. Nathaniel reached ecstasy in a few minutes, then rolled off her and fell asleep almost immediately.

Moira got up and cleaned herself. Why do men ha' t'be such pigs? she angrily thought. Don't they know or care it could be so much better? Only Lord Pendock had bin gentle and lovin' an' knew how t'give a woman pl'asure.

Lord Pendock had been her first love; she had looked forward to sex with him, until he wanted her to share his bed with another woman. The remembrance of it increased her anger. She returned to Nathaniel's bed and pushed him toward the wall to provide a larger part of the bed for herself.

Several months later, Moira and Nathaniel stood in their small garden behind his hut.

"I've bin weedin' an' dumpin' our used water on the plants, but only the onions an' potatoes are doin' any good," Moira said with frustration in her voice.

"Our garden is doing better than most thanks to you, Moira. The corn is stunted, but we've still got a few wee ears and the cabbage may still come around if we can keep the animals away. What we need is some rain."

Moira bent down and pulled up a clump of weeds. " 'Tis poor soil. We need animal manure mostly. 'Twould help the plants grow."

Nathaniel heard his name called out. Turning, he saw George and his wife Martha and another couple standing in the lane.

"Excuse me," he said to Moira and walked to the front of his hut to talk to them.

"Nathaniel," George said in a friendly tone, "I want to introduce you to our friends Lieutenant John Macarthur and his wife Elizabeth. They arrived on the *Scarborough* with Martha and my son. They also have a boy."

Lieutenant Macarthur was well dressed in the uniform of the New South Wales Corps. He appeared to be a few years younger than Nathaniel.

Macarthur offered his hand to shake Nathaniel's. "I've seen you, of course, Lieutenant Armstrong. Regrettably, we haven't had the opportunity to be formally introduced. I daresay it's been a busy time for us all."

Nathaniel shook his hand. "Yes it has. It's a pleasure to meet you, Lieutenant and Mrs. Macarthur. Welcome to our humble colony." Turning to Mrs. Evans, Nathaniel asked, "How are you feeling now, Mrs. Evans?" George had introduced her to him in the hospital, where she was being treated for ship fever.

"Much better now, thank you, Lieutenant Armstrong. Thank you for asking."

"We were just passing by," George said. "I'd ask you to walk with us, but I see you are busy." He looked at Moira, then back at Nathaniel with a lewd look that said: You've got yourself quite a sexy wench there, haven't you?

Embarrassed by George's lascivious look, Martha blurted out, "George told me how you saved his life. I and my son are indebted to you, Lieutenant. You shall always be welcome at our modest home."

"That's very kind of you, Mrs. Evans, thank you."

When Nathaniel returned to Moira, he had no idea that she was angry and offended. She hid her hurt feelings and accepted the reality of her situation: I'm just his Irish doxy—not good enough t'be introduced to his hoity-toity English friends.

◉

On a brisk spring morning in September, Phillip, Nathaniel, and Collins sailed to South Head to select a site for a large brick obelisk to serve as a beacon to ships at sea. Returning to Sydney Cove in the afternoon, they were hailed by officers in a hunting party. The officers told the governor that they had gone ashore at Manly Cove attracted by a beached whale and a large number of natives feasting on it. They talked to Bennelong there, who asked how the governor was and expressed a desire to see him again. Phillip had not seen Bennelong since his escape and decided to go to see him.

As they sailed within sight of Manly Cove, Nathaniel became apprehensive. There were more than two hundred natives, seated around many campfires, cooking and eating the whale meat.

"Your Excellency, there's a great number of them and only fourteen of us."

"We have nothing to fear, Mr. Armstrong. They are in a jolly mood, it appears to me."

"If I may caution, sir, this is where Arabanoo was captured. His tribe does not know what happened to him, only that he never returned. We know these people seek revenge."

"The party of officers just visited here, Lieutenant, and we are invited by Bennelong," Phillip said, annoyed. "This is rather a bit of luck, I believe. I'm not concerned. When we land, I'll go ashore alone and look for Bennelong. Keep your muskets out of view, gentlemen."

When the boat landed, Phillip climbed out and walked toward the nearest group, with his arms out to show he was unarmed, and spoke several native words. The natives retreated from their campfire as he approached. The governor returned to the boat to look for presents that would attract them. As he did, a man in the distance called out "BEENENA!"

"That's Bennelong," Phillip said, looking for him. "Which man said that?"

No one could identify the man who had yelled, because they all looked similar from a distance: naked, thin, and fully bearded. The governor called out "BENNELONG?—DOOROOW?" in the direction the call had come from.

A native motioned with his arms for Phillip to come to him. He was Bennelong's height, but not the robust man who had lived in Government House for five months.

"Can that possibly be Bennelong?" the governor asked. "He's so thin."

Waving back, Phillip said a few native words and motioned for the native to come to him. The native shook his head and said a few native words back, which included the English word "Father."

"By Jove, that *is* Bennelong!" Phillip said. "He won't come to us for fear of being recaptured." Pointing at a bag stuck into an alcove of the boat, he said, "Coxswain Cowley, come with me and bring along that bag of beef and bread."

Nathaniel wanted to caution the governor again but forced himself to keep quiet. Phillip walked willy-nilly into the mass of natives, who appeared agitated to Nathaniel. He watched with trepidation as he approached Bennelong. When Bennelong and the natives around him warmly greeted Phillip with whoops of joy, vigorous handshaking, and multiple pats on his back, Nathaniel was relieved. Bennelong took the governor by the arm and walked him around introducing him to other natives. They sat down on the sand near a campfire and began to eat the meat and bread that Cowley had carried.

The governor called back to the boat for wine. Nathaniel grabbed a jug of wine and cups and walked toward the seated group. Bennelong stood and pointing at him as he approached and said something angrily to Phillip.

Phillip rose. "Lieutenant, stop there please. Give the jug and cups to Coxswain Cowley. Bennelong wants you to go back because you were the one who captured him."

Submissively raising his palms toward Bennelong, Nathaniel backed away for several paces, turned, and as he walked away, heard Phillip scream out:

"*AHHHH!*"

Turning back, he saw the governor falling, a long spear through his collarbone. The natives, including Bennelong, were scattering in all directions. Nathaniel withdrew a hidden pistol and fired at an Indian poised to throw his spear. With all the commotion, he could not see if he hit him.

Cowley helped the governor to his feet. Most of the twelve-foot spear projected out in front of him. Phillip and Cowley ran back toward the boat with Phillip holding up the spear with both hands. Having withdrawn a second concealed pistol, Nathaniel pointed both pistols, only one loaded, in an arc at the natives running for the woods. A spear thumped into the sand next to his foot. He turned to shoot the thrower of the spear but decided not to discharge his only remaining shot at the retreating man.

The attack had happened so unexpectedly that the three marines standing by the boat were only now retrieving their muskets.

In his shocked, stumbling condition, Phillip could not keep the long spear from repeatedly sticking into the ground as he ran, preventing his escape. Frightened, Cowley had run ahead, abandoning the governor. Phillip had fallen to one knee when Nathaniel ran up to him.

"*Break the damned thing off!*" Phillip said.

Nathaniel finched from the impact and pain of a spear shaft ricocheting off his neck. Furious, he ignored the burning sting and placed his knee under the spear projection from Phillip and broke off four feet of it. Phillip ran toward the boat while Nathaniel shot at a man, forty yards away at the edge of the woods, who had just thrown a spear. Spears were landing all around their party as the marines fired their muskets in return. Nathaniel helped push the cutter off the beach and jumped into it.

Collins was attending to the governor, who seemed to be in no great pain.

"Did Bennelong spear you, sir?" Nathaniel asked.

"No," Phillip said. "He was surprised as much as I. It was a man who had been suspiciously eyeing me from a distance the whole time. He did it without provocation. Perhaps it was the revenge you warned me of. Nevertheless . . . I want no one to fire on the natives as a result of this, unless they throw their spears first."

Surgeon Balmain was the first to treat the governor. He extracted the spear, dressed the wound, and announced that His Excellency was fortunate and should fully recover.

Bennelong told government fishermen he had nothing to do with the attack and asked whether he could visit the governor. Phillip sent word back that he could visit without concern of punishment. Trusting the governor, Bennelong paddled his canoe into Sydney

Cove and went to his bedside. The two reconciled, and, thereafter, Bennelong became a frequent visitor at Government House.

◉

The stalwart *Supply* returned to Sydney Cove from Batavia on October 19, 1790, to the collective joy of those who had missed her reassuring presence in the harbor. At the wharf, the recovering governor greeted Lieutenant Ball, who had rushed to return with foodstuffs fearing the colony was starving. He left Batavia ahead of the *Waaksamheyd*, a merchant vessel he had hired, which arrived two months later carrying a cargo of flour, rice, salted meat, and salt.

"The food taste so much better wid salt in it, don't it," Moira said to Nathaniel, trying to draw him out of his sour mood.

"Yes" was his one-word reply.

He had been unusually quiet during dinner. She had come to know the subtle difference between his quiet reticence and brooding. He was upset about something. Concerned, she asked, "D'ye ha' a bad day?"

"The governor barked at me and said to keep my opinions to myself."

"But y'ar' his advisor. Ye *ha'* to give him yer opinion."

"Only on Indian matters."

"Oh . . ."

"He got himself wounded—stupidly—and *still* he allows them to do whatever they want, even though it causes problems for us, in one way or another. He said I have no respect for them, and he doesn't want my opinion on them anymore, unless he asks for it!"

"I'm sorry. I know ye think o' him like yer fadher."

"It's just this issue. It's the only one we disagree on. I *don't* respect them! He's right!—but that's how I feel about it."

"But they're here . . . we're the newcomers."

"More's the pity."

"Come here, darlin'," Moira said as she sat down on the bed and leaned back against the wall. Nathaniel lay down on the bed and placed his head in her lap. She stroked his thick hair and noticed the scar on his cheek was not so evident, since he had put on weight.

"Y'ar' gettin' handsome, Nathaniel, wid the weight my cookin's puttin' on ye." She kissed his forehead and began to softly sing a lullaby her mother had sung to her. He lay there thinking about a hunting party he would be part of over the next two days.

Officers accompanied the convicts hunting for the government store to ensure that they were not hoarding the animals they killed. Nathaniel had three times before hunted kangaroos and emus with the convict game hunters. Having been a young hunter in Scotland, he enjoyed these occasional forays into the woods as a diversion from his regular duties.

At six in the morning, Nathaniel joined three convicts waiting for him at the Tank Stream bridge. John Macintire led the hunting party southwest toward Cooks River. Forming into a hunting line, side by side and separated by thirty feet, the four men quietly walked abreast through the woods without seeing any large game and rested in the shade during the heat of the day. Macintire selected a meadow along the river to lie in wait for kangaroos and emus that typically come out of their hiding places in the late afternoon to drink and graze. When no large game appeared, the men formed a line again and hunted until twilight, without success.

As it grew dark, they quickly made simple lean-tos of green boughs and beds of dry grass and ferns, lit a fire, and ate a late dinner. The hunt would resume at first light in the morning.

Unbeknownst to them, they were stealthily followed for an hour by three natives who had themselves been hunting. The native hunters knew Macintire. He had shot a clansman who died after weeks of suffering. Two of them identified Nathaniel as the redcoat who had captured Bennelong. The warriors felt fortunate that revenge would soon be theirs; they would wait until the whites were asleep and kill them all.

Nathaniel was awakened by a rustling noise in the bushes not too far away. By the flickering light of the dying fire, he gently shook Macintire and quietly cocked his musket. Rising to his knees, Nathaniel looked for the source of the noise. Gradually his eyes adjusted to the darkness and made out three Indians, fifteen yards away, frozen in positions close to the ground, looking back at him.

Nathaniel raised his musket to shoot the nearest one.

"Don't shoot, sir," Macintire said, "I know 'em." He stood up with his hands raised, stepped forward, and speaking in their language addressed one of them by the name "Pemulwuy." The natives stood and relaxed their spears. Macintire took several steps toward Pemulwuy speaking in a friendly tone. The Indian said something back to him.

Nathaniel did not like the feel of the situation; Macintire was foolishly exposing himself. He stood up holding his musket across his body to discourage any foul play. Seeing this, the warriors raised their spears.

Macintire turned around toward Nathaniel. "Put doon yer musket, sir, they jist wint some food."

So not to alarm the natives, Nathaniel said in an even voice, "They were sneaking up on us, man. I'm not putting it down. You come—" He abruptly stopped when Pemulwuy launched his spear into Macintire's side.

Nathaniel quickly raised his musket and, even though Pemulwuy had instantly disappeared, fired where he hoped he would be. A second later, one of the convicts fired blindly into the dark where the Indian's had vanished.

Macintire stumbled back holding the spear shaft and moaned: "I'm a deid mon."

Nathaniel grabbed his shoulder as he dropped to his knees. No one suggested pursuing the natives into the darkness.

Inspecting the wound in the firelight, one of the convicts said:

" 'Tis'nt too bad, mate, didn't pass thro' ye. Ye'll be right if it didn't go in too far."

A large, strong man, Macintire wanted to walk to Sydney Cove immediately, while he was still able. His two convict friends used their knives to cut off the spear shaft leaving two feet sticking out in case the surgeon wanted to pull the spear out. Supporting Macintire on two sides, the four men arrived back at Sydney Cove at four o'clock in the morning.

Surgeon General White was roused from sleep. After examining the wound, he feared that Macintire might die immediately if he tried to remove the spear. The margins around the spear were not bleeding profusely, and although his patient was coughing up some blood, White told Macintire to rest and regain his strength while he conferred with other surgeons.

Macintire took this to mean he was dying and called for Reverend Johnson to ask for forgiveness of his sins and God's mercy. He reproached himself for a life of crime but admitted to having shot at the Indians only in self-defense.

Later in the day, as Phillip and Bennelong walked toward the hospital, Bennelong told the governor "Macintire, 'im bad fella" who had shot his people. At the hospital, Bennelong described Pemulwuy as a few years older than himself, tall, and disfigured by a vertical scar down his face from a tribal battle. The injury had left him with a split eyelid and a whitish cast in the eye. He was a much feared warrior of the Bediagals, the "hunting people" of the woods, who were the enemy of the "fishing people" living along the coast. Bennelong said, "Bediagals, *myalls*, kill whitefellas if can."

The next day, the governor met with Collins, George, and Nathaniel to decide what his response should be to the unprovoked attack on Macintire.

"These damnable attacks on unarmed men, like the attack on yourself, Your Excellency, cannot go unpunished," Collins said, "especially when the offender, Pemulwuy, is known."

"May I add, sir," George said, "that the time is ripe to show the blacks the superiority of our weapons and instill a universal terror, which would act to discourage such future malicious attacks."

Phillip looked at Nathaniel for his opinion.

Nathaniel looked back. *Keep quiet*, he reminded himself, you're suppose to keep your opinions to yourself about the Indians.

"What do you think we should do, Lieutenant?" Phillip asked.

"I agree with Captain Collins and Captain Evans, sir. This wanton attack was remarkably similar to the one on yourself. I admit I don't understand these Indians, Governor. They act irrationally. However, we know they fear the loss of members of their own clan. I think we must instill fear in their hearts that if they kill one of us, we shall kill five of them. I'd like to volunteer to lead an attack on the woods Indians and kill this Pemulwuy."

"No, Lieutenant," Phillip said. "You are an aggrieved party. I agree that the time has come to attack them, but I do not want this to appear to be a personal vendetta."

Instead, Phillip sent for Captain Watkin Tench and Lieutenant William Dawes, who he knew were sympathetic to the natives and could be relied on to act fairly. He told Tench that there had been seventeen serious native attacks on whites, including the one on himself, resulting in death and injury. The tribe located north of the head of Botany Bay was the principal perpetrator of these attacks. He ordered Tench to lead fifty marines, with provisions for three days, to capture or kill Pemulwuy. If he eluded them, they were to kill ten warriors and capture two others for punishment. The heads of the ten slain were to be cut off and brought back in bags. No women and children were to be attacked, nor *humpies* destroyed.

Tench negotiated the terms of the expedition with Phillip, in the event of Pemulwuy's escape, to capture or slay only six warriors. Dawes, who had been studying the ways of life of the natives, at first refused to participate in what he considered an unduly punitive raid until Reverend Johnson told him it was his duty. The expedition remained in the field for three days without firing a shot. The natives had fled ahead of the marine's noisy approach.

Dissatisfied, the governor sent the expedition out again with the same orders. Tench decided on a strategy of sneaking up on the natives around their campfires at night. But once again, he and Dawes were unsuccessful in shooting or capturing a single native.

After the spear was extracted, Macintire's condition gradually improved. It had penetrated his body to a depth of seven inches, passing between two ribs and into a lung. Just as it appeared that he would survive, he suddenly took a turn for the worse and died a few days later.

A nine-month drought caused a poor harvest at Rose Hill. In spite of the food brought by the second fleet, the *Supply,* and the *Waaksamheyd,* there remained only nine months of rations in the storehouses in March 1791. Concerned about the continuing drought and not knowing when the third fleet would arrive, the governor reduced weekly rations by two pounds of grain and two pounds of meat.

Fearing the near starvation he had experienced only months earlier, Nathaniel was pleased that Moira was a clever cook and much better than Flora at adding to their meager rations. Flora had boiled their salted meat, peas, and rice together, which shrunk the meat to half its size and made the rice and peas overly salty. For extra nourishment, they had drunk the bitter brine.

Moira cut around the bone to remove every morsel of meat, so they could toast each piece on a fork over the fire, catching each drop of juice on a slice of bread or in a saucer of boiled rice. To improve the consistency of the peas and provide some variety, she added greens she foraged and boiled them with flour or rice to make a creamy vegetable dish that Nathaniel enjoyed. He also relished her meat and vegetable soup.

"What kind of meat is in this soup," Nathaniel asked one day, and then quickly added, "maybe I don't want to know."

"Ye like the taste of it, don't ye?"

"Aye, but I'm so hungry, I think I could eat shoe leather if it were put into the soup," Nathaniel said with a laugh.

"Well, in troth, 'tisn't shoe leather," she said with a girlish giggle. " 'Tis some kind o' shellfish that clings to the rocks in the cove. It don't look too good t'look at it, but it adds taste an' meat to the soup. I put in the meat bones, too."

Knowing their garden had sprouted few greens, Nathaniel asked, "Where do you find the greens you serve every night and put into the soup?"

"In the woods. I've got very good at it. I follow others to learn from 'em, even whin they don't want me t'follow."

"You know the Indians have killed people who stray too far into the woods. I want you to be careful and return quickly if you sense the natives are around."

She flashed her sparkling smile at him. "Nathaniel, dear, that's the *sweetest* thin' ye've ever said to me. Ye *do care* a bit for me."

Deciding to say nothing that would encourage her, Nathaniel gave her his inscrutable half-smile expression, which she had come to know meant "no comment."

Filling the silence, she said, "I'll be careful."

That night, as they sat in front of the fireplace doing chores, a nagging question once again entered Nathaniel's mind: How could *she* possibly be a felon? He wanted to believe she had been a hapless victim . . . maybe of a mistaken identity. She never said a thing about why she had been transported. Never declared her innocence. Not once. Nathaniel asked himself, If I were innocent, wouldn't I let everyone know, and loudly?

Without any lead in, he nonchalantly said, "After eight months together, you've never told me why you were transported."

Moira looked up from her mending with distress in her eyes. "Och, Nathaniel . . . if I could tell it easy, I would indeed. But 'tisn't so easy in the tellin', darlin'."

"Tell me, I want to know," Nathaniel said more deliberately.

She tried to make light of it, her voice as melodious as ever. "I was a foolish girl wid a hankerin' for beautiful things. I found a necklace that Lady Pendock lost in the mansion. 'Twas worth *only* thirty-five shillin's . . . *just* a trinket. I should ha' tould her I found it."

That was all she intended to say about it and returned to mending his shirt. She recalled to herself how happy she had been when she had found the beautiful gold necklace with inset stones that had fallen from Lady Pendock's neck. The servants were searching throughout the house when she had found it and slipped it into her pocket. It was easily worth *twenty pounds*, equal to her wages for three years! It was going to be the means of her escape to a new life.

Nathaniel was amazed that Moira had worked in a mansion. He knew so little about her.

"Who's Lady Pendock?"

"She's the wife of Lord Pendock o' West Berkshire near London, where I was a chambermaid."

"How did an Irish lassie come to work for a English lord near London?"

"I was the youngest of seven children. My poor ould pa was a tenant farmer on Lord Pendock's land in County Louth. Pa didn't know what t'do whin his lordship tould him he wanted me as a chambermaid. I know now that my mather was right when she tould me what was in store for me, a fifteen-year-ould child. But I didn't believe her. I wanted t'git away from the farm an' go wid him. Mam and Pa argued all night. Pa saw it as a chance for better manners and speech, maybe become a lady. He thought maybe I'd git some good from his lordship's attention.

"Though in two years, I worn't no better off. I didn't like Lord Pendock no more. I wanted to leave but didn't ha' no money. They found the necklace in my room, and that's how I come here." She did not tell him that Lord Pendock had reduced the value of the necklace to thirty-five shillings so her sentence would be seven years instead of the death penalty, which was given for stealing items worth more than forty shillings.

Nathaniel added up the years. "You're only twenty-two?" he asked incredulously,

"I'm twenty-one."

Not believing her, Nathaniel, asked her birth date expecting her to stumble.

"June 23, 1769."

He figured it in his head . . . she's telling the truth! "I thought you were closer to my age."

"Dear me!" She looked at him askew. "D'ye now?"

"Oh, not because you *look* that old," he laughed, "but because you act so . . . mature . . . for your *young* age."

"Ah, righto, troth be tould," she said, smiling brightly.

Nathaniel rationalized her crime. She had obviously been taken advantage of by Lord Pendock and needed to find a way to leave. He went to bed thinking that she's not a *real* criminal . . . not a hardened pickpocket, prostitute, or murderess.

The drought continued into the fall. Their garden greens slowly wilted in the sun, turned yellow, and dried to a tawny color. The edible wild greens, over picked by the whites and natives, became impossible to find.

The natives, showing signs of malnutrition, came into Sydney Cove and camped around Bennelong's house. Months earlier, the governor had built Bennelong a twelve-foot-square brick house on the northeastern point of Sydney Cove in the hope of keeping him near to serve as his native affairs advisor and goodwill ambassador. Instead, it was a troublesome gathering place for natives who begged for food during the day and stole from the gardens at night.

The governor's advisors, including Nathaniel, had recommended against building the house for Bennelong there. Their concerns were realized, when each day the Indians went out in their canoes to demand a share of the returning fishermen's catch. Phillip did nothing to stop this practice, even though the Indians were requiring ever larger shares of the fish and threatening the fishermen aggressively when they resisted.

After a difficult day, Nathaniel returned to his hut frustrated and upset. He forced himself on Moira that night when she was not feeling well. The next day when he returned to their hut, she had removed her things and was gone.

Besides being angry at Nathaniel for his inconsideration, Moira thought she was pregnant. She had to find out how much he cared for her and whether there was a chance that he might marry her; otherwise, she would try to miscarry.

He found she had moved back into one of the women's huts next to the hospital. Two women friends were talking to her in a consoling way when Nathaniel walked in.

"What's going on here?" Nathaniel asked angrily.

The women looked loathingly at him.

"I don't want t'live wid ye no more," Moira said, her face wet with tears.

"What's wrong?"

"I don't want t'live wid ye; all ye care about is yerself. Ye want me to listen to yer problems an' soothe ye, but ye don't care about me."

"*That's barmy!* That's no reason to leave. You said you were happy with me."

"I thought I was falling in *love* wid ye! . . . 'cause I thought ye'd change."

"You thought you were fallin' in love with me because you thought I'd change? What in God's name does that mean?"

"I don't want a man who uses me!"

Incredulous, Nathaniel said, "I don't *use* you!"

"Yis ye do. Ye *use* me, to take care o' yerself. Ye never think o' me, an' what I need."

One of the two consoling women left when she realized she was listening to a lovers' quarrel.

"This is a ridiculous conversation," Nathaniel said testily.

Moira wiped her eyes with her hankie. "I thought ye'd come t'care for me, but I'm only a whore to ye—yer doxy. Somebody to satisfy yerself on." Tears were running down her face.

Nathaniel began to feel contrite. "I'm sorry about last night, Moira; it won't happen again."

" *'Tisn't just about last night!* 'Tis *all* the time. Ye don't really care for me or enjoy makin' love to me."

"That's not true, Moira. I care for you more than any woman I've ever known."

The second sympathetic women drifted away from the doorway of the hut.

"Y'make me feel cheap. Ye don't ask; ye don't enjoy; ye just take—an' then roll over and fall asleep whin y'ar' done wid me. How d'ye think that makes *me* feel?"

She's right; he had to agree. I just do it to satisfy myself, as quickly as possible.

"I ha' t'find a man who loves me, while I'm still young, afore I git used up an' ugly."

"Hah ha—" He didn't mean to laugh and stiffled it. With a grin, he said, "My sakes, Moira, you won't be ugly any time soon."

"Faith, it's bin a *curse!* I've bin used by every man I've ever known." She started to cry in earnest.

"Don't cry, Moira," Nathaniel said sympathetically. "You've got many qualities besides being beautiful. You're caring, perceptive, a hard worker, and *smart.*"

"*Saints preserve us*, you never said that afore. I give ye my opinions, an' ye never say anythin.'" Before Nathaniel could respond, she blurted out, "*But it don't matter!* Ye'll be leavin' soon whin the marines return t'England. I shouldn't ha' ever got ınvolved wid you."

"I'm *not going*, Moira. I've *told* you that. I'm goin' to settle here. So you don't have to worry about that."

Moira sat up on the edge of the bed. "*Faith?—God's troth?* Y'ar' not *lyin'* to me, are you?—just to git me t'come back?"

"No. I don't want to return to dark, rainy, and cold England or Scotland. I told you I have no family left there and no reason to return. I like it here, and I've decided to join the New South Wales Corps." He reached out for her.

She rose from the bed and stepped into his arms.

He drew her close, and they embraced. She cried softly against his chest. He tenderly brushed back her reddish blond hair with his hand, and when she pulled back to look at him, he kissed her on the lips.

That night they enjoyed sex without rushing. She showed him the places to caress and kiss that gave her pleasure and told him the endearments to whisper. He gave her time to please him in ways he hadn't experienced before. For the first time in his life, he enjoyed sex in a shared, caring, and loving way, spending hours lovemaking until they were both satisfied.

Three months later, he kidded her about putting on a little weight.

"I'm pregnant wid yer baby, Nathaniel," she finally admitted to him, looking deeply into his eyes for his reaction.

He did not hesitate. "That's *wonderful*, Moira. I *want* a family."

"But we aren't married," she said in an ashamed, mournful tone.

"Well . . . we'll have to fix that by getting married then, won't we?"

"Oh, *Aye*, Nathaniel!" Moira said breathlessly and threw her arms around his neck. "Aye"—kiss—"yis"—kiss—"yis, yis, yis."

"Hold on, hold on . . . I'll have to get permission. Officers aren't allowed to marry convicts, but I think Governor Phillip will do it for me."

George tried to talk Nathaniel out of marrying Moira. "Think what you're doing, Nate. She's beautiful, yes, except she's a convict, and *Irish*, and a *Catholic* Irishwoman."

"This isn't the British Isles, George. The Irish won't be fighting for independence here, and I'm hoping religion won't play as large a part."

"Can she read and write?"

"A wee bit. She's tryin' to read my books and asking questions. She's smart, in many practical ways. Ach, George . . . she's carrying my child, and I want to start a family."

"Indeed . . . but you don't have to marry her, you know. She'll accept being your mistress if you support her and the child."

"You don't know her; she's headstrong and would leave me in an instant if I even looked at another women. I know it's not perfect, but I've grown fond of her and have made up my mind."

Phillip received Nathaniel's request to marry Moira from George, who did not recommend for or against the proposed marriage. The governor discussed the matter with Nathaniel.

"This comes as a bit of a surprise, I must say, Nathaniel. How old are you now, Lieutenant?"

"Twenty-seven, sir?"

"Anxious to start a family, I understand."

"Aye, sir."

"Are you certain you want to enlist in the New South Wales Corps and settle here?"

"Yes sir."

"You know, of course, that I value your good character and judgment . . . but *this* . . . well, it's a matter of the heart, isn't it?" He continued without giving Nathaniel a chance to answer. "I presume that you've fully considered and accept that marriage to a convict may hinder your career in the military and in public life?"

"Yes, sir."

"Her past will always be a source of . . ." Trying to be tactful, Phillip searched for the right words: "contention . . . perceived sullying of one's honor . . . perhaps embarrassment." Phillip shifted in his chair. "You know my opinion of convicts. They can be redeemed by casting off their old ways. I judge a person by his present deeds not past acts. Though you must feel the same way or you wouldn't have been able to work so well with the convicts. Isn't that so?"

"Yes, sir, I respect those who put out the effort to do their part."

"So you're sure about this, are you, Nathaniel?"

"I am, Governor."

"Well then, there's nothing more to say, is there? except to wish you and Moira O'Keeffe a life of happiness together and many children."

The next Sunday, July 2, 1791, Moira and Nathaniel attended the morning religious service, held outdoors because a church had not yet been built. Following the service, they were married by Reverend Johnson, under the marrying tree, with Governor Phillip and many other officers and officials in attendance.

◉

A week after Nathaniel and Moira were married, the *Mary Anne* transport arrived from England. She carried 144 female convicts. Only three had died on the voyage. By mid-October, ten transports and the HMS *Gorgon,* a man-of-war of forty-four guns, had arrived carrying additional members of the New South Wales Corps and nearly two thousand men and women convicts, many of whom were sent to Rose Hill to work at the government farm. The additional provisions carried by the third fleet allowed Phillip to return the colony to full rations.

On November 10, 1791, Moira gave birth to a healthy boy. Both parents easily agreed on the name "Arthur" in honor of Governor Arthur Phillip. The day after the birth of Arthur, Nathaniel transferred into the New South Wales Corps with his first lieutenant rank.

The health of the colony had come to depend on the public farm and several private farms at Rose Hill. The governor laid out a town immediately east of Rose Hill at the river landing place, called Parramatta by the natives, meaning "place of eels." The population of Parramatta and Rose Hill together was 1,630 people, which was larger than the 1,260 people residing in Sydney Cove. The population of New South Wales, including 1,170 people at Norfolk Island, was now 4,060.

Governor Phillip sent David Chesterfield, a public gardener who had arrived on the third fleet, to do an independent study of the farming practices around Rose Hill to determine whether any additional governmental actions should be undertaken to improve cultivation and production. Phillip asked Nathaniel to accompany Chesterfield and assist him in the preparation of his report.

Chesterfield began his study at Rose Hill's government farm where he and Nathaniel were shown around by Robert Fox, the supervising convict gardener. The harvest of wheat and barley had commenced. Stalks of maize were green and flourishing, but vegetables were not doing well. Overall, Chesterfield thought the crops were doing much better than he had expected after more than a year of drought and a spring of only moderate rainfall.

Nathaniel was eager to visit Ruse's private farm, located just east of Parramatta. James Ruse saw them coming and rushed out of his field to warmly greet Nathaniel. He invited the men into his comfortable brick house where his convict wife, Elizabeth, made tea for them.

Ruse beamed as he said, "We're off the gov'ment store now. It only took fifteen months fer me to grow enough fer us, an' have a little extra to sell. I work fer meself now, thanks be to you, Lieutenant Armstrong."

"Thank you, but it's really Governor Phillip you have to thank. I'll pass your thanks on to him," Nathaniel said. "He considers Experiment Farm a great success, due to your hard work, James."

Over the next three days, Chesterfield and Nathaniel went on to visit the other twelve private farms on land grants made by Phillip to settlers. Only two of the settlers' farms were producing enough to sell. Seven others were barely producing enough to sustain their owners, and the remaining three were still largely wooded with little under cultivation.

Chesterfield's report to the governor focused on water conservation, including ponds and tanks, and the need for plows and draft animals. He wrote that with adequate rainfall, water conservation, and modern farming techniques, the fertile soil at the Parramatta River headwaters would be the salvation of the colony.

Major Ross returned to Sydney Cove on December 18, 1791, from Norfolk Island. A few days later, the first fleet marines formed up near the Government Wharf to board His Majesty's Ship *Gorgon* for England, except for fifty-eight privates, one drummer, three corporals, and one sergeant (Westover) who had accepted the government's offer of grants of land to become settlers in the colony. Many of them had decided to stay because of their affection for female convicts, true of Nathaniel as well.

The few marine officers, including Nathaniel and George, who had elected to stay, stood in line with Governor Phillip to shake the hand of every departing marine officer. Their goodbye comments were filled with heartfelt emotion about shared experiences and best wishes for the future.

The New South Wales Corps, three-hundred specially trained army soldiers, who had arrived in the second and third fleets, now assumed responsibility for the security of the penal colony. Its commander, Major Francis Grose, thirty-seven, debilitated by wounds received in the American Revolutionary War, finally arrived in February 1792 abroad the *Pitt*. He was Major Ross's replacement as lieutenant governor.

At first, the good-natured Major Grose showed himself to be less of a problem for Phillip than Major Ross had been. However, after listening to his officers' complaints for several months, Grose asked the governor to cancel his policy of equal rations for all. When Phillip would not change his long-standing policy, Grose requested that his officers, at least, be permitted to buy goods for themselves at the first opportunity.

Grose was a creative leader and an elitist, with little regard for the convicts. After several months, he had decided how the colony should be managed to benefit himself and the New South Wales Corps. He found men of like mind in George and Lieutenant John Macarthur. Grose chose George as his secretary. Macarthur, who had a brilliant mind for facts and figures, was made regimental paymaster and allowed by Grose to take over business management of the corps. When the *Britannia* came available, Macarthur arranged to charter her to purchase supplies from Cape Town. Grose made the proposal to the governor.

Phillip discussed Grose's request with Judge Advocate Collins and Nathaniel. Collins fashioned his reply to Phillip as a ruling: "If they purchase goods for their own use, and not for resale, it's legally not an infringement on the monopoly rights of the East India Company."

Nathaniel gave his personal opinion: "Officers in the past have bought livestock, food, and personal items for themselves, Governor. It's never been an equitable system, really."

Nodding his head in agreement, Phillip said, "True, I have to agree, still it's never been so blatantly inequitable as commissioning an *entire* ship just for the officers' advantage. An entire ship is sure to cause resentments, and I fear their supplies will inevitably find their way into daily commerce."

After obtaining Grose's assurance that the goods purchased would not be resold, the governor allowed the *Britannia* to sail for Cape Town.

Both George and Macarthur pressed Grose to ask Phillip to grant land to the officers of the New South Wales Corps and convicts to work it. Grose felt that "free enterprise" for personal gain would far outproduce government farming. Not appreciating that George had already asked Phillip several times for land grants, Grose proposed to Phillip that he make grants of land to his officers to increase agricultural production.

Phillip told Grose the same thing he had told George previously:

"My instructions are quite clear, Major Grose, I have been directed not to make grants of crown land to officers. I have long feared that if the convicts are made to work for officers, they shall become little more than slaves, working for masters who will find ways to enrich themselves at the expense of the public good."

"Your Excellency, the New South Wales Corps was recruited with, if not the implicit understanding, at least the impression, that they would become landowners in the new colony."

To resolve their disagreement, the governor agreed to write the home secretary for further instructions. Grose wrote his own letter to include in Phillip's dispatch to London. The governor also included a strongly worded letter reiterating his ideas for a reliable system of regular supplies, less crowded transports for healthier convicts, and more artificers; recommendations that had been largely ignored.

Several days later, in a conversation with Nathaniel about Major Grose's land grant proposal, the governor abruptly asked:

"How well do you know Lieutenant John Macarthur?"

"Not well, sir. I know he was behind the preferential rations request and the *Britannia* enterprise, but I haven't had much to do with him."

"Well, the upstart has refused my invitation for dinner," Phillip said irritably, "because he fancies that I sullied his honor in a misunderstanding concerning the storage of two kegs of spirits in the regimental store. It was his wife, the cultured Mrs. Macarthur, I wanted to entertain, not him. A rather arrogant fellow, I daresay."

Nathaniel noticed that trivial matters were bothering Phillip more than ever before. He had been complaining about a pain in his side ever since the first expedition to Rose Hill and let it be known that he would return to England soon to regain his health.

Some weeks later, after a meeting with the captain of the *Atlantic* in his office, Phillip came unexpectedly into Nathaniel's office. "As soon as the *Atlantic* can be refitted to my specifications, I've decided to return to England."

Nathaniel was surprised. Before he could form an appropriate response, Phillip said, "After nearly five years, I feel that the colony is close to achieving the level of well being we have so long and ardently worked for. I want to return to press for changes that will bring our plans to fruition. I shall retain my commission and intend to return in two years."

On December 10, 1792, after two days of gala events and speeches, the governor stood on the Government Wharf preparing to sail away. Nathaniel was dumbfounded when he saw that Phillip was taking Bennelong and another male native, Yemmerawannie, to England with him. The governor had not discussed it with him.

Lieutenant Governor Grose, who had been sworn in as acting governor, asked Phillip to make an unbiased presentation to the Home Office of both sides of the argument of making land grants to officers and providing convicts to work the land. Phillip assured him that he would fairly present their opposing views.

Phillip walked over to Nathaniel for a final word. "What measures would you like me to press for, my good and faithful adjutant?"

"You know, Governor, I want New South Wales to be more than a penal colony. The government should send artificers and encourage settlers to come by providing free passage and land grants. We also need a more reliable system of government supply or the right to trade to obtain the goods and supplies we need. Those are the keys to our future here."

"I'll press for settlers and artificers, but I doubt that the East India Company will permit trade. God willing, I shall see you again in two years, Nathaniel. Raise my namesake well. If I haven't said it before, my dear boy, I shall forever be indebted to you for your service to me—not to mention saving my life." He put out his hand and, as they shook, drew Nathaniel to him with his other arm and hugged him.

His eyes misting over, Nathaniel embraced Arthur Phillip and, in an emotional breaking voice, said, "Godspeed, Your Excellency . . . I'll miss you terribly, sir." When Phillip stepped back, his eyes were tearing, but he turned quickly and marched toward his waiting cutter. The crew of the cutter rowed Phillip toward the *Atlantic* to the sounds of fifes and drums, gun salutes, and a cheering crowd of well-wishers.

"There goes the only father I've ever known," Nathaniel said to Moira. "Now I've lost my only patron. I don't know what my future will be in the corps."

Holding one-year-old Arthur in her right arm, Moira consoled Nathaniel by putting her left arm around his waist and squeezing him. "I'm not worried, dear, I believe in ye."

Chapter 4

Rum Corps Gentry

" 'Tis winter; y'ar' goin' to catch a chill sittin' outside," Moira said, concerned for Nathaniel's health. "Sit inside wid me an' the childer."

It was the second Sunday in July 1795. The Armstrong family had returned from church, finished their midday meal, and moved into the drawing room. Nathaniel stood with a book in his hand prepared to go out the door to read on the northeast veranda.

"It's too beautiful a day to sit indoors, love," Nathaniel responded. "The sun is shining on the veranda. I'll be warm enough in my coat." He did not tell her that he wanted to read in peace.

"But I don't see you all week," Moira said with a pout.

"Then do your knitting over here," Nathaniel said, "in this chair by the door. I'll leave it partially open, and we can be near each other." Hearing his boys arguing, Nathaniel lowered his voice.

"A-a-ah, Charles, *stop* hitting Arthur with that. Do you want me to take it *away* from you?"

Charles, their second boy, one year and nine months old, looked petulantly at his father and banged his toy hammer instead on one of Arthur's toys.

"Stop it! *Daaaad!*" Arthur yelled.

"Ruth, help Arthur move his toys over here away from him," Nathaniel said to the children's nanny. "*Charles,* if you *can't* play nicely with your brother then you can play *alone!*"

Nathaniel stepped out the door and sat down in a chair on the veranda and opened his book. After reading a chapter, he closed his eyes and rested his head on the high back of the chair to let the sun warm his face. He considered how much he had accomplished in the two and a half years since the departure of Governor Phillip, thanks to the radical policy changes made by Acting Governor Grose.

He had been pleasantly surprised when the home secretary approved Grose's request, over Phillip's objection, to grant land to the military and civil officers. Along with George and John Macarthur, he was among the first officers to receive grants of one hundred acres. Their three grants were near one another east of Parramatta. John Macarthur was granted proven fertile land next to Ruse's Experiment Farm with frontage on the Parramatta River. Nathaniel's and George's grants bordered Parramatta Road and Duck River. Nathaniel's land was west of the river and George's was directly across on the east side.

Grose allowed each of them to choose ten convicts to clear their land and build a house. After a house was built, each selected three additional convicts, both men and women, as household servants. Their convict help continued to draw rations from the government stores. Grose wrote the Home Office that he had assigned up to thirteen convicts to deserving officers. Home Secretary Henry Dundas wrote back ordering Grose to reduce the number to two convicts per officer. Grose blissfully ignored Dundas's direct order for more than a year before providing a lengthy report detailing the success of the officers' land clearing and planting. He ended the report indicating that he had not yet carried out the secretary's order because of the success of the program and asked him to reconsider his order.

Because Macarthur and Nathaniel had moved quickly to clear and plant their land, Grose granted each of them an additional one hundred acres. They were now the largest and most successful farmers, although John Macarthur owned an additional fifty acres purchased from a neighbor.

The Armstrongs lived in a comfortable six-room, single-story, brick house built on a hill overlooking the Duck River. An entrance hall occupied the front center of the house, a dining room was to the left and a drawing room to the right. A central hallway ran from the entrance hall to a back door connecting a sitting room and three bedrooms along its length. The roof was extended out over a raised flagstone veranda at the front and northeast sides of the house to provide shade during the heat of summer. To avoid the danger of fire, the kitchen was a separate building connected by a short path to the dining room. A garden was conveniently situated behind the kitchen to provide fresh herbs, vegetables, and fruits used in every-day cooking and flowers to decorate the house. Behind the main house, connected by a path to the back door, was another building for three household servants and a laundry. The three buildings, linked by paths, had the appearance of a compound. Some distance down the hill was another grouping of three buildings: a bunkhouse for the ten convict field workers, their kitchen, and a barn for farm animals and grain storage.

A dirt track from Parramatta Road snaked its way up the hill through fields planted with corn, wheat, and potatoes to a carriage circle in front of the Armstrong's house. The fields produced an abundance that was sold to the commissory, who also purchased eggs from their hundreds of chickens and fresh meat from their eighty sheep, fifty pigs, and sixty goats. The family had fresh milk, butter, bread, eggs, meat, and vegetables daily for the table. Gone were the famine years, with its rancid salted meat, rotten bread, and dried-up peas.

Nathaniel looked down the entrance track for George. He ex-pected him to ride up at any moment. Reluctantly, he said through the open door, as nonchalantly as possible:

"Oh, Moira, I forgot to mention . . . George Evans will be going down to the barn with me this afternoon, so I can show him how to use draft cattle to plow."

"*Nathaniel*, I'm not purpared for guests," Moira admonished.

"He's not *guests*, Moira. He won't be coming in. When he ar-rives, I'll walk him down to the barn. This isn't a *social* visit."

"Why on the *Sabbath*? the Lord's day," Moira asked, annoyed.

"I'm gone all week and was busy yesterday. I was the one who suggested today."

"He's always askin' you questions. Don't he know *nothin'* about farming?"

"*Doesn't* he know *anything*, you mean," Nathaniel said.

"Yis." She acknowledged his correction without resentment because she had a standing request for him to correct her poor grammar.

Nathaniel answered her question. "George knows very little about farming and doesn't seem to have a knack for it either."

Moira did not like George Evans nor their other neighbor John Macarthur. She had never met their wives nor been invited to their homes. They had tactfully rebuffed her and Nathaniel's every invitation. It had become clear that Moira's "convict taint" was the reason, although she had been given a full pardon in late 1793. Nathaniel had assured her that as time passed and their wealth and prestige grew her convict past would be forgotten, and they would be welcomed into the upper class of society.

Still, it irked him that his so-called friends, George Evans, John Macarthur, Acting Governor Paterson and others, invited him but not Moira to their elegant society events. Reluctantly, he attended their affairs without her because the welfare of his family depended on it.

Despite the Evans's pomposity, which Nathaniel thought was primarily driven by Martha Evans, he remained close to George. He did not feel the same friendship for John Macarthur, although he appreciated many things about him: his abundant talents and boundless energy, his obvious love for his wife and children, and his fairness and generosity toward those who supported him, including the convicts who worked for him. What bothered him was Macarthur's precipitous, irrational hatred of anyone who opposed him and his self-righteous, unreasonable desire to utterly ruin any opponent. He had seen this first when Governor Phillip had reprimanded him and many times since. He was under no delusions that his "friend" Macarthur would turn on him in an instant if he stood in his way.

Through the open door, Moira reminded him:

"Remember, we're havin' Judge Advocate David Collins and Captain George Johnston here next Saturday evenin'."

"Yes, I'm looking forward to it."

Collins and Johnston lived with their emancipated convict mistresses, with whom they had had children. Like Nathaniel, they were members of the second tier of society made up of powerful men whose companions were unacceptable in polite company. Nathaniel was bothered by it more than Moira. She had mentioned once that she would feel uncomfortable among snooty, upper-class women. She was content socializing with the second tier. Nancy Yates and Esther Julian, Collins's and Johnston's respective mistresses, were among her closest friends.

Moira is satisfied, Nathaniel reasoned, because we're one of the wealthiest couples in the colony and more comfortable than she ever expected to be. She's happy with our healthy boys, a nice house, and a few woman friends. God knows she has enough to keep herself busy during the week . . . raising the boys, supervising the household servants, answering the overseer's questions, and managing the kitchen garden, her most enjoyable chore.

He heard someone step onto the veranda. Turning, he saw Felix Morley his overseer.

"Yer wanted ter see me, sir?"

"Hello, Felix." Nathaniel remained seated. "Yes I do. How is everything?"

"Fine, sir." The man loomed over him.

"I want you to prepare for a demonstration of plowing for Captain Evans. He has a plow but no experience with draft cattle."

"Bin plowin' wi' men, has he?"

"Yes . . . well, I believe so. Have you seen it?

"Seen 'em tryin'," he said coolly.

"Well, he purchased two draft cattle from the *Endeavour* that arrived recently. What about using Neal for the demonstration?"

"Arright."

"Can you spare him for a day next week to teach Evans's man?"

"Best use Jacob, if yer want a teacher. Neal has no patience fer that kind o' thing."

"Very well, we'll use Jacob today then too."

"Arright. When d'yer want ter do it?"

"I'm not sure, exactly. This afternoon, perhaps within the hour.

We'll come down to your quarters an' find you."

"Very good, sir. I'll 'ave everythin' ready."

Nathaniel watched Morley walk away and marveled at his size: a giant of a man, six feet three and at least 250 pounds, all muscle. I was really fortunate to get him—stone cold and tough as nails— yet good with the men, who both respect and fear him. He'd sooner drag a difficult shirker into the bush and beat him into submission than report him for a flogging. A good plowman too.

I certainly have benefited from the years I worked for Mr. Fiddes. My knowledge of farming has served me well. I may have been the only experienced plowman in the colony when we arrived. The *Endeavour* will change all that with its 132 head of cattle from Bengal. Wonder how Macarthur learned how to plow with cattle so quickly? He always seems to find his way when an advantage is to be gained. His farm is doing as well as mine . . . probably better. The man's an opportunist extraordinaire.

David Collins is an odd one though. Never came around to accept the changes that Grose made. Still refuses to enrich himself, although everyone else is doing it. He seems to think he has to take a higher road as judge advocate, above reproach, even though every- one knows he has a wife in England while having children here with Nancy Yates.

Nathaniel recalled how he had initially agreed with Collins that Grose's new policies were misdirected. The acting governor did not share Phillip's egalitarian principles and immediately increased the rations to the army and civil administrators. Where Phillip be- lieved in government control of production and distribution, Grose believed that there would be continued shortages until trading was allowed and farming was done for personal profit. Where Phillip thought the officers should stick to soldiering and civil administra- tors to their professions, Grose saw them as the only educated group available to him to improve the fortunes of the colony. He had little regard for the abilities of the emancipated convict farmers and the few free settlers who had arrived.

Because Nathaniel had initially opposed Grose's policies, he had missed out on the first three trading ventures that were hugely profitable for participating officers and civil officials. He did not invest in the officers' hiring of the *Britannia* that Phillip had reluctantly approved and did not buy provisions from two speculative trading ships: the American ship *Hope* that arrived unexpectedly nine days after Phillip's departure and the *Shah Hormuzear* from Calcutta that sailed into Sydney Cove two months later. After the government had bought what it wanted from these two ships, Grose did not permit the ship captains to sell their remaining goods to anyone who wanted to buy them. Instead, he allowed Macarthur to form a purchasing syndicate to negotiate a bulk price for the remaining provisions. The goods were then divided among the officers proportionally, based on their percentage share investments. The officers resold the goods at the highest prices the market would bear. The goods included "rum," the generic name used for strong alcoholic drinks, which Phillip had tightly controlled by issuing landing permits and by arresting and severely punishing any convict found with rum.

Nathaniel had seen the huge profits made by the officers, selling goods for two or three times their cost and rum at a markup of five hundred percent. Having little money, convicts worked extra hours and on Sundays for goods and rum. He had heard Macarthur argue with Collins that the officers were charging only what the ship captains would have charged; however, the profits were staying in the colony instead of sailing away with the captains. His argument convinced Nathaniel to participate in the next trading venture.

Nathaniel's years as an advisor to Governor Phillip had paid off when he received a captain's commission from the army commander in chief in London, pursuant to Phillip's recommendation made a year before he left the colony. This advancement brought Nathaniel to the attention of Grose, who began to seek his advice. He quickly found Nathaniel's five years of experience invaluable. To keep Nathaniel near as an advisor, Grose made him the commander of the Sydney Cove garrison.

Nathaniel's thoughts were interpreted by the sound of horses coming up the track to his house. He was surprised to see Macarthur riding up with George. He turned to announce their arrival to Moira, but she had left her chair. He laid his book down and stepped down from the veranda to greet them.

They exchanged greetings while the men tied their horses to the hitching post. Macarthur was overdressed as usual. Lean and of average height, he was impeccably dressed and carried himself in a straight-backed, proud manner meant to impress.

Macarthur explained his unexpected presence. "I met George on the road, and we decided this might be a good time for us to discuss John Hunter's imminent arrival. I've been meaning to get the three of us together for weeks. Although, if this isn't a good time for you, Nathaniel, we can do it some other time."

"Now is fine, John." Nathaniel directed them up the stairs toward the entrance door. John Macarthur suggested instead that they sit on the veranda.

As they arranged their seats, George said to Nathaniel, "You've mentioned that you've been corresponding with Governor Phillip. How is he?"

Nathaniel considered where to start. He wondered whether they knew, or cared, that Phillip's wife had died by the time he arrived home and that he remarried a year later. He assumed they had read that Phillip had accepted an annual pension of five hundred pounds when he resigned his governorship.

"Do you know that the governor was found unfit for active service because the pain in his side often incapacitates him?" Nathaniel asked them.

"I heard that, a pity," George said.

Nathaniel continued. "Nevertheless, the governor maintains a vigorous interest in us and continues to push for measures he feels are in the best interest of the colony. It's no secret that he has disagreed with most everything Grose did. He wanted Philip Gidley King as his replacement, but went along with Admiral Lord Howe's recommendation of Hunter."

"Do you correspond with Hunter as well?" Macarthur asked.

"No, I've never corresponded with him."

"Has Phillip given you any idea of Hunter's orders?" George asked.

"No. My last letter from him was six months ago."

"What would you speculate his orders are?" Macarthur asked.

"I don't like to do that, John—speculate. I don't know."

"Come now, Nathaniel, we need to be prepared for the new governor, don't we?" Macarthur said with an engaging smile. "Surely, Phillip has written you that the Treasury is displeased with the escalating costs of the colony. I've heard rumors that the Home Office will order a reduction in the number of our assigned convicts from thirteen to two. They want to produce more at the government farms, I understand, which will undercut the commissary's purchases of our grain and animal products. I don't have to tell you what that would do to our fragile economy."

"I'm not aware of the escalating costs of the colony to the Crown. I do know, though, that Phillip is against soldiers farming and using the convicts as 'slaves'—his word. He's also spoken out against Grose's relaxation of rum importation and use."

"Hunter's a religious man and sure to object to the rum trade," George said. "He'll see it as a vice, as Phillip did, when it is, in fact, what makes our system work."

"I've come to agree with you, George, with rum we don't have to flog them to work." Nathaniel asked a rhetorical question:

"Soldier and sailors are given a daily ration of rum, why not our convict workers? My overseer regulates each man's daily ration based on the amount of work he performs. He doesn't allow them to get drunk. It's not the problem I originally thought it might be."

Macarthur became more forthright and told them what he knew. "From my sources, I've learned that they chose a naval officer as governor to rein in the army's free enterprise system. The Home Office and Treasury want to reduce costs and think they can do it by returning to government farming. They think the felons should be able to raise the foodstuffs we need without the incentive of rum. They are short-sighted: they object to paying for our grain and meats, not realizing that private enterprise will soon produce a surplus eliminating the need for more costly food supplies shipped from home.

"I'm also afraid that Hunter's orders may include curtailing our trading ventures that provide the goods we need to live comfortably. Trading and private farming are the backbone of our new economy.

An economy that didn't exist three years ago. Left alone to continue on our present path, we will be self-supporting sooner than anyone expected. The government in London is too far removed from"—

Nathaniel had heard all this before. He let his mind drift into considering how this lieutenant (well . . . captain now, as of two months ago), only twenty-seven years old, became the most powerful and richest man in the colony in just two and a half years.

He knew that as regimental paymaster Macarthur had proved his worth to Lieutenant Governor Grose. In that there was little hard currency in the colony, the two of them had encouraged officers to borrow against their future regimental pay to obtain the investment capital needed to hire the *Britannia* and to purchase provisions from trading ships arriving in port with speculative cargoes to sell. Macarthur issued paymaster's notes to the officers drawn against the regimental treasury in London and accepted the officers' personal IOUs as security. The ship captains accepted paymaster's notes that were worth their full face value in sterling. These financial transactions created the trading syndicate that benefited the officers so greatly.

Grose then helped Macarthur take over responsibility for Parramatta from Captain Foveaux, the commander of the Parramatta garrison. Grose had deputized Foveaux to act in his place on all matters affecting the convicts there and to hear and act on all complaints and offences that had previously been the responsibility of civil magistrates.

It seemed curious, then, when Grose created a new Parramatta office for Macarthur called "inspector of public works." It placed Macarthur in command of the government farms and granaries at Rose Hill and Toongabbie, with authority over the soldiers, overseers, and convicts working there. The overlapping responsibilities of Foveaux and Macarthur were resolved several months later, when Grose replaced "Captain" Foveaux with "Lieutenant" Macarthur giving the younger man unprecedented authority over both the military and civil administration of the community. Grose let it be known that he had written the commander in chief of the army requesting approval of the rank of captain for Macarthur.

When Macarthur became embroiled in a rivalry with Captain Nicholas Nepean, his superior officer, that presaged Macarthur's court martial, Grose supported his protégé. Shortly thereafter, claiming ill health, Captain Nepean obtained Grose's permission to return to England.

The affable Francis Grose projected an easygoing, gentleman-ly, upper-class persona that placed him above his officers' grasping "tradesmen" activities. While his officers grew rich around him, Grose neither granted himself land nor invested in their trading ventures. His indifference to enriching himself was a pretense, Nathaniel thought.

It was well known that Grose came from a modest background and was not wealthy. It seemed incongruous to Nathaniel that he was not profiting from the financial opportunities his lenient policies were creating. Grose allowed Macarthur alone to manage all of the financial accounts of the colony. Before meeting in council with his advisors, Grose usually met privately with Macarthur for an hour or longer on financial matters.

Nathaniel assumed that there had to be some kind of venal arrangement between Grose and Macarthur, but he kept his suspicions to himself and was careful not to insinuate any impropriety. After all, Grose's policies were working well; Sydney Cove and Parramatta had never been more prosperous. No longer was there the threat of famine. And Nathaniel respected Macarthur, who was unbelievably hard working and productive.

Shortly after learning he was to be replaced by Hunter, Grose left the colony claiming that his old war wounds required attention in England. He chose Captain William Paterson, who previously commanded the military on Norfolk Island, as administrator of the government until the arrival of Hunter. Paterson was an ama-teur botanist with little interest in governing the colony. His most fervent pursuit was collecting flora and fauna specimens to ship to his patron, Sir Joseph Banks. In letters to Banks, he proposed that they publish a book together on the natural history of the region. He made no changes to Grose's policies and allowed Macarthur to continue unhindered in his administrative and trading capacities.

—"that's why I think *you*, Nathaniel, should lead our effort."

Hearing his name, Nathaniel returned his undivided attention to Macarthur. "I'm willing to participate, though why should I lead the effort?" Nathaniel asked.

"George and I agree that you are closer to Hunter than we are. I scarcely know the man."

Nathaniel shook his head. "I don't know him well at all."

"George says he likes you. Isn't that so, George?"

"You were close to Phillip, and Phillip and Hunter were close," George answered. "I think you stand a better chance of persuading him than anyone else."

"Of course I'll talk to him, because I believe it's in the best interest of our colony. However, whether I talk to him first or last, it will have to be a group effort."

"Good," Macarthur said. "You can be very persuasive, Nathaniel, when you believe in something."

"If we are lucky, our new governor has been delayed by the French revolutionaries," George said, smirking. Britain had been at war with the French republican government for more than two years.

"George, we shouldn't wish the French even *that* success," Macarthur said coyly. There was an awkward pause. ". . . but I've imposed too long on your gentlemen's business." He rose abruptly and put out his hand to shake Nathaniel's. "By the way, in the spirit of leading, whom have you chosen to lead the foray against the woods Indians along the Hawkesbury?"

The Hawkesbury was a new farming district along the Hawkesbury River located some twenty miles northwest of Parramatta. Grose had opened the area with twenty-two land grants along the river's fertile alluvial flatland. As the number of farmers increased, there were more and more conflicts with the "hunting people" resulting in the deaths of seven white men, two woman, and a few children, and many injuries. No one knew how many natives had been killed.

Acting Governor Paterson ordered all Indians to leave the Hawkesbury District. He erected gibbets along the river to hang bodies of dead warriors. The only problem was that no Indian bodies could be found after skirmishes to hang from the gibbets. A punitive expedition by the Parramatta garrison saw few Indians and recovered no bodies of those shot at. It was becoming apparent that a corps of foot soldiers could not successfully pursue natives into the woods. There was talk of forming a cavalry, but there were too few horses in the colony.

After the disappointing expedition of the Parramatta garrison, Paterson decided to send Nathaniel's Sydney Cove garrison and leave a detachment of soldiers along the Hawksbury River.

"I'm going to lead the foray myself," Nathaniel answered Macarthur's question.

Macarthur looked skeptical. "You're the garrison commander; shouldn't you assign it to one of your officers?"

"Paterson wants me to leave some forty of my men among the settlers for their protection. I want to carefully match the soldiers and settlers to ensure we don't create problems for ourselves."

"Hmm, I see your point," Macarthur said, while thinking that many of the corps's soldiers were now emancipated convicts, who could not be trusted. "Well, good hunting."

After seeing Macarthur off, Nathaniel and George walked down the track toward the convicts' quarters for the planned demonstration of plowing.

◉

Nathaniel told Moira that night that he would not be home the following weekend. When she expressed apprehension about the Hawkesbury expedition, he reassured her:

"The Indians are still using their primitive spears and clubs, which causes us little concern for our safety. In any case, I expect them to keep their distance from us."

Tactfully, he could not tell her that he was keen to trade his boring administrative work for the excitement of leading his men against the marauding warriors along the Hawkesbury River, a district he had not seen before. He was also looking forward to visiting some of the farmers he knew, among them his old sergeant Westover and emancipist farmer Robert Fox.

The expedition was a major undertaking involving fifty-five soldiers and twenty sailors in four longboats and one cutter, all rigged for sailing and rowing. They would sail out of Port Jackson, north along the shore of the Tasman Sea, into Broken Bay, and then travel west up the Hawkesbury River. Nathaniel's plan was to go directly to the most isolated western homesteads before leaving any of his soldiers with settlers. The worse Indian problems were in the west, so he wanted all of his soldiers with him to carry out an attack there. After the attack and having seen the entire stretch of river, he would be better prepared to drop off his men with settlers on the way back to Broken Bay.

Sailing into Broken Bay, the expedition encountered natives fishing from their boats. Nathaniel's orders were to drive the woods Indians out of the Hawkesbury, so he left the fishermen undisturbed. The next morning, before starting up the river, Nathaniel told his men that they were at liberty to shoot at any warriors sighted but not women or children.

Their flotilla was hailed to shore time and again by settlers. Nathaniel had not expected so many to be living along the river. As he proceeded upstream, Nathaniel recorded those settlers who wanted soldiers to live with them for added protection.

Early the third day, they saw four Indians walking along the shore carrying spears. Although in the middle of the river, the soldiers in the lead boat fired on them. The natives ran for the protection of the woods, but not before one fell and then got up and limped for cover.

Later that day, the flotilla arrived at Robert Fox's fifty-acre homestead. Fox greeted his old friend warmly and invited him to use his only bedroom. Nathaniel declined his offer but ate dinner with him, his wife, their three-year-old boy, and the male convict assigned to them, named Pete.

"I sought you out, Robert, because I'd like to leave a soldier or two with you for protection. They have some supplies with them and will be resupplied from time to time, but you may have to help out some. We are going to try this for an initial period of four months. In return, I'd like you to lead us to where you've seen the Indians, so we can surprise them in their camp or set up an ambush along one of their trails."

"Y'know, Capt'n Armstrong, the woods Indians don't live no-where very long. They 'ave some favorite spots, but they're always movin' dependin' on the seasons an' food supply."

"Well, you can take me to one of their favorite spots then."

"What good would that do, Capt'n? If you go into the bush wi' so many soldiers the Indians will 'ear you a mile off."

"That's why I intend to stay near one of their camping sites or along one of their well-traveled trails for a day or two in hope of am-bushing them."

"These are the *woods* natives; you *can't* ambush 'em, Capt'n Armstrong. Yer men will be smokin', talkin', and makin' noise. No way you can ambush 'em in their own woods."

Nathaniel did not want to admit it, but Fox was right. Nevertheless, it irked him.

"Are you telling me you're not willing to help, Robert?"

"I'll be truthful wi' you, Capt'n Armstrong; I don't want no trouble. The Indians know I let 'em raid me fields. They seen me an' Pete wi' muskets in our hands lettin' them do it. Lord, me wife seen twenty o' 'em—men, women, and children—carryin' blankets to fill wi' corn, their favorite food. I lost a pig to 'em jus' the other day. They leave me wheat alone, though, 'cos they don't know what to do wi' it. They aren't that much of a problem if we let 'em steal some corn an' an animal or two. They only seem to bother people when someone shoots at 'em."

In a sincere, confidential tone, Nathaniel said, "I can't in good conscience let you believe what you just said, Robert. I know many instances where Indians have killed people simply because the op-portunity presented itself."

"Me an' Pete are always armed, Captain, an' the wife too. The problem is sumpin' the Indians call 'payback.' They do payback among themselves too. 'Tis the same as revenge. If y'shoot one o' 'em, they will sure as the dickens pick a time to do the same t'you. I'd rather give 'em some food, an' hope they leave us alone."

"Well, I think that's wishful thinking, Robert. The Hawkesbury

District is contested territory now. Farming is pushing the Indians out of their traditional areas, and they are fighting back by raiding farms and killing the settlers when they can. My orders are to leave soldiers with isolated homesteads to protect them, but if you don't want one or two, I can't make you take them."

The next morning, Nathaniel and Fox said goodbye as friends and the flotilla continued on past four farms before arriving at the furthest west farm near Richmond Hill. The farmer there gladly accepted two soldiers from the detachment.

The fifth day began the return trip to Broken Bay. Stops were made at farms along the way to drop off soldiers. The 64° F temperature was warm for the middle of winter. Everyone enjoyed the gentle downstream current that eliminated most of the rowing. In the mid-afternoon, after having eaten, many of the men were being lulled to sleep when a soldier suddenly screamed "AHHHH!" when a spear passed through his thigh. Other spears fell among the boats, one wounding a sailor in the shoulder. A few muskets fired as the warriors fled into the bush.

The Indians had chosen an ideal point of land for their attack: a high rock face jutting into the river, topped with heavy bush cover. Nathaniel knew it would be pointless to pursue them and ordered the flotilla to the opposite shore to treat the wounded. Neither of the two men was grievously wounded. Nevertheless, Nathaniel was anxious to row them downstream quickly to the Green Hills settlement, which had grown up around a government storehouse, to provide them with better medical care and rest.

Besides the two wounded men, Nathaniel left a sergeant and eight soldiers at the settlement. Acting Governor Paterson had directed him to leave a unit there that would patrol the Hawkesbury River and supply the soldiers left at homesteads. A longboat was left for their use.

By the time the flotilla reached Westover's farm, Nathaniel had twenty-three soldiers left. Old "Serge" Westover was anxious to lead the soldiers to an Indian camp site and even had a plan of attack:

"The savages camp aroun' a pond that has hills on three sides. By keepin' the hills between them an' us, Capt'n Armstrong, we can sneak aroun' 'em, then send a party up the valley ter chase 'em toward the waitin' soldiers on the hills. I reckon we'd need at least forty men ter do it, thirty on the three hills an' ten ter go up the valley. Since yer only got twenty-four soldiers countin' yerself, Capt'n, I can git maybe ten settlers ter join us, an' we can use some sailors, eh?"

Nathaniel shook his head. "Governor Paterson has issued a proclamation that settlers are not to shoot at the Indians except when attacked, so I can't use settlers, Serge. Anyway, I'd be afraid of them shooting each other with people moving up the valley and over the surrounding hills. I don't want to use the sailors either. You know how difficult it is in dense bush to keep from shooting each other. What's the largest group of natives you've ever seen in this valley?"

"They hold their singin' an' dancin' *corroborees* there, Capt'n— there could be hundreds—though mostly it'll be around twenty or thirty, maybe ten or so men, camped by the water."

"Well, I'd like to give it a go. What about you?"

"Hell yus! It'll be like old times, Capt'n. And I owe the blacks a few licks."

Nathaniel got his soldiers together and told them he had a risky plan of attack and would do it only if at least twenty soldiers volunteered.

"Serge here tells me there are three hills defining a valley where there could be a hundred Indians or more. The north and west hills are much steeper than the east hill. So, I'm guessin' the Indians will escape up the easiest east slope. I'll quietly position my unit on the back side of the east hill before Serge leads a unit into the valley from the south. My group will not fire into the valley and Serge's unit will not fire up the east slope, to avoid shooting each other. If the Indians choose to escape up the steep north or west slopes, Serge's group can fire on them at will. If they choose to stand and fight, Jimmy here will be with Serge to blow his bugle to let my unit know to attack down the east slope to help out."

"So that's the plan, men, do I have twenty volunteers?" To Nathaniel's satisfaction, all twenty-three soldiers volunteered for the mission.

Nathaniel's unit started out early the next morning and spent a good part of the day finding its way through the woods and quietly climbing the east hill. Below the top of the hill, Nathaniel left his men and completed the climb himself. He found a trodden trail running along the top of the hill. Walking silently along it, he found a path leading down into the valley. Returning to his men, he positioned them every ten paces in a line below the trail with himself in the center of the line opposite the descending path into the valley. He told them not to fire until he fired the first shot.

Nathaniel placed himself behind a tree with bushes on either side. The march, climbing the hill, reconnoitering, and positioning his men took much longer than he had expected. Westover's unit was to start up the valley in mid-afternoon and it was approximately that time now. Nathaniel heard somebody quietly talking off to his left. He attracted his attention with "Psst" and quieted him with "*Ssshh!*"

Nathaniel placed his musket and sword into a crease in the tree trunk. He slowly stretched his left arm forward and then hard down to the right, bending over and stretching the muscles along the left side of his back. The expedition had aggravated his old gunshot wound. Standing on the downhill slope, he angled his legs away from the tree and rested the right side of his back firmly against the trunk. He watched white, lacy clouds moving across the blue sky and enjoyed the tranquility of the moment. He didn't really expect their mission to amount to anything.

There's unlikely to be any natives down there, he thought. And only one chance in three that they'd come up this way. Actually less than one in three. I found a downhill path, but there could be five paths leading down from this hilltop for all I know. Five added to three equals one chance in eight. Realistically, though, if there are any Indians down there, they could probably pick from twenty or more ways out of the valley. So if I'm figuring paths, it's more like one chance in—

He heard something. Turning toward the sound, he listened intently. Faint multiple sounds in front of him from the far downhill side. Bloody hell!—*people*, yes definitely people—a *group* of people, climbing up the other side of the hill, and not too far away either. He lifted his musket, pulled back the cock, put the butt to his shoulder, and steadied the barrel against the tree trunk while thinking: I told Westover not to climb the east slope; if this is him, I'm going to be mad as hell.

Roos. It could be roos. No, they hop, this is definitely *people.*

Spears! A man's head! *Jesus,* this is it!

A large warrior stepped up onto the ridge trail directly in front of him, six yards away. The native reached down to help an old man up beside him. The old man shuffled off to one side and sat down. He wiped his brow and appeared to look directly at Nathaniel but was distracted by a women carrying a baby followed by two children. A smaller warrior stepped onto the ridge path followed by a woman. The two warriors exchanged a few words and the smaller one motioned the group to follow him up the ridge trail.

Nathaniel couldn't decide what to do. How many more of them were coming up the hill? And these were women and children for Chrissake! Families—not warriors! Where's the glory in this? I don't want to kill him in cold blood, probably a father—like a goddamned assassin or murderer!

While he was thinking these thoughts, a woman and a teenaged girl stepped up followed by a young warrior.

BANG.

A shot from further up the trail!

The large warrior looked directly at Nathaniel the exact moment he pulled the trigger. The impact of his shot flung the man back and down the far slope. Nathaniel pulled out his pistol and grabbed his sword and ran around the bush.

There was a crescendo of shooting, screaming and wailing. Nathaniel's mind focused on the horrible high-pitched wailing of small children as he ran to the top of the hill and looked down for more Indians. He saw the body of the warrior he had just shot doing the "death bounce," arms and legs threshing about sending the body down the slope. He was dead or nearly dead, but the nerves of his body didn't know it yet. Through the noise, Nathaniel listened for shooting in the valley, then heard several shots one after another somewhat up the slope.

Nathaniel looked up the trail trying to assess the situation. He couldn't see anyone. Without knowing quite why, he yelled:

"CEASE FIRE!" and then ran up the path shouting "*Cease fire! Cease fire! Goddammit, CEASE FIRE! Take prisoners and form on me!*"

Rounding a bend in the bush trail, Nathaniel nearly tripped over the two small children huddled together on the footpath. They were wailing loudly. He saw a woman lying nearby who had been shot through the shoulder. Next to her lay a baby—dead—shot through the back. A soldier stood with his bayonet pointed at the wounded woman who seemed unafraid, or perhaps in shock.

"What should I do, sir?" the young private asked in a frightened voice.

"Nothing. Stay as you are, Private Finch." Nathaniel yelled out loudly: "COME TO ME WITH YOUR PRISONERS!"

One by one, all of his soldiers joined him. None of them was injured. They brought the old man and a woman and reported that a warrior lay dead on the slope. Nathaniel heard Westover yelling to him and told him to come up.

"We shot one that came dahn our way," Westover told Nathaniel as he walked up to him.

"A warrior?"

"Na, a young girl. But we seen a big black dead one next to the path comin' up."

Nathaniel felt sick about the young girl.

"Whatcha goin' ter do wi' these ones 'ere, Captain," Westover asked.

"I don't know," Nathaniel said. He felt dizzy and overwhelmed. What had they just done?

"Why don't yer let me an' a few of the lads finish up 'ere, sir?" Westover said, looking knowingly at Nathaniel.

"I'm letting them go," Nathaniel said as he stared icily at Westover. "We aren't going to kill children, women, and an old man!"

Westover raised his right hand so the palm showed to Nathaniel. "Didn't mean no offense, Capt'n, sorry sir, just tryin' t'be helpful."

Nathaniel motioned for the Indians to go. The uninjured

woman took the hands of the two crying children and led them away. The woman wounded in the left shoulder slowly rose and picked up her dead baby with her good right hand. She looked at Nathaniel with eyes that could kill. She murmured something that he was thankful he could not understand. The old man remained lying on his side looking oddly up at him with tired, vacant eyes that said he did not care anymore.

They left the old man lying there on the trail.

The experience greatly disturbed Nathaniel. He arrived back at Sydney Cove with the full realization that the massacre had profoundly changed him. His children were close to the same ages as those two wretched native children who had been scared half to death by the killing of their family. Moira could have been that mother. He was thinking of leaving the military and decided to avoid any future operations involving the possibility of killing, if he could avoid it.

⊙

John Hunter finally arrived on September 7, 1795. From his ship, he was amazed to see the improvements that had been made over the four and a half years of his absence. He had left a military camp and was returning to a village with the look of permanence about it. New roads provided a sense of order. Substantial buildings lined the roads, especially on the eastern side of the cove.

The two-story, white Government House looked much the same, except its sprawling garden was now defined by a road leading down the hill to a collection of government and naval storehouses at the Government Wharf. The trees behind Government House had been replaced by open fields and scattered houses. His eyes were drawn with satisfaction to the top of the slope where a cross projected above a white church.

The rocky hill on the western side of the cove, however, did not look as much improved. Among the rocks, scattered haphazardly, was a disorderly array of single-room huts and shacks that he assumed were mostly convict housing.

As he approached the wharf, he saw that while many of the buildings were still constructed of wattle and daub, most of their thatch roofs had been replaced with tile or slate, glistening in the sunlight. A report had informed him that the brick kilns were producing roofing tiles along with an ample supply of bricks. A good vein of slate had been found and sandstone was being quarried from the rock cliffs bordering Woolloomooloo Bay. He assumed that the substantial buildings, made of brick and stone, were public buildings.

Nathaniel was among the officials who greeted the new governor upon landing at Government Wharf. He congratulated Hunter both for his appointment as governor and his honorable acquittal from any responsibility for the loss of the *Sirius* at Norfolk Island. Hunter gave him a personal letter from Phillip and set a time to meet at Government House in two days.

Hunter was handsome at sixty with a full head of white flowing hair. Never married, he arrived without any family or even a personal secretary. His only attendant was his personal servant.

That evening at a welcoming affair, Nathaniel saw Bennelong, who had returned with Hunter. He was dressed in fine clothes and carried himself in an erect, lofty manner. Watching him discreetly, Nathaniel was amused to see that he carried a fine, embroidered handkerchief and made flamboyant gestures with it. Bennelong had adopted the affected, superior airs of an aristocrat!

Bennelong later came over to Nathaniel and greeted him without any of his past resentment for having been captured by him years earlier.

"I want my people t'live happy an' in peace," he said. "When they visit me at Gov'ment House, I want 'em t'be clean an' not say bad things." He used a haughty tone to indicate that he was a man of consequence and expected everyone to do as he said.

Hunter joined them, and they talked about Yemmerawannie, who had died of pneumonia in London. After Bennelong walked away, Hunter told Nathaniel that Bennelong had also nearly died from displacement and heartbreak. He improved immensely, though, when they set sail for his homeland.

At their meeting two days later, Hunter and Nathaniel rekindled their previously warm relationship. They started talking about Phillip and old times and then went on to cover the years since they had parted. Hunter confided in Nathaniel that he did not expect to see Sydney Cove in such an improved state.

"The good Reverends Johnson and Marsden have been writing their patron William Wilberforce, member of Parliament and close friend of Prime Minister William Pitt, about the ungodly state of things here. I expected to find a hellhole, but, frankly, Sydney Cove is much improved compared to when I left. The Home Office secretary, the Duke of Portland, has ordered me to build a proper church and school to replace the makeshift one on the hill built by Reverend Johnson out of his own pocket. I'm sorry that the army administrators held the church in such contempt that they did nothing but place obstacles in the way of church attendance and the education of the young."

Nathaniel avoided responding to Hunter's criticism of the previous administration. "Yes, Sydney Cove is much improved; although, I believe, Your Excellency will be even more pleased with the appearance of Parramatta. It's grown into a fine town, larger and with more people than Sydney Cove. The beautiful rolling hills and farms that surround the town are a delight to see. The days of famine are behind us, I'm happy to say. There's no doubt in my mind that New South Wales, in time, will be a valuable addition to the British Empire. The key is private enterprise that has provided the bounty."

"I'm told the officer farmers are giving spirits to their convict help. My instructions are to curtail the unrestrained importation of spirituous liquors and its distribution."

"I understand your concern about spirits, Governor. Initially, I forbade it on my farm because I was sure it would lead to drunken and unruly convict help. But it turned out to be just the opposite. We give only a daily ration, equal to that given by yourself to sailors and marines at sea. Controlled in this manner, it has become an integral part for the betterment of the colony. Convicts will work for rum, without being flogged, just as impressed sailors will."

Hunter was not impressed by Nathaniel's argument in favor of rum. "I agree with Phillip's policy of restricting the importation of rum and denying it to convicts. I also have orders to increase government farming, which will provide free produce from convict labor."

"We've developed a local economy based on private enterprise and trading since you left, Your Excellency. As you travel around you will see its beneficial results. We now have farmers, tradesmen, merchants, shopkeepers, and all manner of artificers. Because we have no coinage, the local economy is functioning on the exchange of rum. It has become the main commodity of barter and a de facto currency—"

Nathaniel stopped talking when he saw Hunter's eyes glazing over. He obviously wasn't convincing him. In fact, it occurred to him, Hunter hadn't said a word about commerce or finance since he had arrived. He was, after all, a ship captain, who had never managed anything more complicated than his own ship.

Sensing he should respond to Nathaniel's comments regarding the local economy, Hunter said, "The Treasury has complained about the high cost of the colony. The Duke of Portland has ordered me to reduce government support to only two convicts for each farmer. I intend to use the freed-up convicts to increase production at the government farms and to carry out needed public works."

This confirmed Nathaniel's worse concerns. "Your Excellency, may I respectfully advise you to visit Parramatta before issuing such an order? The colony is doing amazingly well under the private enterprise system. The officer farmers have worked very diligently and taken substantial financial risks to benefit the colony and their families, and, I think, they deserve to be rewarded. You may want to consider that the *army* officers are naturally concerned about a *naval* governor and wonder how you intend to treat them. You need them on your side, Governor Hunter, to fight Indians and to maintain order. Governor Phillip led a *government-run* administration, which was right then but not now. It would destroy the private economy that is just getting started. I remind you of the starvation years, which you and I suffered through, when we depended entirely on government farming."

"Thank you for being candid, Nathaniel," Hunter said,

having decided not to argue further with him. He was saddened that Nathaniel held opposing views regarding nearly all of his instructions. His intention had been to ask him to serve as his secretary, regrettably, that was now impractical.

Nathaniel was not impressed by Hunter. My goodness, he thought, I haven't heard an original idea from him yet. Why . . . he's no more than a small-minded functionary, concerned only with his rigid instructions. What are his grand plans and aspirations? He hasn't said a word. Nothing like the all-encompassing vision of Phillip, or even Grose, who knew what he wanted and did it.

"I'd like to invite you to visit my farm, Your Excellency, at your earliest convenience. I'm sure my neighbors, George Evans and John Macarthur, would enjoy showing you around their farms as well. Captain Macarthur is the inspector of public works."

Macarthur met with the governor the next day. At the end of their meeting, Macarthur handed the governor a finely hand-printed invitation to a grand dinner that his wife, Elizabeth, was planning in his honor. The invitation asked him to stay overnight with them. Impressed with Macarthur, the governor immediately accepted.

Hunter visited Nathaniel's and Evans's farms and attended the dinner at Macarthur's farm that evening. John Macarthur introduced his wife saying that their farm, Elizabeth Farm, was named after her.

Before dinner, when a group of men were talking to the governor, Hunter mentioned that his orders were to increase government farming to reduce the cost to the Treasury.

"I'm sorry to tell you, Your Excellency, but after years of farming, the soil of our two government farms is depleted of nutrients," John Macarthur spoke with a voice of official authority. "We have not seeded them for the past two growing seasons to provide a fallow period for the farms to regain their natural fertility."

Hunter was about to speak, but Macarthur forged on. "However, this has turned out to have the most beneficial results for our colony. It brought to the attention of our administration that if the government farms produced sufficient food for all, we farmers would have no market for our produce, and it would be impossible to develop a self-reliant colony. Governors Grose and Paterson found that private farming was much better managed and productive, so much so, that Your Excellency can write London the happy news that in the very near future it may discontinue food shipments and focus instead on sending manufactured goods and other essentials. I would be delighted to write a draft of such a letter for Your Excellency's consideration, if he would but request it of me."

Governor Hunter beamed at Macarthur's offer. "Why yes, I would be quite interested in reading such a draft letter from yourself, the inspector of public works. The letter should estimate future amounts of grain and animal products and provide a date when food shipments from London might be discontinued."

Hunter was captivated by the delightful and talented Elizabeth Macarthur. He was amazed to find the same pianoforte in her drawing room that he had played on the *Sirius* during the voyage to Botany Bay. Its owner, Surgeon George Worgan, had left it with Mrs. Macarthur when he returned to England in 1791. Mrs. Macarthur played several pieces she had been taught by Worgan, including "Foot's Minuet" and "God Save the King." To everyone's great enjoyment, Hunter then played a variety of music for much of the evening.

Mrs. Macarthur embarrassed him when she earnestly deemed the evening a "complete success" and invited him to visit them often. She then lowered her voice as if about to say something intimate:

"I must admit, though, that I have an ulterior motive, which is to impose on His Excellency to teach me a few of his simpler pieces."

Hunter's visit to Parramatta convinced him that the new system of private enterprise had greatly improved the well-being of the colony. Private farming had obviously been more productive than government farming. The officers had found the way to encourage the convicts to work, by giving them the same rum ration given on board ship for good behavior. Hunter was particularly impressed by Macarthur, who obviously had a brilliant mind for facts and figures. He used Macarthur's draft letter to write a glowing report to the home secretary supporting the present free-enterprise system and lauding Macarthur in his capacity as the inspector of the public works, "a position for which he seems extremely well qualified."

◉

After four months in Sydney Cove, Hunter began to wonder whether he had made a terrible mistake by writing the Duke of Portland so hastily in support of the officer farmers, which meant essentially disobeying his instructions. In the pews, he heard the sermons of Reverends Johnson and Marsden damning the officer-ruling class and the drunken, debauched society they had created, calling it a "den of iniquity." He had chosen Judge Advocate David Collins as his secretary, who criticized the officers' avarice and lamented their control of the courts. Hunter saw how the officers, as magistrates, controlled the police and courts in ways that favored themselves. They monopolized trade, especially rum and luxuries from Cape Town and Bengal, and charged exorbitant prices to free settlers and emancipist farmers. Some of the officers ran "grog shops," which he suspected were also brothels.

The governor was also becoming unhappy with Macarthur in his powerful dual roles of financial manager of the colony and inspector of public works. Even though Hunter had not implemented the Duke of Portland's instructions to reduce the number of convicts to only two per officer farmer, Macarthur was reluctant to make many convicts available for needed public works projects. With few convicts arriving because of the war with France, Macarthur was playing a stalling game by giving management reasons why convicts could not be transferred quickly or in large numbers from officers' farms. Finally, in February 1796, Hunter became utterly frustrated and sat down with Macarthur to tell him exactly what he wanted him to do. They argued, until the governor ordered him to do his bidding.

Realizing he could no longer stall Hunter, Macarthur met with George and Nathaniel to decide what to do.

"The governor said, in effect, that he wants to work with me in my capacity of inspector of public works to slit my own throat," Macarthur said. "He proposes to take most of our assigned convicts from us to work on public projects, including government farming, to produce what he calls '*free* grain and meat.' In addition, he thinks the government should pay us less per pound for our grain and meat. He actually is asking us to produce less and be paid less for what we produce. It's his damnable way of reducing cost to the Treasury—at our expense!"

Evans banged his fist on the table. "He's out to destroy us!"

"I told him that this was wrongheaded from both a financial and economic point of view." Macarthur shook his head. "Financially speaking, he would not save money, due to the fact that the government farms have never been productive and certainly will not be productive if the government cannot use rum as an incentive. Economically, he would be destroying our farming enterprises, by taking the profit out of it. The colony would soon become dependent again on foodstuffs sent from England, which would in the long run be more expensive for the Treasury than producing it here. I told him I could not carry out such ill-conceived proposals. In fact, I offered him my resignation if he no longer respects my opinions and has lost confidence in me."

They asked Nathaniel to seek a meeting with Hunter to sway him back to their way of thinking. Nathaniel agreed and ten days later sat down with the governor at Government House.

Hunter began their meeting by sharing a piece of good news he had just received in a dispatch from London. After the French Republic revolutionary forces had invaded the Netherlands and William V of Orange escaped to England, the deposed Dutch ruler issued instructions that the Cape Colony was to be temporarily handed over to Britain to prevent the French from occupying it. A fleet of seven Royal Navy ships under Admiral Elphinstone had carried these instructions to the Dutch governor at Cape Town, but he refused. After a sea and land battle, the Dutch surrendered. General Craig, army commander of the 78th Highlanders, had assumed the office of governor.

While discussing this happy occurrence, they heard an outburst: "*You cannot go bleeding across the governor's rugs!*" and then an unintelligible protest from Bennelong. Hunter interrupted their meeting to step out of the room to see what the problem was. Nathaniel followed him. The governor's servant was pushing Bennelong off a rug onto the stone floor. Bennelong was nude and had an ugly wound to his mouth, which had divided his upper lip and broken two teeth. Seeing the governor, his servant pointed at drops of blood across the rug.

The governor asked Bennelong what had happened. He explained the best he could that he had been assaulted by his old friend Colebee for having sex with one of Colebee's favorite wives. Hunter ordered him to go to the hospital for treatment.

Walking back into the meeting room with the governor, Nathaniel said, "I thought Bennelong had stopped walking around shamelessly nude. How can he still do that after so many years living among civilized people in England?"

"I asked him the same thing. He leaves his clothes here when he goes out among his own people. Evidently, it's the only way they will accept him. It has something to do with superstition and their belief in evil spirits. If a man covers himself, they think he must have something to hide, perhaps a weapon or evil intent ... or sorcery.

"The poor fellow is trying to fit in both worlds, and it's not going too well for him, I'm afraid. He lost his wife Gooroobaroobooloo, you know, to a younger man. The natives don't appear to have much respect for him anymore, which means he's losing his effectiveness as my ambassador.

"I'm sorry for that interruption, Nathaniel. It used up part of the hour set aside for our meeting. You wanted to talk to me about my proposal to reduce the commissary's payment for wheat and corn, I believe."

"I'm not here to add my voice to the hue and cry against this reasonable, although highly unpopular reduction in payment, Your Excellency. Instead, I wish to suggest that you should proceed slowly on the more radical changes in policy that you recently proposed to Captain Macarthur. We have had three years of free enterprise under two army administrators that has greatly improved the general well-being of the colony. Your army officers are concerned that you, a naval officer, may not have their best interest at heart."

"You are not confusing your duties as His Majesty's officer with your own financial objectives as a gentleman farmer, I hope."

"No sir."

"You surely are not hinting that the officers would not obey my orders?"

"No sir."

"My dear Captain Armstrong, I have no choice in the matter. I must find ways to economize to reduce costs. To make long overdue public improvements, I must free up convicts from private farmers. These are things I must do whether the officers like it or not. I am not intent on destroying private enterprise, I assure you, as Captain Macarthur believes."

"That may be; however, I'm told you intend to restart government farming at the expense of private farming and disallow the use of rum as an incentive, because it is in conflict with London's policy. I have to say, Governor, that this would be a return to the failed policies of the past."

"Rum, sir, is the *root cause* of the debauchery of the lower classes, especially women. I have seen with my own eyes the outrageous effects of alcoholism on them. These drunkards are at the bottom of every infamous transaction committed in this colony. Cohabitation is more common than marriage. They are incapable of responsibility for their own children, who I see dirty and wild in the streets getting themselves into all manner of mischief. These drunken women and their children have grown disorderly beyond all suffering. Alcoholism and prostitution go hand and hand. I intend to find ways to limit the available of spirits of all kinds. The military magistrates have been too lenient. That is why I have appointed Reverends Johnson and Marsden, and Assistant Surgeon Balmain to replace military magistrates. I have authorized them to suffer these women such exemplary punishments as their crimes may merit."

"I understand, Your Exce—"

"Allow me to complete my thoughts on the 'failed policies of the past' as you called them. Regarding farming, my orders are to increase government farming. I admit that I was impressed by your farms and the improved appearance of Sydney Cove and Parramatta. But I should not have allowed myself to be misled. I regret writing the Duke of Portland so quickly praising your system before I'd determined the real conditions here.

"Well, I see more clearly now that Macarthur and his officers, and some civil officials, have used their power over the colony in every sphere to establish and manipulate your so-called 'free enterprise economy' to unfairly benefit themselves. The small farmers, tradesmen, and artificers are at your mercy, which undermines the moral being of the colony."

"Governor, I fear that you do not give Macarthur enough credit for what he has done for the colony. You should know that he has been a tireless worker—"

"For himself, foremost," Hunter interrupted. "I think he intends to make as much money as possible and then return to England and couldn't care less about public improvements here. Reverend Marsden told me that Macarthur lied to me about the government farms being used up and no longer good for farming. Regardless, he could have found new crown land to farm, I assume, although I admit I know little about good soil and farming. I asked Macarthur to work with me to make an equitable transition, but he turned me down coldly. Now you've come to advise me not to rock the boat."

"Sir, you need your officers' support. Most of them have self-interests to protect at this point. I simply advise you to go slowly on major policy changes so not to cause a rift."

"What has happened to you, Nathaniel? Did you lose your sense of fair play to your family's comforts? Surely you are aware that your coterie is exploiting the convicts and has placed the small farmer at your mercy by manipulating the levers of government, police, and courts for your own benefit. Let us be honest, your group is creating a baronage for itself. You have given yourselves first choice of the best land, convict labor, and government store goods. Your syndicate monopolizes the purchase of goods from visiting trading ships and then resells to those who have no recourse but to pay your extortionate prices. You contract ships to buy yourselves luxuries and rum, which you use to extract from the inebriated lower classes what little money they have or their labor. I daresay that your coterie has broken an implied fairness pact with the British government."

"I know that view is held by Reverends Johnson and Marsden and such men as Doctor Balmain and Richard Atkins, but it is not a fair or accurate one. I would argue instead that a freer economic system has allowed the more productive members of our small community to advance through creative hard work that has benefited all, in varying degrees. Our two views, however, do not have to lead to conflict, Your Excellency. You have already made changes that have negatively affected my 'coterie,' as you call it, and they have been accepted. As I said before, I counsel slow incremental changes to avoid confrontation."

"These are not the words I had hoped to hear from you, of all people, Captain Armstrong. I *must* say that you, of all my officers, have disappointed me the most. I had looked forward to your support and helpful counsel. Under Governor Phillip, you had the colony's best interest close to your heart, but now you are among the most avaricious members of the corps.

"As you are here on an errand for Captain Macarthur, you may tell your friend that I have accepted his resignation as inspector of public works 'without reluctance' and shall appoint Richard Atkins in his place."

"I respectfully must say, Your Excellency, that would be a mistake. Mr. Atkins is a well-known drunk, womanizer, and a fool. He and Captain Macarthur are—"

"Pray enough, Captain Armstrong, he is an aristocrat, his brother is an admiral and a good friend of Admiral Lord Howe, under whom I served and have great admiration."

"But, Governor, such an appointment would be seen as—"

"That's quite enough, Captain Armstrong," said the governor as he rose abruptly from his seat, obviously highly agitated. "Good day to you, sir." He walked out of the room leaving Nathaniel sitting there, offended and disappointed.

"**When I'm gone,** you'll be one of the few remaining first fleeters, Nathaniel," Judge Advocate David Collins said. "It's amazing; in three months, it'll be nine years that we've been here."

"It *seems* like nine years to me, David, so much has transpired. But there's more than a few of us remaining: George Evans, Captain George Johnston, Reverend Johnson, Sergeant Westover, who's now a farmer on the Hawkesbury, and several more if I put my mind to it. Do you have a ship yet?"

"No, but I've told the governor … and Nancy is halfway through packing. It's next to impossible to find two cabins next to each other for us and the children and their nanny."

Nathaniel wondered whether Collins had written his wife that he was bringing home his mistress and their two children.

They were leaning against the rail of the balustrade at one end of the Nathaniel's veranda. Moira and Nancy Yates were seated at the opposite end, talking. It was a warm afternoon in September. Collins and Yates had brought their two children, a six-year-old girl and her brother age three. Being city children, they had arrived anxious to go down to the barn to see the animals. Their nanny had walked them down led by Arthur, with Charles, nearly three, trailing along behind.

"I didn't think I'd have two children when I returned. I'll tell you that," Collins said with a wry grin.

Is he providing an opportunity to ask about his wife? Nathaniel wondered and then decided to respond safely.

"They're two beautiful, well-mannered children, David."

"Thank you, they are. You seem very happy with your family as well."

"I am, thank you, although Charles is a little bugger."

"It's a pity that the governor has no family to support him. He'll be lost without me, I fear. The officers have isolated him socially and only deal with him when they must. He has only the pastors and his religious friends, who I feel are too biased in their viewpoints to serve him well." Collins took a slow drink of his wine to give Nathaniel a chance to respond.

Nathaniel had no intention of reconciling with Hunter and

looked away while taking a drink of his beer.

"It's a vexing situation," Collins continued. "The governor is being frustrated at every level and hasn't been able to move ahead with most of his projects. He hasn't even been able to find the funds and convict labor to build the church he promised Reverend Johnson." He stopped again to take a drink of his wine. "*I'm* frustrated too; that's why I'm leaving."

Nathaniel sensed that Collins was trying to draw him into discussing Hunter's problems and then solicit his aid in some way. He decided to say something innocuous:

"Governing is never an easy matter."

Obviously, Nathaniel had to see his livelihood at risk before he would assist Governor Hunter, Collins concluded. "I probably shouldn't tell you this, Nathaniel, but I want to warn you as a friend. The governor has written the Home Office and the Admiralty asking that the recalcitrant New South Wales Corps be replaced by marines. He's sure the marines will be more responsive to him. I expect that he would like to see Macarthur lose everything by being recalled. Inasmuch as you want to stay, you may want to consider resigning from the corps or supporting the governor in some manner that you are comfortable with."

"*Well*—that's a bit of news," Nathaniel said, taken aback. "Thank you for the warning, David. Actually, I've been giving some serious thought to leaving the military."

"I think that the governor is sorry that you and he have parted ways. Frankly, Nathaniel, I've never understood why you are friends with Macarthur. You'll never be accepted by him and his exclusive crowd. Surely you know they dream of creating a colonial aristocracy, of which you can never be a member because of Moira; no offense intended, Moira is a wonderful woman."

"Yes, of course . . . I know that and can live with it. By the way, I do not consider Macarthur a friend, although I do respect the man. He's an exceptional fellow—a visionary."

"Well, you know *what* I think of him . . . so we can leave it at that then."

There was commotion at the other end of the veranda. The

children were returning, and Collins's girl was running toward her mother crying about something or other. Nathaniel and Collins walked over to them in the middle of the tumult. The girl was holding her mother's hands through the balusters.

Pointing at Charles, Collins's boy said accusingly, "He pushed her down, and she got dirty!"

"She pushed me first!" Charles said in defense, crossing his arms petulantly.

Nathaniel bent over the railing and grabbed Charles harshly by the arm. "*Charles*, you're going to apologize to her. *Boys* don't push *girls*, do you hear me! *Say you're sorry!*"

"Ah . . . I'm . . . sooorry," he said.

Nathaniel let go of his arm and, while turning back to Collins, quietly said, "Even when they're twice your age." Collins smiled.

A month later and a week after Collins had departed, Macarthur told Nathaniel that Hunter had written the Duke of Portland begging for the recall of the New South Wales Corps. Nathaniel did not let on that he already knew. Macarthur was incensed that Hunter had identified him as the reprehensible ringleader. He suggested that Nathaniel should join him and other officers in writing Portland and the army commander in chief to refute Hunter's accusations and expose his maltreatment of the corps and mismanagement of the colony.

◉

During the early months of 1797, there was a inexplicable increase in violent attacks by the woods natives in the area between the Hawkesbury River and Parramatta. Their principal leader was identified as Pemulwuy.

A pattern had developed with Pemulwuy-led encounters. When the number of his warriors greatly outnumbered those of the whites, Pemulwuy would fearlessly show himself and make his demands. If his demands were refused, he would immediately signal an attack and kill as many as possible. Although Pemulwuy was often wounded, his warriors came to believe that he could not be killed by firearms. Cloaked in this imaginary security, he became even more aggressive.

After a group of natives had killed a farmer, his wife, and their child, some fifty settlers armed themselves and set off to track the group down. They followed the natives' trail and saw their camp fire that evening. The settlers attempted to sneak up on them during the night but found they had slipped away, leaving behind a large quantity of corn and plunder. Undeterred, the posse doggedly pursued them through the night and sighted the group the next morning. Although there were more than one hundred native men, women, and children, they chose to flee when they discovered their pursuers were well armed. The posse continued to follow them to within a mile of Parramatta. Fatigued from their march, the fifty men entered the town for water and food.

Nathaniel and George were together in Parramatta purchasing farm equipment when they heard that a large group of heavily armed settlers had entered the town after chasing a band of Indians throughout the night. Hunter had issued a proclamation that it was a crime for settlers to shoot natives except when defending themselves. Since this clearly was not that case, Nathaniel and George walked over to advise them that they should disband.

While they were talking, Pemulwuy and fifty or more of his warriors brazenly entered the village in bold contempt of the armed men who had been following them for a day and a half. Pointing at the posse, the native men let it be known that they were annoyed by being followed.

Nathaniel started to move toward the Indians.

Knowing what Nathaniel was about to do, George grabbed his arm. "Don't get in the middle of this, Nate!"

Nathaniel jerked his arm away. Spreading his arms, he walked out between the two groups saying to the whites "Stay back men" at the same time as a majority of them, not interested in parlaying, advanced to seize Pemulwuy.

In a great rage, Pemulwuy threw a spear at one of them. Several musket shots simultaneously hit him, knocking him down and severely wounding him. In the ensuing battle, five warriors were slain before they retreated. A settler was speared in the shoulder.

The whites converged on the unconscious Pemulwuy intending to kill him. Nathaniel shot his pistol into the air to get their attention.

"*Get back men!* Anyone who kills him will be breakin' the governor's proclamation and will be charged with murder." He made his way into the mob. "Step back now! I'm arresting him for his crimes. He'll hang for what he did!"

Pemulwuy had suffered six small shot wounds to his head and multiple hits to other parts of his body. He was placed in chains and taken to the hospital. Nathaniel sent a rider to advise Governor Hunter of the capture of Pemulwuy and requested that Bennelong be dispatched immediately to serve as interpreter at his trial. Word was sent back that Bennelong could not be found.

Bennelong had been spending longer periods of time among his people and was often unavailable to Hunter. Often he returned wounded and a couple of times was pursued by warriors requiring the guards at Government House to save him from harm. He had developed a thirst for spirits and when drunk was belligerent and abusive. Instead of an ambassador to his people and an aid to the governor, Bennelong was becoming a drunken nuisance to all.

Two days after his capture, Pemulwuy escaped from the hospital. Hearing nothing about him for several months, Nathaniel was told by Colebee that Pemulwuy had recovered from his wounds and was leading his people again. Colebee at this time was living in Sydney Cove among his soldier friends, sometimes in their huts and other times in the corps's barracks.

Colebee was living close to the soldiers because he had murdered a popular young warrior named Yeranibe in a disreputable way. He had met him on a field of honor to resolve an argument. They were equally matched until Colebee knocked Yeranibe's shield to the ground. When he bent to pick it up, Colebee cowardly struck him on the head with his club and then bludgeoned him to death. The natives watching the contest immediately yelled "*Jeerun, jeerun*"—Coward, coward—and chased him from the field. With Colebee unavailable, Yeranibe's clan members attacked Colebee's family members and relatives, seriously injuring three of them.

When Yeranibe's clan learned that Colebee was staying in the soldiers' barracks, they assembled on the adjacent parade ground and called for him to come out to face tribal justice.

"*JEERUN* come out! COLEBEE, the *jeerun*—COME OUT!*"

Although Bennelong had come with Yeranibe's clan, he chose to stand quietly off to one side. The soldiers filed out of their barracks and huts to watch the show. When Colebee did not come out, the clan members forced one of Colebee's relatives to face them. They gave him a shield and threw spears at him until he was hit. Still alive, he was removed and another younger male relative was pushed out onto the parade ground and given a shield. This young relative screamed for Colebee to come out and save him. Colebee then came out of the barracks armed for battle with a shield and spears. He was unclothed as were all the natives.

When Colebee was within range, the warriors of Yeranibe's clan began to throw their spears. Colebee jumped from side to side while throwing four of his spears back at them without effect. A spear struck Colebee in the chest, knocking him to the ground. Swinging their clubs menacingly, three of Yeranibe's brothers walked toward Colebee to kill him. But before they could reach him, soldier friends of Colebee forced them back with their muskets and bayonets. Four other soldiers lifted Colebee and began to carry him toward their barracks.

An enraged Bennelong stepped in front of the soldiers saying they could not interfere with tribal justice. Knowing Bennelong was no longer a friend of Colebee, the soldiers pointed their bayonets at him and forced him aside. As they walked away, Bennelong threw a spear through the leg of one of the men carrying Colebee. Bennelong would have been shot had the provost marshal not been standing next to him. He immediately arrested Bennelong and ordered him bound and taken to jail.

Nathaniel rushed from his office to the jail where he found Bennelong yelling and screaming incoherently. He had never before been confined in a cell. When he saw Nathaniel, he screamed for his immediate release, and when that was not effective, he said:

"Let me go, or I *kill you!*"

Through Bennelong's tantrum, Nathaniel said, "You're going to *stay in jail* until it's assured that the soldier you wounded survives. It's going to be days before we'll know that, so you'd better get used to your cell!" With that, Nathaniel went to the hospital to visit the wounded private. He later met the governor, who agreed that Bennelong would be tried if the soldier died of his wound.

A week later, with the wounded soldier on the mend and sure to live, Nathaniel went to the jail to release Bennelong. Still incensed for being jailed, Bennelong told Nathaniel:

"I'm goin' t'spear yer the next time I see yer, an' Gov'ner Hunter too."

For these threats, Nathaniel ordered the jailers to throw Bennelong back into his cell. After discussing the threats with the governor, Nathaniel showed Bennelong the governor's proclamation banishing him from Sydney Cove and Parramatta and allowing any soldier to shoot him on sight if he entered either town again.

◉

"Intolerable humbug!" **Hunter** exclaimed to the empty room as he read a copy of John Macarthur's letter that had been sent to him by Home Secretary Portland for reply. He fumed and mumbled aloud as he read the letter. "*Good Lord!* . . . this is gross insubordination . . . false and malicious libel! . . . . . . monstrous poppycock! . . . the man has no scruples at all!" He was shocked in equal parts by the unfair accusations and the persuasiveness of them.

Every one of his failures as governor was enumerated. He was criticized for not carrying out Portland's direct orders—the very orders Macarthur opposed! As one of the colony's most successful farmers and former inspector of public works, Macarthur attested that Hunter had no knowledge of farming and mismanaged government farm production. Referring to his years as regimental paymaster and financial manager, Macarthur wrote that the governor exhibited little knowledge of finance and economics, was profligate, and obstructed the enterprises of free men. Hunter was criticized for restricting the purchase of goods by the upper classes from Cape Town and Bengal, at their own expense and for their own use, which had caused an unnecessary drain on goods from the government's commissary. He faulted Hunter, a naval man, for being antagonistic toward the army and for interfering unnecessarily in its mission. Macarthur closed with criticism of His Excellency's governing style calling it autocratic and self-defeating because he seemed incapable of accepting sound advice from more knowledgeable advisors.

Hunter could fume and fuss, but he had to admit to himself that Macarthur was a brilliantly persuasive writer; although, most of his criticisms were unfair, biased, and self-serving. None of his successes as governor were mentioned nor the difficulties of his untenable position acknowledged. No one cared, he lamented, that he was isolated with few advisors and reliable assistants. Regardless of all that, he knew he was in deep trouble.

Hunter put his hands to the sides of his head and massaged his temples. Anger screamed inside his head. This scoundrel is attacking me personally. Why . . . it's an attack on my honor! By God, I'll call him out for this. He'll have no choice but to face me on a field of honor! . . . ridiculous . . . I can't do that, a sixty-three-year-old governor dueling with a thirty-one-year-old captain; it'd look like I've lost my mind.

I'll charge the cur with gross insubordination, sedition, and libel! I've got all the evidence I need right here in this letter to charge him. I'll arrest the bastard and throw him in jail! But the letter would have to be submitted as evidence and the criticism of my administration would come out. And would the magistrates actually convict him? many of whom are his friends.

Why didn't Portland see this letter for what it is?—seditious. He must think there's some truth to the charges and that my administration may be culpable. *Damme*, am I to be reduced to defending myself?—*I'll resign first!* I must think this through completely.

Reverends Johnson and Marsden agreed to write Portland on Hunter's behalf to damn Macarthur to the best of their ability. Hunter would still have to respond to Macarthur's letter; now, however, he could do so at a higher level more commensurate with his august position. Hunter wrote to the home secretary saying Macarthur had "a restless, divisive disposition and that only the full power of the governorship would satisfy him."

Macarthur's critical letter was not the only disappointing news that Hunter received in Portland's dispatch. The home secretary informed him that a regiment of marines was placed on ships to replace the New South Wales Corps, as he had requested; but regrettably, due to the exigencies of the war with France, they had to be dispatched elsewhere. Hunter would have to live with the New South Wales Corps for the time being.

Portland reiterated his initial order to reduce the number of convicts per officer down to two, who must be fed and clothed by the officer for whom they worked. He also told the governor again to restrict the importation of rum and to keep it from the convicts.

Hunter issued a proclamation advising the officers of Portland's orders and directing them to reduce the number of their convict workers by one each month until they were down to two. The officers raised a ruckus about his proclamation and then proposed a compromise. A committee, headed by Macarthur, proposed to fed and clothe all of the convicts presently assigned to each of them if their number would not be reduced. Thinking the officers would revolt if he explicitly followed Portland's orders, Hunter reluctantly agreed.

Because Hunter's proclamation also included his intent to restrict the importation of rum and its distribution, Macarthur asked the officers to sign a pact. He told Nathaniel:

"Hunter is about to restrict all trade by the officers, especially rum. We need to formalize our commitment to act as a syndicate to buy from speculative ships that come into port. If we all sign a pact there is nothing he can do about it. Will you sign?"

Nathaniel added his signature as a member of Macarthur's syndicate. He had little choice. If he did not sign he would be ostracized and forced to purchase goods at inflated prices.

In response to Macarthur's pact, Hunter issued an order that the officers had to share their monopoly with any free man who desired to purchase at the same price the goods were purchased. It was a meaningless order because it was impossible to enforce. The monopoly of the Rum Corps, as the New South Wales Corps had come to be called, continued unabated.

In October 1798, Johnson's temporary church, built by him five years earlier, was burned to the ground. Hunter offered a large reward for identification of the culprit, but the firebug was never identified. At this point, Hunter felt despair at being unable to control the officers, who threw obstacles in his path at every step. He continued to complain to Portland that he had little control over the colony, while the New South Wales Corps thwarted his every order and initiative.

Hunter received a furious letter from the Duke of Portland in July 1799 explicitly ordering him to arrest any officer found engaging in the rum trade and return him to England to face court martial. This was an impossible order, Hunter thought, because *all* of the officers were involved in the rum trade. He considered arresting a low-level officer as a warning to the others but decided it would be a cowardly act. He would have to arrest the acknowledged ringleader Macarthur. Through indecision and fear that the New South Wales Corps would refuse his order to arrest their leader, Hunter chose instead to ignore Portland's order.

When Hunter's complaining letters continued, Portland decided to replace him with Philip Gidley King on the recommendations of Arthur Phillip and Sir Joseph Banks. The frustrated home secretary had arrived at the conclusion that Hunter was an ineffectual leader who could neither obey orders nor enforce them. He dismissed him for not reducing the number of convicts assigned to officer farmers to two, for not restricting the importation of rum, for allowing the distribution of rum to the lower classes, and for his continuing budget overruns. King sailed for New South Wales with a commission to succeed Hunter as governor upon Hunter's departure from Sydney Cove on the first suitable ship of his own choosing.

◻

Nathaniel was delighted to have his former mentor Philip Gidley King back in the colony and was pleasantly surprised, when at their first meeting he felt equal to the governor-designate. At thirty-seven, Nathaniel was a seasoned senior officer and a rich farmer who was better off than the poor, forty-two-year-old King. Suffering from gout, King walked like an old man, while Nathaniel was strong and vigorous. They were both responsible family men; King had arrived with his wife, Anna, and their children.

King enthusiastically and openly discussed his hopes and plans with him, indicating by his attitude that Nathaniel would be a member of his administration. As King spoke, Nathaniel felt the same admiration and respect for him that he had before; feelings he had not felt for Hunter.

King intended to accomplish what Hunter had been unable to do: control the importation of spirits by the Rum Corps and remove its monopolists' grip on the economy, so goods could be provided to all at a reasonable cost. Lieutenant Colonel William Paterson, Nathaniel's commanding officer and friend, had agreed to serve as lieutenant governor to help reform the New South Wales Corps. King asked Nathaniel to serve as his personal secretary and closest advisor.

Nathaniel spoke to Moira about King's offer.

"This is one of those *major* decisions in our marriage that we should make together, for the good of our family and our future. If I throw our lot in with King and he is unsuccessful, we could be ruined."

"You've spoken often about him being yer friend," Moira said. "You think he's a good leader, don't you?"

"Aye, both a good friend and leader."

"Aren't you honor bound to support him then?"

"It isn't that simple, Moira. We have to be realistic and practical. His policies will hurt us. We'll lose many of the advantages we have now. He wants to reduce the number of assigned convicts. We'll lose household servants and field workers and be forced to either hire people or cut back on farming. We may have to accept less for our farm products. No one knows how this will affect our local economy. We can't be naive, Moira, or consider friendship over what is best for us.

"I didn't like opposing Hunter, but I did. Perhaps I realized he didn't have the mettle necessary to successfully oppose Macarthur and the corps."

"You feel Governor King does?"

"I don't know . . . but, yes, more than Hunter. It helps that Paterson, the corps commander, has agreed to serve as his lieutenant governor. He is a good and fair man. Unfortunately, he's not a strong leader. When he was acting governor for nine months, he let Macarthur run the colony. I'm sure that King realizes that he has to attract other officers to his side."

"Is Captain George Evans on the other side?"

"Yes, he'll stand with Macarthur, though I don't like to think of it that way. We're all entrepreneurs who have tried to improve our lot while working to improve the colony. Those who are able and have worked the hardest have done the best."

"I think we've helped ourselves enough already, Nathaniel. We ha' a lot; I don't need anythin' more. I don't like people takin' advantage of others, like John Macarthur does. I think Governor King wants t'do the right thing."

"King told me that there are no plans to replace the corps with marines. As long as the corps remains, it will be difficult for him to achieve half of what he intends. I told him that, but he doesn't understand it yet. As his secretary, I would inevitably be drawn into conflict with Macarthur and George and other leaders of the corps. I don't look forward to being in conflict with my neighbors."

"Over rum an' spirits?"

"Over many issues, rum is just one of them."

Moira looked sternly at him. "Well, y'know how I feel about that. I want to see less drunkenness an' disorderly behavior in Sydney Cove and Parramatta."

"I don't want to discuss that, Moira. There are many more important issues, which have to do with land rights, free trade, allocation of convict labor, price controls, economics, expansion of our colony, and how we are to handle the troublesome Indians."

"I don't understand most of those things. But you're talkin' to me 'cause you want my opinion, do you not?"

"Aye."

"Faith then, become Governor King's secretary and advisor. You're a good man, Nathaniel, an' that's the right thing t'do. 'Tis best for our community. This is where we want to live the rest of our lives. I want our children and grandchildren to live in a better place than it is today."

Nathaniel agreed with Moira and became King's secretary.

Governor King wasted no time in making it clear to the officers that he had been sent with orders directly from His Majesty to clamp down on their abuses. In one proclamation order after another, he restricted the trading in spirits to those issued licenses, outlawed the importation of goods except by government approved traders, limited the mark-up on the sale of goods to a maximum of fifteen percent on non-perishable goods and thirty percent on perishable goods, and introduced copper coins as a medium of exchange to lessen the reliance on rum as the main commodity of barter.

Nathaniel set about reasoning with Macarthur, George, and other officer farmers that their days of dominance were over. They had had over seven years of largely unrestricted ability to improve their lot. Most of them were wealthy landowners. It was time to think of a more equitable distribution of wealth for the good of the colony. Yes, they were being hurt by Governor King's initiatives, but they could still make a handsome living, and besides, they had no choice if they wanted to avoid being court-martialed.

Believing that his opportunities were being stifled, a disheartened Macarthur decided to sell out and return to England. He offered Governor King his farm and stock for four thousand pounds, including his prized herd of pure Spanish merino sheep.

Macarthur felt his price was reasonable. After all, he had originated the idea that wool was the ideal export to correct the import imbalance, because it could withstand the long voyage to England without spoilage. He had put years into crossbreeding sheep purchased from Ireland and Bengal to improve their rough woolen coats and perfected the breed with bulky, fine-wooled, Spanish merino sheep from Cape Town. His diligence had developed hardy sheep suitable for the colony's climate. Now he was offering the government the lot, his farm and six hundred crossbreeds and merino sheep, to produce an invaluable export commodity.

Nathaniel pressed hard for the governor to immediately purchase Macarthur's farm. He tactfully explained that Macarthur was capable of perfidious plotting against his administration, but King decided he had to write Portland for approval. Fearful that the opportunity could be lost in the year's time it would take to receive the home secretary's approval, Nathaniel asked the governor to, at least, sign a binding sales agreement. This too the governor decided against, not appreciating that this was a golden opportunity to rid the colony of a brilliant but divisive man, who could destroy him.

◎

The governor's lady, Anna King, found it intolerable that Sydney Cove streets were full of young, abandoned children subsisting on begging and stealing. She appealed to her husband to establish an orphanage where the most vulnerable of them, young girls, could find safety and obtain an education.

Governor King had the government purchase a large house on High Street to establish the Female Orphanage and School. When Nathaniel heard the governor mention that his wife was considering women, as well as men, to serve on the orphanage management committee, he thought of Moira.

After Arthur and Charles had gone to bed, Nathaniel told Moira about the orphanage. She was pleased until he suggested she could serve on the orphanage management committee.

"I wouldn't enjoy serving on the committee," Moira said coldly.

"The governor's wife Anna is a very nice lady. Why *wouldn't you* enjoy serving with her on a committee that helps orphan girls?" Nathaniel asked, annoyed. "It's a ideal way for you to become involved in upper-class society."

"I'm *too* busy. You are in Sydney Cove all week; you don't know whatall I do here. I have to manage the house an' servants, solve problems with the overseer, direct the plantin' in the kitchen garden, manage—"

"I *know* you do a—"

"Don't interrupt me! I have to manage the butchering, smoking an' curing, make sure the chickens are fed, to say nothin' about carin' for the children. Charles wouldn't sit still for ten minutes in front of the tutor without me there. I don't have time to travel to an' from Sydney Cove."

Nathaniel knew that Moira sat in on the boys' tutoring as much to discipline Charles as to improve her own English, reading, and writing.

"You would have to attend only one monthly committee meeting. It would give you a chance to meet the wives of the men I work with."

"I don't want to meet the wives of Governor King and John Macarthur and the likes o' them."

"Why not?"

"Because I wouldn't feel comfortable with them—that's why! And they wouldn't like me. You *know* that, Nathaniel. They think they're better than me. It doesn't matter to them how rich we are. I'm glad that you feel comfortable with them, but I *don't*."

"Why *don't* you? You are altogether more attractive than any of them. Your English is much better now. You dress beautifully. When *will* you feel comfortable with them?"

"I'm very happy here at home and with the people we entertain, and who entertain us. I know it's hard on you, love, to have to attend social events of the snooty elite without me, but they don't want emancipists there anyway, especially an Irish Catholic emancipist."

"They don't know you are Catholic. How would they know that?"

"Maybe they don't, but they know I'm Irish from my brogue. I'll never lose that."

"Arthur is old enough now to begin to understand what's going on. Do you want him to realize that his mother feels inadequate because of her past or be proud of her because she fits in?"

"That's *hateful*, Nathaniel. Don't *ever* talk to me like that again! He's only nine . . . maybe I'll feel different when he's older. I don't want t'talk about this any more." She angrily turned and walked away from him.

Two days later, when Anna King decided to wait in Nathaniel's secretary's office until the governor's meeting ended, Nathaniel found himself saying that his wife had been very pleased to hear that Mrs. King was establishing a safe place for orphan girls. She too had been concerned about the vulnerable female street urchins. Then Nathaniel suggested that Moira would enjoy serving on Mrs. King's committee.

Mrs. King too deftly sidestepped his suggestion.

"Ah, unfortunately, Nathaniel, I've already chosen all of the committee members based on their particular skills. If one does not accept, however, I'd be delighted to include your wife."

He sensed Mrs. King was uncharacteristically nervous in providing her polite but dismissive response to his offer. She knew that he was married to an emancipist—everyone knew. He wondered whether she was as fair-minded as he thought.

When she chose Mrs. Paterson, Mrs. Evans, Surgeon William Balmain, and Reverends Johnson and Marsden, all elitists, to serve with her on the orphanage management committee without any emancipist, Nathaniel knew the reason why Moira had been rejected out of hand.

◉

Governor King's early administration was everything Nathaniel had hoped it would be. The new governor enthusiastically pushed his radical reforms and refused to be intimidated by innuendo and veiled threats from the landed gentry officers as his predecessor Hunter had been. Small farmers, tradesmen, merchants, and shopkeepers all benefited from the governor's host of orders that controlled spirit imports, reduced prices of goods, and made needed public improvements. As he had anticipated, Nathaniel and other large landowners had to bear the consequences of King's adverse orders that reduced the number of convict servants and workers to two. They now were forced to hire additional help while their farm production fell. In addition, the government stores paid less for farm produce and meats. The governor also removed the right of the syndicate to purchase and distribute rum to their workers.

Although the Rum Corps gentry grumbled among themselves, they seemed lost as to what to do about it. All of that changed after June 1801 when a dispatch from Home Secretary Portland was received rejected Governor King's request to purchase Macarthur's farm and stock.

It was obvious that the home secretary remembered Macarthur from his letters critical of Hunter. Portland wrote, "I can by no means account for his being a farmer to the extent he appears to be, and I must highly disapprove of the commanding officer of the corps to which he belongs allowing him or any other officer to continue in such contradictory situations and characters." He agreed to purchase only Macarthur's English cattle and the merino sheep to improve the breed of the public stock and wrote that his farm and everything else should be sold to private buyers willing to pay his exorbitant asking price.

Knowing now that he was committed to New South Wales, Macarthur wasted no time in organizing his fellow officers to resist Governor King's initiatives that were hurting them. He and George Evans decided to press tactics that would make it obvious to the King that he could not hope to prevail against a united Rum Corps. They recruited officers of like mind to laxly carry out the governor's orders, obstruct enforcement of his new regulations, miss his meetings, and generally ostracize him as they had Hunter. Both Macarthur and Evans tried to convince Nathaniel and Lieutenant Governor Paterson to join them, without success.

Seeing that Macarthur was up to his old tricks, Nathaniel decided that the governor had to act quickly and decisively.

"Your Excellency, you must force a showdown immediately with Macarthur before he has time to persuade a majority of the officers to join him. Please do not underestimate this man."

"I am not overly concerned by this agitator; he knows I am

executing the commands of His Majesty. I have told him directly, as I have all my officers, that the home secretary has ordered me to send home any officer who opposes me to be court-martialed. When he commits some reprehensible act, I shall act without delay to arrest him and send him on the first ship back to England!"

"With all due respect, Governor, I know this man. He is smart and cunning. He will not commit the obvious reprehensible act you are waiting for. He will work behind the scenes until he has convinced all of the officers that you are a despot intent on destroying them and the colony. In the end, he will win by frustrating you to death, as he did Governor Hunter."

Appreciating Nathaniel's strategic sense and long association with Macarthur, King asked, "I expect that you may have something in mind, Nathaniel—what is it?"

"The officers are now choosing who to ally with, you or Macarthur. You need to hold a grand governor's dinner at Government House to separate friend from foe. You can do that by inviting all of the officers except Macarthur. That will make the issue clear. At this early date, I feel sure that the great majority of them will attend *your* dinner, more fearful of offending you than Macarthur."

The governor's dinner was a great success. Macarthur was incensed and embarrassed that he could convince only George and three other officers to boycott the governor's dinner by claiming an earlier commitment to attend a dinner at Macarthur's Elizabeth Farm.

Realizing he was losing the battle for control of the officers, Macarthur uncharacteristically lost control of himself. To discredit Nathaniel, he circulated the information that Moira was a former felon and rumored that she had been a prostitute. Macarthur also showed around a private letter from Elizabeth Paterson to his own wife Elizabeth that compromised Lieutenant Governor Paterson. With his honor deeply wounded, Paterson demanded that Macarthur submit to a duel. Paterson chose Nathaniel as his second, and Macarthur chose George Evans.

They met two days later at ten in the morning at Kangaroo Meadows, halfway between Sydney Cove and Parramatta. The morning mist from the Parramatta River was just burning off when they arrived in separate carriages. Surgeon John Harris awaited them. He had arrived with a driver and a four-wheeled cart containing a mattress to transport a wounded or dead man. Without any discussion or attempts to amiably resolve the matter, the duelists' seconds approached each other. Nathaniel tossed a coin that George called "Heads" in the air. The coin fell to the ground showing heads, winning Macarthur the right to shoot first.

At twelve paces, Macarthur and Paterson stood facing each other. With his pistol in his right hand hanging down at his side, the stately lieutenant governor turned his right shoulder toward Macarthur and stoically looked at him, awaiting his shot. Nathaniel hoped that Macarthur would fire decorously off to one side, but he raised his pistol and took deliberate aim.

Nathaniel held his breath anticipating the blast from his pistol, but Macarthur did not fire. The meadow hushed as the wind stilled and birds seemed to quiet, as if awaiting the report of his pistol. Just as Nathaniel thought that Macarthur must have some ploy in mind, a piercing *BANG* startled him. Paterson rose off his front leg and his arm flew up, the pistol flipping out of his hand. His back leg gave way sending him crashing hard onto the ground.

Surgeon Harris and Nathaniel rushed to aid Paterson. Macarthur and Evans walked to their carriage and drove off. The ball had passed through Paterson's shoulder and entered his chest at the armpit. Harris bound the wounds to stop the bleeding but could not tell Nathaniel whether Paterson would survive.

Governor King used the army's articles of war, which banned duels, to place Macarthur under unconfined arrest and advised him that he would be sent on the first available ship to England to be court-martialed. Macarthur had, after all, shot not only his commanding officer but also the lieutenant governor of the colony! For two weeks, Paterson was poised between life and death, then began to slowly recover.

In the dispatch to the Duke of Portland containing the charges against Macarthur, the governor enclosed a private letter that said in part:

"Experience has convinced every man in this colony that there are not resources which art, cunning, impudence, and a pair of basilisk eyes can afford that he does not put in practice to obtain any point he undertakes." He called Macarthur a "perturbator" and "a master worker of the puppets he has set in motion." The last sentence of his letter read: "I shall close the subject by observing that if Captain Macarthur returns here in any official character it should be that of governor, as one-half of the colony already belongs to him, and it will not be long before he gets the other half."

It was an ironic turn of fate that the first ship available to transport Macarthur to his uncertain future should bear the name of the previous governor, *Hunter*, who had wished to shoot Macarthur in a duel or court-martial him. The *Hunter* sailed from Sydney Cove, with Macarthur on board, on November 15, 1801.

◙

Although Captain George Evans had sided with Macarthur, he never said or did anything against Nathaniel. After Macarthur was arrested and sent off to England, George gradually rekindled his friendship with Nathaniel. He needed his neighbor's advice, especially since his farm was suffering under King's orders and regulations.

They sat together on George's veranda drinking beers after George had asked Nathaniel to stop by to advise him of new farming techniques to increase his crop production. Nathaniel had walked his fields and pointed out ways to improve water retention and distribution and told him of the latest planting and fertilizing techniques. His visit was not entirely charitable because he had a hidden agenda.

Curious to know how Macarthur's family was coping without John Macarthur, Nathaniel said, "Macarthur's crops appear to be coming up well without him."

"It's all due to his wife Elizabeth," George answered, shaking his head in wonderment. "That woman knows more about farming and animal husbandry than I do. John sends her instructions on every ship headed our way of what to do. He's got her selecting rams and ewes from his merino sheep herd to breed to improve their fleece. You know he took samples of the fleece with him to show in England? D'you think he's on to something that we should be doing?"

"I don't know, George. I raise my sheep for meat and its ready market. Wool sent all the way to England? It's too speculative for me."

"That's what I think too, Nate, I doubt anything will come of it."

"I was surprised to see Mrs. Macarthur in civil court pursuing payment of some promissory note or bill of exchange. She's an able woman. Has Macarthur been in England long? I heard he was delayed by a storm."

"He's been in London for a month or two. The *Hunter* was damaged by a typhoon and forced into a port in the East Indies. He had good luck there, though. He met the son of Sir Walter Farquhar, physician to the Prince of Wales. They traveled together to England."

Nathaniel did not respond to Macarthur's good fortune in meeting a man who could be helpful to him. They sat there uncomfortably silent for several minutes drinking their beers until George said, "I heard that Pemulwuy was killed and two settlers have put in for the bounty."

"Aye. I had the gruesome duty of identifying his head."

"Was it him?"

"Yes. I could tell by the scar down his face and the cast in one eye."

"What happened to his head?"

"The governor had it placed in spirits to preserve it and sent it off on the *Speedy* to Sir Joseph Banks, who'll probably display it in his collection at the British Museum. King wrote Banks that he regarded Pemulwuy as a terrible pest to the colony, but a man of brave and independent character. I'd have to agree with that."

"I'm glad we're done with him. There'll be fewer murders on the frontier now."

Nathaniel decided it was time to unload on George what he had come to say. "I have something difficult to discuss with you, George..."

"What is it, Nathaniel, you can discuss anything with me, mate."

"I know that you and several other officers have a smuggler off the coast waiting to sneak in and unload in Broken Bay or Botany Bay."

"*That's not true!* I don't know anyt—"

"I'm *not* lookin' for confirmation, George! I thought you'd deny it, just listen to what I have to say. I've decided not to tell Governor King what I know, because it would ruin you financially, and you'd be sent to England to be court-martialed. I wouldn't want to be a party to that and the suffering it would cause Martha and your children. However, I want you to promise me that you will never again place me in this position. Agreed?"

"Yes. . . . thank you, Nathaniel."

◉

Late one evening, Nathaniel and Moira sat quietly reading in their drawing room. Moira put down her book and sighed loudly.

"Disconcerting part of your book?" Nathaniel asked lightly without looking up from his reading.

"I have somethin' that's been botherin' me about the boys' religious instruction."

"Can it wait a few minutes until I finish this chapter?"

"Yes." She returned to her book.

Twenty minutes later, Nathaniel closed his book and asked, "What's on your mind, love?"

"You know, I've agreed the boys can be raised Anglican 'cause there's no Catholic churches here. The important thing is that they read the Bible an' receive religious instruction. What I don't like is them bein' instructed by Reverend Marsden—the *floggin'* parson. He's not a good example of Christian love for our boys. How can a man o' God flog young Irish boys in hope of finding hidden weapons? How can he do that when they haven't done anything wrong, just because he thinks they know somethin'?"

"These floggings have been ordered by the judge advocate and Reverend Marsden in the course of an inquiry into a suspected Irish uprising. The men flogged were withholding information."

"But how can a man o' God oversee floggings? 'Tisn't right!"

"He's doing it as a Parramatta magistrate, not as an Anglican parson. Although, I'll admit that it seems odd . . . but these aren't children he's flogging, Moira. They're seditious Irishmen who have brought their rebellion here. One out of four convicts is Irish now; there are too many of them not to be concerned. Marsden has found hidden weapons by flogging some of them to within an inch of their lives."

"Some have died on the triangle."

"Aye, maybe one or two. But the Irish are planning a rebellion, there's no doubt of that now. You're gettin' all this from O'Donovan, aren't you?"

"Shure, an' I won't deny it. But I have ears and hear what others say too. Mr. O'Donovan is an educated man—so you said yerself. He's a United Irishman an' was transported here as a *political* prisoner. He didn't do anything more'n argue for an independent Ireland that doesn't want t' be part of the United Kingdom."

"I *won't* have him causing discord in my own house. Talking to him won't do any good; I'm going to replace him!"

"*Don't* treat me like a child! Nathaniel, that you can control by replacing somebody. Even if you replace the best overseer we've ever had, I'll still know what's going on. I know the difference between right and wrong, and it isn't right that an Anglican parson should be crucifying Catholic Irishmen. I think you should be outraged an' say somethin' to the governor to make him stop. 'Tis for his own good and the good of the colony."

"Ach, Moira, I don't want to control you—even if I was daft enough to think I could—or change your thoughts. I understand and respect your Irish Catholic sentiments. Don't forget that I'm a Scot, and we've had our own problems with the English. . . . really, Moira, this is only *one* of the many problems the governor faces. I *can't* suggest that he let up on the Irish convicts when they're hiding weapons and planning a revolt. You don't know . . . the weight of office is making him a very sick man."

"He's *very* sick? You've talked about his poor health, but haven't said he's seriously ill."

"He's concerned that if there's an Irish revolt his officers may not do their duty—just to embarrass him. The Rum Corps's unremitting criticism and insolence is making him seriously sick. Most of the officers continue to disobey his orders, smuggle in spirits, and write letters home to influential people supporting Macarthur and criticizing him. He's suffering from gout and constant stomach pains and often conducts business from his bed now. He's lost his sense of humor and has become overweight, short-tempered, and sometimes seems on the verge of a nervous breakdown."

Obviously concerned, Moira said, "I didn't know it was *that* bad. Macarthur's still to be court-martialed, is he not?"

"I don't know," Nathaniel said, shaking his head. "Governor King's dispatch of detailed charges against Macarthur was stolen or lost. Macarthur has been very fortunate in meeting the right people to support him. He's avoided court-martial so far and is even making headway in promoting his wool-exporting scheme because the war with France has interrupted the flow of wool from Spain."

"What's goin' to happen? Could he return without being punished?"

"The governor sent another dispatch of the charges; however, since Paterson has fully recovered and so much time has passed, I fear the charges may be dropped. Unfortunately, I could not stop King from sending an imprudent letter to the home secretary in which he asked for a leave of absence to return to London to defend himself. He threatened that if Macarthur were permitted to return that his recall, or permission to return, would be absolutely necessary, to prevent him from taking steps against Macarthur that would not be good for the colony."

Over the following months, rumors intensified that an Irish convict revolt was imminent. Floggings could not identify the top leaders of the "Croppies" (from the Irish rebel anthem "The Croppy Boys"), because they were organized into cells to protect their leaders' identities.

As Nathaniel and his family were finishing Sunday dinner on March 4, 1804, the clatter of hooves was heard coming fast up the track to their house. Approaching the house, the rider called out loudly "*Captain Armstrong!*"

Nathaniel rushed from the table and met an army corporal on the veranda.

"The Croppies 'ave risen up, sir! They're comin' this way! They burnt the gov'ment farm buildings at Castle Hill, an' they're comin' to attack Parramatta." Winded, he coughed loudly and bent over with his hands on his knees as he continued to cough.

Nathaniel placed a hand on his back. "Get your breath, Corporal. . . . Did you see them yourself?"

Standing erect, the soldier placed his hands on his hips. "No sir, but Private Cooper an' another feller rode down from Castle Hill; they seen 'em—*cough*. Killed Duggan the gov'ment flogger, they did. Said there's lots of 'em, sir. Some got muskets too."

"What were your orders?"

"To tell Captain Evans, but he weren't home, so I come 'ere."

"Who's in charge of the Parramatta garrison?"

"Only Lieutenant Lardner. He sent me, sir."

"Has anyone been sent to Sydney Cove to warn the governor?"

"I think so, but I'm not sure, sir."

"Can you do that?" Nathaniel asked, then changed his attitude; he should take charge. "I want you to ride to Government House and warn the governor. Tell him that I'm taking command of the Parramatta garrison if Captain Evans cannot be found. We'll establish a defensive line north of Parramatta. A Sydney Cove detachment should make a forced night march to be here by dawn. If the governor is indisposed for some reason, tell Major George Johnston at the barracks. Can you remember all that?—wait—I'll write it down. Sit down on the steps, Corporal, and rest."

Attracted by the commotion, everyone on the farm was gathering around. Nathaniel searched for O'Donovan among his workers. "Where's O'Donovan," he demanded.

"Ain't seen 'im all day, sir," came the answer.

"Denise, get a glass of water for the corporal. Michael, saddle up a fresh horse for him."

"Sir . . ." The corporal got Nathaniel's attention. "If yer don't mind, sir, I'd like to ride me own horse. He's fresh enough."

"Very well. Give his horse some water. You saddle a horse for yourself, Jacob, and go with him." Nathaniel went into the house to write his letters.

Moira and the boys stood by Nathaniel as he wrote at his desk. Nathaniel sensed that Arthur, twelve, was frightened. He's old enough to understand the gravity of the situation, Nathaniel thought. Finished writing, Nathaniel put the letters into envelopes and addressed one to Governor King and the other to Major Johnston. Moira helped him put on his coat. He put the leather strap holding his sword over his head, placed his pistol into its holster, and grabbed his hat.

Arthur ran up to him and threw his arms around his waist. "Ah, Dad, I don't want you to go," he whispered.

Patting him on the head, Nathaniel said, "I'll be fine, old chap, there's nothing to worry about. Now you mind your mother, and I'll see you tomorrow, Monday, when I'm usually in Sydney Cove. Won't that be nice?"

"Yes, Father."

Charles, ten, stood holding Moira's hand. It struck Nathaniel that he was unusually composed, in stark contrast to Arthur. Nathaniel walked over to him and dropped down onto one knee; he and Charles embraced.

Pulling his head back from the embrace, Charles looked directly into his father's eyes and said with unexpected seriousness:

"I'll protect Mum, Dad."

Nathaniel was dumbstruck; he almost laughed but quickly said, "*Good!* . . . both you and Arthur take good care of your mother. She loves you both very much, as I do."

Sharing the delight of Charles's comment in their eyes, Moira and Nathaniel embraced, kissed, and said goodbye. They walked out together. Nathaniel gave the envelopes to the corporal.

"These letters must get to Sydney Cove quickly, men. I'm counting on both of you to convey the urgency of the situation to the governor and the major. Don't be shy."

The corporal saluted. "Don't worry, sir." He rode off with Jacob.

With Moira standing beside him, Nathaniel called over the assistant overseer. "Assist Moira to prepare a carriage. I intend to locate the rebels tonight and keep them from Parramatta and this area. You shouldn't be in any danger. I'll send a rider to alert you, if I have any concern. Just in case though, be ready to escape down Parramatta Road. God forbid, if you see the town aflame or hear any sounds of battle, don't wait for the messenger, just leave. I don't expect that to happen. If I did, I'd send you all to Sydney Cove now."

Nathaniel rode toward Parramatta across his own land and jumped the fence separating his property from Elizabeth Farm. He was concerned about Mrs. Macarthur and her children, alone without her husband.

He was pleased to find Reverend Marsden and his wife visiting Mrs. Macarthur. Although Nathaniel explained that he intended to stop any advance by the Irish rebels north of Parramatta, Reverend Marsden insisted that they escape immediately by boat down the Parramatta River to Sydney Cove. Leaving the matter in their hands, Nathaniel rode on to Parramatta.

Lieutenant Lardner had the garrison assembled and prepared for action when Nathaniel arrived. Taking over command, Nathaniel lead the garrison out of Parramatta and established a defensive line along a rise on either side of the north road. He sent out mounted scouts to find the Croppies. George Evans showed up at eleven o'clock at night and took command from Nathaniel. He told him he had returned home late from business in Sydney Cove. Nathaniel wondered whether George was telling him the truth; he no longer trusted him.

The morning sun, bright in a cloudless sky, had cleared the eastern horizon when Major Johnston atop his horse led a sweaty detachment of foot soldiers up the north road from Parramatta. While the Sydney Cove troops fell out to rest and eat their biscuits for breakfast, Nathaniel and George met with Johnston and three other officers who had accompanied him.

"I sent out four mounted scouts last night," Nathaniel said. "They followed a trail of burning buildings from Castle Hill south toward Parramatta and then northwest on the road to Green Hills. There's some three hundred Croppies, and others are joining them along the way. They're looting and burning farms and stealin' weapons and spirits. Most are armed with pitchforks, axes, and scythes, but a few have muskets and pistols."

Johnston decided to divide the soldiers into three commands. Captain Evans would remain in position to defend Parramatta, another captain would proceed north to secure Castle Hill, and the third under Johnston would take the road to Green Hills settlement on the Hawkesbury River. Because Nathaniel was the governor's secretary and not directly under the command of Johnston, he was left without orders. He decided to accompany Johnston's unit. As they prepared to start off, Nathaniel met Father Sean Dixon, a Catholic priest. He had asked to accompany Johnston in the hope of avoiding bloodshed by negotiating a truce with the Irish rebels.

Eight miles from the Hawkesbury River, Johnston's scouts found the rebels resting on a low hill. Many of them were drunk and exhausted from carrying-on without sleep. Their number had grown to nearly four hundred. They jeered the small number of "lobsterbacks," a few over fifty counting the officers, who marched in two columns to the bottom of the hill. Without discussion, Major Johnston and his adjutant rode forward.

Father Dixon was standing next to Nathaniel, who was seated on his horse. The priest asked, "What should I do, Captain?"

"I can't tell you what to do, Father Dixon," Nathaniel answered, "though if you want to parley, now's the time to do it."

The priest hurried forward and heard Johnston bellow to the rebels on the hill:

"WHO IS IN CHARGE? I WISH TO SPEAK TO HIM!"

Through the convicts' taunts, jeers, and insults hurled down the hill, Johnston heard "Ye come on up here if ye want t'talk!"

Johnston noticed the priest standing beside him and taunted the rebels back:

"I'm within pistol shot now if you want to kill me. Your captains must be of little spirit not to come forward to speak to me and your priest!"

Trusting that Johnston intended to negotiate with them, the rebel leader Phillip Cunningham and his second-in-command, walked down the hill with swords in their hands. As Cunningham walked up, he nodded toward the priest to acknowledge him.

Before the priest could utter a word, Johnston said, "You are insurrectionists and escaped convicts, I advise you to surrender. I will mention you in favorable terms to the governor if you do so immediately."

Cunningham laughed. "We ha' ten times as many men as you. *Surrender?* I would ha' death or liberty."

Withdrawing his pistol, Johnston pointed it at Cunningham's head. "Then you shall have *death*, you scoundrel, if you do not walk immediately toward my men. *You choose!*"

Johnston's adjutant followed suit and trained his pistol on the other rebel.

The priest protested: *"This is not negotiating!"*

The officers maneuvered their horses behind the two rebel leaders, who, still holding their swords, were marched back to Johnston's lines.

Father Dixon ran up the hill yelling:

"LAY DOWN YER WEAPONS, M'LADS, AND SURRENDER!"

When Johnston passed by the captain in command of the soldiers, he ordered, "Fire a volley into the Croppy rabble and advance in good order on them, Captain."

Nathaniel was on the opposite side of the line and did not hear Johnston's order, but he heard the captain's order and before he could think, a well-directed volley ripped into the disorganized rebel mob, dropping a number of them where they stood. It was followed by a desultory return of fire from the hill.

With fixed bayonets, the soldiers moved forward and halfway up the hill fired a second volley into the rebels who were by now running in all directions. Nathaniel suddenly thought of Father Dixon. He could be killed by mistake. Nathaniel spurred his horse and rode behind the soldiers and up the hill in the direction where he had last seen the priest. He found him off to one side sitting on the ground, crying.

A victory yell came from the soldiers as they charged to the top of the hill. Twelve rebels lay dead and six were wounded. The soldiers corralled twenty-six prisoners without sustaining any deaths or injuries themselves.

Nathaniel was dejected as he sat on his horse next to the distraught priest. The carnage was unnecessary. He could hear the screaming and crying of the badly wounded. It did not have to be a massacre. Johnston meant to teach the rebellious Irish a lesson, and he did.

Riding to the top of the hill, Nathaniel saw the body of O'Donovan, his overseer. One side of his forehead was blown away. Looking down at what had been a good and fair man, Nathaniel thought to himself, what am I going to tell Moira about all of this?

Under the state of martial law that had been declared by Governor King and was being carried out by Major Johnston, the rebel leader Philip Cunningham was taken to Parramatta and hung by the neck from the gable window of the government store. Eight other rebels were tried and found guilty of murder and revolt against the Crown. They were hung, three in Parramatta, three Castle Hill, and two in Sydney Cove. Their bodies, in chains, were taken down from the gallows and placed in rough iron cages and then hoisted up to hang from gibbets. There in the three towns, their bodies rotted for months as food for birds and warnings to all those with thoughts of further rebellion.

Moira was sickened by the sight and smell of these dead Irish martyrs in their cages and pleaded with Nathaniel to ask Governor King to order their burial. After two months, Nathaniel asked the governor, but it was not until the entreaties of an aristocratic couple, recently arrived from India, that the governor conceded that the point had been made and ordered the burial of the remains of the eight convicts.

The battle on the unnamed hill near Castle Hill was reminiscent of the famous Vinegar Hill battle in Ireland in 1798, where the rebellious United Irishmen were decisively defeated by a large English force. The Irish in the colony came to refer to their own defeat as taking place on Vinegar Hill in New South Wales.

Several months after the Irish rebellion, Governor King received a thick dispatch from the Home Office. In it was a letter from the Duke of Portland in reply to King's earlier letter requesting a leave of absence to defend himself in London and asking to be recalled if Macarthur was permitted to return. The home secretary treated his letter as though it was a resignation. He granted the governor's request to be recalled and wrote that he was disappointed "the spirit of the party... has reached such an alarming height" and about "the unfortunate differences which have so long subsisted between you and the military officers of the colony." He asked King to remain in office until his replacement could be selected and sail to New South Wales to relieve him.

King was a sick man who was tired of fighting his officers. He accepted his recall in good grace.

Nathaniel was disillusioned. Although he was well off from farming, many of the other officers had prospered over the years by smuggling, distilling spirits illegally, and using surrogates to run grog shops and brothels. He and the governor knew who the perpetrators were, but, because most of the officers were united in their misdeeds, there was little that could be done against any one individual. Along with the governor, Nathaniel had been ostracized by his fellow officers. He had not received an advancement in rank to major, although strongly recommended by King to the army commander in chief.

Weary of traveling between Parramatta and Sydney Cove every weekend to be with his family, Nathaniel had been thinking of not renewing his army commission for years. He wanted to live an easier and more comfortable life on his farm in Parramatta. Moira encouraged him to leave the corrupt Rum Corps. At the age of forty, he resigned his military commission and his position as secretary to Governor King. Other than the governor, Nathaniel had only one other close friend, honest trader Robert Campbell, a fellow Scot.

Born in Scotland, Campbell had gone to Calcutta as a young man to join his elder brother in Campbell, Clark and Company, traders and merchants. He came to Sydney Cove in June 1798 to open a branch of their firm. By 1804 he owned the largest warehouse in Sydney Cove and was the principal trader between the colonial government and India. Wanting to expand his trading, but unable to engage in free trade because of the East India Company strictures, he developed side businesses in ship building, whaling, and sealing.

Nathaniel had met Campbell through his dealings with the governor, who was encouraging Campbell to send a shipment of colonial goods to England to fight the outdated monopoly of the East India Company. Nathaniel had convinced the governor that the smuggling of goods could be eliminated by free trade once the stranglehold of the East India Company was removed. Governor King had received an assurance from Sir Joseph Banks that he would assist Campbell in London. Campbell decided to try. In support of Campbell's effort, Nathaniel invested in the risky venture.

In January 1805 Campbell and his family sailed for England in his *Lady Barlow* carrying a cargo of seal skins and oil in direct violation of the East India Company's charter monopoly.

◎

"I am greatly indebted to you, Nathaniel, for your valiant defense of my family during the Irish rebellion," John Macarthur said. "Although time was short, and I know you must have had many other concerns that night; you thought first of my defenseless wife and children. You advised them of the danger and assisted Reverend Marsden in their safe passage to Sydney Cove."

"You are too kind, John, really," Nathaniel said, overwhelmed by his earnestness. "I appreciated your gracious letter; it was quite enough. We are neighbors. I'm sure you would have done the same for my family."

Macarthur ignored Nathaniel's protestation that his letter sent from England nine months earlier was enough to show his appreciation. He had come to Nathaniel's house unexpectedly three days after arriving back to express his gratitude in person.

Macarthur continued. "Of course, you didn't know then, that the rebel's plan was to set fire to my house, taking advantage of my wife's lonely situation, expecting that the garrison would rush to her defense and thereby make it easier for them to capture the armory. It was only your defense organized on the north road that disrupted their plans. So I am grateful to you on two counts."

Macarthur had returned to Sydney Cove on June 9, 1805, triumphantly in his own ship *Argo*, which flaunted a large golden ram figurehead. The War Office had decided it could not fairly court-martial him because of the passage of time and the lack of witnesses to testify. He was returned as a civilian; the expectation being that without his power over the military, he would no longer be a thorn in the side of governors.

The golden ram figurehead on his ship assertively expressed his triumph. He carried orders from the Earl of Camden to Governor King directing him to assist his former adversary in his "national project" to produce fine wool for export to Britain. Lord Camden had replaced the Duke of Portland in the Home Office, which had been renamed the Colonial Office. Governor King was ordered to grant Macarthur five thousand acres of prime crown grazing land, known as the "Cowpastures," and to provide the number of convicts he required to make the national project a success. An additional five thousand acres would be granted to Macarthur if his national project succeeded.

"We are both civilian farmers and graziers now," Macarthur said with a wry grin. "The future is merino wool, Nathaniel. I'd like to make a gift of a merino ram and two ewes to you, so you can begin breeding your own merino herd."

"Oh, I couldn't accept, John, really, I'd feel obliged . . . I mean your gift would be too much." Nathaniel sensed Macarthur was offended, so he tried to ameliorate the situation. "I greatly appreciate your coming here; I'm sorry that I didn't welcome you back first."

"Well, permit me to leave my offer open then. Actually, I'm *not* anxious to create competition for myself, but I'd do it for you, in light of what you did for me, *and* Elizabeth. I shan't forget it, Nathaniel, ever.

"If you won't take my merinos, what are your plans? Do you intend to simply continue farming and grazing sheep for meat?"

"I'm involved in whaling and sealing with Robert Campbell.

You may have heard that he's taken a shipment to England to contest the monopoly of the East India Company."

"Yes, good on him. I hope he's successful. He's supported by Governor King and Sir Joseph Banks, I understand."

"That's right," Nathaniel confirmed.

"You may not believe it, but I'm actually saddened that King is leaving, because he is being replaced by the notoriously imperious Captain Bligh, of the *Bounty*. Banks recruited the man, you know, for *twice* King's salary. A ridiculous amount of two thousand pounds! Damned nonsense . . . why do they continue to send us naval governors to reign regally over our army corps?"

Nathaniel did not respond. He looked at Macarthur with his impenetrable half-smile. Macarthur saw impartiality written on Nathaniel's face, a trait he greatly disliked in the man.

"Well, I must be going, Nathaniel. Please say goodbye for me to your wife and thank her for the tea and biscuits. I'm very pleased to have you as my neighbor—remember, the merinos are yours for the asking."

Nathaniel walked him out thanking him for his kind words and offer of the merinos. When he returned to the drawing room, Moira was seated in a chair waiting for him.

"He said to say goodbye to you and thanked you for the tea and biscuits."

"I was in the sitting room and heard most of it," Moira said. "Do you believe the audacity of him? after all he did! To come barging in here, unannounced, scheming to win you over."

"He loves his family, Moira. I think it was genuine, not scheming."

"He offered you three merinos as a *gift*?"

"Aye. Now *that* may have been scheming."

"He's put on a bit of weight . . . Did you sense he's changed his attitude much after three and a half years away?"

"No."

Chapter 5

Mutiny Against Bligh (of the Bounty)

Captain Bligh stood on the quarterdeck of the HMS *Porpoise*, a telescope to his eye as he surveyed his new dominion. It was August 6, 1806, and he had just cleared the heads into Port Jackson. Standing apart from others anxious to see their new home, he began to prepare himself for the latest challenge in his tempestuous life. He went over in his mind the reasons Sir Joseph Banks had given for the failure of the previous two naval governors.

Governor Hunter had been recalled for his lack of backbone. He had allowed himself to be cajoled and intimidated by the Rum Corps officers and did not fulfill his royal instructions. Initially, Governor King had carried out his instructions admirably, satisfying both Banks and his main patron Phillip. However, he proved too sickly to sustain the officers' persistent opposition. Exhausted and defeated, King asked to be recalled.

The governor-to-be concluded in his mind: So the Rum Corps has regained control of rum as the main medium of exchange and reestablished its monopoly over trade as well. They ruthlessly exploit others in the colony, especially the small farmer. It's my job to put the rum dealers and monopolists in their place. My instructions are clear: eliminate the rum trade, curtail the illegal local distillation of spirits, institute anti-profiteering measures, assist the struggling small farmer, and reduce the cost to the Treasury . . . and *by God* I'll fulfill my orders!

And I will not disappoint my good patron Sir Joseph. He chose me because I have the self-confidence, and yes, *arrogance* to face any situation and any man without fear. Hadn't I sailed as a master with Captain James Cook? Hadn't I faced the guns of the *Bounty* mutineers with defiance and sailed in an open, overloaded longboat nearly four thousand miles to safety with the loss of only one man killed by natives? (An amazing feat of navigation, perseverance, and seamanship that never fails to uplift me when I reflect on it.) Hadn't I shown my command abilities and courage in battle at Camperdown in 1797 and again in 1801 at Copenhagan? Indeed! Lord Nelson himself publicly praised my command of the HMS *Glatton.* Yes, I have a tough job to do, but *by God* I'm up to it!—pity the poor sod who tries to stand in my way!

Bligh was fifty-one, short and paunchy, with black hair and blue eyes. Ambitious and always thinking of his image and ways to achieve results that would advance him in rank and prestige, he used his hot temper, impatience, and bullying manner to demand excellence and impose his will. He possessed an unusual ability: by using his acerbic wit, sharp tongue, and repertoire of invectives, he was able to browbeat any man of equal or lesser rank until he felt like an overwhelmed, speechless child. Although Bligh would walk away from such confrontations immensely pleased with himself, his victim would hate him.

Because his dear wife was terrified of sea travel, he had reluctantly left her at home. He was happy that he had been able to convince his eldest daughter and her naval lieutenant husband to accompany him.

Bligh's arrival date had not preceded him, so he landed quietly. Immediately, however, he set about organizing his own ceremonial landing involving three days of pomp and pageantry to welcome himself and to send off King. There was the question of King's health, whether he was well enough to sustain the demands of the festivities and the voyage back to England, but Bligh pressed ahead regardless.

After two days of ceremonies, Nathaniel stood in a long line of people waiting to have a final word with Philip Gidley King before his departure. He was shocked to see how exhausted the ex-governor looked. With the military band playing and cannons sounding, the King family was rowed out to the HMS *Buffalo*, which had been prepared for their voyage home. Once King was abroad the *Buffalo*, the guns of the *Porpoise* thundered a salute as Bligh left the *Porpoise* and was rowed toward King. The former governor welcomed Governor Bligh aboard the *Buffalo* and there was a brief ceremony, then the guns of the *Buffalo* thundered a salute as Bligh left to be welcomed ashore. The New South Wales Corps stood at attention on Government Wharf and lined the road to Government House. A welcoming committee awaited the new governor at Government House to tender its congratulations. Major George Johnston represented the officers, Richard Atkins the civil administrators, and John Macarthur the free settlers.

The ceremonies was marred when word circulated that Philip Gidley King had collapsed on the *Buffalo*. The King family's voyage home was canceled, and they were moved from the ship to the Government House in Parramatta. King's recovery would be slow, and the voyage to England delayed for six months.

The new governor's first order of business was to deal with the recent devastating Hawkesbury River flood. He visited the small farmers along the river and promised his support as well as emergency relief supplies.

Within a week, Bligh ordered that every tenth bushel of grain ground by the government be donated to the distressed Hawkesbury farmers. Building materials and convicts were provided to aid in the reconstruction. Maximum hourly wages were set at a reasonable amount that small farmers could afford, to eliminate the ability of large landowners to pay more; several who did so were arrested and heavily fined.

During this time, he received a congratulatory declaration signed by 135 Sydney Cove and 234 Hawkesbury "free inhabitants."

Part of the declaration complained that John Macarthur had acted entirely on his own in purporting to represent the free settlers:

> We beg to observe that had we deputed anyone, John Macarthur would not have been chosen by us. We consider him an unfit person to step forward on such an occasion, as we may chiefly attribute the rise in the price of mutton to his withholding the large flock of wethers he now has to make such a price as he may chose to demand.

Feeling that Bligh cared about them, the Hawkesbury free inhabitants appealed to the governor to fight the monopolistic practices of the Rum Corps that were keeping them poor while making the officers richer. They set forth what could be called their Bill of Rights asking for free trade, right to buy and sell commodities on an open market, an end to extortion, trial by a jury of free inhabitants (instead of a military jury), and all debts to be paid in a stable currency.

◎

Nathaniel had been invited to lunch with the Kings at Parramatta's Government House, after church on Sunday. When he arrived, he was pleased to meet Governor Bligh, who had arrived uninvited the previous morning to spend the weekend with the Kings.

It was Nathaniel's first opportunity to become acquainted with the new governor. The lunch was a pleasant exchange of information. Bligh spoke mostly about the latest news from England, the war with France, and his abhorrence for all things French, especially Napoleon. In response to Bligh's questions, King and Nathaniel educated him about the short history of New South Wales.

Bligh seemed to grow impatient with the conversation and asked whether anyone would like to join him for a walk in the garden. Mrs. King excused herself. Nathaniel and King said they would join him in a few minutes after they finished their drinks.

Bligh went out into the garden by himself. At the same time, John Macarthur arrived unannounced seeking to talk to Governor Bligh. Having seen the governor entering the garden, the doorman directed Macarthur there.

Pointing at the window, King said, "Upon my soul, isn't that John Macarthur walking with Governor Bligh? Where in heaven's name did he come from?"

Nathaniel nodded his head, watching the two men converse.

"This should be interesting," King said with a twinkle in his eye. "The meeting of opposites."

"How so, Governor?"

"Macarthur is cool and devious while Bligh is hot and direct."

"Though equally condescending, wouldn't you agree?"

"Yes, more the possibility of friction between them, I'd say. Which one will out condescend the other? one might ask."

"Governor Bligh will find Macarthur insufferable first, I'll wager."

While King and Nathaniel watched, the two men's exchange became more animated. There was an obvious clash of personalities going on in the garden.

"My, my, look at Bligh gesturing about wildly," King commented. "If anyone can stand up to Macarthur, it's Bligh. We should join them before there's a problem, don't you think?"

"Aye, before they come to blows."

As King and Nathaniel approached the two men, they heard Governor Bligh angrily say, *"What have I to do with your sheep, sir? What have I to do with your cattle? Are you to have such flocks of sheep and such herds of cattle as no man ever heard of before? No, sir!"*

Bligh and Macarthur were too hotly engaged to acknowledge King and Nathaniel.

Holding his temper in check, Macarthur said, "I've been given the land on the recommendation of the Privy Council, sir." Gesturing toward King, he added, "Governor King can attest that the secretary of state for the colonies, Lord Camden, provided instructions directing the government to assist me in our national wool project to develop a stable export product." (Camden had been replaced by Viscount Castlereagh over a year earlier.)

"*Damn* the Privy Council," replied Bligh, "*and damn the secretary of state too!* What do I care for him; he commands in England, and I command here!"

Nathaniel and King were shocked by such impolitic statements. A gentleman, especially a governor, should never say such things.

Bligh was not done yet. "You have made a number of *false representations* respecting your wool, by which you have obtained this land. I have *heard* your concerns, sir. You have got five thousand acres of land in the finest situation in this country. *But by God, you shan't keep it!*"

Flushed with anger, Macarthur stared at him. His jaw was set and his determined chin stuck out. Slowly his narrowed brown-eyed stare softened, and he forced a smile.

"I've interrupted your pleasant walk, Your Excellency, for which I sincerely apologize." Affecting an insouciant countenance, he said, "It's a beautiful day, and my farm is only minutes away, Governor. Please accept my invitation to visit Elizabeth Farm later today, or before you return to Sydney Cove, to inspect my sheep for yourself."

"I must return directly to Sydney Cove today, perhaps some other time. I give you good day now, sir."

Macarthur made a slight bow to the governor and said a cordial goodbye to King and Nathaniel. He had barely left the garden, with the door closing behind him, when Bligh's restrained temper exploded.

"*Damn* his impudence! Didn't mean to disturb me! *My God*, King, who let that dreadful scoundrel in here uninvited? You should have told the bastard that he had no right to interrupt us— *you didn't say a blasted word!*—little wonder these Rum Corps rascals have been able to—"

He was interrupted by King bursting into tears. Already disturbed by Bligh's profanity and immoderation, King's tender emotional state could not withstand Bligh's violent and insulting accusations.

◎

"**I didn't throw** up my breakfast, like Artie did!" Charles said impishly, trying to draw a response from his older brother. Charles was in the hospital recuperating from a swollen foot caused by an insect bite. Nathaniel, Moira, and Arthur were visiting him.

"The boat was too small," retorted fourteen-year-old Arthur. "I don't like the ocean."

"*I do*," twelve-year-old Charles said too quickly and enthusiastically.

They were referring to a recent, and their only, fishing trip through the heads and into the Tasman Sea. They had accompanied Nathaniel and Robert Campbell and his son in Campbell's ketch.

Campbell had returned to Sydney Cove a month earlier. As expected, the East India Company had demanded the seizure of *Lady Barlow's* cargo when it entered the Port of London for violating the company's importation monopoly. True to his word, Sir Joseph Banks had testified convincingly at the hearing in support of Campbell and Governor King. The cargo of the *Lady Barlow* was returned to Campbell. Parliament was expected to act soon to overturn the East India Company's trade monopoly and allow free trade between New South Wales and Britain.

Trying to reinforce the point that he was more adventuresome than his brother, Charles said, "I want to be a sea captain like Mr. Campbell some day—not a farmer like you, Artie."

Nathaniel did not like Charles's antagonistic attitude. "Just because your brother enjoys plants and farming doesn't mean you have to dislike it, Charles. You don't know anything about the sea. It's a hard and dangerous life, son, and you're always away from home. You wouldn't like that, would you?"

Not knowing how to answer his father's loaded question, Charles looked disappointed.

"Why would you want to be a captain of a ship, dear?" Moira asked, trying to be supportive.

"I like ships and the water and sea birds—everything! You can go places and see things. It'd be fun and different every day."

"There's storms and you're wet and miserable most of the time," Nathaniel said. "That's not so much fun, believe me."

Charles looked exasperated. "I don't care. There's sunny days too."

Nathaniel laughed out loud. "Aye, there's sunny days too."

Following their visit with Charles, as they were walking down the hall, a voice called out "*Cap'n Armstrong!*"

Sticking his head into the hospital room from where the call came, Nathaniel saw Bennelong sitting up in a bed.

"Bennelong! It's been a long time since I've seen you. Why are you in the hospital?"

"I bin sick from spear in leg."

Moira and Arthur joined Nathaniel in the doorway. "You've heard me speak of Bennelong," Nathaniel said to Moira and Arthur. "This is my wife and boy, Bennelong."

Bennelong smiled at them showing the few teeth remaining in his mouth. The split in his upper lip from the fight with Colebee had healed grotesquely. He was older and grislier than Nathaniel could have imagined.

Nathaniel said to Arthur, "Bennelong met the king and queen in England when he went to London with the first governor."

Open-mouthed, Arthur rudely stared at Bennelong. He did not acknowledge what his father had just said.

Remaining in the doorway, Nathaniel asked, "Is your wound healing well, Bennelong?"

"Good. I leave 'ere soon, doctor say."

"Well, I'm happy to hear that," Nathaniel said, about to go.

He was surprised when Moira asked, "Where do you live, Bennelong?"

"North side Parramatta River, missus. I bin long time *king* of blackfellas, one hundred people—men, women, children—many clan all together."

"*How* do you live?" she asked in a concerned tone.

"Old way, missus, not whitefella way no more. People fish, hunt some, an' Mr. Holt an' Mr. Squire let us pick fruit in orchard. Hard life." Then he added with a mischievous look "Sometime go to town" recalling how Nathaniel had banished him from Sydney Cove and Parramatta after he had threatened him and Governor Hunter years ago.

"Well, very nice to see you again, Bennelong," Nathaniel said, finishing their visit. "I hope you are up and about soon. Goodbye."

"Goodbye, Cap'n Armstrong, missus, an' Armstrong boy."

As they walked away, Moira said, "That poor man."

"That old man is *ugly*, Father. How old is he?"

"He's around my age, Arthur."

"Oh, he *can't* be! How old are you, Dad?"

"I'm forty-two."

"He looks *a lot* older than you," Arthur said with conviction.

"That's what happens when you drink too much, Arthur—remember that."

◉

"His Excellency, Governor Bligh, regrets that he must inform you that you are one of several holders of leases mistakenly issued by the previous governor on land retained by the Crown on the original 'Official Plan for Sydney Cove,' " the first line of the letter from Surveyor General Grimes read. Apprehensively, Nathaniel read on: "As a consequence of this most unfortunate lease allocation, Block 66, held by one Nathaniel Armstrong, occupying land within an area designated on the Official Plan as the 'The Domain of Government House,' is declared invalid and is hereby canceled and rescinded effective three months from the date of this letter shown above."

"Well, I'll be *damned*," Nathaniel said aloud, although he was alone in the sitting room of his Parramatta house. Indignant, he continued to read:

"Leaseholder Armstrong is hereby directed to pull down the illegal small structure on Block 66 within three months from the date of this letter, thereby returning the land to the Crown in its original, unencumbered condition.

"Subject to the fulfillment of the above conditions, leaseholder Armstrong may visit the Surveyor General Office on Bridge Street to select a similar-sized replacement block from the available unoccupied blocks shown on the '1807 Plan of the Town of Sydney.'

"The government of His Excellency Bligh regrets the mistaken lease issuance and any inconvenience this order may cause leaseholder Armstrong and shall attempt to facilitate this matter to his utmost satisfaction."

"*Utmost satisfaction!*"—by pulling down my own house? Nathaniel grumbled to himself. He was outraged and thought to discuss it immediately with Moira but decided instead to control his emotions to better consider an appropriate next step.

Having heard his anxious voice, Moira knocked on his partially opened door and asked, "Is there a problem, Nathaniel?"

"No, dear, just gettin' old and talkin' to myself."

He mulled it over for a day and came up with a reasonable strategy. It would serve no purpose to visit the Surveyor General Office because he knew that all similar-sized, unoccupied blocks were undesirable pieces of land either in The Rocks or on the outskirts of town. His lot was immediately behind Government House in a prime location. Bligh would appreciate its value and should be willing to exchange it for an unsightly and boggy area of tidal crown land where Tank Stream emptied into Sydney Cove. The land there was used infrequently to repair small government boats. He would build a seawall and fill the land for a warehouse that he could use in an import-export business, now that the East India Company's monopoly would soon be overturned. He arranged a meeting with Governor Bligh.

Nathaniel's proposal was immediately rejected by Bligh.

"That's the careening area for repairs to government yawls and cutters. It isn't among the available blocks shown on my new Sydney Town plan. You would have seen that, sir, if you had bothered yourself to visit the Surveyor General Office as his letter recommended, before coming here. I suggest that you proceed forthwith to his office."

Offended by the governor's haughty attitude, as though Nathaniel had never met him before and was wasting his time, he found himself feeling unusually combative. "You know, of course, Your Excellency, that my five-year lease was renewed by Governor King in January 1806 for fourteen years."

Screwing up his face to convey a satirical question, Bligh asked, "Now why do *you think*, he would do such a thing? . . ."

Nathaniel refused to respond to Bligh's condescending quizzical look. He sat in stony silence looking at the governor.

Bligh continued unfazed: "*Why* would he do that? . . . when your block clearly violated The Domain of Government House shown on Phillip's plan for Sydney Cove? Why in God's name would King lease it away for an additional fourteen years, I ask you?"

"I can't speak for Governor King, although I *can* tell you that my original five-year lease was so I could build a house close to Government House to be readily available—"

"*You* built it? Didn't the *convicts* build it at no cost to you?"

"It cost me time and money, Governor, obviously to plan and furnish it, and later to add a slate roof. I needed to be close to Governor King to serve as his secretary."

"Yes, yes, I know, you served previous governors while being granted hundreds of acres of land and becoming one of the richest men in the colony. I fancy it should not be too much of a burden now for you to return the land to the government that you had no right to occupy in the first place."

His aggravation beginning to show, Nathaniel asked, "If I may be so bold to inquire, for what public use do you intend to put the block?"

"Government purposes that will improve the aspect of Government House."

"But what specifically? considering that I am to be so grievously inconvenienced."

"*Grievously*, eh? You are no longer a member of the government, Mr. Armstrong. It is quite enough for you to know that it is wanted for government purposes." Bligh did not want to tell him that his daughter and the surveyor had prepared a formal geometric garden plan for that part of The Domain.

"The surveyor general's letter did not address many of my concerns, Governor, such as am *I* to incur the cost of pulling down my own house? is the block to be cleared of debris? am I to receive compensation for the loss of my house? will convicts be provided to—"

"*Enough with your concerns, sir,* take them up with the surveyor general," Bligh said curtly. "I have *no* time for such piddling matters."

"Your *Excellency,* I hold a *valid* lease under the laws of England and can and should expect redress!"

Suddenly red-faced, the governor nearly screamed:

"*Damn your laws of England!* Don't talk to me of your laws of England. *I will make laws for this colony, and every wretch of you, son of a bitch, shall be governed by them. Or there*"—pointing at the jail—"*is your habitation!*"

Angrier than he had been in a long time and close to losing control, Nathaniel stood up abruptly, looked down at the foul-mouthed, pudgy, little bastard he wanted to crush, then turned on his heels and marched for the door.

The governor yelled after him:

"*If you were still in the army, I'd have you arrested for insubordination, Armstrong! Your insult will not be forgotten!*"

Later, Nathaniel learned that there were some ten other lease-holders who had received the same letter from Surveyor General Grimes. Macarthur was one of them involving his vacant Block 77 leased on Church Hill within an area of crown land designated for the exclusive use of St. Phillips Church. Bligh wanted to expand the church and needed Macarthur's land to do it. Angry talk abounded that Governor Bligh had no respect for property rights, a corner-stone of liberty, so now no man's home was safe.

◎

When the anticipated letter from Sir Joseph Banks finally arrived, it caused great excitement in the Armstrong household. Nathaniel had written to him that his son Arthur wished to study botany and attached letters of recommendation attesting to Arthur's education and expertise in agriculture and horticulture. Banks wrote back that the name of Nathaniel Armstrong had become well known to him in his dealings with Governors Phillip, Paterson, Hunter, and King. He would be pleased to sponsor Arthur's naturalist education.

Arthur was overjoyed that he was to receive a scholar's educa-tion in England. His enthusiasm, however, began to wane as the day of his leaving grew nearer. He was frightened both by the voyage and being away from home, most likely for three years or longer. He was three months short of sixteen when the day of his departure arrived, August 3, 1807. It took all of his fortitude and the encouragement of his parents to force him onto the ship.

Charles was no help in the matter. He belittled his brother's fears and went on about how he wished he was leaving home to sail the seas. Shortly after Arthur left, Charles stopped caring about his education and made his tutor's life a misery. Finally, the tutor resigned saying he had taught Charles all he could learn and all that he cared to teach him.

Nathaniel could not interest Charles in farming or keeping animals. When he turned fourteen, he announced at his birthday party that he had decided to become a sailor and would sign onto the next ship leaving Sydney Cove.

After Charles had gone to bed, Nathaniel and Moira discussed their problem son.

"Who knows why he likes the idea; some men are just drawn to the sea for it's freedom and adventure. I don't know," Nathaniel said in answer to Moira's question.

"We'll have to find something else for him to do," Moira said, "since he doesn't like farming."

"I'm happy he's identified something he wants to do, Moira. We should let him do it and get it out of his system early. If it isn't to be, he can get into something else."

"He's *just* fourteen, Nathaniel. Why are you seriously considering this?"

"Because the sea can be a worthwhile life and a profitable one for an adventurous young man like him."

"He's only a *boy!* I won't hear of it."

"He's not too young; he's the right age if he wants to be the captain of his own ship someday. Bligh was a cabin boy at the age of seven. Marine drummers are often boys. Midshipman are learning to be officers at his age. He's the right age to start, if the sea is to be his trade. If it isn't to be, it's best to know now. It will make a man of him."

"Or *kill* him," Moira said scornfully.

"I'm not suggesting that we send him off on any ship, Moira. I'll talk to Robert Campbell to see whether he will arrange something on one of his ships. I'll make sure there's someone to look after him and protect him and help him learn the ropes. This is the best way to satisfy his headstrong desire to go to sea. We shouldn't stifle something he really wants to do, Moira. One voyage will tell us whether it's to be or not."

A trading voyage to India, for seven months or longer, was arranged on one of Campbell's ships. Charles would serve as the master's cabin boy. Nathaniel and Charles met the master, who seemed to hit it off well with Charles. Three months after Charles had announced that he was going to sea, whether his parents liked it or not, he was sailing cheerfully away to India.

With both boys gone, Moira seemed lost. She slept in and moped around the house looking forlorn.

"Moira, you have to get yourself together," Nathaniel told her. "You knew the boys were going to leave home some day. You still have all your responsibilities; immerse yourself in work and you won't miss them so much."

"It's easier for you. You didn't give them birth. You were gone all week while I raised them. I'm used to havin' them around. It seems so dead around here now."

Later that day, while looking in the sitting room for writing paper, Moira came across a partially written poem on Nathaniel's desk. Seeing the title "Children," she picked it up and moved close to the light of the window. Feeling a little guilty, she read it:

<u>CHILDREN</u>

Children, a blessing to ~~their par~~ behold.
You watch them crawl and help them ~~up~~ to their feet.
~~Reaching~~ They play, laugh, fall, cry, and learn along the way,
All the while creating memories so sweet.

Too soon they are gone, leaving an aching pain of loss.
You did not want them to ~~go~~ depart,
But they were nearly grown and wanted to go,
Leaving you with a broken heart.

revel in

Mourn not their ~~going~~ absence but^ ~~think of~~ the bright
  future ahead,

Of family extended and grandchildren's love.

For as men they will return to enrich with their own
  plans,   Pleasing

~~Reinvigorating~~^their parents in ways unthought of.

"Nathaniel, what is this I found on yer desk?" Moira held up his partially written poem.

Angrily, Nathaniel reached out saying, "Give me that!" He took it from her and looked at it. "Did you read it?"

Smiling victoriously, she said, "You're just as heartsick about the boys leavin' as I am" and then laughed. "All that rubbish about me mopin' around and needing to buck up! You're just maintaining yer manly facade."

"You didn't have any right to read it, Moira. What I wrote wasn't meant for you or anyone else to read—it's personal. I just started it."

Seeing that Nathaniel was truly offended, Moira tried to make amends. "I didn't mean to pry, dear, but it was laying on the top of yer desk, and I was looking for writing paper. I couldn't help reading it when I saw what it was about. I'm sorry. But I love it and love you for writing it. Why don't you ever show me yer poems?"

"They're *too* personal, like a diary. I couldn't write them if I knew others were going to read them. Also they're no good, that's why I don't keep them. You've read Burns, Milton, and Pope—*that's* poetry; mine are just musings."

"What's *musings*?"

"My muddled thoughts. I use my quill to help me think through things that are bothering me. The quill helps me find the best words to express my thoughts to myself, if that makes any sense to you."

"It *does* make sense to me. I sometimes write things down that are botherin' me, so I can think more about them later. I like yer poem. I'm going to try to think less about the boys bein' away and more about the future when they return. Can I have it? It'd be a comfort for me."

"Well, just this once. I'll give it to you when I've written it the best I can."

◉

"**This test of** wills between Macarthur and His Excellency must stop, Nathaniel, don't ye agree?" asked Robert Campbell. He and Nathaniel were meeting in Campbell's warehouse office concerning trading ventures when Campbell turned the conversation to politics. Governor Bligh had appointed Campbell the port naval officer in control of Port Jackson. In this official capacity, he and Macarthur had had several disagreements.

Nathaniel sidestepped his direct question but agreed generally. "Aye, Sydney Town and Parramatta are in a very disturbed state."

"It's been going on fir nearly a year now, disturbing the general tranquility. 'Tis going tae hurt oor business if it continues. Macarthur has been openly hostile tae Bligh and me, ever since I seized his illegally imported still and the governor impoonded it. Macarthur's not foolin' the governor; he's well aware who's leading the writing campaign against him."

"You should know, Robert, that I'm among those who have written the Colonial Office complaining about Bligh. I wrote regarding his pulling down my house along with four others in The Domain."

"I'm not spe'king of *those* kinds of specific issue letters. Nae one objects tae your position that your hoose shou'dnae have been torn down until a ruling came from London aboot the validity of your lease."

Nathaniel wondered whether Campbell knew about Macarthur's lease on a vacant block. "Bligh also rescinded Macarthur's lease on Church Hill."

"So I heard."

"And they have been unable to agree on a replacement block."

"So I understan.'" Campbell had seen Bligh's Sydney Town plan, which showed many scattered unoccupied blocks. "Whose fault is that?"

"I don't know, probably a little on both sides."

"Weel, now *I* have a problem on *my* hands. The governor is aboot tae deny Macarthur's appeal and direct him tae pay the £950 penalty fir allowing a stowaway convict tae escape tae Tahiti from his ship the *Parramatta*. Macarthur has said that if Bligh rules against him, he will simply abandon the ship tae the government and will look tae his underwriters tae make him whole. Of coorse, he's bluffing. But what am I tae do in the meantime wi' his impoonded cargo and a crew wi'oot pay or provisions, which under port regulations may nae come ashore under these circumstances. If he pays the penalty, he'll probably still make a profit from his cargo. You are his neighbor; cou'd ye talk some sense into him?"

"I'd like to help you, Robert, really I would. But, I wouldn't be successful. You don't know him as I do. This is fatal combat to him. He feels he has been treated unfairly and will never pay the fine."

"Weel then, there's nae easy solution is there?" Campbell said.

"You could advise the governor to back off a bit, Robert. He could find some extenuating circumstances and reduce the fine by half. Give Macarthur a measure of victory and then allow tempers to cool."

"The governor wou'd never agree tae that, Nathaniel. He wints tae *punish* the mon."

"Bligh should be careful and not underestimate him. Macarthur still holds sway over the corps officers and would prevail if this comes to a head."

"Comes tae a head?—ye don't mean—attempt tae overthrow Bligh, do ye?"

Nathaniel gave him a serious look and did not answer.

"I'm nae a military man, but I cannae imagine the Rum Corps wou'd be so foolish as tae attempt tae overthrow His Majesty's emissary. Ye cannae be serious."

"Indeed I am. It's general knowledge that Bligh has written to the War Office, the Colonial Office, and the Admiralty asking for Royal Marines to replace the corps. He's vindictively recommended that the corps should be sent to India. They would lose their farms, privileged lives, *everything*."

" 'Tis better than being hung fir mutiny," Campbell said.

"Hung by whom? When? And they wouldn't *'attempt to'* arrest Bligh; they would simply march over to Government House and arrest him! Done. Who's to stop them? The corps is the real power here, Robert. Bligh has no power base. You should help him to accept that."

"More than eight hundred free settlers and emancipists, many o' them small farmers alang the Hawkesbury, signed a pledge tae support the governor at the risk of their lives and properties."

"Have you heard Bligh mention these men as allies?"

"Aye."

"Well, I'm dumbfounded. He's a foolish man if he thinks for a moment that they will face off against the army."

"Weel, I cannae believe that Major Johnston or any other corps officer wou'd be so foolish as tae try tae arrest Governor Bligh, I'm sorry."

"Robert, I should like to convince you that the governor needs to be realistic. These are military men of action, who act now and think later. Johnston is their commanding officer. I saw him brutally put down the Irish revolt at Vinegar Hill. He didn't think or reason; he acted. Governor King understood how far he could push these men; evidently, Bligh doesn't. Between you and me . . . Bligh is a hot-tempered bully who hasn't shown any capacity for moderation. It will be his undoing, believe me, if he continues down this path he's taken."

Nine days after their meeting, in contravention of port regulations, the master and crew of the *Parramatta* came ashore and made affidavits in the judge advocate office that they had left the ship because Macarthur had deprived them of their pay and provisions. Bligh instructed the Judge Advocate Richard Atkins to summon Macarthur to appear before a bench of magistrates to explain his actions. Macarthur treated Atkins's summons like an inquiry and wrote back a rudely dismissive explanation.

Resenting Macarthur's inappropriate and disrespectful reply to a legal summons, Bligh directed Atkins to issue a warrant through Francis Oakes, chief constable at Parramatta, to arrest Macarthur and bring him to Sydney Town.

One hour before midnight, on December 15, 1807, Chief Constable Oakes knocked on Macarthur's door at Elizabeth Farm. He presented the warrant to an irate John Macarthur. Seeing Atkins's name on the warrant, Macarthur said, "Had the person who issued this warrant served it instead of yourself, Constable, I would have spurned him from my presence. If he came well-armed and tried to enforce the warrant, I would never submit till blood was shed."

Inviting Oakes into his house, Macarthur pointed out where the warrant was invalidly written and therefore could not be legally enforced. "No matter, Constable Oakes, I will acknowledge in writing that you did your duty." He quickly wrote a letter to the constable.

Mr. Oakes,

You will inform the person who sent you here with the warrant you have now shown me and given me a copy of, that I never will submit to the horrid tyranny that is attempted, until I am forced; that I consider it with scorn and contempt, as I do the persons who have directed it to be executed.

J. Macarthur

When Bligh saw this letter, he angrily directed that a second warrant for Macarthur's arrest be prepared and ordered Oakes to "safely lodge him in His Majesty's jail." When the constable and his deputies arrived at Elizabeth Farm, they learned Macarthur had gone to Sydney Town. They found him in George Evans's Sydney house and took him before a bench of magistrates, who rather than send him to jail, admitted him to bail until his trial before a monthly-scheduled criminal court.

Four days later, Macarthur went to the judge advocates office and loudly demanded payment of an IOU for £26 6s signed by Atkins years earlier. When Atkins refused payment under such rude circumstances, Macarthur filed for payment in civil court. He then wrote Governor Bligh entreating him "to appoint a judge advocate who should be disinterested in the event of my criminal trial."

While Bligh considered what to do, Macarthur had a fence built around his disputed Church Hill leasehold property. This was more than Bligh could stomach. He had the fence torn down and advised Macarthur that Atkins would serve as judge advocate at his trial.

Atkins was widely regarded as an drunken incompetent. He proved this to Bligh when he sheepishly informed him the day before Macarthur's trial that due to the normal rotation of magistrates, he would be the only civilian, the other six were all Rum Corps officers, led by Captain Kemp. It was too late for Bligh to engineer a more impartial criminal court. The entire colony was anxiously awaiting the trial. Bligh and Atkins decided to proceed, hoping that Macarthur did not know the court's composition and had not fraudulently influenced the officers.

On January 25, 1808, the courtroom was packed. Nathaniel and Moira had arrived two hours early to ensure themselves seats.

"This court is called to order," Judge Advocate Atkins announced while banging his gavel on its wood block. The audience went silent. "The charges against Lieutenant Macarthur—"

"*I object!*" Macarthur interrupted him.

"*You* are out of order," Atkins said.

"*And you are not impartial!*" Macarthur said as he stood.

Atkins said, "You, sir, are—"

"*Aw shut up, and let him speak!*" Captain Kemp yelled at Atkins.

Macarthur spewed out a caustic diatribe, laced with sarcasm, explaining why Atkins was unfit to try him and why a fair trial was an impossibility. Atkins's efforts to interrupt Macarthur were to no avail. Finally, between one of Macarthur's breathes, Atkins said:

"You are in *contempt* of court! I commit you to jail. Bailiff—"

"You commit?" Captain Kemp said as he leaped to his feet. "*You commit?* No, sir! I will commit you to jail!" A loud cheer went up from the soldiers in attendance.

Atkins bolted for the door, leaving all of his papers spread out on the table. Macarthur walked over to the table and picked up Atkins's papers and in a loud voice over the commotion read his indictment:

" 'That said John Macarthur being a malicious and seditious

man, and of a depraved mind and wicked and diabolical disposition, had been deceitfully, wickedly, and maliciously contriving and abetting against William Bligh, Esq., His Majesty's governor in chief of this territory . . .'" Macarthur waved the paper in the air. "This is *ridiculous!*"

The rest of the day continued the drama. Kemp and the five other officers wrote a joint letter to Bligh stating their position that Macarthur's objections were valid and a new judge advocate should be appointed. Bligh wrote back saying that the court could not take any actions without Atkins, he was the only person authorized to sit as judge advocate, and that his papers should be returned immediately. The governor summoned Major George Johnston, the commander of the corps, from his home in Annandale. Johnston refused, saying he was recovering from a fall from his carriage. Bligh took this to mean that Johnston stood with his rebellious officers.

The next day was the twentieth anniversary of the founding of the colony, but nobody celebrated. Bligh issued summons to the six officer magistrates ordering them to appear before him at Government House at nine o'clock the next morning to explain their actions, which amounted to usurping His Majesty's Government and creating conditions of rebellion and treason. The governor then wrote Johnston telling him that he had summoned six of his officers before him, and as Johnston was "totally incapable of being in Sydney" he would give command to an officer of his choosing. When this news reached the officers and their soldiers, the streets became alive with anticipated consequences. Officers scurried among the government and military offices, pubs, and barracks discussing what should be done. Macarthur's Sydney house became a beehive of activity.

As Johnston was driven in his carriage into Sydney Town at five o'clock in the afternoon, he was surrounded by soldiers and well-wishers, many of them clamoring for Bligh's arrest. Johnston went to his army barracks. Shortly after, Macarthur arrived.

"*God's curse!*" exclaimed Johnston. "What am I to do, Macarthur? These fellows advise me to arrest the governor."

Macarthur put his hand on Johnston's shoulder and replied, "They '*advise you?*' Then, sir, the only thing left for you to do *is to do it!* You know that to *advise* on such matters is legally as criminal as to do it! Allow me to provide you with support in fulfilling your duty." He wrote out a petition that read:

26th January, 1808

Sir,

The present alarming state of this colony, in which every man's property, liberty, and life is endangered, induces us most earnestly to implore you instantly to place Governor Bligh under an arrest and to assume the command of the colony. We pledge ourselves, at a moment of less agitation, to come forward to support the measures with our fortunes and our lives.

We are, with great respect, Sir,
Your most obedient servants:

John Macarthur

The first to sign his name, Macarthur walked around the room dramatically choosing, as though it were a great honor, among the men who wished to add their names to his petition.

So empowered, Johnston acted. He ordered the corps to form ranks under arms and directed Captain Kemp to lead them "in quick step" to Government House.

Kemp was delayed at the gate of Government House by the governor's guards. Advised that mutinous troops were at the gate, Bligh rushed from the dinner table while ordering Mr. Griffin, his secretary, to have his horse saddled. He ran up the stairs to put on his uniform. Bligh's daughter and Reverend Fulton rushed from Government House in a valiant attempt to slow the advance of the corps. When the troops removed the struggling woman from their path, Reverend Fulton ran back inside Government House and locked the front door. He refused to open it to a group of soldiers led by Captain Kemp.

The governor was coming down the stairs when he heard soldiers coming in a side door. Retreating back up the stairs, hoping he had not been seen, Bligh went into his personal servant's room and moved quickly to its window in the rear wall. Seeing the stable boy leading his saddled horse out of the stable, he opened the window, put a leg out and sat on the sill; looking down, he considered the hazard of hanging from the window sill and dropping to the ground.

Three soldiers came running toward the stable boy, not seeing Bligh in clear view to their right. He quickly pulled his leg back into the room and, hearing the clamor of soldiers' voices and the sounds of many feet coming up the stairs, shut the window and looked for a place to hide. There was no clothes closet, only a chest of drawers, desk, and bed. He slid quickly under the bed.

Looking at the door, he saw the boots of two soldiers enter. They looked behind the door and out the window and then left. He could hear the soldiers yelling to one another as they searched every room. A half an hour later, the second floor was quiet. Extremely uncomfortable, he moved around silently to find a more comfortable position. After hiding beneath the bed for an hour, he slid himself across the floor toward the window, careful not to creak the floor boards. It was turning dark. He thought it must be at least seven thirty; soon he would have the cover of darkness to escape. Raising his head up very slowly, he looked out a corner of the window. To his disappointment, he saw two soldiers stationed outside the stable.

He could hear voices downstairs but none on the second floor. Sitting upright, he rested his sore back against the wall and listened for his daughter's voice. Unable to hear it, he assured himself that they would not harm a woman.

Would they dare harm me? he wondered. It won't be long now until they'll assume I've escaped and will leave. They'll post guards about but in the middle of the night, once they're asleep, I'll be able to slip out the window and escape. I'll find a horse somewhere and ride to the Hawkesbury and safety. That farmer Lyford will hide me. Then I'll have time to decide what to do. The infernal rotters must be furious that I've eluded them!

He heard several loud, frustrated voices below, all talking at once, moving from the back of the house toward the front. They stopped at the bottom of the stairs. They seemed to be arguing. Then one voice announced loudly:

"*Damn my eyes, I'll find 'im!'* E *has* to be somewhere upstairs!" They started up the stairs. Bligh quickly pushed himself across the floor and under the bed. He moved his body as far back as possible and pressed his back against the wall. The boots of three soldiers entered the room.

The governor held his breath. One of the soldiers walked toward the window and suddenly a musket barrel swept under the bed without touching him. He breathed a silent sigh of relief. The barrel reappeared held by the extended arms of a soldier. The musket was pushed further under the bed and began a second sweep that hit him! The soldier's knees dropped to the floor with a *thud* and then his delighted face exclaimed joyously:

"I *FOUND* THE BUGGER!"

Hands grabbed him and dragged him out from beneath the bed. The governor thought with great chagrin—*how ignominious!*—I must deny it happened this way!

Late that night as Nathaniel and Moira were retiring to bed, they were concerned to hear a rider coming up the track to their house. Nathaniel walked to the front door and opened it holding a loaded pistol behind his back. He saw John Macarthur stepping up onto the veranda. He invited him inside.

"My deepest apologizes for interrupting you so late at night, Nathaniel. I was on my way home and thought to inform you that Bligh was arrested today by Major Johnston."

"Ach, I knew this was coming!"

Macarthur described the events of the day.

"I have a petition that we signed in support of Johnston and the corps. I would like you to add your name, if you are so inclined." He handed it to Nathaniel to read.

Nathaniel quickly read the petition and the signatures of the most prominent men in the colony.

"I'll sign it, John, because Bligh must bear most of the responsibility for this mess, but *you* are not without blame yourself. However, I suspect you're prepared to pay the price."

Macarthur's expression did not change, and he said nothing in response.

"I must admit though," Nathaniel said as he signed the petition, "I'm relieved this nasty business is finally over."

Martial law was enforced by Major Johnston, who declared himself acting lieutenant governor. He suspended the judge advocate and other officials and appointed John Macarthur colonial secretary. Macarthur wrote a lengthy dispatch to London, for Johnston's signature, explaining in great detail the reasons why Bligh had to be removed from office. In closing, the dispatch asked for an army governor to replace Bligh and promised that the colony would be fairly administered until Lieutenant Governor William Paterson, serving in Port Dalrymple, could return to the town of Sydney.

The mutineers confined Bligh to Government House for months before allowing him to leave Sydney if he would agree to return to England. He refused. Expecting a military force from India or Britain that would defeat the Rum Corps, Bligh wanted to be in Sydney to hang the mutineers. In March 1809, after waiting for more than a year, Bligh finally agreed in writing to return to England on the HMS *Porpoise*. Once on board, however, he broke his word and took control of the ship from its lower-ranking captain and sailed to Van Diemen's Land seeking help from Lieutenant Governor David Collins, who had been lieutenant governor there since 1803.

Having received convincing dispatches from New South Wales that Bligh was at fault, Collins decided not to take sides, but treated Bligh with courtesy. Bligh decided to wait in Hobart until help arrived from Britain.

Chapter 6

Mockery of Macquarie

"Charles, you're home!" Nathaniel said as he started down the stairs toward his son, entering through the front door.

"Guid tae have ye hame, yoong laird," said Nathaniel's valet-butler who had answered the door of the Armstrong's Sydney town house.

"Thanks, Iain." Charles dropped his sea bag on the polished foyer floor and stepped forward to meet his father at the bottom of the stairs.

"You look wonderful, lad—*healthy!*—and taller." Nathaniel reached out and embraced him.

"How's Mum, Dad?"

"She's very well and will be even better when she sees you. She worries about her boys when they're away, you know."

"Is she here?"

"No, Parramatta. I met with your employer, Mr. Campbell, just this morning. You weren't expected for another week! I'm glad when you're early. Did you find many pearls and mother-of-pearl shells in the Society Islands and the Tuamotu Archipelago?"

"*Lots* of pearls and pearlshells! You and Mr. Campbell are goin' t'be *rich!* . . . or richer. We traded for them mostly on Tahiti, also on Rangiroa and Fakarava atolls in the Tuamotus. Mr. Rodden paid next to nothin'—knives, metal tools, cloth—bloody cheap. There wasn't anything worth trading for in the Cook Islands though."

"Well, it's still splendid news. We'll have to celebrate. You'll benefit as a member of the crew if we've done better than expected."

"Good! It was really a great voyage, Dad, and those flamin' Society Islands—you wouldn't believe it, especially Bora-Bora and Tahiti. They're so damn beautiful you can't believe your silly eyes. And the saucy donahs—*crikes!*—they don't wear no tops. It's a paradise. None of us wanted to leave the *bloody* place."

"*Whoa.* Your seafaring language gets worse with each trip, Charles. Don't talk like that around your mother—please! You know how I had to convince her to let you become a sailor, and she sure as the dickens isn't going to be happy hearin' you speak like one."

"I'll try to watch the swearin', Dad, but that's who I am now. Mum's already use' to it."

"Just because she doesn't say anything, doesn't mean she likes it!"

"Look at this, Dad," Charles said to change the subject as he took a small leather pouch out of his pocket and untied the strings on top. Upending it on his hand, out rolled seven or eight small pearls. "I found these *myself*, by G—by gum. The native divers showed me and my chums how to do it. I dove with *sharks* around!"

"*Good lord,* Charles, sharks! Don't tell your mother that story. Not if you ever want to go to sea again. You'll worry the poor woman to death with a story like that. When you show her the pearls tell her that you traded personal items for them."

"Master Rodden didn't allow us to do that."

"I know. So think up something else. Just don't tell her you dove with *sharks* around!"

"What's the news of Artie and when will he be back?"

"He's doing very well in his studies and works with an associate of Sir Joseph Banks. His last letter said he plans to sail for home in March or April, so he could be here in September or October."

"Great!"

"I'll tell you all about him on the way home. I was going to return to Parramatta tomorrow, but we can go there together later this afternoon and surprise you mother."

Nathaniel left Charles to his own devices and went out to conclude some business he had in Sydney Town. They left in Nathaniel's carriage at four to complete the two-hour ride before dark.

During the ride, Nathaniel brought Charles up to date.

"The new governor arrived a month and a half ago, an army lieutenant colonel commanding the 73rd Highlanders, named Lachlan Macquarie. The British government finally realized it was necessary to send an *army* governor with his own troops to support him."

"What's he like?" Charles asked.

"I've only met him once. He's a Scot like me, I'm happy to say. A few years older than me, perhaps fifty, my height and build. He seems a decent, unassuming sort of chap. His first wife died, I'm told. He has a new young wife, early thirties, named Elizabeth, pretty."

"Was there a battle to take control?"

"No. Lieutenant Governor Paterson had returned from Port Dalrymple and taken control of the government and military and let the mutineers, Johnston and Macarthur, escape."

"Wasn't Mr. Macarthur the one who almost killed Paterson in a duel?"

"Aye."

"Why would he let *him* escape?"

"Paterson isn't a vengeful man. I think he was happy to see them both go, so he didn't have to deal with them. Macarthur knew that Macquarie had orders to arrest them. They probably feared there'd be a summary trial, and they'd be hung."

"Does anyone know where they escaped to?"

"I shouldn't have used the word 'escape.' It was all very aboveboard. They went to England to make their case. Johnston is sure to be court-martialed. I don't know what they'll do to Macarthur, a civilian."

"I never liked Mr. Macarthur, always puttin' on airs. Is Governor Bligh still in Van Diemen's Land?"

"No. He returned two weeks after Macquarie arrived. Wouldn't you know, he demanded a full honor guard before landing. He was disappointed to learn that Johnston and Macarthur had flown the coop, so to speak. The new governor is ignoring him, though, so Bligh won't stay long, just long enough to collect evidence for Johnston's court-martial."

"What's happening to the Rum Corps?"

"Its officers are being sent back to England."

"Mr. Evans too?"

"Yes, he's being sent back too."

"Bugger me!"

"*Charles!* Do you know what the means?"

"It doesn't mean what you think anymore, Dad. It's just an expression."

"Well . . . don't use it around me, if you please."

After a few seconds, Charles said, "I'm sorry Mr. Evans is leaving. I like him. He told me I made the right decision to go to sea 'cos it's something *I* wanted to do. He wished he had done somethin' like that before gettin' married. What's he goin' to do with his farm?"

"He tried to sell it; however, with so many farms up for sale at the same time, they're going for very low prices."

"You should buy it, Dad."

"Well, as a matter of fact, that's what I'm doing. He wasn't happy with the highest price he was offered and asked me if I would better it. I expected he'd be coming to me. I'm the logical buyer, after all, as his neighbor. We've negotiated a fair price for everything. I don't want to take advantage of him; he's an old friend."

For the next three-quarters of an hour, Nathaniel enjoyed listening to Charles's exciting stories about his voyage. He told about his native girlfriends and from what he said and hinted at, Nathaniel surmised that his son had "become a man."

When there was a lull in their conversation, Nathaniel said, "I wasn't going to discuss this with you until I got a little further along, but now seems like a good time. You know that I've been in business with Mr. Campbell, primarily as an investor, for five years now. Well, I've learned a bit about trading and merchandising and have set up my own business named Star Trading Company. Lieutenant Governor Paterson approved my charter three months ago. So in a—"

"Are y'goin' to buy a *ship*?" Charles interrupted, sensing he was going to benefit from his father's endeavor.

"Yes. *But it will take time*, Charles, so don't get excited about it. I'll start off renting one of Mr. Campbell's ships, and if the new venture works out, I'll go out on my own. I'll rent part of Mr. Campbell's warehouse initially and build or buy my own after that. In a few years, I'll buy a ship and will need a good captain. Know anyone who might be experienced enough by then?"

"Me! I'll be experienced enough by then."

"I can't promise anything, Charles. This is a risky business, you know, but there's a lot of money to be made if everything works out well. If luck is on my side, this is a business you could take over at some point, and your brother could take over the farm.

"Parliament is about to eliminate the East India Company's monopoly everywhere except its valuable tea trade with China. So Mr. Campbell and I are organizing a trade route to take advantage of that. It would run from Fiji to Calcutta, then to Canton, and back here. Sandalwood is the key; it's like gold to the Chinese. They make it into joss incense sticks to burn in their religious services, carve it into statues, boxes, and ornaments, and use it to make perfumes and soaps. When I'm ready, I want you to serve on my ship that'll go to Fiji for sandalwood and pearls, then take the sandalwood to Calcutta where it will be placed on an East India Company ship. It will sail to Canton to trade the sandalwood for tea and bring it back here, along with any other items I order, such as silk, chinaware, cabinets, and lacquer boxes."

"What will we bring back from Calcutta in your ship?" Charles asked.

"Whatever is needed in the colony at the time or the government contracts for, like spices, sugar, salt, rice, cloth, furniture, cattle and, if we have an import permit, spirits."

That night sixteen-year-old Charles dreamt of being the captain of his own ship and sailing back into the waiting arms of alluring, fun-loving, and willing native girls in their south sea paradise.

◉

Moira sat reading a book in the drawing room when Nathaniel joined her. He sat down on the sofa, opened his own book, and nonchalantly said, "We've been invited to Government House for tea on the fourteenth of March to meet the governor and his lady."

"That's nice, dear," Moira commented without thinking, then wondered: Did he say *we*? "Did you say *we*, Nathaniel?"

Nathaniel looked up from his open book. "Why yes, I *believe* that's what the invitation said. Let me have a look." He lifted an envelope from within his book and slowly withdrew the enclosed invitation.

From his teasing tone, she knew it was true. "Here, let me see that."

"I *can* read it. Give me a second." He fumbled unfolding the invitation and took his time pretended to find where it invited them both.

Impatient, she laid down her book, got up, and walked over to him with her hand extended. "Let me see that, you devil."

He turned away from her. "Why yes, here it is, Mr. and *Mrs.* Nathaniel Armstrong, I *dooo* believe that's you."

"Nathaniel, give it to me!" Still standing, Moira put a hand on his shoulder and reached over him to take the invitation. She had never been invited to any event at Government House in her twenty years in the colony and had never even been inside the building.

She raised the invitation up and read it. "Holy Mother of God!" Her hand over her mouth, she sat down on the sofa with a *plop* next to him. She lowered her hand and looked inquisitively at him. "Do you think they know?"

"I don't know; although I've been expecting it. They've already invited other emancipists and mixed couples to their table. Will you go with me?"

"Oh, Nathaniel, I don't know whether I'm ready. I don't want to make a silly fool of myself."

"Moira, this is the best thing for you to do. It'll show you how exceptional and smart you are. You'll be the most beautiful, composed women there—I know it. I've been to hundreds of these affairs and will help you through it. The best thing is to simply look radiant and choose your words. You don't have to say much. I want you to go with me. You owe it to all the other emancipists."

Tears forming in her eyes, she turned away from him, took out her hankie, and dabbed at her eyes. He moved closer and kissed her on the cheek.

"So you'll go then?" asked Nathaniel.

"Yes. I *do* owe it to other emancipists."

"And the Irish."

"Yes, for my people too."

"*And* the Catholics," he said with an impish smile, containing a laugh.

With tear-filled eyes, she looked at him to confirm his teasing. "Oh stop it, you rascal!" She playfully slapped his arm. ". . . I never thought this day would come."

On the fourteenth, they rode proudly to Government House in their barouche that Nathaniel had ordered from England. There were only five or six others in the colony, one of which was used by the governor. It was an elegant four-wheeled carriage, pulled by four horses, with two facing double seats, a retractable hood, and a box seat at the front for the driver and another person. They were pleased that Governor and Mrs. Macquarie saw them arriving in the barouche as they greeted guests on the pillared veranda of Government House.

Moira curtsied demurely and opened her mouth to say the greeting that she had practiced for days, but nothing came out. She had forgotten every single word. After an awkward silence, she mustered a feeble "Your Excellency" and "madam."

"What a lovely spencer jacket, Mrs. Armstrong," Elizabeth Macquarie remarked, smiling warmly. "The color becomes you so."

"Oh . . . why thank you, Mrs. Macquarie, " Moira replied diffidently, pleased that she had chosen something subdued, as Nathaniel had suggested. She searched in vain for something to say. Nathaniel touched her elbow, indicating that another couple was standing behind them. They were directed into the combined reception-drawing room where drinks were being served.

The Macquaries entered the room after all of the guests arrived and spent some time talking with each couple. Nathaniel described to Moira the two male guests he knew, both doctors. He did not know the women with them nor the fourth couple. Doctor D'Arcy Wentworth was the principal surgeon at the hospital and Doctor William Redfern was chief surgeon under him. Redfern was an emancipist. There were stories that Wentworth had committed a crime and was given the choice of prison or volunteering as a surgeon on a convict ship bound for New South Wales. (Moira was disconcerted by the tall, handsome, blue-eyed Doctor Wentworth, whose eyes followed her about the room.)

They were introduced to Mr. and Mrs. Franklin Pemberton. Mrs. Pemberton, a thin, pale woman, was a niece of the former Judge Advocate Richard Atkins. They arrived only one month earlier. Unfortunately, her uncle was on his way back to England while she and her husband were en route to New South Wales. They carried government instructions to the governor to grant them one thousand acres of good grazing land to enable them to participate in the national wool project. It was unclear whether they were nobility as Atkins had claimed to be. As they talked to Nathaniel and Moira, Mrs. Pemberton's eyes darted nervously and rarely connected with theirs.

Name cards placed the four couples along either side of the long table with the governor at one end and Mrs. Macquarie at the opposite end. Moira was seated second in from Elizabeth Macquarie with D'Arcy Wentworth between them. Doctor Redfern was seated directly across from Moira. Between him and Mrs. Macquarie sat Mrs. Pemberton. Nathaniel was seated on the opposite side of the table at its farthest end, to Governor Macquarie's left. He was too far from Moira to be of any help, except for an occasional supportive look.

As a light meal was being served, Doctor D'Arcy Wentworth asked, "Do you have any children, Mrs. Armstrong?"

"Yes, two boys. The youngest, Charles, has just returned from his third voyage on one of Robert Campbell's trading ships. My oldest son, Arthur, is studying in London and shall return within the year."

"I'm anxiously awaiting the return of my son, William, from his education at Greenwich School."

"How old is he, Doctor Wentworth?"

"Nineteen."

"My Arthur is eighteen. They grow up so fast."

"What is your Arthur studying?" Wentworth asked.

"Horticulture and botany under the gracious sponsorship of Sir Joseph Banks."

Upon hearing Sir Joseph Banks's name mentioned, Mrs. Macquarie turned from her conversation with Mrs. Pemberton to ask:

"I wonder whether your son might assist me, Mrs. Armstrong? Both the formal garden and kitchen garden have been dreadfully neglected. The plants I brought with me should cheer things up a bit, but I shall require some assistance to see them flourish in this sunny climate. I'm eager to learn about your native plants as well. Do you think your son would be so kind as to advise me?"

"Ah, Mrs. Macquarie, shure I am that he would be most honored to assist you. He's quite knowledgeable about our native plants . . . and a natural-born farmer."

"When do you expect him to return?"

"Not till September or October, unfortunately, ma'am."

"That is not a problem, dear. I'm so busy right now. I shan't have time to address the gardens until then. September is the start of your spring here, is it not?"

"Yes, madam."

"Well . . . excellent then. I shall look forward to meeting your Arthur when he returns, to assist me in my spring planting."

The governor was having a loud, animated conversation with guests at his end of the table that drew everyone's attention.

"It didn't take me long, Mr. Pemberton, to determine that there are many more freed convicts, called emancipists here, than those such as yourself who have come out free—exclusives—they call themselves. It seems to me that the fate of the colony depends on these two main groups working together for mutual benefit. Wouldn't you agree, gentlemen?"

"Yes, I would, Your Excellency," Nathaniel said.

The others nodded their heads with the exception of the

Pembertons. They looked concerned and confused.

Encouraged, Macquarie continued. "Emancipation, when united with rectitude and long-standing good conduct, should lead a man back to that rank in society which he had forfeited, it seems to me. Emancipists are too often treated with rudeness, contempt, and even oppression. I intend to counteract this envious disposition of one class over the other, by admitting, in my demeanor and occasional marks of favor to both, making no distinction when their merits and capabilities are equal."

The servants' removing of used dishes and silverware and the serving of sugar cakes quieted the governor's end of the table.

Unexpectedly, Wentworth quietly asked, "Your maiden name was O'Keeffe, wasn't it?"

Moira was astounded. How did he know that? She did not want to hear her surname, which immediately identified her as Irish. She composed herself and tried to remove the anxiety from her voice. Just as quietly, she answered, "Why, yes . . . have we met before, Doctor?"

"I was the assistant surgeon on the *Neptune*, part of the second fleet of transportees, that arrived with many critically ill convicts. You were very helpful to me and all the doctors in treating the sick and dying. I wondered what became of you. I went on to Norfolk Island on the *Surprize*. You were listed to go on the same ship but didn't."

Now she remembered him clearly. He had tried to get her alone many times back then, but she had been able to avoid him. There was a heavily pregnant women from the *Neptune* claiming to be his wife. She could have been carrying his son William nineteen years ago. He was one of the reasons she wanted to avoid going to Norfolk Island.

Mrs. Franklin Pemberton had taken in every whispered word. This handsome "doctor" was obviously lusting after this buxom woman. He had not had the civility to say even one word of greeting to her. This "Moira" must have been an Irish convict. The other doctor's woman was vulgar, the lowest order of person, probably also an ex-convict. She doubted that they were married. All this crude, impolite talk of sick and dying convicts, emancipists, and politics was simply more than she could bear. In fact, it suddenly occurred to her, they could *all* be former convicts. She had not wanted to come to this dreadful, godforsaken, criminal outpost to begin with, and now her uncle had departed. Suddenly, she felt faint. She made eye contact with her husband indicating she wanted to leave immediately.

"Dear, are you not feeling well?" Mr. Pemberton asked his wife.

"I feel faint, dear."

He turned to Governor Macquarie and said in a way of explanation: "She did not feel well on the way here, perhaps the rough ride in the carriage."

"We are two doctors here, Doctor Redfern and I," Wentworth said, "perhaps you would like to lie down, Mrs. Pemberton. We could check your pulse and recommend a remedy."

"I think it may be the excitement of moment," Mrs. Pemberton said to Doctor Wentworth.

Mrs. Macquarie had thought that Mrs. Pemberton looked ill when she arrived. She was now flushed of color and seemed about to swoon. "Please retire to a guest bedroom upstairs, my dear, and lie down for a spell."

"You are very kind, Mrs. Macquarie, but the brisk air will refresh me, I'm sure."

As they rose, her husband said, "We had a very arduous voyage here; I fear my wife has not yet fully recovered. We beg your pardons, one and all, and especially Mrs. Macquarie's."

Governor Macquarie led the way out to their carriage.

The abrupt departure of the couple was disruptive and cast a pall over conversation. Being a high tea, rather than a full dinner, entertainment did not follow and guests were expected to excuse themselves promptly. Nathaniel announced that he and his wife had enjoyed the tea immensely but had to be off. He invited the Governor and Mrs. Macquarie to visit them in Parramatta at their earliest convenience. The other two couples immediately followed suit.

Moira was satisfied with her performance and a little flattered, in spite of herself, that Doctor Wentworth remembered her and even her maiden name, after so many years. She was favorably impressed by the governor's humanitarian sentiments and marveled at the aplomb of his lady, Elizabeth. During their ride back to Parramatta, Moira talked excitedly about the tea while Nathaniel mostly listened. He was pleased that she thought the tea was a success.

◉

"I'll be returning to Sydney Town tomorrow," Arthur announced at dinner. "Mrs. Macquarie has arranged a meeting with the surveyor that she wants me to attend."

"On what?" Nathaniel asked in a piqued tone.

"A detailed survey of The Domain."

"Why do you have to be there? You agreed to work with me this week to plan next season's planting."

"We have time to do that, Dad. This is important. I think Mrs. Macquarie is willing to talk to the governor soon about establishing a botanic garden at Farm Cove for horticultural and botanical research. I want the surveyor to include Farm Cove in his survey."

"See here, Arthur, that's not your job. You aren't being paid to act as Mrs. Macarthur's horticultural advisor. I want you to take more responsibility for the farm. It's a big job for your mother when I'm away or working in Sydney on Star Trading ventures. You spend twice the time in Sydney as you do here, where you're needed."

"Oh, I don't mind, dear," Moira said. "With the boys grown, it keeps me busy."

"Darn it, Moira, I'll thank you not to undercut me when I'm givin' the lad hell. There you go, mate, saved by your mother again. . . . I assume you'll be obligated to serve as director or some such office, if this botanic garden goes ahead?"

"I doubt it, Dad. They'll pick someone a lot older than twenty."

"So you reckon there are people better at this than you?"

"I fancy so; although, I haven't met them."

"*That's* the kind of attitude I'd like to hear more of from you. You're good at this scientific kind of work, Arthur, so keep at it, but don't forget your responsibilities here."

"I won't, Dad."

"Do you think we should be breeding merinos for their wool like Mrs. Macarthur and Reverend Marsden?" Nathaniel asked him. "Is that something you might want to get involved in?"

"No . . . I'm a lot more interested in botany and farming than in being a grazier."

"Fair enough. I don't need anything more to do and neither does your mother."

"I forgot to mention," Moira said. "I saw Mrs. Macarthur across the fence yesterday directing her field workers. When she saw me riding by, she waved hello. Wasn't that nice?"

"Aye. She's a nice lady," Nathaniel said

Arthur said, "I heard the governor say that she's more than doubled the size of her merino herd since her husband's been gone,"

"Evidently, she's breed a large herd at the Cowpastures," Nathaniel said.

"When do you think her husband will return," Moira asked. "I feel sorry for her. He's been gone for three years already."

"Th—" Nathaniel began but was interrupted by Arthur.

"He might never come back, Mum. He'll be arrested by the governor if he does."

"Why?" she asked.

Arthur allowed his father to answer this time.

"After Johnston was found guilty of mutiny and cashiered from the army, the British prosecutors decided they had no jurisdiction in England to try Macarthur, a civilian, for treason here. So they provided Governor Macquarie with instructions to immediately arrest Macarthur for treason if he returns to New South Wales. He's not likely to leave England any time soon, at least not until he's able to press his patrons to remove this obstacle to his return."

◉

"Arthur, come in here, won't you?" Governor Macquarie called out to Arthur when he saw him and Mrs. Macquarie walking by his partially opened door. Both of them stepped into the governor's office

where he was meeting with a gentleman. "Could you spare Arthur for a half an hour, Elizabeth?"

"Of course, Lachlan. You'll find me in the kitchen garden when you are done here, Arthur."

"Yes, madam." Arthur walked over to the governor.

"Arthur Armstrong, do you know Mr. Gregory Blaxland?" Governor Macquarie asked.

"I believe I know *of him*, Governor, a major grazier. Good day, sir," Arthur put out his hand and the two men shook.

"I know your father," Blaxland said.

"Arthur is assisting my wife with her gardens. He studied under Sir Joseph Banks. He's a very knowledgeable farmer, botanist, horticulturist, and a student of all the natural sciences. I want him to hear what you have to say, sir."

Embarrassed, Arthur said, "The governor is much too kind, Mr. Blaxland."

"Not in the least," Macquarie said. "Go ahead, Mr. Blaxland."

"My property is hemmed in by the barrier of the Blue Mountains. This drought is drying up my grasses and my waterholes, killing my stock, and withering my grains. I've been to the top of the ridge nearest my property and have an idea. I'd like to try to find a way across the tops of the Blue Mountains. Most explorers have tried to go *through* them. My idea is to see whether there's a continuous series of linked ridges that will take me across the mountains to the interior and, hopefully, to the lush grasslands there."

"Is that a fact that all previous explorers have gone up valleys?" Macquarie asked.

"I've read all the accounts I could find of previous explorers all the way back to 1789 when marine Captain Watkin Tench led one and Lieutenants Dawes and Johnston made a more ambitious penetration of the Carmarthen mountains, as the Blue Mountains were called back then. All the explorers over the years have been stopped by obstacles such as waterfalls, impassable thorny bush, dead-end canyons, or vertical cliffs. I do not intend to follow waterways or climb cliffs but instead stay on the ridgelines.

"Lieutenant William Lawson, an army surveyor, is

accompanying me and will keep us moving along the highest ground. At every decision point, I intend to stay high and head for the next peak."

"It sounds like a practical approach, Your Excellency," Arthur said.

The governor asked, "Are there only the two of you, or are there more in your group?"

"William Charles Wentworth will accompany us."

"D'Arcy's son?" Macquarie asked.

"Yes, sir."

"What does he add to your effort?"

"He *wants* to go, is young and strong, and can afford to supply himself along with his servant and horses."

"Arthur, *you* should go," the governor said brashly. He turned, smiling, to Blaxland who appeared alarmed. "Of course, if Mr. Blaxland agrees."

Blaxland did not respond.

"Perhaps I should keep my thoughts to myself," the governor said. "Although I was thinking that with this drought, withered grasses, and shortage of water, perhaps Arthur could identify edible plants for the horses and find sources of water or plants high in moisture content. I know he could identify the quality of grasslands on the other side of the mountains if you are so fortunate as to reach the interior."

"Could you do that, Mr. Armstrong?" Blaxland asked, curious.

"I believe I could. I know more about our local flora and the natural sciences than most farmers."

"I should tell you at this point, Mr. Blaxland, that I cannot fund your highly speculative venture; however, I can reward it, if you are successful, with grants of at least one thousand acres for each man. Mr. Armstrong is about the same age as William Wentworth and would also be able to finance himself, I presume, if he's so inclined."

"Would you like me to go, Governor?" Arthur asked brightly.

"That's for you and Mr. Blaxland to decide. I was just thinking that with your expertise, I could rely on your report. Well, Mr. Blaxland, I don't know whether I've been helpful or not. Of course,

I applaud your original strategy and wish you great success."

"Thank you, Your Excellency." Blaxland shook Macquarie's outstretched hand, and he and Arthur walked out of the governor's office together.

When Arthur confirmed that he would like to join the expedition and could fund his own involvement by bringing a servant, his own horses, a hunting dog, and a packhorse carrying his supplies, Blaxland invited him to join his group of explorers. There would be a total of four gentlemen, four servants, eight horses, four packhorses, and at least five hunting dogs.

Nathaniel was pleased that Arthur had the gumption for such an adventure.

Moira was concerned for his safety. "Unlike your brother, Arthur, you've always shown good judgment. Are you sure you aren't gettin' yourself into something dangerous. I don't want you to injure yourself."

"I'll be fine, Mum. We have it planned for three weeks. Two weeks to find our way across the mountains and a week back. If Blaxland's idea of moving from one ridge to the next isn't possible, I'll be home earlier."

Nathaniel and Arthur chose emancipist Ellis Lench, their assistant overseer at the farm, to accompany Arthur. A large, strong, forty-year-old man, he had been a corporal under Nathaniel's command. The Armstrong's best hunting dog Robbie would go with them.

On the morning of May 11, 1813, the explorers Blaxland, Lawson, Wentworth, and Armstrong started out from Blaxland's house located a mile from the Nepean River. The party forded the river and entered a broad plain, a mile wide, situated at the base of the mountain. Years before, emus frequented the plain in the hundreds. Off in the distance, they saw emus in groups of ten or more running off. Blaxland led them up a valley that he said ran to the ridge. After three miles of difficult, steep terrain they stopped to set up camp for the night. The next day, they ascended to the first ridge of the mountains and walked over to a bluff that provided a view of the land below.

"This is as far as I've explored previously," Blaxland said to them.

This is as far as he's gone before! Arthur exclaimed to himself, aghast. Higher land loomed over them, except to the east from whence they had come. True this was something of a "ridge," because the land fell away to both sides, but it immediately rose up again to the west. He had expected a "RIDGE," *on top of the mountain!* so they could see where they were going. He wanted to say something, but the others seemed unconcerned.

"I'll get out my equipment to take elevation readings," Lawson said. "Then we can decide the best direction to go." Lawson and Blaxland determined that the highest ground was to the northwest, so the party headed off in that direction through increasingly thick woods. When riding became impossible, they had to dismount and lead their horses through the dense bush. They used their hatchets and axes to leave a narrow trail and cut slashes of bark off trees on two sides to indicate the direction they had come from and where they were headed.

Hearing their dogs barking wildly, they went to them and found them tearing apart a small kangaroo. They assumed the dogs had killed the animal until they saw a large eagle staring down at them from a nearby tree. Lawson speculated that the dogs had scared the eagle off its kill. It was late in the afternoon, so they decided to let the dogs finish their meal and camped nearby for the night.

Arthur and Wentworth found they enjoyed each other's company. They were both serious men and bookish. Wentworth was a bear of a man: thickly built, over six feet in height, with a large, broad face, and huge hands. His wild, reddish hair gave him a disheveled appearance. Arthur enjoyed talking to him about a wide range of topics. The only thing he didn't like about him was that he was completely self-absorbed; talking incessantly about himself and what he hoped to accomplish in life.

Making their way uphill the next day, the explorers rode into an area of undulating hills with wider-spaced trees. The grass was good for their horses, so the party had their midday meal there while the horses grazed. Further along they found several native huts, recently occupied. Beyond these, the forest turned into bush, and then thick, thorny bush. They decided to attack it the next morning.

Lawson climbed a tree in the morning and shouted down that the thick, thorny bush went on as far as he could see. Through the treetops he could see a mountain top. Because the bush looked impassable, Blaxland led the party westward hoping to find a way around the barrier.

Crouching in his saddle, Arthur threaded his horse through small openings in the bush where he could find them. It was impossible to ride in single file. The men often became separated and had to yell to each other to keep track of one another. Seeing some light coming through the dense, dark bush, Arthur directed his horse in that direction.

His horse suddenly lurched back and to one side, throwing Arthur into sharp twigs—"*Aahhh! Whoa!*"—he screamed. His eyes saw through the opening to a distant cliff beyond. His horse was trying desperately to back up from a precipice but had become ensnarled in the enveloping mesh of vines, bush, and small, thorny trees.

"*Steady Dusty! Steady!*"

Afraid his horse was going to panic, Arthur tried to jump off, but could not extract himself from the tangle. Through sheer strength, his large, strong horse powered himself backward into the dense mass and then turned and bolted, throwing Arthur. He landed on his back three feet from a one thousand-foot fall, straight down. Badly shaken, Arthur nevertheless had the presence of mind to yell to the others that there was a precipice to their left.

Wentworth brought Arthur's horse to him. The group turned back and then headed eastward only to run into another deep rocky precipice. Returning to their morning camp site, they decided over lunch that there was no choice but to cut their way through. Alternating two men working at a time, they cut a narrow path nearly three-quarters of a mile long by the end of the day.

The next three days they averaged two miles a day. Their water was running low and the horses were hungry with little to eat. Only the dogs were faring well, returning each night with fresh blood on their faces.

Blaxland chose Arthur and his employee Ellis Lench to go back with two packhorses approximately eight miles to a stream to replenish their water supply and collect grass for the other horses. Returning just before dark, Arthur found the men exhausted and demoralized, because the undergrowth had been particularly dense and thorny that day.

In the morning, Blaxland asked Arthur and Lench to begin the day's work. After an hour of backbreaking work, hacking and sawing and clearing, foot by foot, Arthur was cut, bruised, and dead tired. Replaced by Wentworth and his servant, Arthur dragged himself to his tent and collapsed. He slept until his next shift. In the late afternoon, the party finally broke out of the dense, thorny bush and were able to remount their horses.

They rode only a short distance before coming to a treacherous, rocky ridge no wider than thirty yards across with precipices on either side. The men got off their horses and led them across the ridge composed of loose, flat, slippery stones. Lawson's packhorse slipped and fell to its side, sliding several yards down the slope before lodging itself between two small trees. It rolled over onto it haunches and stood. Lawson and Blaxland were able to pull the horse by its reins back up the slope. The narrow ridge was a mile long before it widened out. Further along, the explorers came to a swamp with good water. The dogs had run ahead and killed a kangaroo. Blaxland and Lench rode quickly ahead to take the partially eaten kangaroo carcass from the dogs for the party's evening meal. Camp was made next to the swamp.

That night, Arthur, exhausted and weak, caught a chill. With the fire out, he shivered on the cold ground. By morning, sure that he had a serious fever, Arthur ate a little breakfast and vomited.

While the others were packing up and preparing to move on, Arthur said in a weak voice:

"I've decided to stay here by the water until this fever passes. I'm too sick to work, and I'd only hold you back. When I'm better, Ellis and I will follow your trail to catch up."

After some discussion, the leaders agreed to Arthur's proposal. Blaxland thought to himself that Arthur had been a disappointment. His naturalist training hadn't added up to much. He was a bit of a whiner and a slow worker who they would be better off without. Blaxland was sorry, though, to lose Lench, who was a tireless, strong worker.

Lawson checked his notes and estimated that they had come some twenty-two miles since crossing the Nepean River. If Arthur had to return, the trail back was well marked. The men said their goodbyes and wished Arthur a speedy recovery and quick reunion with them.

"Robbie. *Robbie!*" Arthur shouted when his dog started off with the others. Arthur slapped his leg a couple of times saying, "*Come here, boy!*" The dog returned to his side and sadly watched as the party rode off into the bush.

Three hours after the explorers had left, Arthur was feeling no better. He had a headache and could not stop shivering. "I've decided that we should return, Ellis, while I still have the strength to ride."

Ellis was not anxious to leave. "The sun is jus' gettin' high, sir. Why don't yer rest today an' make the decision tomorrow morning?"

"I'm so weak; I won't be able to work for days. My mind's made up, Ellis. I don't want to get worse and not be able to ride. Load the horses. I want to leave as soon as possible."

That day and the next, on their way back, Arthur was shaky and nauseated. He was unable to keep food down and could ride for only a few hours of each day. On the third day, he began to feel better. They arrived back in Parramatta on the fourth day.

Weeks later, after Blaxland had been quoted in the newspaper as saying, "We found grasslands sufficient to feed the stock of the entire colony for the next thirty years," Arthur invited Wentworth to the Armstrong's town house to hear him tell the story of what happened after he had left the explorers.

"In all, we traveled sixty-two miles through the mountains," Wentworth said. "You wouldn't have made it, Arthur, sick as you were. There was plenty more dense bush to hack through with larger thorns than what we went through together." He raised his hand to show the scars. "One night we heard natives around our camp and expected an attack, but the dogs chased them off.

"When we saw what looked like grasslands below we couldn't get the horses down the steep grade. We had to dig a narrow trail crisscrossing the slope for them and carry their loads down ourselves."

Governor Macquarie was true to his word. He granted Blaxland, Lawson, and Wentworth each one thousand acres in the new territory. He felt badly that he could not rightly grant Arthur any land.

◉

"Oh, Bennelong died," Nathaniel said to Moira as he read the *Sydney Gazette.*

"What a shame, that poor man," Moira said looking up from her sewing. "How did he die?"

"It doesn't say. It just says that 'He died on the third of January at Kissing Point on the Parramatta River.' Talks about him going to England and being alienated from his own people when he returned. Says he was 'troubled by consumption of alcohol'—he's not alone on that score. It notes that he 'was the leader of a group of natives who frequented the north shore.' That's what he told us when we saw him in the hospital years ago, remember?"

"Yes, he said it was a difficult life. It must be terrible to have to forage for food and beg to get by."

"He was buried amidst James Squire's orange trees."

"Does it say anything about a Christian burial?"

"No. He wasn't a Christian when I knew him."

"Is there no eulogy for him?"

"Yes, but it's hardly a tribute. You won't like it."

"Read it to me, though, won't you?"

"I must say, the *Gazette* is rather unfair and scathing: 'His propensity for drunkenness was inordinate; and when in that state he was insolent, menacing, and overbearing. In fact, he was a thorough savage, not to be warped from the form and character that nature gave him by all the efforts that mankind could use.'"

Moira put down her sewing. "Why must we so thoroughly reject and abuse the native people in their own homeland? It's little wonder that they drink to forget their problems after what we've done to them with so little thought of remorse. And it isn't right that we neglect their education and religious instruction. I wish we could do somethin' for them."

"It's a bit late for that, Moira, at least in this region. There are so few of them left."

Governor Macquarie also felt the need to do something for the Aborigines. He had been considering a request from a missionary, Reverend William Shelley, for a grant of crown land to establish a Native Institution for the education and conversion to Christianity of Aboriginal children. Shelley's idea was to separate native children from their parents at an early age so the connection with their backward primitive culture could be severed. He needed sufficient land to teach the boys farming and the girls household domestic services, so they could be hired by whites as farm workers and maids. He believed that their salvation, both in practical and religious terms, lay in their useful assimilation into the white society.

Macquarie granted Reverend Shelley twenty-seven acres along Parramatta Road. The Native Institution began operation in April 1814 with twelve children.

Nathaniel and Moira passed the entrance to the Native Institution every Sunday on their way to and from church in Parramatta. One morning after church they met Reverend Shelley. He was a tall, thin, cheerful, pink-cheeked man. Moira liked him immediately and complimented him for his good work, which prompted him to invite her to stop by sometime to see the institution.

A few Sundays later, after church, Moira asked Nathaniel to follow Shelley's carriage to see his Native Institution "for just a few minutes to satisfy my curiosity."

"I have a lot to do this afternoon, Moira," Nathaniel said, but acquiesced when he saw the look on her face. "All right, but just for a few minutes, if we don't leave the carriage."

The visit lasted for over two hours. After being shown around the facility, meeting the two teachers, and all twelve of the native children, Nathaniel was persuaded by the sociable reverend to become a benefactor. Moira willingly agreed to come two afternoons a week to teach the girls domestic skills and to assist in their reading of the Bible.

Moira was feeling anxious the first afternoon she rode into

the Native Institution to donate her time. Her anxiousness was ameliorated, though, by the joyful sounds of children singing: ". . . feur-five-six"—shuffle-shuffle-*clap*—"seven-eig't-nine"—shuffle-shuffle-*clap*—"ten-'leven-tulve"—shuffle-shuffle-*clap*—"t'irteen-feurteen . . ." She walked into the administrative building to meet Reverend Shelley thinking how clever the teacher was to utilize the natives' love of chanting and dancing to teach them counting.

◉

"Capt'n Armstrong! Capt'n Armstrong!" Nathaniel heard his name and banging on the front door of his town house as he roused himself from a deep sleep. It was after midnight. He knew the emotional and high-pitched man's voice was that of Corporal Jenkins who had served under him in the Sydney garrison. Jenkins saluted him when Nathaniel opened the door.

"Capt'n Armstrong, Charlie 'as bin knifed an' is in the hospital!" the thin, wiry, agitated man said.

"My son Charles?"

"Yus sir, he tol' me ter come an' tell yer! He's bin arrested fer *killin' a feller!"*

"Where was he knifed?"

"We wos in The Rocks at—"

*"NO!—where—on Charles's body—*was he knifed?"

"All ova—I don't know exactly where—he wos knifen him pretty bad when—"

Nathaniel grabbed the man's shoulders and shook him once, while looking directly into his eyes. He could tell he was intoxicated. "*Corporal Jenkins, listen to me!*"

"Yus, sir!" The man came nearly to military attention and looked with a shocked expression at Nathaniel.

"Calm down, Corporal, and *answer* my questions. Is Charles's going to live?"

"I think so, sir."

"Were you there when he was knifed?"

"Yus sir."

"Could he walk after the fight?"

"Yus sir. Well, a bit, he wos stabbed in the leg."

"Any place else?"

"Ah . . . an' he wos bleedin' from a cut on his arm . . . an' he wos stabbed in the chest."

In the chest!—where?

"Up high between his neck an' shoulder."

"Was he bleeding from the mouth or coughing up blood?"

"Dunno . . . but don't think so, sir."

"Good! I'm going to get dressed now before I go to the hospital. Thank you for coming to tell me, Corporal Jenkins. Is there anything else you want to tell me?"

"It worn't his fault, sir, we was jus—"

"I'm glad to hear that, Corporal, but I have to rush to the hospital now. I'll talk to you more tomorrow or the next day. Thank you for coming to tell me. Good night, Corporal."

"G'bye, sir. *I'm sorry*, sir."

Nathaniel closed the door and rushed upstairs, taking two steps at a time—a chest wound could be fatal!

He dressed quickly and rushed to the hospital. The front desk directed him to the basement lock-up section. Before he could see Charles, Nathaniel had to sign a log and submit to a search. An armed jailer gave him a chair to carry and led him to Charles's cell.

Charles heard them coming and was awake and smiling when his father walked into his cell. Nathaniel sat down next to Charles's bed. After Nathaniel confirmed that Charles felt as well as could be expected, he asked him what had happened.

"The man made a comment, and I answered him back. It was over nothin'. He was lookin' for a fight and pulled a knife with a eight-inch blade and stabbed me in the chest before I knew what happened. I pulled back, slipped, and fell to the floor. I thought that was it, but he motioned me up and said, 'I'm goin' to cut you up slow before I kills yer.' Everyone was standing back 'cos he was a big bastard with a long fucken knife. There wasn't no where to run. I had a folded knife in my pocket, but my right arm was pretty useless, an' I couldn't have got it out an' opened before he would've killed me. The son o' a bitch was big as a fucken house, Dad, and I thought *I'm dead!* He wasn't even mad—grinnin' when he slashed my right arm and then stabbed me in the right leg."

Nathaniel did not speak, anxious to hear his son's story and pleased to see that he was all right.

"I was going backwards and fell on my arse again and hit something really hard that I realized was a bottle. As I scooted back away from him, the bottle bit into my back, so I knew it was broken.

"The bastard grabbed my shirt and raised me up like he was going to gut me. I reached down with my left hand and grabbed the bottle, and without even looking at it, jabbed it as hard as I could into his throat. The blood just gushed out like a faucet all over me. I couldn't believe it. He grabbed his neck, coughed out some blood, and then just fell on top of me. He shook for a few seconds and then just died. There was blood all over me and all over the floor. I couldn't push him off and his blood just kept pumping out all over the place.

"I'm not worried about anything, though. Everybody said it was self-defense—even the police. There's plenty of witnesses. No one knows this guy. My mates will say this crazy sod was barmy as hell an' out t'kill somebody. What I'm most pissed off about is no one tried to help me or break it up. The bastard and his knife were just too fucken big. I feel lucky to be alive, Dad. I don't feel sorry at all about it. I'm *glad* I killed him; it was either him or me."

Nathaniel said, "You *should* feel sorry when it's the first man you've killed. Maybe you will tomorrow after the excitement passes."

"You didn't see his face, Dad. He was one mean, ugly bastard, and I know he wanted to kill me."

"I doubt he would have killed you, Charles; he was in control. It was a public place, and he'd hang for it. Sounds like the type who enjoys inflicting pain. But I wasn't there and maybe *he was* crazy. He misjudged you, that's for sure. You did what you had to do, lad, to protect yourself, and you didn't mean to kill him. That's what you must say before the magistrates.

"Just tell them the same story you told me, but leave out the part that you felt the broken bottle cutting into your back and don't say you're glad you killed him. Say you're sorry and show remorse. Stress that you grabbed the bottle to hit him with it and didn't know it was broken. And don't say you aimed for his throat. You were just trying to hit him with the bottle to defend yourself. Right?"

"That's the truth. I was just bloody lucky it was the broken end."

"And you feared for your life?"

"Damn right I did!"

"And you are *sorry* you killed him ... *right?*"

"Yes ... I'm sorry I killed *the fucker.*"

"Don't be an arse, Charles, this is no laughing matter. You don't want to go to jail."

"Dad, *don't worry!* Everybody said it was self-defense. I'm *not* going to jail. But I'll tell them I'm sorry and all that. I'm not *stupid,* you know."

Nathaniel looked away from Charles and ran his hand across his forehead. He had a headache.

"Look, Charles, after this is over, assuming you are found innocent of any wrongdoing, I want you to think about something. You almost died tonight. You need a break from your voyages. I want you to think about learning my side of the business. I want you to take a year off and work with me and my partner Henry."

"You mean in the *office?*"

"Yes, just for a year to become better rounded in the business. You'll need it if you ever want to become the top man."

"*No way,* Dad. I couldn't stand bein' cooped up in an office. No, I already work well with Henry. He's happy in the office, and I'm happy doin' the seafarin' an' tradin' side. It's a good marriage, and we both like it that way."

"*I have* something to say about it, you know!" Nathaniel said. "You could've lost your life tonight. You drink too much, and you're too wild and undisciplined. I *don't* like it! I want you to settle down some."

"Not going to happen, Dad. You know how I am. I'm only happy when I'm sailing. It's who I am. I'm good at it too. We're makin' a lot of money, aren't we? Soon I'll be a master. It's not the kind of life you want, but it's *my life* to live—not *yours.*"

Nathaniel was aggravated and ready to berate Charles when he realized that what his son had just said was true. "Well . . . my word, Charles, that was *well* said. It *is* your life to live; I shan't argue that, even though I don't agree with it . . . . You'll have to deal with your mother then. She wants you to spend more time at home. She says it's my fault . . . because she thinks you're like me, and I was the one who let you go to sea." Nathaniel fumbled for the right words. "You may look like me, with your auburn hair, but you're not like me. You're headstrong and impetuous like your mother."

"You were like that too, Dad, when you were young."

"No . . . not like you, Charles . . . I was always responsible, even when I was your age. I wish you'd think more about where you're heading, if you keep drinkin' and behaving like this."

At Charles's hearing before the magistrates, the provost marshal presented evidence that the dead man was an ex-convict with a long list of arrests. Witnesses testified that he had drawn a knife and wounded Charles who was unarmed. The court ruled self-defense, and Charles was released from custody to go free.

◉

Following the shooting death in 1810 of Tedbury, Pemulwuy's son, the frontier along the Hawkesbury River quieted. With the best land in the Hawkesbury District granted and settlers arriving in ever greater numbers, the governor opened the Nepean River southwest of Sydney to land-grant settlement. Beginning in 1814 there were increasing numbers of conflicts with the natives there. After several whites in the Camden area were killed in 1816 by marauding bands of Aborigines, causing settlers to flee their farms, Macquarie was besieged with requests for protection and forced to act. He sent the 46th Regiment on a punitive expedition with orders to "strike terror amongst the Aboriginal tribes but spare women and children, if possible." Any children orphaned or separated from their parents as a result of clashes were to be taken to the Native Institution in Parramatta.

Moira had been volunteering at the Native Institution for two years when eighteen disoriented Aboriginal children, twelve boys and six girls, were brought into the institution under army guard. Reverend Shelley met with the officer in charge. After the officer and his men had gone, Reverend Shelley explained to Moira and the teachers why the children had been brought to the institution. She was outraged and heartsick when she realized that the parents of the children had been killed and the children brutalized. Arriving home an hour before dinner, she knocked on the door of Nathaniel's study.

"Yes."

"May I talk to you."

"Of course, come in, dear."

"I'm very upset and have to talk to somebody, or I'll lose my mind."

"That serious, eh?"

She sat down hard in a stuffed chair. She explained what had happened. "These are *children*, Nathaniel, traumatized *children*. Some of them have been kept in jails for weeks. They're confused and frightened. The three oldest boys and the largest girl arrived in *chains!* The military just dropped them off and left as quickly as they could. We don't have beds for half of them. Some of them are going to have to double up or sleep on the floor with just blankets. And we're going to run out of food quickly. What is Governor Macquarie thinking? This doubles the number of children in one day. Reverend Shelley was surprised, although he said he had discussed the possibility of some children being brought to the institution—but not eighteen at one time! There are only two teach—"

"Moira please, stop, calm yourself. What can I do?"

"Have you ever talked to the governor about this?"

"No, I haven't, although I will if you think it would help."

"Well, it *would* help. We need a lot of help. I'm going to spend all day there tomorrow, and the reverend is going to Sydney Town to ask the governor for a long list of things. This is just ridiculous. Some of them may escape tonight. God only knows where they would go. Oh, those poor dears. The little ones are *so scared*, you have no idea."

I *know* how scared they are, Nathaniel thought to himself. His mind went back twenty years to the Hawkesbury and two, small, terrified children huddled together on a trail after he had just killed a man who could have been their father.

"There are a few extra beds stored in the barn," he said. "I'll have them taken over there tomorrow. We could also help with food."

"I'll make a list for the kitchen maid to fill," Moira said. "Will you talk to the governor?"

"Not until after Reverend Shelley talks to him tomorrow. I can't imagine that the governor won't provide everything he asks for. I fancy Macquarie didn't know the children were being delivered at all. He wouldn't know the details of his general order."

"How can the soldiers be so *heartless*, that's what I can't understand."

Nathaniel's mind would not leave him alone. If she only knew . . . her husband had been one of those "heartless" soldiers. She will never understand that *no one* wants to hurt small children—*that's not true*—but I don't want to think about that . . .

"Are you sure you want to continue putting yourself through this, Moira? You don't have to, you know."

"I *want* to. That's reason enough. Would you talk to the governor about doing something *positive* for the Aborigines?"

"Like what?"

"I don't know. Something that gets whites and blacks together as human beings."

"Hmm . . . Whites would come out for a native *corroboree*."

"What's that?"

"A meeting of two or more tribes where they gather to chant and dance, trade, throw their spears and such. It goes on for days."

"The governor could call for one. And to give the natives a reason for coming, he could offer them food, blankets, and tools. It would get whites and blacks together for peaceful reasons."

"That's a good idea, Moira, I'll talk to him about that."

◉

The Royal Botanic Gardens were established in 1816 as random paths through wild, overgrown plants. Governor Macquarie appointed Arthur the assistant superintendent and botanist. It was a paid position, but Arthur cared more about the opportunities it provided for botanical research. Arthur's association with Elizabeth Macquarie was to provide an additional benefit: he would meet his future wife through her.

Catherine Nesfield was the only child of widower Alfred Nesfield, an army captain who had served as Macquarie's aide-de-camp in India. At Macquarie's request, Captain Nesfield came to the town of Sydney in February 1817 to accept the position of secretary to the governor. The Macquaries gratefully welcomed the Nesfields into their household. Catherine was a shy, twenty-four-year-old woman who enjoyed her own company. An avid reader, she would closet herself away for days with a good book, leaving only for her daily walk through the botanic gardens. Not an unattractive woman, she was, nevertheless, prepared to enjoy her life as a spinster caring for her father. Elizabeth Macquarie would not hear of it; she knew just the right man: Arthur.

Mrs. Macquarie took the withdrawn woman on as a challenge and dressed her in the latest fashions, gave her a modern hairstyle, and improved her already fine features with beauty aids. Without telling her what was on her mind, Mrs. Macquarie invited Arthur to their quiet evening meals with the Nesfields.

At twenty-five, Arthur was inexperienced with women; in fact, he had never courted. He was pleased that Mrs. Macquarie was playing the matchmaker, but could think of nothing to say to Miss Nesfield at their dinners. She was equally ill at ease with him.

Mrs. Macquarie found the key to creating a relationship between Arthur and Catherine when she realized that the young woman had a knowledge of plants that she was too reticent to express at their dinners. She orchestrated Arthur's and Catherine's courtship through casual meetings in the botanic gardens while Arthur worked.

When near Arthur, Mrs. Macquarie would ask Catherine about a plant and draw Arthur into the conversation. They would then discuss genus and species, cultivating methods, grafting to improve flowering and fruiting, fragrance, and other such matters. After several such visits, Mrs. Macquarie found that the two young people did not object if she drifted away to carry out some chore or other responsibility. Their dinners became more animated and weeks later, Arthur introduced Catherine to his parents. With Mrs. Macquarie's encouragement, Arthur proposed marriage to Catherine just five months after meeting her.

Catherine accepted Arthur's marriage proposal gleefully. He was handsome, intelligent, and an admiring suitor from a wealthy family. She was told by her father that her future mother-in-law was an emancipist. He did not object to it but felt she should know. She did not care. Arthur and Catherine were married in St. John's Church in Parramatta on October 22, 1817.

Surprisingly, both Mr. and Mrs. Macarthur attended the couple's wedding and the reception afterward. John Macarthur had arrived back the previous month after receiving Colonial Secretary Lord Bathurst's approval to return on the condition that he not engage in politics.

Any hope Nathaniel had that John Macarthur had changed, after being banned from the colony for eight and a half years, was dashed when Macarthur expressed his dissatisfaction with Governor Macquarie.

"Many have written the House of Commons demanding the removal of Governor Macquarie because of his autocratic rule, grandiose building plans, spendthrift ways, and misuse of convict labor."

Nathaniel made light of it. "Ach, John, every governor we've had has had damning letters written about him to members of the House of Commons."

Governor Macquarie had told Nathaniel that Macarthur had sent a steady stream of letters to him over the years presenting reasons why he should be permitted to return. His foremost argument was to head the national wool project; however, Macquarie thought Mrs. Macarthur was doing remarkably well without the help of her troublemaking husband. After the governor had written back to Macarthur numerous times indicating that he had no way to change his orders to arrest him upon return, Macarthur changed his tactics and asked the governor to appeal to the Colonial Office on his behalf. This the governor simply refused to do, and wrote Macarthur to that effect. Macarthur then stopped writing and became the governor's enemy, intent on undermining him and working for his recall.

Macarthur continued. "Yes, but I believe Parliament or the colonial secretary will soon take action to appoint a select committee or royal commissioner to investigate the complaints and to consider Macquarie's policies and administration. The colonial secretary feels the governor disregards his instructions and does just as he pleases."

Nathaniel made a disagreeing face and asked, "For instance?"

"For instance . . . Macquarie was instructed not to form a bank, and he went right ahead on his own and authorized the formation of the Bank of New South Wales. That's one good example of many."

"You of all people, with your financial mind, John, know that with the proliferation of bogus promissory notes, legal disputes involving nonpayment, and lack of a stable currency, that we need the bank. I serve on its board of directors. We have official notes and coins now to serve as the colony's first legal tender. A depositor's money is safe and commercial loans can be made at a fair, stable interest rate. I don't see where that is a good example at all."

"I didn't say I *disagree* with the *need* for a bank, Nathaniel. What I said was, it's a good example of Macquarie not taking the time and effort to convince the colonial secretary of the need for the bank and instead doing just what he damn well pleases."

"Well, I don't want to get into this at my son's wedding reception, John. This is too festive an occasion to talk politics."

"You're right, Nathaniel. Pardon me."

"Your glass is empty, John; let's get ourselves another wine."

◎

As John Macarthur had predicted, the British government appointed a royal commissioner to inquire into the affairs of New South Wales. Criticism had grown loud in Parliament concerning the rising cost of the colony and Governor Macquarie's humanitarian policies, which were seen by some members of Parliament and Colonial Secretary Bathurst as lessening the fear of convict transportation. On September 26, 1819, Commissioner John Thomas Bigge arrived in the town of Sydney. A welcoming ceremony was held in front of Government House where Bigge's commission was read aloud and both the governor and Bigge gave speeches.

During Macquarie's speech, Bigge sized him up. I wonder whether he fully appreciates that I have the power to overrule his decisions? That makes me more the governor than he is. If he disagrees with me, his only recourse will be to appeal to the Colonial Office, which he will be reluctant to do.

Nathaniel studied Bigge, a small, impeccably dressed man with a roundish face and pink cheeks. He's a bit young for such an important position, Nathaniel thought. The chief justice of Trinidad . . . that's not good for us. He would have dealt with slaves there. I hope he doesn't liken slaves to convicts.

Bigge was articulate in giving his speech, but Nathaniel sensed a sullen, pedantic personality. A gloomy, little peacock of a man, Nathaniel concluded.

Bigge accepted Macquarie's offer to live in Government House. At Bigge's request, Macquarie provided him with three soldiers of his choosing to serve as his security detail. During the initial months of the investigation, the governor cooperated fully by making available all of his government records and introducing Bigge to anyone he wished to interview.

Months later, Macquarie asked Nathaniel to accompany him and Bigge on a tour of projects under construction in Sydney Town. When the governor entered the reception room of Government House, he said in his usual exuberant voice "Ah, Nathaniel, so nice to see you." They shook hands. "Commissioner Bigge should join us shortly. You've met, of course?"

"Yes, Your Excellency, at his welcoming ceremony and at a social function since then."

"I understand that he hasn't interviewed you yet."

"That's correct, sir, although I expect he will get around to me soon."

"Well, I told the commissioner that I consider him remiss. You arrived with the first fleet and have been a valued advisor to several governors, including me. He should have interviewed you by now."

"I'd like to contribute my thoughts, Governor."

" *'Pon my word,* I forgot . . . I understand Catherine has borne your first grandchild—congratulations!"

"Thank you, Governor, I'm just pleased that both the infant and Catherine are healthy."

"Have Arthur and Catherine named the child?"

"Gilbert. Gilbert Nathaniel Armstrong, actually."

"Ach—*well,* even greater congratulations are in order then."

Nathaniel smiled warmly.

"Oh, here comes the commissioner now," Macquarie said as Bigge approached.

After greetings, the three men walked out of Government House and into a waiting carriage, which headed west on Bridge Street. The governor said, "Mr. Bigge, I've asked Mr. Armstrong to accompany us today because he has participated in many of the improvements in Sydney Town and might want to add a comment from time to time."

Nathaniel said, "Thank you governor and Commissioner Bigge, it's a pleasure to accompany you," but, in fact, it was no pleasure at all. He knew the real reason Macquarie had invited him along was to hear his supportive comments and to keep the peace. During Bigge's first five months in Sydney, he and Macquarie had disagreed on most everything. Bigge had been gone from Sydney for the past three months visiting other areas of the colony.

"How was your trip to Van Diemen's Land, Commissioner Bigge?"

"Fine, fine, Mr. Armstrong," he responded, looking disinterested. "It was a productive trip."

The open carriage turned north on Macquarie Place and stopped at Macquarie Park where a sandstone obelisk stood.

The governor pointed at the obelisk. "This is the surveyor's starting point for measuring the distance of all roads from Sydney Town. From this one point, all maps and plans can be coordinated one to the other."

The carriage took them around the park then traveled east. It turned right and proceeded south on Macquarie Street. They rode past a large structure under construction.

"That will be the new government stables in the Gothic Revival style of architecture," Macquarie said. "It's beautifully situated, surrounded, as it is, on three sides by the botanic gardens. It will be a handsome structure when completed."

Nathaniel added: "The governor has sponsored the breeding of fine horses in the colony. We're reaping the benefits now, in that the army has first-rate mounted units."

Bigge nodded.

Further along, Macquarie pointed out the new hospital, an accomplishment he was sure Bigge would approve of, because it was an essential facility for the good health of all. "It's a fine piece of architecture, don't you agree," he said to Bigge, who did not respond.

Acting as though Macquarie had asked them both, Nathaniel said, "Indeed, a very necessary and good-looking building, sir."

They passed through the gates of the Hyde Park Barracks, a project nearly completed, and made a circle around its forecourt as Macquarie explained the need for the facility and the details of its Georgian sandstone and brick facade.

Bigge stared ahead.

The governor stopped the carriage as it left the barracks and pointed south. "The site for St. Mary's Chapel is immediately south. Private funds are being raised for it now. The Treasury will incur no cost; the government's only contribution will be crown land on the periphery of The Domain."

"A large proportion of our population is now Catholic," Nathaniel said. "For practical as well as religious reasons, we need to make them feel welcomed. It's a hardship for them to be without a place of worship."

"Your wife is Catholic, is she not?" Bigge asked pointedly.

Nathaniel wondered how he knew that and why he would want to make a point of it. "Yes sir, she is. She has long desired a proper Catholic church in which to worship."

"Where does she worship now?"

Although Nathaniel could see where Bigge was heading, he could think of no way to avoid playing into his hands. "St. John's in Parramatta."

"*Ah*, an Anglican Church, I *see*," Bigge said, making his point that the Catholic chapel was unnecessary.

The governor spread his arms wide. "Ahead will be Queen's Square. Planned as a grand European-like quadrangle, designed by Francis Greenway and me. He's a brilliant English convict architect whom I pardoned recently for his valuable service to the Crown. He designed the barracks behind us and the Georgian courthouse under construction ahead." Macquarie tapped the elbow of the coach driver. "Proceed toward the courthouse, please." He continued: "Greenway also designed the school being built across from the courthouse. The large quadrangle will serve as the civic center for the entire community, where festivals of all kin—"

"That's enough, sir," Bigge rudely interrupted. "Coachman, please stop the coach!"

Bigge opened the coach door and alighted in an obvious huff. The governor and Nathaniel followed.

"Would you please excuse us, Mr. Armstrong?" Bigge asked. "We have government issues to discuss."

"Yes, of course," Nathaniel complied courteously, even though the governor looked at him with anxious eyes.

Nathaniel walked some distance away from the two men but clearly heard Bigge unleash a tirade on Macquarie.

"These extravagant and expensive buildings are an outrage, sir. They're nothing less than embellishments to your own pride! This, this is a *penal* colony, for God's sake!"

What? The governor was taken aback. He thought Bigge would be impressed by the construction projects that were improving and beautifying the town; projects constructed under challenging circumstances and using mostly unskilled convict labor.

"Most of what you've shown me today, so proudly, are unnecessary and expensive buil—*baubles!*"

"I *protest*—" Macquarie said indignantly.

"What could you be thinking, Governor? While Britain stands

on the brink of financial ruin, you've been wasting His Majesty's precious money on these . . . these monuments to *yourself.*"

"To myself? They're neces—"

"Don't tell me they're *necessary*. This is a *penal* colony, man—not your personal estate! And naming everything after yourself and your wife! If it's not Macquarie this, it's Macquarie that, and there's Elizabeth Street, Elizabeth Bay, and Elizabeth this and that!"

"SIR! I cannot allow you to—"

"GOVERNOR! Are there no limits to your eponymous vanity? Have you no humility, sir?"

"This is grossly unfair, Commissioner. I MOST STRONGLY PROTEST!"

"*Protest* all you like! *I* have complete authority to override *any* of your actions. If you disagree, you may appeal to Lord Bathurst," Bigge said. "I doubt you'll find a sympathetic ear though. You've overstepped your authority and shown poor judgment in these lavish undertakings."

Macquarie was speechless. How rude!—and *attacking* Elizabeth!

"You *will* immediately convert this courthouse to an Anglican church," Bigge ordered. "It's much too grand for a courthouse." (After Greenway added a spire, the courthouse-turned-church was consecrated as St. James's Church by Reverend Samuel Marsden.)

Macquarie was incredulous, his mouth gaping as he looked at Bigge and then at the courthouse. "But it *looks* like a courthouse . . . not at all like a church. Moreover, I've already laid the foundation stone for St. Andrew's Cathedral."

"I want you to stop work on that and the city square around it that you've planned with this Greenway fellow. A town of fifteen thousand residents does not need anything so lavish—a cathedral—*my word!*" He pointed at the school under construction. "And that will serve nicely as your courthouse."

Nathaniel thought, it's only a matter of time before Macquarie will tender his resignation again, and this time Bathurst will accept it. It's clear that the commissioner sees the Sydney Town as little more than a penal settlement.

Some weeks later, Macquarie showed Nathaniel an essay

written by John Macarthur at the request of Bigge. "I'd like you to take a few minutes to read it and tell me what you think. It's confidential. Bigge doesn't know I've been given a copy."

Nathaniel read the two-page document. It was Macarthur's vision for the colony. Like everything he wrote, it was well written and cogent. He recommended to Bigge that a body of men of real capital be established who would support the government as aristocrats, each granted at least ten thousand acres to produce wool for export to England. Most of the convicts should be removed from towns, where they were involved in all manner of depravity, to work in the country as shepherds, laborers, and domestic servants for the landowning gentry. Only the upper classes should be permitted to serve as magistrates and superintendents of police who would prevent the lower order of people from disrupting the public tranquility.

Nathaniel and the governor discussed how Macarthur's vision must appeal to Bigge, a social climber and former chief justice of a slave colony.

The next time that Nathaniel saw Bigge was at the Parramatta *corroboree*. Macquarie had embraced Moira's idea and organized the first government-sponsored *corroboree* shortly after Nathaniel had proposed it to him. It had become an annual event in Parramatta. It was tame compared to the wild native *corroborees* Nathaniel had witnessed in the first years of the colony. Because the local tribes had been decimated, it was now primarily a display of native dancing and chanting for the white dignitaries, who provided gifts and a feast after the event. Early native *corroborees* attracted many clans and hundreds of natives and lasted for days. Macquarie's *corroborees* typically attracted well less than a hundred natives and a handful of curious settlers, soldiers, and officials. Moira and another teacher brought the children from the Native Institution to read aloud from the Bible before the governor, Commissioner Bigge, and tribal elders.

At the height of the corroboree, Macquarie ceremoniously hung a crescent-shaped, brass breastplate, inscribed "King of Sydney," around the neck of the native Bungaree. He was well-known as the native interpreter who had sailed with Matthew Flinders, naval explorer, to accomplish the first circumnavigation of Australia in 1802. "King" was a grandiose title because Bungaree led only his four wives and their numerous children and a few others of his despoiled tribe, but Macquarie knew Sydney's remaining Aborigines needed a leader and hoped to elevate Bungaree to the role.

Nathaniel found himself standing beside Commissioner Bigge and asked, "What do you think of the *corroboree*, Commissioner?"

"It's all very interesting and entertaining," he answered with a hint of condescension, "and shall be a good story to tell back home."

"And the education of the natives?"

"Reverend Marsden has tried to educate these people but concluded they were too primitive and finally gave up all hope of success. It's well meaning, I grant you, but when these children return to their native tribes they will forget all they've learned."

That was Nathaniel's concern as well. "I too have reservations about the Native Institution. My wife volunteers there to save their Christian souls as well as to educate them. But over the years, I've seen that the native people have no interest in farming or trades, being employed at our farms, or any other kind of paid employment. They don't care about our work ethic, values, and, for that matter, our God. So, I tend to agree with you."

For the first time since he had met him, Bigge smiled at him and asked, "What are your hopes for the future of the colony, Mr. Armstrong?"

It was an unexpected question coming from Bigge, who had already accomplished one of his main objectives: Macquarie's resignation had been accepted by the colonial secretary. Nevertheless, Nathaniel welcomed the opportunity to be interviewed.

"The Sydney and Parramatta region has become attractive to emigrants from England. I'd like to see the British government provide free passage to emigrants of all classes to provide the workers, artificers, tradesmen, and craftsmen we need here."

"Yes, the British press *has* identified New South Wales as a colony of genial climate and opportunity. However, the government cannot afford a *paid* emigration policy, but men of capital can be attracted by land grants and government assistance to come here on their own."

Nathaniel saw the opportunity to promote the elimination of convict transportation to the region. "I fear that such men of capital will quickly find it repugnant to live in a penal colony and yearn for an end to convict transportation."

"I understand that yearning, sir, and agree that most convicts should be removed from towns, except for essential labor, to avoid temptation and vice. They should be sent to work in the country as shepherds and the recalcitrant ones to harsh, isolated penal outposts. *Terror* needs to be added to their punishment. It's the only thing people of the lowest order understand. Transportation must act as a deterrent to crime."

Nathaniel agreed; he wanted the convicts out of the area. "Why not repeat the Sydney Cove experience in other locations then? Use the convicts to clear the bush and lay the foundations for new ports and towns?"

"My recommendation exactly, my good man," Bigge said. "We are in complete agreement. Of course, this would put an end to the extravagant building projects in Sydney Town, which you seemed to support."

"If we are given some degree of self-government, we can raise taxes to provide our own public improvements. That is why I strongly advise for an assisted emigration policy. Within ten years, we could easily triple our population."

"The House of Commons and the colonial secretary have sent me to investigate convict transportation not to recommend an emigration policy."

Nathaniel thought to flatter his ego. "But of course, Commissioner, your recommendations may be a turning point in our colony's evolution. I see a day when Australia will be one of the jewels of the British Empire and transportation of convicts will be unacceptable to Australians, on both moral and excessive cost grounds, and will be discontinued by the mother country. If you were to recommend such a farsighted emigration policy it could replace the need for convicts altogether."

"Ah, you fancy yourself a visionary, I see, Mr. Armstrong. Well, your vision is too far into the future for me. Transportation will continue for years to come, I assure you. Most likely, long after we are dead and gone. I am concerned with how these convicts are used to further commerce and relieve the financial burden to the British Treasury."

"To promote commerce, free trade should be permitted and unfair import duties in England should be eliminated to enhance our economic growth," Nathaniel said.

"You raise sheep for meat, I believe."

"That's correct, sir."

"Why have you not embraced your neighbor's national wool project? I've been curious to ask you."

"I'm somewhat at a loss to answer that. I've involved myself in other endeavors and projects and doubted whether fine wool would ever be embraced by Great Britain. High import duties on our wool continue to make it a marginal business."

"Here again, sir, I agree with you. I will recommend that they be removed—entirely!"

"A very sensible recommendation, sir. I commend you."

"Thank you, I will also recommend that men of capital be granted interior land of at least ten thousand acres each and the convict labor to assist in producing wool for export. I believe it to be the key to economic growth of the colony. These large-capital pastoralists would be assigned convicts in proportion to their assets invested and would maintain the convicts at no cost to the government. They would raise sheep to produce fine wool for export, which would earn income for the colonists and reduce the financial burden of Britain."

This was Macarthur's vision of creating a landed aristocracy that would exclude emancipists.

"Would men of capital presently residing in the colony, who are emancipist, be granted such acreage for wool growing as part of the national wool project?"

"I was thinking of it primarily as a way to entice emigration from England."

"I assume, of course, that the main proponent of the program, my neighbor Mr. Macarthur, would be able to participate."

"Certainly."

"But not wealthy emancipists, such as Andrew Thompson, Simeon Lord, and Henry Kable?"

"Humph! A most interesting and revealing choice of men. They are adventurers all, untrustworthy men, not to be assisted by the government to accumulate more wealth than they have now. It would only serve to upset the governance of the colony. I shall recommend the granting of crown land and government assistance only to *gentleman*."

"Surely you realize, sir, by denying land to emancipists, even when they have the capital, you are assisting in the creation a landed aristocracy, an elite ruling class in the English mold. In light of the American and French revolutions, you cannot seriously be considering such an outdated form of government."

"*Outdated!* My God, my good man, the *English model* of government has created the grandest society in the history of mankind. The French revolutionary rabble, led by their pretend emperor Napoleon has been defeated. The bankrupted Americans may still yet beg to return to the British Empire."

Nathaniel shook his head in disagreement. "Would you deny emancipist, as I've sadly heard is your intention, the right to high office, to practice law, and to sit on juries?"

"*Of course.* It's repugnant to the morals of free men to expose their life and property to a jury of ex-convicts. Why should one who has chosen to break the law be permitted to practice it or judge the lawfulness of others. Why, it's *ridiculous and offensive!*"

"You realize, of course, that we have a special situation here in our colony. Emancipists greatly outnumber exclusives."

"Come now, ten percent of the population in England easily rules over the others."

"I'm disappointed, Commissioner Bigge, I fear your proposals are both out-of-date and insensitive to our unique circumstances here. The exclusives' days are surely numbered."

"And you, sir, are spouting *Jacobean* sentiments against the king and our English form of government. I should not be surprised. You are after all, a Scot, and do not fully embrace the English model that has been so lavish in its gifts to you."

"I believe we Scots have added *immeasurably* to the union of our two countries."

"And your wife is an *emancipist*, is she not?"

"You use that as a pejorative term of condescension, sir, which I find offensive."

Bigge did not want to infuriate this large man with a scarred face. "I did not say *ex-convict* out of respect for her. What other term would you have me use?"

"I have no objection to the use of the term, only the sniveling, rude, and *disrespectful* way you said it!"

"I only used the term because it places our conversation appropriately within context. But since you object to my use of it, allow me to assure you that I meant no disrespect to your wife or to you, sir." He turned to two of his bodyguards who had drawn near when they heard the angry exchange. "There's no problem, men. Let's go."

Chapter 7

Emancipists Prevail

Having just returned from Calcutta, Charles sought out his father and found him in his gentlemen's club. They ate dinner together there, and then Charles oddly said he was going back to the ship to sleep, instead of sleeping at their Sydney house. The reason he gave was that he had to rise early to oversee the unloading of the ship. When the work was completed in two days, he would go to Parramatta to visit his mother.

Two evenings later, Charles showed up unexpectedly at their Sydney house while Nathaniel was having dinner alone. Another place setting was brought out, and Charles joined his father. Near the end of the meal, Charles abruptly said:

"I got a surprise to tell you, Dad, get yourself ready. . . . I got myself married!"

"Ach, to whom!—in the past two days or on your trip?"

"In Calcutta."

"Is she Indian?"

"*Hell no!* She's a white girl. Her father was a sergeant who died in the war, and she's been livin' with her mother. I've bin seein' her my last two trips there. Her mother died, so she was waitin' for me to return. She didn't have any family left there, so she wanted to get married. We did it in front of this bloke; he wasn't a pastor, something like a justice of the peace. He didn't make us sign any papers, though, so I think it's not legal."

"What's important is . . . do *you* consider yourself married?"

"I don't know. I think you have to have a marriage license or have it recorded in a church to be legal. Do you and Mum have marriage papers?"

"Yes we do. But what I'm asking you *is*—do you *want* to be married to this woman, or are you still making up your mind?"

"I *like* her, but I'm wonderin' whether I've made a big mistake. This is going to change my *whole life!*"

"If she's a good woman . . . By the way, *is* she a good woman?"

"She's not a whore, if that's what y'mean. I think I'm probably her first."

"Well then, *being* a good woman, she thinks she's married, I suspect."

"Aye, she thinks we're married, and I don't want to hurt her feelings."

"What's her living situation in Calcutta? Does she live alone in a house?"

"No, they were renting, so we just left."

"Where is she now?"

"On the *Southern Star* in my first mate's quarters."

"Oh . . . that explains it. I've been wondered about that."

"I've been trying to make up my mind what to do. Mom's goin' t'be really upset."

"My goodness, lad, *don't* worry about your mother. She can handle anything you boys throw at her, except injury or death. Don't worry about her. What do *you* want to do! How much do you care for this woman? She must know you're having second thoughts by now. You have to shit or get off the pot, mate! It isn't fair to keep her hanging like that. Is she pregnant?"

"Na, at least not when we got married; she hasn't said anything."

"What are you afraid of? You're nearly *thirty-two,* Charles, *start* taking some respon—" Nathaniel stopped himself.

"*What?* Go ahead and say it!" Charles said.

"No, I'm sorry, Charles . . . I *know* it's a big decision, not to be taken lightly."

"I've thought *a lot* about it, Dad. All the way back, *day and night*. It's driving me barmy, but I can't seem to make up my mind! I guess I'll do it."

"Think it through, son. Answer the important questions. I can answer one of them for you—you can *afford* to get married. If you can answer 'Yes' to your own questions, then you ought to commit yourself to this marriage."

"What kind of questions?"

"Is she the best woman you've met so far? Do you want to have children with her? Will she treat you right, and can you trust her? Are you able to enjoy each other's company, or do you argue all the time? Do you have more than sex in common? I could think of many more. Write them down and answer them yourself. Just *decide* and stop torturin' the poor woman."

Charles's face lit up with an idea. "I want *you* to meet her, Dad, go to the ship with me right now!"

"*No*, not me. I'm not going to make *your* decision for you, lad. If you decide to give her some money and put her in a hotel room and walk away that will be on *your* conscience, not mine. It's *your* decision."

"Aw . . . Dad."

"I'm telling you *this* though, Charles. You are *not* going to introduce her to your mother until you are *committed* to this marriage. In fact, as soon as you introduce her to your mother, you two are going to get married properly in a church in front of your family—so there it is.

"I hope you make the right decision for *you*. I say 'you' because I care more about you than her at this point. However, as soon as we meet your *wife*, I'm sure your mother and I will start caring for her too."

Two days later, Charles did introduce his wife, Sarah, to Moira and Nathaniel. Ten days after that, Reverend Fulton married them in St. John's Church in Parramatta with the Armstrong family and close friends present.

○

Moira finished her sewing session at the Native Institution and watched her students put their sewing materials into baskets. While wrapping a length of thread around a spool, she wondered what would become of the girls in the new year after the institution closed. Commissioner Bigge's recommendation that the government should discontinue funding of the institution had been approved, and Reverend Shelley had not been able to raise adequate private funds to continue.

She did not mind terribly, for it was too long a ride since the institution had been relocated to Blacks' Town, a land grant set aside by Governor Macquarie for Aborigines.

Looking back over her eleven years of volunteering, Moira could see that 1823 had been the turning point. That year several students died of an intestinal ailment and a thirteen-year-old student was killed in a dispute with another native. His violent death was followed by ritual payback injuries. Remembering that troubling time gave her a sick feeling in the pit of her stomach. The deaths combined to make the Parramatta institution a place of death and ghosts feared by the Aboriginal students and their elders. The nearby landowners had been happy when the institution was closed and relocated to Blacks' Town.

"That's right, girls . . . walk orderly and quietly," she heard Reverend Shelley saying as the girls filed out the door. She walked with him out to her waiting carriage.

"You will give my best regards to Dorrie, won't you?" he asked. Dorrie had left the institution at the mandatory age of fourteen. A delightful girl, she had been a favorite student of the reverend and Moira.

"Yes, of course, I shall, Reverend," Moira said as she thought how old and gray he had become in the past few years.

The coachman shook the reins to start the horses toward the main road. Moira glanced back at the institution wondering what use it would be put to after the end of the year.

A very pregnant Dorrie sat sewing on a bench, her back against the wall of her hut, when Moira was driven down the rutted dirt track into the small settlement. Dorrie looked up from her sewing and waved. She enjoyed the occasional visits by Mrs. Armstrong and other whites from the Native Institution. Their visits were her only pleasurable interaction with the white world.

Moira looked about for Dorrie's "husband"; she did not know whether they were properly married or not. For one reason or another, she had never been able to engage him in a conversation. He seemed to avoid her. Usually, Moira would see him in the distance, working in their small garden or sitting with his friends in front of one of their huts.

If she ever talked to Dorrie's man, Moira intended to compliment him. Their hut was better maintained than most, and they had a cow, a few pigs, some chickens, and a garden. Dorrie had told her that he did odd jobs when he could find the work.

"My, don't you look the picture of health, ready to give birth to another little darlin," Moira said cheerily, concealing her dismay at how drawn the petite young girl looked in her dusty white dress.

"T'baby bin due fer a week now," Dorrie said. In the three years since leaving the institution, her English had deteriorated. "Do ya likim a cuppa tay, Mrs. Armstrong?"

"No, thank you, Dorrie," Moira said as she playfully ruffling the hair of Dorrie's one-year-old son, who was playing with a toy in the dirt. She sat down on the bench and opened a basket between herself and Dorrie. "I have some jams and syrup for damper cake, and some other treats I know your son will like."

"Oh, t'ank you, ma'am. 'E'll like t'at."

The coachman carried over two large boxes and looked questioningly at them.

Dorrie pointed at the open front door of her hut. "T'em two udder boxes is rig't inside t'door."

He stepped inside, placed the two boxes down and picked up two similar boxes, which he carried to the carriage.

One of the industries of the Native Institution was the seaming and repairing of cloth sacks used for seed and wool. After leaving the institution, Dorrie had been permitted to continue this work to earn a little extra money. Moira paid her for the two boxes assuming Dorrie's work was at its usual high standard.

Moira stood and picked up a long coat she had laid down on the end of the bench. "I have some seamstress work you could do for me, dear, if you like." She put on the coat.

With some effort, Dorrie stood as Moira buttoned the coat.

"See how it's too tight under the arms right down to the waist. I need you to let out the seams an inch or so." Moira giggled. "I've been eating too many pies lately, I'm afraid."

Dorrie smiled and muffled titters with her hand.

Moira unbuttoned the coat and handed it to Dorrie, so she could examine the seams. She lovingly handled it and after a few seconds told Moira her price to do the work.

"That will be fine, Dorrie. It's a winter coat so I won't be needing it for a while. With the baby due, don't worry about completing it by the time I or someone else comes for the sacks next month."

"*Cooee*"—come here—"Dorrie!" A man's brusque voice called from inside the hut. Dorrie gave Moira a rueful smile.

"I must be goin' anyway, Dorrie," Moira declared. "Do let me know whether there's anythin' I can do after the little darlin' arrives."

◉

"Sarah!"

"Don't *yell* up to her, Charles, it's rude," Moira criticized as she took off her raincoat.

Charles walked up the grand staircase several steps and hollered less loudly. "Sarah! He's slept long enough. Get Duncan up. Mum and Dad are here." He walked down to his parents who were handing their raincoats to the maid after being received into Charles's house by the butler.

"I'll pass your message on to your wife, sir," the butler said to Charles as he started up the stairs.

"Good, Robert." To his parents, Charles asked, "Is it still raining hard?"

"Yes, thank goodness," Moira said. "It's been so hot. The crops need the rain. This will cool it off for the baby. How is the little dear?"

"He's great, though he wakes me up every night with his

crying—sometimes twice a night! How much longer will *that* go on?"

"He's *only* two months old!" Moira laughingly answered. "It could go on for months. You were hungry twice a night, so Duncan could be just like you."

It was a week before Christmas 1827. Charles had invited his parents and Arthur's family to his house to view his Christmas decorations and for drinks and dinner.

"*Oh,* here comes Arthur and Catherine," Charles said as he ran halfway up the stairs while yelling, "*Robert!* My brother's carriage just pulled up to the portico."

"*Coming, sir!*" the butler answered frantically. "Coming, sir." He stepped lively down the stairs as the front door was knocked. A maid appeared and moved quickly across the domed salon to take her place next to the coat closet.

Nathaniel had moved toward the door to open it, but stepped back when he realized that it was important to Charles that his butler and maid properly receive his guests, even though they were his own kin.

"Let's move into the drawing room," Charles encouraged his parents.

"They're *here!* Charles," Nathaniel said disdainfully and turned to greet Arthur, Catherine, and seven-year-old Gilbert coming through the door.

"*Grandpa!*" shouted Gilbert, who rushed to Nathaniel and threw his arms around his waist.

Nathaniel picked him up and hugged him. "My, you're almost *too heavy* to pick up now—such a big boy!"

After greetings and discussion about the rain, they all moved into the drawing room for drinks and to view the Christmas tree and other decorations. Sarah came down the stairs with a maid who was carrying the baby Duncan.

While the baby was passed around, Charles pointed out not only the expensive Christmas decorations but the rugs, paintings, furniture, moldings, and other decorations and finishes of the exquisite room. He took pride in saying that this item came from Bengal and that item from China and some other item from England. The large, extravagant house had taken nearly two years to build and furnish. He and Sarah moved in just before she gave birth to Duncan.

Charles's interest in fine things followed his marriage to Sarah. Before then, he had no interest in money, provided he had enough to cover his basic needs and to live a free and easy life. He relied on his father to provide his pay and sufficient funds for each voyage. Prior to his first voyage, he had told Nathaniel:

"You keep my share of the profits and invest it for me, Dad. I know you'll be fair with me. Don't tell me how much there is, 'cos I'll ask for it an' jist piss it all away."

Shortly after Charles married Sarah, Nathaniel said, "It's high time we go over your financial situation."

They met in Star Trading Company where Nathaniel showed Charles an accounting of all their ventures over the past fifteen years and the value of the company's ships, warehouse, equipment, and inventory. Unable to hold Charles's attention, Nathaniel finally gave up and simply told him he was a rich man worth approximately fifteen thousand pounds, of which eight thousand was readily available and the remainder constituted his percentage interest in Star Trading Company.

"Gawd, that's a lot of bloomin' quid, Dad," Charles said. "What should I do with it?"

"Why don't you buy a house in town for you and Sarah. You'll have a family before too long. A house in town will always go up in value over time. It'll be a good investment."

Rather than buy an existing house, Charles hired a contractor to build a large house to his specifications that would showcase his wealth and success.

◎

"How is Arthur, Mr. Armstrong?" William Charles Wentworth asked Nathaniel. "I see him so seldom these days."

"He's in very good health, Mr. Wentworth, thank you for asking. His wife and son are fine as well. He's quite busy at the Royal Botanic Gardens and managing our farm, you know."

"Yes, of course, the botanic gardens have become a delightful place to spend a Sunday afternoon. He's not much interested in politics, though, is he?"

"No, not much, unlike his father."

"Which brings me around to the reason for my visit. I'd like to interview you regarding your views, as a senior member of the Legislative Council, regarding the Judicature Act recently passed by the British Parliament."

Three years after being one of the explorers who had found the way across the Blue Mountains, Wentworth sailed to England to study law. He returned in 1824 with another lawyer Dr. Robert Wardell, who had been the editor of a newspaper. The two of them had a grand plan: To start the first independent, uncensored newspaper in Australia to achieve a free press and then use the newspaper to foster a home-grown constitution, representative self-government to replace autocratic rule, and trial by jury; all fundamental rights provided in the British Constitution. They intended to champion emancipists in their quest to be accepted as rehabilitated, full citizens with all the rights of the exclusives. Wentworth and Wardell named their newspaper *The Australian* and audaciously published it without government approval. Governor Brisbane decided to allow "freedom of the press" as an experiment and lifted censorship on the *Sydney Gazette* that had been controlled by the government for twenty-one years.

Nathaniel answered his question:

"I think the Judicature Act is a good first step in the direction of what I and others have worked hard for, and what your newspaper has been advocating: trial by jury, a more representative Legislative Council by increasing the number of members from seven to fifteen, and real power beyond advisory to reject a proposal of the governor."

"Are you disappointed that trial by jury applies only to civil cases and not to criminal ones?"

"No. Once trial by jury is successful in civil cases; criminal cases will follow."

"I believe you proposed that at least some of the additional members to the Legislative Council should be elected instead of appointed by the governor."

"Yes, I proposed that. Unfortunately, it was not accepted by the governor or the British Parliament."

"Are you disappointed?"

"I'm willing to advance slowly in the right direction, one step at a time."

"Aren't these improvements to the Legislative Council rather meaningless, since Governor Darling has created an Executive Council of exclusives to advise him and seldom seeks the Legislative Council's advice or makes proposals to it?"

"You may recall that a year and a half ago, I threatened to resign from the Legislative Council because of the formation of the Executive Council. Instead, I joined with other councilmen to press the British Parliament to give us the power to reject a government proposal unacceptable to us. The Judicature Act conveys that power to the Legislative Council, which makes us relevant once more."

Wentworth asked, "Why has the Governor Darling not placed John Macarthur on his Executive Council? He is after all the leader of the 'pure-merino' exclusives."

"You should ask Governor Darling that."

"Have you heard that Darling and Macarthur violently disagreed over the composition of the Executive Council and the governor accused him of erratic behavior?"

"No, I haven't heard that."

"So you were not among those who heard the governor say that he 'doubts the soundness of Macarthur's mind because he acts like a wayward child and remains at home brooding.' "

"I cannot confirm or deny such a statement by the governor. And I'd advise you to think twice before printing such a libelous quote questioning the mental state of such a brilliant and litigious man."

Despite Nathaniel's evasive answer, he had seen a steady decline in John Macarthur's mighty mind over the past few years.

◉

Charles's ship *Star* *of the Orient*, heavily laden with cargo from Canton, sailed out of the Pearl River on June 21, 1829, with Master

Max Hewer at the helm. The weather was fine, but hot, with a clear sky, calm sea, and moderate west-southwest wind. Charles stood on the quarterdeck next to Hewer taking in the fresh sea air and enjoying the view. The bustling Portuguese colony of Macao was to his right, and the open waters of the South China Sea lay ahead. Astern, the afternoon sun glistened on the water amid the East Indiamen and junks plying the waters. The *Star* was gleaming, her wood deck having been polished with holystones, gunwales newly painted, and ropes neatly coiled on deck.

This was Master Hewer's first voyage with Charles. Henry Stevenson, Charles's first mate, had died of a stomach ailment and fever in port. Hewer was a navy-trained master, who came highly recommended by the Admiralty office in Canton. He had sailed in the Orient for years and knew its waters well. At forty-eight, he was thirteen years older than Charles. Rather than call him "master," Charles chose to refer to him as "first officer."

Charles set the course of his square-rigger southeast by south for Mindoro Strait in the Philippines. The first leg of their voyage to Sydney was the most perilous, 750 miles of open water across the South China Sea, without so much as an island to lay up to for repairs or a harbor to shelter from a storm.

"She's sailin' sluggishly, bein' so heavily loaded," Hewer said to the helmsman when he turned over the wheel to him.

Charles had approved every item purchased by the ship's purser. They had bought more tea than intended because the price was depressed. In addition to tea, they bought silk, chinaware plates, cups, tea sets, bowls, vases, statutes, cabinetry, and hand-painted fans. The heavy boxes of porcelain were placed in the bottom of the cargo hold as ballast, with the lighter boxes of tea, silk, and fans on top. The cabinetry, in boxes cushioned by straw, was placed in various locations on the second deck. Some of the extra cargo, casks of water, and barrels and boxes of food were lashed to the upper deck under the longboat and in other locations protected from the weather by tarps.

Over six weeks, Charles had been involved in the price negotiations with the *hongs,* Chinese trading houses, and loading the ship. He was anxious to get back to sea and felt sure that this was going to be one of his most profitable voyages.

He trusted that the *Star of the Orient* could easily carry the weight of the extra cargo. She was a three-masted, three-deck merchantman, 132 feet in length, built to Charles's specifications. The bilge was two feet high and served by two midship pumps, one on either side of the keel, to keep the cargo hold dry. The hold was twelve feet high at its greatest clearance. The middle deck, six feet in height, housed the crew of eighteen, six twelve-pounder guns set at three gun ports on either side of the hull, the galley, mess, carpenter's shop, sailroom, and sick berth. Charles's cabin was at the back of the quarterdeck beneath the poop deck, which also covered his captain's wardroom, the stores for spirits, tobacco, and other valuables, and the wheelhouse. The forecastle housed the officers: the first officer, purser, boatswain, carpenter, and helmsmen.

The guns were needed to defend the ship from pirates. Additional defense was provided by four nine-pounder guns and two six-pounder guns situated on the waist of the ship and two swivel guns mounted on both the poop and forecastle gunwales. She carried a crew of thirty-seven.

Her maximum speed was twelve knots under ideal conditions, but she was presently doing only three and a half knots per hour. The unfavorable wind direction and her heavy load would restrict her to less than one hundred nautical miles per day.

In the late afternoon of the fourth day, the sea grew choppy. The wind direction, which had held steady within twenty degrees throughout the voyage, moved through southwest to southwest by south requiring Charles to sail as close to the wind as possible to hold course. Sailing close-hauled through the chop slowed their speed to two knots per hour, or less than fifty miles per day.

First Officer Hewer looked concerned as he said, "I don't like the wind direction, Captain, and there's the smell of a storm in the air. It's the end of June and not too early to run into a typhoon. If the wind moves south, we'd best play safe and turn around and run before the wind back to Canton."

"Let's not be overly concerned now, First Officer. If it moves south, we can beat to windward. I won't be concerned until it moves southeast, which could indicate a typhoon. They usually come out of the southeast."

"Beggin' your pardon, sir, but they come out of the south too. I was in Manila in 1821 when one came straight out of the south in early July. I wouldn't advise tacking into a south wind at this time of year, sir. Safest thing to do is to turn and head back as soon as the wind direction moves south."

"I wouldn't want to do that, Mr. Hewer. We'd lose two weeks, at the very least. I'd head for safe harbor in Lingayen Gulf in the Philippines first."

"We're some three hundred miles from there, sir. If the wind moves around to the southeast, we'll be slowed to nothing and the storm will be on us in no time."

"Thanks for your thoughts, First Officer," Charles said with finality in his voice. He had not asked for his opinion and resented it. He felt he had hired an alarmist, and didn't like that Hewer had corrected him.

"Let's see what the wind does, shall we? I'm none too happy sailing close-hauled anyway; let's hope it returns to west-southwest for us. I'm off to dinner; keep me advised of the wind direction."

Hewer wanted to say more but simply answered "Aye, sir." He turned his face into the wind. I'm sure there's a gale coming, he thought, tasting the wind.

Before turning in for the night, Charles told the helmsman to wake him if the direction of the wind moved to south and held steady. At two, the helmsman's mate woke Charles to inform him that the wind was blowing steady from the south, and it had started to rain. Charles told him to come back in twenty minutes for orders and went to his chart table. He had already decided that Hewer was right: it was too risky to beat into a south wind at this time of year. They would have to find safe harbor or return to Canton. They were 325 miles from Canton and 250 miles from Lingayen Gulf in the Philippines. Charles ordered the helmsman to set his course east-southeast for Lingayen Gulf and went back to sleep with orders to wake him at six, or earlier, if the wind moved around to blow from the southeast.

A little after six, Charles entered his personal galley for a cup of strong, hot coffee to wake himself and then walked into the wheelhouse with the cup of coffee in hand.

Without being asked, the helmsman said in a sullen voice, "The wind's blowin' from the south-southeast, Capt'n. We're makin' little headway toward Lingayen Gulf."

Charles drank the remaining coffee, secured the cup, and buttoned his foul weather gear. He walked out into the rainstorm and over to the gunwale. The southeastern morning sky was dark and ominous. The sea was large, the rain hard, and the overloaded ship was taking on water. A seaman walking past gave him a withering stare. Looking around at the working crew, he sensed fear in them. No one's happy on a foul weather voyage, he reassured himself.

First Officer Hewer stepped onto the quarterdeck and walked toward him. He looked haggard as though he had not slept.

Now's the time to show leadership, Charles told himself. "MORNIN', FIRST OFFICER," he said in a loud, cheerful voice to be heard above the noise of the howling wind and rain.

"NASTY MORNING IT IS, SIR!" the first officer hollered in reply. "WE MADE ONLY *SEVEN* MILES SINCE YOU CHANGED COURSE, CAPTAIN!" Hewer was angry that Charles had decided to try for Lingayen Gulf rather than return to Canton. He did not say more, expecting that Charles had no choice now but to lighten the ship and turn around to run downwind back to Canton.

This bloke likes confrontation, Charles thought and pugnaciously said, "I'M GOING FOR A BIT OF BREAKFAST. WHEN I RETURN I'LL DISCUSS IT WITH YOU."

The first mate couldn't believe his ears. "EXCUSE ME, SIR, BUT THERE'S *NO TIME!* WE HAVE TO LIGHTEN THE LOAD *NOW* AND HEAD BACK! WE CAN'T MAKE LINGAYEN—THAT'S CLEAR, AND THERE'S A TYPHOON COMIN' ON!"

"LIGHTEN THE LOAD, YOU SAY?"

"AYE, SIR! OTHERWISE, WE'LL NEVER OUTRUN IT!"

"IF THE WIND MOVES BACK TO THE SOUTH, WE

CAN MAKE LINGAYEN AND *SAVE* THE CARGO, *YES?*"

"NO REASON TO THINK THAT, SIR. THE WINDS BEEN MOVING COUNTERCLOCKWISE FOR FOURTEEN HOURS—LOOK AT THE SEA BUILDIN', LOOK AT THOSE DARK CLOUDS, AND SMELL THE WARM STORM AIR. IT'S A STRONG TROPICAL GALE OR TYPHOON, NO DOUBT ABOUT IT NOW!"

Charles resented the first mate's tone and aggressiveness. "I DON'T AGREE! IF IT BECOMES OBVIOUS TO *ME* THAT THIS IS A TYPHOON, I'LL THROW THE CARGO OVERBOARD TO PROTECT YOUR LIFE AND MINE. *BUT NOT BEFORE!* I KNOW MY SHIP! SHE'LL DO TWELVE KNOTS BEFORE THE WIND AND OUTRUN ANY TYPHOON!"

"NOT IN THIS SEA SHE WON'T! AND IT TAKES TIME TO LIGHTEN THE SHIP. *TIME WE DON'T HAVE!*"

"I'M GOING TO EAT!"

"CAPTAIN, I *CAN'T* BELIEVE THAT Y—"

What the devil! Charles said to himself as he turned. "*DAMMIT, MAN,* I'LL BE BACK IN TWENTY MINUTES!" He marched away and while walking through the wheelhouse said, "Keep her on course for Lingayen Gulf, Helmsman."

The first officer was livid. He had told the boatswain's mate that they had an inexperienced captain who was placing them all in grave danger. He knew the mate would tell the boatswain and his concern would circulate among the crew. The worried looks on the seamen's faces told him that they did not need much encouragement to mutiny or, at the very least, form a committee to talk to the captain. If that happened, so be it. The captain should have started back hours ago, and he wanted them to know it.

Charles returned to the quarterdeck a half an hour later to see that the wind direction had continued counterclockwise toward southeast, which he feared could indicate a typhoon. The intensity of the wind had increased and the rainstorm was worse. He had to decide what to do. He motioned to Hewer to come to the wheelhouse.

Hewer was beside himself; what was there to discuss? It was obvious: they couldn't make Lingayen Gulf now, they had to lighten the ship, turn her, and sail as fast as they could before the wind to save themselves. As he followed Charles, he promised himself never to sail again with a captain who owned the ship and cargo.

Charles lit two lanterns over the table for better light on the charts. "So we are here, yes?" he said, pointing at their position. "Approximately 240 miles from Lingayen Gulf and 330 miles from Canton?"

"Yes sir," Hewer confirmed. "And there's no other safe harbor north of Lingayen Gulf on the island of Luzon."

"What about sailing east by north to shelter in this Babuyan Channel on the north end of Luzon. Ever been there?"

"Never been there and it doesn't matter—we can't make it. That's at least 280 miles. Even if we throw *all* the cargo overboard, we won't be able to do more than four or five knots on a heading of east by north. It would take three days to get there, and we only have a day, or two at the most, until the full force of the storm hits us. We need to throw the cargo overboard immediately and head northwest for Canton and hope to outrun the storm downwind at eight knots. We're way late now. I just hope not too late!"

Charles noticed the lack of respect with no "captain" or "sir." However, he knew Hewer was right. They had no choice now. "All right, First Officer, throw all the cargo, food, and water on the upper deck overboard, along with the artillery and one of the extra anchors but keep enough water and food for two days to reach Canton. I expect once we lighten her sufficiently, we'll be able to do 200 miles a day downwind to stay ahead of the storm. If need be, we can empty the hold to increase our speed."

"Very good, sir," Hewer said, relieved. Walking away, he wondered whether Charles had sensed that the crew was near mutiny.

It took an hour to clear the deck of cargo and turn the ship downwind. By noon the wind was blowing from the dreaded southeast direction. The black southeastern sky was full of bolts of lightning. The thunderstorm seemed to be gaining on them. The seas grew larger, and the ship began to pitch heavily.

A topman was coming down the fore topmast shrouds when a rogue wave slammed hard into the starboard side making the ship roll suddenly. The impact threw him off the rigging down onto a yardarm where he hung for a second before falling into the sea. There was no way to save the man as he disappeared beneath the waves.

Throughout the afternoon, the fury of the sea increased and the wind grew to gale force. Charles left the safety and comfort of the wheelhouse to direct his men from the quarterdeck. Above him, he heard the sound of the mizzen topsail starting to tear—*rrriiiiipp*—*FLAP—FLAP.* Damn! he said to himself and yelled:

"BOATSWAIN, REPLACE IT WITH A NEW SAIL!"

"AYE AYE, SIR."

The first officer hollered above the howl of the storm:

"WE HAVE TO GET MORE'N SIX KNOTS, CAPTAIN! THE TYPHOON IS CATCHIN' US. WE MUST GET THE CARGO OUT OF THE HOLD *NOW* WHILE WE'RE STILL ABLE."

A savage gust tore the mainsail off the main yard.

"PUT MEN TO WORK ON IT BUT NOT THE YARDMEN. I NEED THEM TO REEF THE SAILS. THE WIND IS TOO MUCH FOR THEM." Charles ordered the sails folded up to stiffen them and reduce the amount of canvas exposed to the wind.

By five, the sky turned menacing dark as the leading edge of the thunderstorm reached them with its ear-piercing claps of lighting and bolts of electricity.

The mizzenmast through the poop deck developed a length-wise split. Within minutes, the mizzen yards and sails began to gyrate wildly, widening the split in the mast. Charles ordered the mast cut down. With axes in hand, the crew had just begun to chop at the mast when it suddenly snapped. The wind hurled the mast, its yards, and sails onto the poop gunwale, crushing it. The topgallant sails were dragging in the sea. The crew attacked the shrouds and backstays with their axes trying to separate the wreckage from the ship. Unexpectedly, the gunwale gave way plunging the mess into the waves along with two men entangled in it.

Shit! Everything is going wrong at once, Charles thought. I can't keep up with it. The ship heeled; he grabbed a pulley rope and held on. A man skidded across the deck and somersaulted over the waist rail into the angry sea. The ship righted herself, timbers squealing. Working his way over to Hewer, Charles ordered him to raise the guns on the middle deck and throw them overboard, along with the extra anchor. The first officer grabbed his arm and yelled into his ear:

"ORDER THE TOPMEN TO CUT AWAY THE TOPGALLANT MASTS ON THE TWO REMAINING MASTS—BEFORE WE LOSE THEM TOO!"

As the topmen climbed aloft, a savage wind tore the reefed fore topsail from its yard taking a man with it.

The ship sprang a serious leak in the firewood hold situated in the stern of the ship, a very difficult place to work. While the hold was cleared a log at a time, the water spilled out into the cargo hold. Caulking oakum had squeezed out of two seams, letting the sea rush in when the stern sank beneath the water line. The seams were re-packed and a lead plate nailed over the repair to keep the oakum in place. Soon after, water started coming through numerous other seams in the cargo hold. Repairs could not be made fast enough to keep the seawater from filling the bilge and rising up through the floorboards of the cargo hold.

A repair crew worked under the command of the ship's carpenter throughout the evening and into the night trying to plug leaks. No one slept. The thunderstorm would not let up. Within an hour of a new sail being put in place, the strong wind would tear it. A gust carried away the fore topmast and its sail.

The waves built higher causing the ship to pitch and roll turbulently, which opened more seams in the hull. The pumps could not keep the water from rising in the cargo hold. There was four feet of water in the hold by the middle of the night forcing the repairmen to dive underwater to plug some of the holes.

By morning, their condition was dire. The seas were huge, and they were down to only a few undamaged sails. All thoughts of outrunning the storm were forgotten.

The bow was taking a terrible beating. Every few minutes they would sit on the head of a massive wave, as if on a precipice, looking down into a deep valley of sea. The ship would then pitch downward and rush headlong down the face of the sea mountain to crash into the valley at full force, burying its beakhead, bowsprit, and forecastle deep beneath the water. The crashing of the bow and the pitching and rolling was shaking the ship apart. At ten in the morning, a loud *CRACK* of splintering wood was heard, and the beakhead and bowsprit disappeared from the bow of the ship.

The water now rushed into the ship each time the bow crashed into a wave. The repair crew was forced to abandon the cargo hold. The water rose fast through the second deck floorboards forcing everyone up to the upper deck. Both pumps continued to work miraculously well. Their hope was that the pumps would keep air in the ship to keep it afloat.

The storm continued to build. The main topmast broke and its reefed sail and yard were caught in the standing rigging of the foremast and the fore yard and its sail. Being held fast in this way, the broken mast beat against the ship like a battering ram smashing everything it hit. A seaman was killed when the mast crushed him against the gunwale. The crew went about their work and cut it away. With help from the wind and sea, the mast, yard, and sail were disengaged and fell overboard.

The two helmsmen working the wheel were thrown to one side. When they jumped back to take control of the wheel, they found there was no resistance. The rudder had been torn off. The ship was buffeted about wave to wave. Men were being lost overboard without anyone noticing. Charles had a fresh foresail put in place hoping to gain some measure of control by scudding before the heavy wind. But it was not to be. The wind tore the sail to shreds in a matter of minutes. Seeing themselves in deadly peril, without a rudder and sails, many of the crew lost heart and gave up.

Charles saw the pumps were not being worked, although their salvation depended on it. Two seamen near him were tying themselves to fixed timber to keep from being swept overboard.

"YOU TWO, WORK THE PUMPS!"

They ignored him.

He shook one of the men by his upper arm to get his attention. "THAT'S AN ORDER!"

The seaman pushed him away forcibly. Charles walked down to the waist of the ship and found four men who would follow his orders and man the two pumps.

Charles made a rough count, fifteen men, counting himself. The first officer was not among them; he had not been seen for an hour.

Stepping back onto the quarterdeck, Charles turned to see a huge wave crash into the longboat, wrenching it from its berth. The boat floated across the deck pushing a man before it and crashed through the larboard gunwale and fell into the sea.

By two o'clock in the afternoon, the waist of the ship was so low in the water that the pumps had to be abandoned. Waves were sweeping across the waist and quarterdeck of the ship, taking men with them. The remaining seamen made their way to the broken forecastle and poop deck. Charles counted three men on the forecastle deck and six with him on the poop deck.

There was no hope left, Charles admitted to himself. The ship was under bare poles and rudderless. Nothing more could be done. He lashed himself to the split mizzenmast. A debilitating exhaustion came over him. He was sorry that he would never see Duncan and Sarah again. The thought of dying at sea had always been with him; even so, he hadn't expected to die so young. He should have listened to Hewer.

The ship descended into troughs so fast and deep that he thought, time and again, that they would never come up again. Swamped by the howling sea and sure they were on their way to the bottom, Charles was surprised each time the ship bobbed to the surface. They were like the cork ship he had given Duncan to play with in the bathtub. The misery went on for three long hours until Charles began to have some hope that they were through the worst of the storm and might somehow survive.

Coming out of a drenching, his eyes set on a tremendous wave still building in height. It was powerful and black below with angry claws of white foam above. All who saw it must have realized that it would end their lives in a matter of seconds. Although not religious,

Charles found himself saying the Lord's Prayer. The mountainous wave lifted the ship to it as though in an embrace while the top of the wave curled high above them and dropped with such force that it exploded the larboard side and rolled the ship over twice, leaving it upside down. The last air in the hold bubbled away, sending the battered ship and Charles to a watery grave.

Nathaniel began hearing about the storm a few days after Charles's ship was late. News came a ship at a time: there had been a powerful storm in the South China Sea; later, it was described as a typhoon. Nathaniel expected the worse and told Moira the truth that it looked bad. Still later, it was reported that many ships had been sunk.

Moira moved in with Sarah to support her. They walked to Sydney Cove every day and sat on a bench hoping to see the arrival of the *Star of the Orient.*

They often saw the native Bungaree there, dressed in his admiral's jacket and cocked hat, waiting to welcome arriving passengers with his native ambassador's routine that led to selling native items or asking for liquor, tobacco, and cash. No longer able to sustain a traditional Aboriginal lifestyle, marginalized, and rum-soaked, he had been unable to lead Sydney's Aborigines to the better life that Macquarie had envisioned. Several months later, Bungaree died, a ravaged celebrity.

A sister "Star" ship came into Sydney Cove and its captain confirmed that Charles had left Canton on June 21 and would have been in the China Sea when the typhoon hit. After two months, with no word from Charles, Nathaniel and Moira sat down with Sarah.

Moira told Sarah, "We would like you and Duncan to move in with us for as long as you would like—permanently if that would suit you."

"Thank you, Mother. I would enjoy staying with you in the country for a few weeks, but I feel most comfortable here in our house. Charles worked so hard on this house. He picked out almost every item. I feel his presence here, even at this moment."

"But you'll be alone," Moira lamented.

"Oh, I have Duncan and my women friends. We have our sewing

circle and card groups. I've become close to Elizabeth, Duncan's nan-ny. And we will visit each other often, I'm sure. I'll be fine."

Nathaniel said, "Later, when it's appropriate, Sarah, I'll sit down with you and explain Charles's interest in Star Trading Company and your financial situation. The main thing you need to know is that you do not have to worry about money at all. You and Duncan are very well off. You can keep all your servants and live in the man-ner you have been living without the least financial worry. Duncan can be privately tutored or sent to England for his education, what-ever you decide. Of course, we can talk further about all of this later."

◉

"**No, no, Mr.** Armstrong, upon my soul, my mind's made up!" Governor Bourke said. "The Legislative Council is a deliberative body on which I depend. This has been a very constructive meeting, but when *Macarthur* is here we accomplish nothing. I regret to say that the man is a lunatic with little hope of restoration. We can no longer put up with his disruptive antics. I shall remove him from the council as soon as a proper document can be prepared for my signature."

In the past few years, John Macarthur's obsessions finally drove him over the edge into mental illness. He had become a tragic figure, living in dark seclusion, attended only by his private nurses. No lon-ger could his tormented mind restrain its paranoiac thoughts that everyone was plotting against him and wished to do him harm, even his devoted wife Elizabeth. He accused her of infidelity, without any grounds, and forced her and their daughter out of Elizabeth Farm to live at their Cowpastures house, now named Camden Park. From there, Elizabeth Macarthur ran their vast wool empire that had grown to sixty thousand acres.

John Macarthur's final years could have been gratifying. After having been presented with two gold medals by the Society of Arts in London for wool equal to the best from Europe, he gradually lost interest in wool production, which grew each year, until right before his death, it became Australia's largest export commod-ity. His Camden Park property was named the "first agricultural establishment in the colony." Unfortunately, when he achieved the coveted moniker of the Father of Australian Wool, he was too deranged to appreciate it. He died on April 10, 1834, and was buried at Camden Park.

With John Macarthur dead and Elizabeth Macarthur sixty-eight years old, a concern grew in the Legislative Council that the national wool project was loosing verve and direction. Its members discussed with the governor the need for a government agency or a national board of woolgrowers to promote wool as capably as John and Elizabeth Macarthur had done.

Feeling that he should know more about the intricacies of the wool industry, Nathaniel wrote to Elizabeth Macarthur at Camden Park asking whether he could visit her to discuss the current status and future of Australian wool. She wrote back inviting him and Moira to visit her for a weekend or longer if they desired.

Moira was very excited that she was finally going to spend time with the great lady. She admired her fortitude for having raised her family while managing Elizabeth Farm and the Cowpastures merino sheep station without her husband over two long periods totaling twelve years. She felt that Mrs. Macarthur should be recognized as the Mother of Australian Wool and intended to tell her as much.

Nathaniel, Moira, and their coachman, Sam, left Parramatta at ten in the morning with the intention of arriving at Camden Park, thirty miles away, in the mid-afternoon that would provide adequate time to refresh themselves and dress for dinner. Nathaniel tied his horse to the back of the carriage, so he could ride around the sheep station to view the merino herds.

The roads were in much worse condition than they had anticipated because of a recent heavy rain. When they entered Macarthur's Camden Park, it was already three o'clock. The track through the property was deeply rutted and had been washed away in some valleys.

Coming down a grade, the coachman stopped the carriage and pointed across a grassy slope.

"See that Mr. Armstrong. There's a large bull standin' over there right at the edge of those trees with a native's spear in 'im, abaht a hundred yards."

"Impressive eyesight, Sam. I see the bull, but I can't see the spear in him from here. Can you see it, Moira?"

"Yes . . . above his back leg. It's hanging down to the ground."

"I used to have excellent eyesight," Nathaniel lamented. He reached down to the floor of the carriage and picked up his musket.

Realizing the coachman's and Nathaniel's concerns, Moira asked, "You're not worried the bull will *charge us,* are you?"

"Not overly, Moira," Nathaniel said in a reassuring voice. "Although he's a bit too close to where we must cross the stream." Nathaniel checked the flint of his musket while saying, "You have a musket under your seat, don't you, Sam?

"Yus sir."

"Is it loaded?"

"Yus sir."

"Why don't you add fresh powder to the flashpan."

"Arright, sir."

While Nathaniel reprimed his musket, he said, "He's a big, wounded animal, Moira, which is always unpredictable. It's best to be ready if he's a problem." Nathaniel took out his pistol and added powder to it as well. Seeing that the coachman was done preparing his musket, Nathaniel said, "Let's go ahead, Sam. It's our two muskets against his horns."

"I dunno, sir. Could we wait fer a minute or so to see if 'e goes one way or the other?"

"All right," Nathaniel agreed.

They waited for five minutes. The bull was like a statue. It didn't move except to occasionally swing its head in a violent, odd motion from side to side.

"He knows we're here," Moira said, after the bull turned his head to look directly at them.

"Ach, look at the damn thing just standing there," Nathaniel said. "Cattle are such stupid animals. I've seen them stand like that all day. Let's go, Sam, it's getting late. We'll shoot him if he comes in our direction."

" 'E's a big one, sir, three-quarters of a ton, I reckon. I wouldn't trust 'im. You know, I won't be able t'shoot if the horses git spooked."

They sat there for a few more minutes.

Sam said, "I could try t'go down the slope real slow like to see what 'e does."

"Damn, this is a predicament," Nathaniel said. "If we shoot him from here we'll be lucky to hit him, and if we do, it'll just wound him, and then he *will* charge us. If we start toward him it will be difficult to shoot accurately from the moving carriage."

They sat there another few minutes. "We're going to be very late," Nathaniel said. "I'm going to get on Sandy and ride over toward him—that will get him moving."

"Don't you even *think* of doing that Nathaniel Armstrong!" Moira said, frightened. "You're nearly seventy-one!"

"*Moira,* I'll be on my horse! He's just a bull, and I'll have my musket. I'll only shoot him if he comes toward us."

Moira shook her head. "*No,* let Sam do it ... a young man."

He wasn't going to let her treat him like a feckless old man. "No, it's *my* horse. Look at that dumb arse—just standin' there." Nathaniel remembered that he had another unloaded musket attached to his saddle in the back of the carriage.

"You know, it could be too painful fer 'im to move, sir. The spear could be in a leg muscle."

"I'm going," Nathaniel resolved. "I have another musket in the back of the carriage." He got out of the carriage with his loaded musket.

Moira knew that when Nathaniel decided something she would not be able to dissuade him.

"Sam, get your musket ready. I'm going to walk a few yards toward him and wave my arms." Nathaniel walked forward carrying his musket and waved an arm while yelling at the bull, which did not so much as turn its head in their direction.

Shaking his head in irritation, Nathaniel walked to the back of the carriage, removed his saddle and cinched it on his horse, loaded and primed the second musket and placed it in its leather riding case, and mounted his horse.

"*Please* be careful, dear," Moira said as he rode by the carriage.

Nathaniel rode at a walk toward the bull, which was now looking at him. Forty yards from it, Nathaniel stopped. *Damme,* he thought, it hasn't moved, except for its head. Strangest bull I've ever seen. The spear didn't go far in . . . doesn't look too badly hurt. From this distance, I can put a ball into his heart and be done with it. Of course, I'll have to tell Mrs. Macarthur that I had to kill one of her bulls. I'm sure she'll understand. Damn big bull!

Nathaniel reached into the gun case and pulled out the second musket and balanced it across his saddle and a raised leg, so he could grab it quickly if he needed it. He aimed the other musket at the bull's heart, behind its front shoulders, and slowly pulled the trigger— *BANG*. Surprised by the sound next to its ear, his horse swung his head away, its body followed, throwing Nathaniel out of the saddle.

As he fell, Nathaniel saw the bull start toward him. Letting go of the musket, he reached out with his hands to break his fall but hit the ground with his shoulder and head, dazing himself. In a fog, he staggered up onto his knees and felt around for the second musket. He could hear the bull now and turned toward it, still on his knees.

When Nathaniel was thrown from his horse, Moira screamed, and Sam stood, took aim, and fired. The carriage jerked forward after he fired, plopping him back down into his seat.

The bull lowered its horns. Having taken out his pistol and cocked it, Nathaniel raised his arm and shot the bull in the head. The bull hit him and a cloud of dust obscured them from Moira and Sam. Neither the bull nor Nathaniel emerged from the other side of the dust cloud.

Turning the carriage off the track and onto the grassy slope, Sam whipped the horses toward the cloud of dust that was settling on a large black mound. He looked for Nathaniel and saw an arm—*he's under the dead bull!*

Moira jumped out of the carriage and ran screaming toward the mound. "*NOOOOO! NOOO! MARY—MOTHER OF GOD! NOOO!*" She dropped to her knees and pulled on Nathaniel's lifeless arm. "*NATHANIEL! SAM!—HELP ME! FOR THE LOVE OF GOD! Oh Nathaniel! SAM help me get him OUT!—for the love of God* . . . Help me . . . Sam, please." She stopped pulling on his arm as the realization sunk in that he was gone. "Lord, please! Oh Lord. Plea . . ." She collapsed on Nathaniel's arm, crying.

Sam stood behind her. He knew that Nathaniel was dead; he could not have survived the hit and the weight of the huge bull on him.

I'm really, really sorry, Mr. Armstrong, Sam thought. Poor Mrs. Armstrong... there's nothin' I can do fer 'er. Thank God she can't see 'is face. ... I'm goin' to 'ave to git help to git 'is body out.

◉

Arthur sat down to breakfast on January 16, 1836, with a smile on his face thinking that it was a fine day for a ride. Normally, he disliked riding long distances on horseback, but this one-week for-ay was just what he needed. He had been working too hard at the Royal Botanic Gardens, where he was the superintendent and chief botanist of New South Wales.

He was looking forward to visiting a wealthy English friend and colleague, John Sweeney, who had worked under him for two years at the botanic gardens before deciding to buy an operating sheep station named Wallerawangar. It was located west of the Blue Mountains where the grasslands of the Bathurst Plain began, some twenty miles southeast of the town of Bathurst. A young English naturalist, Charles Darwin, had prompted the trip. He had arrived unexpectedly at the botanic gardens asking for Sweeney, who had graduated eight years before him from Cambridge.

Finding Darwin a cultured, genial sort of man, who was well versed in the natural sciences, Arthur invited him to dinner. After learning that Darwin intended to hire a guide, horses, and supplies to take him over the Blue Mountains and into the interior to visit Sweeney, Arthur offered to guide him, so he could see Sweeney as well.

Fifteen-year-old Gilbert joined his father at the breakfast table. "I shall look forward to hearing all about your trip with Mr. Darwin, Father." Gilbert had been excited by the naturalist's stories about ex-otic places visited over four years on the HMS *Beagle,* an English surveying ship on a scientific expedition around the world. It had surveyed the east and west coasts of South America and crossed the Pacific before sailing into Sydney Cove.

Gilbert related well to Darwin, who appeared younger than

his twenty-six years. Looking forward to going to England in three months to begin his secondary education, Gilbert had asked Darwin many questions about England and the schools there.

Catherine came down the stairs with one-year-old Eleanor. "Will you be certain to return in a week's time, Arthur?"

"Yes, don't worry, Catherine. I shan't miss the dinner with the Whartons." Patting his lips with his napkin, he rose from the table and picked up his coat. He kissed his wife and his baby Eleanor tenderly on the cheek. Saying goodbye, he went out the back door of his Macquarie Street house toward the stable. The stable master, Isaac, an emancipist employee, stood as Arthur entered the stable.

"Morning, Isaac, are we ready to go?" Arthur asked.

"Yes sir. I put everythin' in the saddlebags yer give me along wi' the other things yer arst fer."

Arthur patted his horse, Jacaranda, on the neck and opened the two saddlebags to confirm their contents.

" 'Ere comes Mr. Darwin, sir," Isaac said.

"The saddlebags look good, Isaac." He pulled on the bags and his gun case to ensure they were well cinched and then waved and walked out to greet Darwin. "Good morning, Mr. Darwin." Pointing toward Isaac, Arthur said, "This is my stable master, Isaac Cobham, who will be accompanying us. He's wonderful with horses."

Darwin exchanged greetings, dismounted, and shook hands with Arthur and Cobham. They briefly discussed the trip before mounting their horses. As they rode through Sydney Town, Arthur pointed out places of interest.

"Mr. Armstrong, I'm indebted to you for doing this for me."

"Oh, I should be grateful to you, dear boy, for getting me out of the office. Sweeney has invited me several times to his sheep station, but I've been too terribly busy, you know. I do want to see how he's getting on. We had had a very congenial working and social relationship, you see. I quite liked the chap, and he was an exceptional botanist. I must say that I was greatly disappointed when he announced, out of the blue, mind you, that he wanted to become a grazier. Why, I don't have the faintest idea. He never explained it to me."

"I also want to thank you for personally showing me through

the Royal Botanic Gardens. I would have missed Mrs. Macquarie's chair, a sublime spot, if you hadn't taken me there."

"It's become a most popular spot on weekends ever since Governor Bourke opened the grounds to the general public. It's a pity you missed some of our more interesting natives in bloom. Our spectacular red Waratah, *Telopea speciosissima*, just finished blooming, and, in a few months, the lillypilly's fruit will ripen to the loveliest pink-purple color."

Riding through the outskirts of Sydney Town, Arthur asked, "So, Mr. Darwin, what do you think of our little town?"

"Well, sir, the town seems a bustling place with some people doing very well, judging by the number of new, large houses. What is the population?"

"Nearly twenty-five thousand, I believe."

"It's not all that different from a similar-sized English town, is it?" Propriety prevented him from telling his host that he had noticed far too many public drinking houses and far too few booksellers' shops.

They took Parramatta Road. Arthur pointed out his farm and told Darwin they would visit his mother on the way back. But, in fact, he was not anxious to introduce Darwin to his emancipist mother and intended to arrange the return trip so they would not have time to stop before his dinner party with the Whartons.

Leaving Parramatta, they rode onto the Western Turnpike toward the Blue Mountains. Along the way, a large group of Aboriginal men, women, and children scurried across the road ahead of them. Darwin quickly rode ahead in an attempt to see them more closely, but they vanished from view into the bush. He marveled that, in the midst of civilization, the natives were mostly unclothed and carried little with them. True hunter-gatherers, he thought.

The day's journey ended at Governor Bourke Inn at Emu ferry, thirty-two miles from Sydney. At dinner, Arthur talked about his respect for Sir Joseph Banks and education in London. Darwin asked him how he would compare society in London with that in Sydney Town.

"Well, there *is* no comparison, to be honest and candid," Arthur said. "One cannot compare a penal colony with the center of the empire, can one? We are only now developing an educated elite that will raise the standard above the poorly educated underclass and assume positions of guidance expected of society's upper class. My father, who died two months ago, served for many years on the Legislative Council that advises the governor."

"Oh, I'm sorry for your recent loss, Mr. Armstrong."

"Thank you. He was an exceptional man and father. He came here on the first fleet, serving as a young marine lieutenant. He decided to stay, became an advisor to governors and a successful farmer, trader, and merchant."

"I hope your mother is handling the loss as well as can be expected."

"Yes, she is. She's made of hardy stock, my mother. Once my father was settled, he sent for her, and she came out by herself."

"I say, that was audacious for a young woman back then."

Arthur was not concerned that Darwin would catch him in his little white lie. He would be leaving within days of their return. His mother was made of hardy stock and did come out by herself, so most of it was true, he told himself.

The next morning they took the same route into the Blue Mountains that Arthur had explored with Blaxland, Lawson, and Wentworth. As they rode along, Arthur told Darwin and Cobham stories from his exploring days. From a vantage point, they viewed the spectacular Wentworth Falls, a series of ponds, cascades, and waterfalls descending nine hundred feet into the valley below.

Darwin pointed at the rust-colored, sandstone cliffs. "Professor Lyell says that such cliffs hold the history of our earth. Each horizontal layer represents a specific time on the earth's surface and bears evidence to what took place at that time."

"Geology is not my field," Arthur said. "Are you saying that each stratum contains a record of the plants that lived at that time?"

Darwin nodded. "Quite right, Mr. Armstrong, plants *and* animals." He considered whether to mention his inexplicable observations made during his travels: Extinct animals in older strata sometimes resembled more evolved animals in more recent strata and even living animals. How could that be? Each set of animals the Creator introduced was supposed to be unique.

Riding farther into the mountains, the three men saw billows of smoke in the distance. Somewhat concerned, they proceeded and coming around a bend saw a bush fire in the valley below working its way up the slope.

"Bush fires are common here, Mr. Darwin. Often they are set by the natives to encourage the growth of grasses for the kangaroos they hunt. I think we can get past this one well before it gets up to the road ahead. Don't you agree, Isaac?"

"Yes sir, if we ride fast," Cobham answered.

"Mr. Darwin?"

Darwin sat up in his saddle and looked down the slope. "It appears that it will take some time to reach the road. I'm not much of a rider; however, I'll follow you as fast as I can ride."

"Well, let's ride quickly then," Arthur said.

They rode off at a canter and rounding a bend lost sight of the fire coming up the hill. Minutes later, Cobham shouted back over his shoulder:

"We should ride faster!" and set the pace at a gallop.

Arthur prodded Jacaranda into a gallop, but when Darwin could not keep up, Arthur slowed his horse. The smell of burning was strong and wisps of smoke were reaching the road sooner than Arthur thought possible. He started to cough and so did Darwin. As the smoke increased, they lost sight of Cobham ahead.

Now feeling the heat of the fire, Arthur said, "You must kick your heels into the sides of your horse, Mr. Darwin, and hang on." With that, Arthur rode ahead at a full gallop.

Losing sight of the road in the dense smoke, Jacaranda slowed, but Arthur dug his heels into her sides to keep her galloping ahead. He could not hear Darwin's horse behind. The heat was becoming unbearable. Arthur's heart was racing when he emerged into clearer air. Coughing and eyes tearing, he looked back as he rode. Darwin was still within the dense cloud of smoke. Frightened, Arthur didn't know what to do, then suddenly Darwin emerged coughing and gasping for air.

Safely away from the fire, they dismounted for rest and water. Neither Arthur nor Cobham wanted to take responsibility for misjudging the fire, and Darwin was too kind to blame them for endangering his life. While Cobham minded the horses, Arthur and Darwin drank water and wiped their faces with wet handkerchiefs.

"These bush fires are common during summer," Arthur said, to make conversation. "They're not nearly as destructive as you might think. Many of our trees germinate through fire and will begin sending out new leaves in a few months. The bush will look green again within a year." As evidence, Arthur pointed to several healthy looking trees with trunks charred from previous fires.

Darwin looked up at the sparse canopy of long thin leaves and realized that he had seen the same monotonous gray-green color since their trip began. The eucalyptus trees dominated the landscape all the way from sea level to the mountain top evidently.

"Mr. Armstrong, do you ever long for the lush, green colors of England and its great variety of tree types with their cooling shade?"

Arthur was taken aback by Darwin's apparent lack of appreciation for the uniqueness of the Australian bush and his rather parochial preference for his English flora.

"I was born and raised in Australia, Mr. Darwin, and find it has a unique beauty. Although having lived in England, I can understand why you would find it harsh and dull here in comparison."

Sensing he had insulted his host, Darwin said, "But, of course, everything has its *good* and *bad* points. In winter, our deciduous trees are bare and stark while your evergreen eucalyptus must look lovely."

"Quite so, Mr. Darwin."

They rode on to the Scotch Thistle Inn at Blackheath. The next morning the three men rose late and ate a large breakfast. Arthur and Darwin were saddle sore and slow to be on their way. When they cleared the last ridge and started down the mountain it was midday, the hottest part of the day. A hot, searing wind from the lowland blasted them.

Riding along with his head down to brace against the wind, Arthur said, "These winds come from the parched interior, much like the Sirocco winds that originate in the Sahara. I wouldn't be surprised if it gets up to 110° F today." Ahead, clouds of dust swirled over the Bathurst plain.

The journey ended in the midafternoon at the sandstone house of John Sweeney. He was happy to see Arthur and surprised to see Charles Darwin, whose letter he had not received.

The house was surrounded by outbuildings and grazing land as far as they eye could see. "I have fifteen thousand sheep. You've come at shearing time. I've got four thousand left to shear. Good quality wool for the most part."

The next morning after breakfast, Sweeney showed his visitors around. He took them to the woolshed where sweating shearers were at their backbreaking work. Each was hunched over a sheep between his legs, one hand holding its upper body and the other rhythmically removing the wool in long, efficient swipes. The shearers worked so rapidly that their combined shears made a humming, instead of a clicking, sound. The men treated the sheep roughly, thumping them down and positioning their bodies, as the sheep bawled their protests.

Sweeney pointed out a man he called a "gun." "He's an expert shearer who will likely shear two hundred today. A 'dreadnought' can do even more—three hundred."

They went into the wool room, where the clip was being sorted according to quality. Outside Sweeney pointed out different sheep enclosures. "Those over there, I'm going to breed because they had the best wool. Those ones on the side of the hill are diseased. That third lot will be slaughtered for meat."

At the end of the tour, it was time for lunch on the veranda.

Darwin asked, "Is there a waterway nearby, Mr. Sweeney, where I might see the *Ornithorhyncus paradoxicus,* the extraordinary platypus?" (It was later renamed *Ornithorhyncus anatinus.*)

"The Coxs River is two miles northeast. It's pretty dry right now, just a series of *billabongs,* that's an Aboriginal word for 'marshy ponds or watering holes,' but you may see the platypus there. I'll have somebody take you and Arthur there, if you like."

"Very much so," Darwin said.

Arthur said, "Indeed."

"Very well. It will take your entire afternoon and then some, so I'll expect you back for a late dinner."

When they returned late that evening, Darwin said, "We had a very productive expedition today, Mr. Sweeney. Mr. Armstrong and I saw black swans, Australian crows, emus, a pygmy kangaroo . . . *and* this!" From a sack, he withdrew a dead platypus. "We were quite fortunate to find several of them feeding in the water just as we were about to leave. I thought at first that they were water rats. Your man was kind enough to shoot one for me. I consider it a great feat, to be in at the death of so wonderful an animal. A most peculiar animal having the hair and body of a mammal, a duck's bill, webbed feet, and reptilian features. A classification nightmare, I daresay." He handed it to Sweeney for his inspection.

Sweeney manipulated the bill of the platypus. "It's quite pliable isn't it? Not like a duck's bill at all."

"Indeed," Darwin said. "The bill of the mounted platypus specimen I inspected in England was hardened. It was thought at first to be a hoax, hence the name *paradoxicus*."

Sweeney went inside to tell the cook to prepare something for his guests. Darwin and Arthur sat on the verenda staring silently at the plain, the last rays of the sun shining bright orange and yellow on wispy clouds in the dusk sky.

"I must say, Mr. Armstrong," Darwin said thoughtfully, "I've been reflecting on the strange animals of your colony as compared to the rest of the world. Your curious platypus is similar to our water rat, the emu like the ostrich, the lion ant is the same genus but a different species from the European one, and your marsupial kangaroo . . . the list goes on. Why would God waste his time creating similar but quite different species in various locations around the world, each perfectly adapted to its environment? A disbeliever in everything beyond his own reason, might think that there was more than one Creator at work."

"Hmm . . ." Arthur searched for an appropriate response. The question lay somewhere in the nexus between religious belief and scientific knowledge, and Arthur did not want to go there. He had often wondered whether he was interfering with God's divine plan when he grafted a plant, but he didn't feel comfortable asking, let alone trying to answer, such questions. Out of embarrassment for his long silence, Arthur stammered:

"Well—er—I don't know, Mr. Darwin. It's almost . . . we can't know how and why God acts as He does." Arthur was relieved when Sweeney called them in to eat.

◎

"Happy birthday, Grandma!" eleven-year-old Duncan said to Moira as he handed her a small, gaily wrapped box and stepped back.

"Too old for a hug and a kiss?" Moira asked, putting her arms out to him.

He stepped into her arms and hugged her as she kissed him on the top of his head.

"I have a present too, Mother," Sarah said, standing next to the butler, who had just answered the door. She stepped forward and gave her present to Moira, and they exchanged kisses.

It was Moira's seventieth birthday. She continued to live at her Parramatta farm with servants and farm workers and was still active in managing the farm.

"Can I go down to the barn, Mum?" Duncan asked. "I won't—"

"*No.* You're in your good clothes!" Sarah said harshly. "I don't want you getting yourself dirty. Uncle Arthur's family will be here shortly. Just sit down and talk with us like an adult for a while."

"I'll only go down to look. I won't touch *anything*. I'll come back as soon as I hear them comin' up the track—*pleeease*."

"Oh, Duncan, you're such a pest. If you get dirty, I'm going to be very mad."

Duncan hit the door running, jumped down the verenda steps, fell to his knees, sprang up while looking anxiously back at them, and ran off.

"Oh my, Sarah, he reminds me so much of Charles at that age," Moira said, shaking her head. "So rambunctious. We couldn't hold Charles down either."

They walked arm in arm into the drawing room.

"It's my fault," Sarah said. "He wanted to bring some play clothes, but I thought Arthur would be here by now. Duncan's a city boy; he so loves your farm. I do too. The plants, the animals, and the air is so refreshing here. Perhaps we'll come again soon, for a week next time, if you'll invite us."

"*Sarah*, you know you don't need an invitation. You and Duncan may come any time you like and for as long as you like. With Gilbert in England, Duncan is the only grandson I have to spoil. Also, you don't have to hide that male friend of yours. You may bring him along too, if you like."

"Thank you, Mother . . . You look well. How are you feeling?"

"I'm in perfect health—never been seriously sick a day in my life, thanks be to God. The farm keeps me healthy. Arthur doesn't care much about it anymore, but it's my lifeblood." Changing the subject, Moira asked, "Will you be sending Duncan home to be educated?"

"Ah, I'm not sure what to do about that," Sarah said. "I remember you telling me that Charles was smart but a disinterested student. Duncan must be like Charles was. He's very bright and quick but is driving his tutor to distraction. The poor man does his best, but Duncan won't sit still and study. I *do* want to send him off for a proper education, but I'm concerned for him, if he refuses to apply himself."

They talked for over an hour. Dinner was to be served at five. Duncan came back to the house somewhat sheepishly a little after five and was surprised that Uncle Arthur's family had not arrived yet. Shortly afterward, though, the sound of a carriage coming up the track heralded their arrival.

Eleanor was first through the door and walked deliberately to Moira with a smile. The five year old said, "Happy birthday, Grandmother" and hugged her around the waist. She was a proper young lady—sweet, loving, and well-mannered with a composure far beyond her years—exactly what her father and mother wanted her to be. Moira found it disconcerting.

Recently, when Eleanor had stayed with her for a week, Moira had taken her with her to Blacks' Town to visit her old Aboriginal friend Dorrie. When Arthur heard about it, he chided his mother saying Eleanor was too young for such an experience, and it could have traumatized her. Moira scolded him for sheltering her. Catherine also disapproved of the visit with Dorrie but was in the habit of leaving Armstrong family problems to Arthur to resolve.

Arthur sat next to his mother and accepted an aperitif from the butler. After a few words of apology for being late, he told her that he would like to discuss some farm business matters later.

"Will you be staying over tonight?" Moira asked him.

"No, Mother. I have an important meeting tomorrow that I could not change. I'm sorry. We had hoped to stay over, but I must go back tonight."

"You hardly ever visit for more than a day, Arthur. The farm needs your attention. I can do it, though you do it better than me."

"That's what I want to discuss with you after dinner and your birthday celebration, Mother."

They were called by the butler to dinner. After taking their places around the table, Arthur said a short prayer of thanks for both the meal and his mother's health.

"When will Gilbert return?" Moira asked. "He's been gone for years now and is nearly twenty."

"I'm afraid it may not be for a while longer, Mother," Arthur answered. "He's thinking of studying law. If he is accepted, he'll be there for two or three more years."

"I miss him. Of course, I'm also very pleased that he is doing so well."

"We miss him too, Mother," Catherine said.

Duncan asked for some salt at his end of the table.

Moira said to the maid standing near the wall, "Betty, please bring out another set of salt and pepper shakers for the other end of the table."

When the maid returned with the shakers, Moira introduced her. "This is our new maid Betty. She came out last month all by herself from Ipswich."

"That was very adventurous of you, Betty," Arthur said. "How much is the cost of passage these days?"

"I don't rightly know, sir. I come aht ona Emigration Commission women's ship. There was 267 of us."

"All government-paid passages?"

"I think so, sir."

"What was the range of ages of the women?" Catherine asked.

"Yer 'ave t'be eighteen to twenty-five, ma'am."

"All unmarried?" Arthur asked.

"Yus sir."

Sarah joined in the questioning. "May I ask why you decided to come here, Betty?"

"There's no work at home now, ma'am. I seen a notice fer female servants fer good wages. A cousin o' mine come aht three years ago an' she liked it. So I decided t'travel aht."

Moira said warmly, "Well, Betty, you certainly are welcome here."

"Thank yer, Mrs. Armstrong." She curtsied to the family and hurried toward the kitchen, embarrassed.

"It's a good program," Arthur said. "The United Kingdom is happy because it reduces widespread unemployment, and it provides us with badly needed farm workers, shepherds, and mechanics. God knows we need young women too, with so many male convicts transported over the years."

"It replaces convict labor, since the transportation of convicts to New South Wales was stopped," Moira said. "Your father worked so hard for that . . . I hope it pleases him in heaven."

"Well . . . many large graziers aren't too happy about it, Mother, I'll tell you that," Arthur said. "They wonder where they will get sufficient numbers of free men to live the lonely life of shepherds and how they will pay the higher wages."

Moira smiled tolerantly at Arthur. "Most of them are disgruntled rich exclusives, who have been defeated by emancipists' rights. They haven't been able to establish the elite ruling class that John Macarthur and others wanted. Our colony is better off because of it, believe me."

"It's your birthday, Mum, so I won't argue the matter with you."

A birthday cake was brought out followed by the butler, cooks, and maids to join Arthur, Catherine, Eleanor, Sarah, and Duncan in singing "happy birthday" to Moira. She opened her birthday presents while the cake was cut and passed around.

After dinner, as Moira walked into the drawing room holding Arthur's arm, she decided to devil her persnickety son.

"I wonder whether you would take me to Blacks' Town to see my friend Dorrie. You've never met her, and I'm sure you'll see that Eleanor benefited from the visit."

"Really, Mother, if you must go, you can go with your coachman or the overseer or somebody else. Your friend Dorrie and I have absolutely nothing in common."

Moira sat next to Arthur on the sofa. "I'm curious, Arthur, what do you think of Governor Gipps creating a protectorate system for Aborigines in response to Myall Creek and other massacres."

"I have no problem with it, Mother, except it won't work. Establishing native stations is fine, but prohibiting settlers from coming within five miles of them to protect the Aborigines there will never hold up."

"You've never really cared much for the natives, have you, dear?"

"*Mother*, I understand why you care about them—you grew up with them. However, I and others my age hardly ever see them anymore. They just aren't that relevant to my life, that's all."

Having confirmed Arthur's elitist attitude once again, Moira asked, "You said you wanted to discuss the farm with me?"

"Yes. You know how busy I am as superintendent of the Royal Botanical Gardens and chief botanist. I'm required to travel more and more around the colony. I simply don't have time to run the farm anymore. It's worth more for its real estate value than the money we're making from farming. We should consider selling it."

"*Arthur*, I wou—"

"Wait, Mother. This is just something I want you to think about. I'm not suggesting we do it immediately. You are getting older and living here by yourself isn't good for you. I want you to move in with us. I've discussed it with Catherine, and she agrees. Eleanor loves you, as we all do, and she would benefit greatly by having her grandmother close at hand."

"Arthur, you haven't gone and done something foolish and need money, do you?"

"My word, of course not, Mother. I'm thinking of you, your well being, for goodness' sake."

"Well, if that's the case, you need not worry yourself. I'm quite content here. This is my home. I was telling Sarah earlier today that the farm is my lifeblood. It's what I've always done. As long as I have my wits about me and can get around, I'll be living here. Although, when the time comes, I'll accept your hospitality willingly, and we can sell the farm. How's that, Arthur?"

"If that's what you want, Mother, it's fine with me. I just want you to know that you have a place with us when the time comes."

Three weeks later, Moira sat down after dinner in her favorite stuffed chair to read a book of poems by Lord Byron that Nathaniel had given her as a present. After a while, she fell asleep with the book lying in her lap opened to the romantic poem "When We Two Parted." She slept in the chair well beyond her usual bedtime.

The new maid Betty walked up to one side of her and quietly said, " 'Tis time fer bed now, Mrs. Armstrong." Moira did not stir, so Betty laid her hand on her shoulder to wake her. When Moira slumped to one side, Betty ran off screaming for help.

The doctor diagnosed that Moira had died of a brain disorder, heart attack, or something else that had taken her quickly and peacefully. He said simply, "It was her time."

◎

Months later, Duncan, Sarah and her friend Stanley met Arthur, Catherine, and Eleanor at the Armstrong farm to spend the weekend together. Sarah had met Stanley a year earlier at a church function. He was a widower and owner of a paint company. She had recently accepted his proposal of marriage, and they were planning a large wedding.

On Monday, Arthur's family returned to Sydney Town while Sarah, Stanley, and Duncan continued west into the Blue Mountains to vacation at a Katoomba resort. The trip to the resort was expected to take four to five hours in Stanley's four-wheeled carriage drawn by two horses.

Deep into the mountains, as they rounded a crest and started down the other side, a dangerous-looking man with a musket suddenly jumped from the bush ahead.

"*Oh Stanley*, what does he want!" Sarah asked, grabbing his arm.

The man raised his hand in a command to stop and yelled, "*Bail up!*" Two men jumped out of the thick bush on either side of the road and reached for the horses.

"*They're bushrangers!*" Stanley exclaimed, whipping the horses to ride through the three men.

The man with the musket jumped to one side and, as the carriage sped past him, shot Stanley, who lurched forward and fell through the horses. The frightened horses stampeded down the steep road with Sarah and Duncan holding on the best they could. Approaching a bend in the road, Sarah reached over to grab the dangling reins. The carriage careened around the curve throwing her out.

Continuing around the sharp turn, the carriage went up onto two wheels with Duncan desperately hanging on to keep from falling out. The carriage dropped down hard onto all four wheels again and continued down the road. As the horses slowed, Duncan jumped from the moving carriage; panicked and crying about his mother, he ran up the road toward the bend. The sounds of men's voices and running feet from around the bend met his ears. He dove headlong into the bush and lay quietly.

Two men came running down the road and passed by him. He didn't dare move. After a short while, he heard the third bushranger bound by, followed shortly by arguing. It became quiet for a minute, then Duncan heard the carriage being driven down the road. Still lying flat, he turned around and peered through the bushes and saw the three bushrangers in Stanley's carriage disappear around the next bend. He laid his head on his arms and sobbed, still too afraid to move.

Hearing no sounds, except birds in the trees, Duncan rose and ran around the bend expecting to see his mother lying injured—*but she was not there!* The sound of a carriage behind him sent him scurrying back into the bush. He thought the bushrangers were returning.

Duncan was relieved and elated to see a stagecoach coming up the hill. He jumped from the bush and ran down the road waving his arms. While he told the coachman and armed guard what had happened, two male passengers stepped out of the coach.

"That must've bin the carriage we just passed on the road," the stagecoach guard said, shaking his head in dismay. "You get into the coach, young man. You've told us all we need to know." He did not want Duncan to see the two bodies he expected to find.

The men walked along the road looking over the edge. In a few minutes, one of them pointed down.

"There she is!"

Sarah lay among boulders on the rocky slope. There was blood on the rocks, and she was not moving. If she had not been killed by the fall from the carriage, she died by being thrown from the road by the bushrangers.

When Duncan heard the man's quiet exclamation, he jumped out of the stagecoach and ran crying toward the men. They rushed to him and grabbed his arms.

"This won't do yer no good ter see, young fella," one of them said. "Yer can't do nothin' fer 'er now."

Struggling against them, Duncan was forced back into the stagecoach. The women in the stagecoach tried their best to comfort him.

Stanley's body was also found on the rocky slope. Both bodies were wrapped in blankets and tied to the back of the stagecoach.

Back in Sydney Town, Duncan was taken into Arthur and Catherine's home, which was only three blocks from Duncan's former home. His new "sister" became cousin Eleanor, now age six, who embraced him as her big brother. The love of Arthur's family along with support from Duncan's tutor and neighborhood friends, helped Duncan slowly adjust to life without his mother.

When Arthur thought Duncan was over his grieving, he sat down with him to explain his financial situation. Referring to a ledger he had prepared, he said:

"You are very well off, Duncan. Your mother's will left the house to you, most of her savings, and her eighteen percent interest in Star Trading Company." Arthur served on the board of Star and assured him that this was worth a lot of money.

"I have been appointed your guardian. Your interest in the company is held in trust for you until age twenty-four, when you can decide what you want to do with it."

"Thank you, Uncle Arthur," Duncan said, having understood

little of what he had heard.

"I intend to send you off in a year or two to England for your education, as I was sent off when I was a young man."

"I *don't* want to go. I want to stay here with my friends."

"Don't be so hasty in telling me what you want and don't want to do, Duncan," Arthur said firmly. "I'm your guardian, and I'll decide what's best for you."

"I'm *not* going, and you *can't* make me!"

God, Arthur thought, he's just like Charles was, obstinate and aggressive. (Arthur's childhood feelings of ineptitude flooded over him.) He's suffering from insecurity right now; I'll let him think on it.

"All right, Duncan. Perhaps it's too soon after the death of your mother. We'll talk more about this later."

◎

Duncan never agreed to go to England for his secondary education. At age fifteen, he stopped studying after having an argument with his tutor. He went looking for work, any work, that would pay him enough to get out from under Arthur's control. His first job as a shipbuilder's apprentice lasted ten months. He then left Sydney to work as a drover. Tired of that after two years, he became a stage-coach guard at the age of nineteen.

Every time Duncan visited Uncle Arthur he had to listen to him say: "You are wasting your life with these menial jobs, Duncan. They're all well below your station in life. You must stop being so difficult and go off to England for a proper education."

Tired of unfulfilling, low paying jobs, Duncan finally agreed to try seafaring at Star Trading Company. After his first voyage of eight months, he told Uncle Arthur that he had had "enough of the sea to last a lifetime." He took a job as a clerk in the Star Trading Company warehouse intent on learning the business from the bottom up.

"Hopefully, you will be president of your father's company someday," Arthur told him wishfully.

Chapter 8

Antipodean El Dorado

GOLD DISCOVERED NEAR BATHURST! the headline of the *Sydney Morning Herald* exclaimed. The newspaper crier shouted, "Get *rich* quick! Get your *Herald* right here. *Gold discovered near Bathurst!*"

Buying a newspaper, Duncan excitedly read down the front page:

> Colonial Secretary Deas Thomson announced at Parliament House on May 14 that E. H. Hargraves, recently returned from America's Californian goldfields, has discovered gold at Ophir near Bathurst. Mr. Hargraves was heard to say, "I was standing in an alluvial creek bed near the Macquarie River thinking how much this looks like California when I looked down to see flecks of gold lying at my feet."

He had heard rumors of gold discovered a month earlier in 1851, but now it was officially confirmed. This was his chance to leave Star Trading Company. After nearly four years of working at Star, in increasingly more responsible positions, Duncan had had all he could stomach. He had been looking for another job for months now, something less boring and confining. Gold mining was perfect.

Duncan had been living with Uncle Arthur and Aunt Catherine

for several months because his housemate had lost his job and moved away. After dinner, Arthur and Duncan retired to the drawing room as was their habit. Over cigars and port, Duncan broached his plan.

"Uncle Arthur, I've got something I need to discuss with you. I don't think you're going to like it much, but I've thought it through, and my mind's made up."

"Now, Duncan, that's not the way to start a discussion with me or anyone else. If you want to discuss something with someone, don't tell them at the start that your mind's already made up."

"I'm goin' to leave Star," Duncan blurted out.

"What do you mean—leave?"

"I'm going to quit."

"Quit to do what, may I ask?"

"Go prospectin' for gold at Bathurst."

"Oh, Duncan! . . . now don't get caught up in this hysteria. You'd be making a big mistake, m'boy. This gold thing's a lark; it's *not* going to last, believe me."

"How d'you know that? I've heard rumors, for weeks now, about prospectors getting rich. They say all you need is a pan, and you can wash the gold right out of the sand. It's been in the papers for two days. I wanta get up there as soon as I can."

"Duncan, think what you're saying. It's irresponsible. Like the California gold rush, it will be over in a few months. This craziness will pass, and you'll be out of a good job and a career. Mr. Enright and Mr. Whittingham won't take you back if you leave like this, and I wouldn't blame them."

"I don't care. I wouldn't want to go back. I've had my fill of that place. I don't like the business, and I don't like working for them. I've told you that. They don't respect me and will never make me a partner. Mr. Whittingham's son will be made partner before me, and he's a toady. I'd rather work for myself."

"At what?"

"Prospecting for gold, first, and then I'll see after that."

"What will you live on?"

"I've got plenty in the bank to get started, and I can sell my interest in Star if I need cash in the future."

"You can't do that until you're twenty-four."

"That's in five months."

"Duncan, you don't want to do that. Your eighteen percent interest is worth far more over time than at its current selling price."

"Then I'll only sell it if I have to, if I don't strike it rich at prospecting."

"You don't know anything about gold prospecting!"

"I'll learn from doing it, or I'll learn from others. It can't be that hard."

"You'll learn from street cleaners, drunks, shearers, and drovers because those are the kinds of people who are running off trying to strike it rich overnight. You don't want to associate with people like that!"

"I was a drover! Those are my kind of people. I don't like people who *put on airs* and think they're *better* than other people. That's the problem with Mr. Enright and Mr. Whittingham."

And the problem with me? Arthur thought to himself, resentment showing on his face.

Duncan saw that his uncle had gotten his inference and said, "You've been really good to me, Uncle Arthur, but I'm not like you. I don't want to be better than anyone else, or tell other people what to do. I just want to make my own way."

It took Duncan two weeks to quit his job and find the gold digging provisions that were in short supply: a tin dish, shovel, pick, billy can, blankets, tent, hatchet, musket, and ammunition. By mid-June he had ridden to Ophir and joined hundreds of other hopeful gold diggers.

◉

Arthur looked though the mail as he walked into the sitting room to join Catherine. He was happy to see a letter from Duncan, because they had not heard from him for two months.

"We have a letter from Duncan, Catherine."

Catherine looked up from her book. "Oh good. Will you read it to me?"

"I'd rather give it to you when I'm done."

He poured himself a sherry, sat down in his favorite overstuffed chair, opened Duncan's letter and began to read:

> I pray this finds you all well. I just received your September letter and was sorry to hear that Eleanor has been ill with a cold. I hope she is better by now.
>
> I left Ophir at the end of August because the alluvial gold had run out in the valley and pickings were thin in the uplands. I am now working a claim with two mates on the Turon River, near Sofala, about 24 miles north of Bathurst. I want to assure you that I am using good judgment in my conduct and whom I chose to associate with. However, being that there are few 'gentlemen' up here, I have joined up with two diggers my age from Sydney.

Arthur bristled and thought, I probably shouldn't have suggested that he try to seek out gentlemen . . . in the goldfields. He read on.

> John Thorne is from Surry Hills and worked as a stonemason's apprentice. Matt O'Dea was a wainwright in Bankstown. We enjoy each other's company and work well together.
>
> There are thousands of diggers along the Turon and its creeks. Most of the easy gold had already been panned or claimed along the bends of the river and in the creek beds before I got here. I've learned how to prospect for gold and it's <u>NOT</u> all luck. Some miners hack gold nuggets out of veins of quartz and iron-sandstone in the ridges in the hills around, but it's back-breaking work. The easier gold is found in gullies over old streams that carried eroded gold for thousands of years to the river below. When we find gold particles in the top 6 to 18 inches of gravelly quartz earth, we peg our claim and start digging. Paying gold is usually found from 8 to 15 feet down where it's settled into a bed of sand and small gravel on top of a tough clay

layer, which itself is usually on top of rock.

We've had several good gully claims, but the one we are working on now is a real dream claim! We take turns digging, carting the earth to the stream, and washing it in our rocking cradle. It's a lot of hard work but worth it. You wouldn't believe the calluses on my hands.

Anxious to know Duncan's condition, Catherine interrupted Arthur's reading. "Is he well?"

"Seems so. The letter's all about what he's learned about gold mining—trying to impress us." Arthur resumed reading.

We are getting about an ounce of gold per cart load of earth and do 5 to 7 loads a day. The gold traffickers are paying now £2 12s an ounce, so that's £15 per day or £5 each. So I'm making as much as £30 per week compared with £3 5s a week at Star! Although we have found many pennyweights of raw gold, what we are really hoping for is a run of nuggets that will make all of this coolie labor really worthwhile.

Arthur wondered whether he could believe Duncan—*thirty pounds sterling a week* was an awful lot of money. He knew some gold miners were striking it rich, but he couldn't imagine Duncan would be successful.

"It sounds like Duncan is striking it rich, Catherine, if you can believe his boasting."

"Arthur, please don't be like that."

He did not respond and continued reading.

We work very hard but also have some fun. Evenings we join others to play cards and two-up, for pennies, and swap tales. Matt plays the harmonica while we sing along. This kind of living suits me just fine. The only problem is there are too many diggers mucking about, especially the pushy foreign types who don't understand our ways and don't speak English. The Chinese are the worst!

Arthur smugly thought, these are the kinds of people I warned him about. He went on to the next paragraph:

If we don't hit a prize nugget run that makes us our fortune in the next week or two, we are thinking of going to Victoria where a huge goldfield has been found near Ballarat. Everyone is striking it rich there! We hear stories that they are getting fantastic yields of up to 5 ounces to the tin dish! I probably won't be home for Christmas as I will most likely be in Victoria. Write me in Bathurst though, because I will have my mail sent on if I go to Ballarat. I hope you all have a Merry Christmas, if you don't get my next letter before then. Until then, I remain, your devoted nephew.

Arthur settled back into his chair and grudgingly murmured to himself, "Well, I'll be damned. It sounds like he's making a go of this."

"What did you say, dear?" asked Catherine.

"Duncan has more gumption than I gave him credit for. He's going to Victoria!"

"Why?"

He held the letter out for her to take.

"Here . . . read for yourself."

○

Fong Ho-teng, a twenty-year-old apprentice woodworker in Canton, wanted to go to the San Gam Shan, New Gold Mountain, in Australia to seek his fortune. He hoped to repeat the success of his employer, who claimed to have become wealthy in just a few months as a Forty-Niner at Gauh Gam Shan, Old Gold Mountain, in California.

But Ho-teng was afraid to go by himself. He wanted at least one of his elder brothers to go with him, most likely his unmarried, Second Eldest Brother, Sing-woo. Taking time off from work, he walked the fifty miles to his village, Yang-lu. He was anxious to visit his family, because he had heard that villages in the Sun Wei District had been attacked by roving bands of bandits, demanding tribute and killing those who refused. Nearing his village, Ho-teng saw Sing-woo working in their family field.

Ho-teng ran toward his brother shouting, "*Revered Brother, you are well! How is our family, Yigo?*" As he came closer, he said, "I heard there were attacks by bandits in the area."

He addressed Sing-woo as "Yigo," the respectful kinship term for Second Eldest Brother. It was considered disrespectful to address another sibling, especially an elder sibling, by given name. Confucian ethos numbered offsprings to distinguish between elder and younger siblings and to discourage individualism, which was considered egocentric and ill-bred.

Sing-woo walked quickly toward his younger brother, pleased to see him. They stopped a few feet apart and bowed to each other. Sing-woo put his hand on Ho-teng's shoulder. "You look well too, Saamgo"—Third Eldest Brother—"but I am saddened to tell you there *was* an attack on our village. I thank the goddess of mercy and our ancestors that no one in our family was hurt, although twelve men in our village were killed and many wounded."

"*Bai!*" Oh dear! Ho-teng cupped his mouth and nose with his hands in dismay. Speaking through his hands, he said, "That's *terrible*, Yigo, worse than I'd expected. I'm so happy that our family is safe." Ho-teng showed emotion more readily than most Chinese men, who tended to be stoic and impassive. Shorter than Sing-woo by two inches, he was pudgy and round-faced. A long, braided queue hung from the back of his shaven crown.

"What happened?" Ho-teng asked.

"I'll tell you on the way to our village. You are probably anxious to see Father and Mother after so many months away."

Ho-teng expected to hear that Sing-woo was in the midst of the battle. He was athletic and had always been brave when they were growing up. Sing-woo was twenty-two, five feet seven inches tall, thin, and stronger than he looked from years of working in the fields. He too wore a long, braided queue.

As they walked, Sing-woo told the story of what had happened.

"Seven, long-haired, Hakka bandits rode into our village and demanded tribute to support their ungodly mission. They said they were brethren of the Taiping rebels. The Hairy Thieves said they had defeated the imperial Manchu forces in our district and needed food for their troops."

"Were the Hairy Thieves as wild-looking as I've heard?"

"Yes. They were dressed in gaudy red and yellow clothes and wore red headbands. Their heads were not shaven like ours. They had scruffy beards and long, wild hair in defiance of the Manchu's order that all men must wear a queue. They mocked the elders' queues as symbols of their kowtowing to the imperial, foreign Manchurians.

"When they rode into the village, everyone ran into their houses. The elders sent children to alert us in the fields. The bandits called for the elders to come out. They came out slowly, and did everything slowly, to give us time to come together and retrieve our hidden weapons. Father and the other elders told the bandits we did not have the amounts of rice and the number of pigs and fowl they wanted and walked them through the village to show them how poor we are. It seemed for a while that they would accept less, but then seeing us returning from the fields, they also demanded five volunteers to join their unholy rebellion.

"The elders told them that the young men were needed in the fields and would not want to volunteer. The leader of the Hairy Thieves then ordered the elders to line up all the young men in the village for him to choose five to be pressed into service. When the elders protested, their leader ran his sword through esteemed Doctor Choo and—"

"*Aiyaa!*" Nooo! Ho-teng exclaimed in horror. "*Not* old Doctor Choo!—*those dung-eating vermin!*"

"*—and cut off his head!*" Sing-woo said, finishing his sentence.

"*Aiiiya!*" Ho-teng said squeamishly through his hands covering his mouth.

"The elders ran and the bandit leader told his men to take what they wanted. As they went from house to house, the battle broke out. We fought well. They did not expect us to fight or to be organized into fighting units. One unit killed the man guarding their horses and ran them off. On foot, we were too many for them. *We killed them all!*"

"*Waa!*" Wow! "I am greatly relieved, Yigo, my dearest brother, that you were not hurt. You were very brave. Did you kill anyone?"

"Homage to Lord Buddha that I did not. I stabbed them with my bamboo spear and struck one soldier in the neck with my hand ax. We were all hitting and stabbing at them as best we could, so no man should feel he has killed. The imperial soldiers came afterward and thanked our elders and presented us with many swords and spears and a few shields."

"There is much fighting around Canton now," Ho-teng complained. "On my way here, I hid off the side of the road three times because I was afraid of approaching riders. This disorder is bad for the woodworking business; every year has gotten worse since I started apprenticing five years ago. Fewer foreign traders are coming now to buy our cabinetry and lacquered boxes and trays. I will not get rich in this business." Ho-teng kicked at a sod of earth with his foot. "I want to go to San Gam Shan to become a gold miner. If you join me for a year in the goldfields, we can live like emperors when we return."

"Younger Brother, these are dangerous times for our family and clan. There are other roving bands of Hakka bandits about, the Taiping insurgents are fighting the government, and criminal *triads* control Yanping and many other towns. I am needed here to help farm and defend our family. The imperial Manchu cannot maintain order or provide protection for us. Yet the corrupt *mandarins* in Canton continue to demand taxes and threaten us if we pay tribute to the rebels. With you and Eldest Sister gone, there are still ten mouths to feed."

Sing-woo and Ho-teng did not fully understand the reasons for the turmoil affecting their region. They knew the principal group causing the chaos was the Taiping Tienkuo, the Heavenly Kingdom of Great Peace, a nationalistic and religious uprising that had started in southern China. It was ravishing the country and threatening the rule of the Qing dynasty. The Taiping's founder, Hung Hsiu-chuan, was a charismatic Hakka who had been converted to Christianity by Protestant missionaries and then preached to the oppressed underclass that he was the younger brother of Jesus Christ. He professed to be the Celestial King who had come down from the Heavenly City above to save China from the corrupt foreign Manchu and provide salvation to the masses. Hakka, Miao, and Yao minorities and impoverished peasants flocked to his crusade in response to his promise of immediate and divine ascent into heaven if killed in battle.

"You must think of your future, Elder Brother," Ho-teng said. "As Second Son, you will not inherit our esteemed father's land, and I, as Third Son, have no chance at all. You will always toil for your elder brother unless you provide for yourself and your future descendants."

Ho-teng exaggerated when he said, "My employer told me about two men who returned *rich* from San Gam Shan after only six months of gold digging. You and I have no future, our *karma* is not good. We should seek gold riches together in the land of the southern white barbarians."

Sing-woo had once seen the strange whites in Canton. The thought of going to the land of these ghostly-looking foreigners, derogatorily called *kwai-lo*, was not appealing to him.

"The ancient books teach us that our short lives are nothing, except to prepare for future rebirth," Sing-woo said. "If I were to go with you, it would be for the good of our ancestors, our aged parents, our clan, and our descendants."

"Yes, yes, you are quite right, Yigo. We will seek gold riches for our family and to become revered ancestors for all time."

"Why are you so sure that we can find gold easily in the land of the *kwai-lo?*" Sing-woo asked.

"I am told they have mountains of gold that will last for a hundred years, and every day they find more. They have so much gold that they do not care whether others dig for it. Few people live in their land. They are a simple, peaceful people who do not have to work hard to live richly."

"How can we get there?" asked Sing-woo. "Have you saved money for the voyage?"

"I don't have any money, but we could ask Father. Will you join with me to ask him to provide a loan to purchase our passage?"

"So sorry, Saamgo, I cannot ask our father for a loan of such a large amount of money. He would have to sell or borrow against our land, which our ancestors would not approve of. No . . . my place is here . . . I do not wish to discuss this further."

◉

In the middle of a hot December night in 1854, Duncan had been awakened by shouts and drawn out of his tent by a false alarm of an attack on the stockade. He had returned to his tent but could not fall back to sleep. Restless for hours, he sat up and took a drink from his canteen. Clasping his arms around his legs, he rested his chin on his knees and began to question his judgment.

If I'd known that by joining the Ballarat Reform League I'd be committing myself to armed rebellion, I wouldn't have joined. I only joined because Matt did. No, that's not true; I joined because I opened my big mouth to rail against the arrogant goldfield administration and its hated digger's license fee, and I liked the crowd's response. I *sucked up* the applause actually, like some bloody actor on a stage. *Then* I got myself elected to the central committee. *Then* I got involved in writing the list of grievances against the tyrannical Victorian government.

Matt left. After three years of mining, he'd had enough. Said he had all the money he needed and left—why didn't I? Maybe it wasn't such a great idea to build this stockade as a refuge for diggers who had burnt their licenses . . .

Irritated with himself, Duncan threw off his blanket, grabbed his moleskin trousers and put them on outside of the tent. As he pulled on his boots, his eyes slowly adjusted to the dim moonlight. Sunrise was an hour or two away, he surmised. Taking his musket from the tent, he walked over to the crude stockade barricade of hastily thrown up wood planks, shoring timbers, logs, and dead branches enclosing about an acre of the Eureka goldfield at Ballarat. Groping in the darkness, he found a spot to sit down against the barrier and made himself comfortable.

The soft sound of the diggers' Southern Cross flag wafting in a gentle breeze drew his attention to the top of the flagstaff. He thought of the solemn oath he had taken under the starry flag with hundreds of other rebellious diggers:

"We swear by the Southern Cross to stand truly by each other and fight to defend our rights and liberties."

The objectives of the Ballarat Reform League ran through his mind: reform the abusive goldfield administration, abolish its expensive mining license fee, manhood suffrage, representation in the Legislative Council, and the lease or sale of crown land in small parcels at reasonable prices. Noble objectives all. Luxuriating in the stillness of the night and the warmth of his righteous cause, his reverie was interrupted by the sound of somebody walking up.

"I'll replace ye as sentry, if y'want to git some sleep, mate."

Duncan looked at the dark form standing in front of him.

"I'm not a sentry, mate, just couldn't sleep."

"Me either, but I'm always a' early riser." The man lowered the butt of his musket to the ground and leaned on the barrel. " 'Twill be light soon; d'ye think the lobsterbacks an' gold-lace police'll be attackin' us t'day?"

"Don't know whether they'll *ever* attack us. They're waiting for military reinforcements and artillery from Melbourne. If they drop a few rounds of artillery among us, we'll be *buggered*."

The man bent over to look closely at Duncan in the gray morning light. "I know who y'ar' . . . yer name's . . . Dunc Armstrong, ain't it?"

"Yeh," Duncan answered, looking intently at the man to see whether he knew him. "You look kinda familiar . . . Where'd you know me from, mate?"

" 'Twas in a pub in Bendigo in June. I shouted a round o' drinks for yous. Me name's McMullan—Michael McMullan—but m'mates call me Mick. Ye was sp'akin' out against the Chinks, how they wor takin' over an' oughta be run out, all the way back t'China. Bill Denovan was talkin' about joinin' up wid the Americans on the Fourth o' July to drive out the Chows, but then nothin' happened. Why?"

"Commissioner Panton threatened Denovan with arrest and called up the military from Melbourne. We *had* to back down, mate. . . . now I remember you, Mick. How'd you get involved in this mess?"

"Ah, most like ye an' the rest o' us . . .'tis the gold-lace police an' their bloomin' license hunts I can't stand no more. The Brit guv'nor an' commissioners treat us worst than dingoes—we ha' to stand up to 'em. We'll give 'em what for whin they come at us."

"They're not going to attack us, Mick. Commissioner Rede isn't going to lose men when all he has to do is wait for the artillery to arrive. We can't fight artillery."

"The American McGill an' his California Rangers wor sent out t'ambush 'em, worn't they?"

"Yes."

" 'Tis possible McGill beat 'em an' sent 'em back to Melbourne. Rede's itchin' for a fight, so I reckon he won't wait. He'll come at us t'day."

"Na, the military has never fired on free men and isn't going to do it over our reform issues."

"Och, what about *Vinegar Hill*?"

"Those were mostly Irish convicts, not free men. No . . . they'll wait for the reinforcements, line the artillery up on Bakery Hill, and parley with us."

While they had been talking, the darkness of night had slowly brightened to gray and then to the hazy pink of early dawn. The day was coming alive with the sounds of birds greeting the morning light. Mick had just opening his mouth to disagree with Duncan when they heard a shot sound nearby and a piercing cry:

"*REDCOOOATS!*"

A second and a third shot rang out from the sentries announcing that they were under attack from at least three directions. Duncan and Mick raised their heads above the barricade. Dumbfounded, Duncan couldn't believe his eyes! A redcoat British unit of foot was marching toward them in an orderly line, bayonets fixed, *less than two hundred yards away.* Aghast, Duncan looked at Mick, who returned a triumphant, crooked smile that didn't hide the concern in his eyes. Duncan looked toward Lalor's headquarters to seek guidance only to observe total pandemonium among the diggers emerging from their tents, pulling up their pants, grabbing weapons, and shouting incoherently as they ran to the barricade. He turned back to Mick, just in time to see him disappearing into the chaotic throng of diggers.

Unable to believe that the British soldiers were actually advancing on the stockade, Duncan again looked north over the barricade. The soldiers were much closer now and a unit of police, in their blue uniforms, was approaching on foot to his left. Gunfire was erupting all around him. Keeping his head low, he ran south toward the gate, opening onto Melbourne Road, with thoughts of escape. As he ran, he caught glimpses of mounted redcoat soldiers to the east and police riding up Melbourne Road to encircle the stockade.

A deafening volley of musket fire from outside the stockade drove Duncan headlong into the dirt. Several diggers writhed on the ground near him shrieking in pain and calling out for help. Crawling on his hands and knees toward the breastwork, frightened and dragging his musket, Duncan heard the terrifying *whizzz* of bullets and *pings* when they ricocheted and a sickening *thud* and scream when a man was hit. *Godalmighty!* he thought, this is insanity, people are being *killed!* A man running by was knocked off his feet by a bullet to the head and landed beside him, covering him with blood and brain tissue. Frantic, confused, and weeping with fear, Duncan scurried to the protection of the barricade. Horrifying screams of pain were all around him. He covered his head with an arm, drew up his legs into a protective ball and cried out inside his head: I'm here *on principle!*— not to shoot British soldiers—*I'm British myself for Chrissake!*

Suddenly, Duncan felt strong hands grab his arms and jerk him up bodily. His musket was slammed into his stomach; reflexively, he grabbed the stock and barrel.

"DEFEND YERSELF Y'YELLA-FACED BLIGHTER!" a huge, contorted, bearded face screamed above the roar of battle, spittle flying, "*OR I'LL SHOOT YE MESELF!*" The giant forcibly turned him around to face the enemy.

Sixty yards from the stockade, a row of British soldiers had been ordered into firing position just as Duncan, in a dreamlike state, began to raise his musket. The soldiers discharged their muskets upon command. Duncan had his musket against his shoulder when he saw the bright flash of their volley off to his left. The stockade barricade splintered into a thousand shards and blew full force into his upper body; spinning, he landed on the ground in an unconscious, contorted heap.

That evening Duncan regained consciousness in the nearby London Hotel that had been turned into a hospital. Pain racked his body. He had a throbbing headache and could not move his left arm. Feeling the bandaging covering the left side of his face, he called out urgently to a man nearby wearing a blood-stained, white smock who was working over another patient. "*Doctor!* what *happened* to me?" When he did not respond, Duncan called out a second time. The man finally walked over to him.

"Your upper left side was badly traumatized: your left arm and side sustained multiple injuries and a bullet passed through below your collarbone; you've lost your left eye and part of your left ear."

"*Oh God!*" Duncan exclaimed in horror.

"You're lucky to be alive . . ." the doctor said coldly. An odd look crossed his face. " . . . that is, until they hang you!" Abruptly, he turned and walked away.

Nonplussed, Duncan looked at the patient in the next bed, who said, "We're all un'er arrest, mate, fer killin' six soldiers an' woundin' twelve. The nurse said they've arrested one hundred an' twenty o' us. There's goin' to be a trial."

A Catholic priest visited the hospital and informed the recuperating prisoners that the trial would begin with thirteen prisoners accused of murder, sedition, and treason. "There's six Irishmen, a Scot, a black American, a black Jamaican, an Italian, a Dutchman, a Dane, and one Englishman. The prosecution says twenty-two diggers were killed an' twelve wounded, though the defense contends that if the indiscriminate butchery outside the stockade was included, forty diggers were killed an' fifty wounded.

"Ye'll be happy to know that the newspapers are on our side and a groundswell of popular support is brewin'. The British governor is being blamed for mishandling events and supporting a brutal over-reaction. A Goldfields Commission of Inquiry has been formed to look into it. Bless ye lads, shure I am that God will preserve ye."

While Duncan slowly convalesced, the priest continued his visits. He complained about the unfairness of starting the trial with the black American defendant, John Joseph, one of the so-called California Rangers, who was sure to be found guilty. He was the only American, of three arrested, who had not been released to the custody of the U.S. Consul.

To everyone's surprise, the jury returned a verdict of not guilty. Jubilation erupted in the courtroom. Joseph was placed in a chair and carried around the streets of Melbourne in triumph by a cheering throng of merrymakers numbering over ten thousand. One by one the defendants were tried and let off. By the end of March 1855, all thirteen defendants had been acquitted and the leader of the rebellion, Peter Lalor, was pardoned.

The Goldfields Commission of Inquiry published its report immediately following the acquittals. Duncan and his mates were pleased that the commission's recommendations were quickly carried out by the Victorian government. The corrupt and abusive goldfield administration was replaced by a system of mining wardens. The number of police was greatly cut. The expensive miner's license fee was replaced by a "miner's right" costing only one pound sterling per annum, which gave the holder not only the right to mine but also to vote for a representative to the Legislative Council. Peter Lalor, the rebel leader, was the first elected. The loss in mining revenue was made up by a new export fee on gold. In response to the miners' demand for land, crown land near the goldfields was offered in small parcels for sale or lease.

"The British ha' learned something from the American Revolution," the priest said. "The swift redress of most of our grievances has undercut the aims of chartists, socialists, an' republicans who wanted political and social reforms."

Nearly mended, but physically unable to continue gold mining,

Duncan decided to return to Sydney. While he rode the stagecoach home, he wondered whether his disfigured face would be repulsive to his family and friends.

When Duncan emerged from the stagecoach in Sydney, his Uncle Arthur, Aunt Catherine, and cousin, Eleanor, were there to meet him. The women gasped at his sickly appearance, black eye patch, and scarred face. Twenty-year-old Eleanor hide her emotion, but Catherine sobbed openly.

"Oh, Duncan dear, you're so thin, hasn't your arm healed yet?" She could not embrace him because his left arm was in a sling. Instead she laid her head lightly against his chest and wept, while he embraced her with his right arm. Eleanor and Arthur stood to one side.

"Don't cry, Aunt Catherine; actually, I'm feeling quite well. My arm is almost healed. I just put it into a sling to protect it while traveling. Uncle Arthur and Eleanor, how nice of you all to meet me."

On the way home, they talked about gold mining, family, and friends while avoiding the subject of Eureka Stockade.

That evening after dinner, Arthur and Duncan retired to the drawing room, as they had done so often before. "What are your plans now, Duncan?" Arthur asked.

"I'm thinking of getting involved in politics, Uncle Arthur. I quite enjoy public speaking and would like to see the principles I fought for at Eureka Stockade come to fruition."

"What principles?"

"Manhood suffrage, the secret ballot, land reform, and other such reforms."

"Isn't it enough that W. C. Wentworth's Constitution Bill provides for an *elected* lower house assembly?"

"No, not when *only* eight thousand men in the colony meet the property requirements to vote. I'd like to see truly representative government through manhood suffrage, so any man twenty-one years or older can vote and hold office."

"I'm not in favor of that; it would lead to the uneducated, emancipist rabble running the colony."

"Well, I'm not afraid of full democracy for all men. What I am afraid of is Wentworth's bill that has the British queen appointing the members of the upper house council. Wentworth wants to raise the graziers and pastorialists to nobility through hereditary seats in the upper house council—just like England's House of Lords."

Arthur shook his head. "You're too young to appreciate that the upper class has done a splendid job of governing the colony so far."

"I don't agree, Uncle Arthur; the inequities have become all too painfully obvious to me. The greedy, large landholders control everything and restrict the common man's freedoms. We have a unique opportunity in this country to create a truly classless, free society that is more democratic than Britain itself."

"Duncan, there's really no reason to argue the form of New South Wales's government, because the British Parliament has already decided the matter by approving Wentworth's Constitution Bill."

"Ah, but the British House of Commons, in its wisdom, altered Wentworth's bill to permit the elected lower house assembly to change the constitution by majority vote, instead of a two-thirds vote. That's why I'd like to get elected. The liberals in the lower house under the leadership of city men, like Charles Cowper and Owen Vernon, should be able to achieve the majority vote to require *election*, rather than appointment, to the upper house council. Election will end the long-time dominance of the elitist landholding gentry. Reformist associations in the goldfields and in Melbourne and Sydney are organizing to promote the Eureka Stockade principles, and I intend to help here in Sydney."

"I must say, Duncan . . . Eureka Stockade was an effrontery to the queen and our English heritage. I'm disappointed that you got yourself involved in an *Irish* revolt against our birthright."

"It wasn't *only* an Irish revolt, Uncle Arthur, and by the way, though you may choose to ignore it, *we* are part Irish . . ."

Arthur looked at him without expression.

Duncan continued without pause. "There were Englishmen, Scots, Europeans, and Americans there too. You weren't there to see the abuses of government. We all came together to fight for the same democratic ideals."

"Very well, Duncan, you were there. I don't wish to argue with you. I'm at the age when I'm willing to leave politics to younger men."

The strained relationship between Duncan and Arthur continued to the family dinner the following evening. Gilbert and his wife Barbara arrived with Barbara's lifelong friend, Grace Butler, who was visiting them. At thirty, Grace was the same age as Barbara and a year and a half older than Duncan. She was an unmarried, plain-looking woman with a prominent nose and close-set eyes. Her figure, however, was curvaceously attractive.

Conversation during dinner was polite prattle and gossip, until Grace, seated opposite Duncan and observing his grimaces when he used his left arm, asked, "Does your arm pain you very much, Mr. Armstrong."

"No, not so much, Miss Butler. I'm just a little clumsy with my left hand."

Although his face was scarred and he wore a black eye patch, Grace found herself curiously attracted to his masculine, rakish appearance. "I can't imagine being shot. It must have been frightful."

"It was, rather," Duncan said, liking the attention, "but I daresay we didn't have much of a choice."

"Your choice could have been not to be there at all," Gilbert said pointedly.

"We didn't expect Commissioner Rede to send military against us without provocation, Gilbert. I'm sorry I had to fire on them, and doubly sorry if I killed any soldiers; however, we had to fight for our principles and defend ourselves."

Gilbert sat back in his chair. "I couldn't believe when I read that you had been shot *and arrested*. I was the one who had to tell Mother and Father."

"Let's leave it at that, Gilbert, shall we?" Arthur admonished.

Gilbert persisted. "Father . . . I'd just like to ask Duncan what he thinks he accomplished by getting himself all shot up—was it worth it?"

"Yes, I think it was, Gilbert," Duncan answered readily. "We established liberal, democratic principles that came out during the trial and that are going to change the direction of government. We learned that we can challenge government and get a fair response. It shows that Britain doesn't want to lose Australia the way it lost America."

Trying to change the subject, Barbara asked, "Duncan, will you return to Star Trading Company, now that you have given up gold prospecting?"

"I wasn't cut out for Star, Barbara. I'm not sure what I'll do."

"How will you support yourself then?" Gilbert asked in a haughty tone.

"No problem there, Gilbert. I've got a fair bit salted away in several banks, plus I still own my interest in Star, which Uncle Arthur rightly advised me to retain. I intend to stand for election to the first Legislative Assembly. We Armstrongs have a proud heritage in politics through grandfather Nathaniel that I can put forward. With my Eureka Stockade notoriety, I imagine there's a city electorate that would support my democratic ideals."

"It's a noble calling, if I may say so."

Surprised, everyone around the table turned to look at Miss Butler who had quietly uttered the statement.

"My word, Miss Butler, are you interested in politics?" Duncan asked disbelievingly.

"No . . . not really. Although, I've read the English classics and feel that those who govern best often answer to a higher calling."

"Why . . . thank you for that thought, Miss Butler. Yes, I do feel rather compelled to involve myself in politics at this critical time in our colony's development. Public service would be a worthwhile life . . . especially after nearly losing mine in pursuit of my principles."

This was the start of a nine-month courtship and engagement that led to the marriage of Duncan Armstrong and Grace Butler in February 1856.

◉

Life for the Fong family in the Sun Wei District had worsened from 1853 into 1856. The fanatically religious Taiping Tienkuo had attacked and taken the Manchu's southern capital of Nanking. Opportunistic *triads*—criminal secret societies—took advantage of the weakened government and attacked Canton, Amoy, and Shanghai. Bandit gangs roamed the countryside, robbing at will. The catastrophic chaos in southern China brought on by the Taiping Rebellion was causing the deaths of tens of millions. With the trade in tea and silk disrupted, British and Australian captains refitted their ships to take Chinese men to Australia's goldfields.

"Revered Father, Yigo and I ask your permission to go to the land of the southern barbarians for three years to seek gold," Ho-teng said.

"So, Saamjai"—Third Son—"you've finally convinced your elder brother to go with you to the San Gam Shan in the land of the *kwai-lo*. Does your younger brother speak for you, Yijai?"—Second Son?

Sing-woo ignored his father's derisive remark. "We want to find gold to regain our family's fortune, *a*-Ba." He used "Ba," the kinship term for "Father," and the prefix *a-* sound to indicate affection.

"Saamjai, I assume you've found a way to pay for this voyage, *kwa*?"—right?

"Yes," Ho-teng said. "I have this notice to men in the Sun Wei District." He handed it to his father. "It says that Melbourne Chinese businessmen will provide passage to the goldfields in the colony of Victoria on August 18 in exchange for two years of work. They'll provide food, tents, tools, and even pay a small wage. All the gold we find will belong to them for the first two years, but, after that, we can work for ourselves and keep all the gold we find. We should be very good at finding gold after two years and should need only six months to a year to become very rich. We'll then purchase our return passage home."

"This is very kind of our Chinese brothers in Melbourne," their father facetiously said with a slight smile while pulling on his stringy, white chin whiskers. He rose from his chair, clasped his hands behind his back, bent forward, and, as was his habit, began to walk slowly around the room as he thought. His sons composed themselves and sat respectfully silent, waiting. After a few minutes, he said, "I don't want to lose you, Yijai . . . but you are the one to go because your elder brother is married and has two small children. You're also unencumbered, Saamjai.

"The plunder of our village will continue until there is peace once more. Our savings are *gone* . . . our provisions are being depleted by the unending payment of tribute, heavy taxes, and pilferage. I fear there will be widespread death from famine soon. I praise the gods that we have our land, the salvation provided by our ancestors."

Sing-woo said, "There's another matter, *a*-Ba, the passage is called a credit ticket that requires your pledge to reimburse the Melbourne businessmen if we dishonor our contract with them."

"Do you intend to dishonor your contracts, Yijai and Saamjai?"

"No, *a*-Ba," Sing-woo answered.

Ho-teng shook his head. "No, Father."

"I don't have to pledge our land as security, *kwa*?"

"That's right, Father, just sign the pledge, as an elder of our clan," Ho-teng said.

"Then I'll do it. And I want you to take your youngest brother with you. He's not of much use in the fields; he's too young to fight; and he eats too much."

"But Daidai"—Little Brother—"is only *eleven years old!*" Ho-teng said.

"He'll be twelve in August before you leave," his father said. "With you, he'll have food to eat; otherwise, he may starve here with us."

On August 15 Sing-woo and his youngest brother, Min-chin, traveled to Canton and stayed with Ho-teng. On the eighteenth, they joined a large number of other men at the wharves answering the recruitment notice. The head of recruitment, Kwan Cheng-san, representing the Melbourne Chinese sponsors, had been an Australian gold miner. He would lead the expedition to the goldfields.

Leader Kwan and his two assistants evaluated the applicants. Min-chin was passed over as too young and small. When Sing-woo said, "Kwan-*Lingdouyan*"—Leader Kwan—"my brother and I will not go without our little brother," the three of them were passed over. Later, when Kwan realized he did not have enough men from the Sun Wei District to fill the two ships commissioned for the voyage, he accepted all three Fong brothers. Kwan did not want to accept any men from other districts, fearing conflict among clans, but was forced to chose seventeen men from other clans to fill the ships.

During the voyage the Fong brothers were inducted into the Sun Wei Tong, a secret brotherhood association. Although membership was voluntary, all the men from the Sun Wei District felt compelled to join. Each new member stated his name starting with the surname followed by given names; the reverse order of names in English. To Chinese, given names were of little importance compared with the overriding significance of family surnames. Each told something about himself and paid his membership fee. Any inductee who could not pay the one pound five shillings fee had the amount added to his debt.

The Fongs learned secret passwords and signs of brotherhood and swore a solemn and sacred oath. A long list of rules and regulations were distributed covering proper behavior, obligations, and punishments. For those who could not read, Leader Kwan read aloud the rules requiring members "to gain the favor of their foreign hosts. Disagreements with the white barbarians were to be avoided for the good of all." All *tong* members were expected "to practice patience and forbearance" and "to endure suffering when imposed on by the discourteous foreign ruffians," who were mostly ex-convicts. They were "to act with the humility of a guest in another's home." The Sun Wei Tong would "serve as judge and police to fine and whip any member who did not follow the rules." Members were to think only of hard work to gain gold riches and return to China as wealthy men who would be honored for all time by their appreciative families.

"You will be sojourners in a barbarian land of large Europeans, many of whom are recently released convicts or sons of convicts," explained Kwan. "The gold diggers are mostly bearded, dirty, mannerless, disreputable, and drunken louts. In groups, they are threatening, disorderly, and riotous." The description horrified many of the Chinese men. Leader Kwan used their fear to his advantage:

"A wise teacher once said, 'The fox must tread softly when he enters the territory of the wolf to avoid a fight he cannot win.' Cooperation and assistance among *tong* members is essential, infighting will not be tolerated. The 350 men on our two ships will travel and work together for safety and companionship. I and my two assistants understand the barbarians and will make all of the arrangements and do all of the talking."

As the three Fong brothers left the meeting, Sing-woo sharply said, "These *kwai-lo* do not seem like the simple, *peaceful* people you described, Saamgo"—Third Eldest Brother.

"I am sure that Kwan-*Lingdouyan* is just preparing us for the worst people we will encounter," Ho-teng replied. "I have met many white foreigners in Canton who were kind souls and not at all as he described. We will be with our Sun Wei countrymen, so you should not be concerned, Elder Brother." But in truth, Ho-teng was very concerned.

Leader Kwan did not tell them that they were sailing for South Australia, instead of the goldfields of Victoria, to avoid Victoria's punitive entry taxes on Chinese. The Goldfields Commission had included in its reports the often-repeated grievance that nothing was being done to staunch the increasing numbers of unwelcome Chinese gold miners. It warned of "an unpleasant possibility of the future, that a comparative handful of European colonists may be buried in a countless throng of Chinamen." Acting on the advice of the commission, Victoria's legislature passed "An Act to Make Provision for Certain Immigrants." It limited the number of Chinese migrants on any vessel to only one for every ten tons of ship tonnage and charged an exorbitant entry tax of ten British pounds for each Chinese arrival.

During the voyage, Sing-woo assumed the responsibilities of the Eldest Brother. He undertook the education, religious training, and disciplining of twelve-year-old Min-chin. Ho-teng passed his time making friends and *mah-jong* gambling, a game played by four players involving 144 small tiles bearing designs on one side. The winner was the first to complete a pattern using thirteen tiles.

After a two-month voyage without incident, the two ships sailed into Guichen Bay and landed at the settlement of Robe, South Australia. Their group joined a tent encampment of eight hundred other Chinese who had arrived earlier in the week.

After meeting with the Melbourne sponsors, Leader Kwan informed his charges that their destination was the Bendigo goldfield nearly three hundred miles away in Victoria. He estimated that the trek would take less than two weeks. While Sing-woo accepted the bad news stoically, Ho-teng joined distraught friends to grumble among themselves, to no avail.

Following ten days of preparations, Kwan's group joined another group of three hundred and set out for Bendigo. The Chinese carried their belongings in heavy baskets suspended from bamboo poles slung across their shoulders that obliged them to walk one behind the other. As they walked by the Casterton Inn pub, men seated on the veranda shared their observations about the small foreign men:

"They been passin' by for twenty minutes and there's still no end to 'em."

" 'Tis a blessed army, a long line of black ants, chatterin' away in their teeth-breaking lingo."

"Fancy a walkabout in white socks and slippers—don't make no sense at all."

"Silly-lookin' buggers with those long black pigtails, saucer hats, blouses, and baggy pants."

Though it was unusually hot for late spring, the headmen drove the group relentlessly. Many suffered from heat exhaustion and were carried in wagons. Stragglers were allowed to fall behind and limped into camp late each night.

After the first few days of walking, Ho-teng collapsed every evening and whined about his discomfort. His brothers had to pitch the tent, cook, and break camp each morning with little help from him. The arduous trek took the lives of several along the way who were buried by the side of the road. Exhausted, the travelers arrived in Bendigo after twenty days to find that they were not welcome— even by the Chinese community.

Bendigo was in turmoil because of the burgeoning number of Chinese and lower mining returns. There were over five thousand Chinese in Bendigo with hundreds more arriving weekly. The district goldfield warden was having a difficult time controlling random anti-Chinese violence and claim jumping, due in part, to a recent murder of a prostitute by a Chinese man. A day before they arrived, a Chinese digger had been killed and many other Chinese injured defending a valuable claim.

After a week of negotiations with the Bendigo Chinese Council, Leader Kwan agreed to lead his group eastward 150 miles to the Buckland River goldfield. The secluded goldfield in the Barry Mountains had been discovered by Canadians in 1852 but abandoned because of poor yield. Sun Wei Chinese had reopened the goldfield and were trying to keep its high productivity a secret.

The arrival of Kwan's group of 350, increased the number of Chinese in Buckland River to over two thousand diggers, greatly outnumbering the three hundred or so whites. The Chinese controlled the best-producing areas. For the first few months, as the Fongs learned the routine of gold mining, there were no serious conflicts. However, by April 1857, when the number of whites had grown to over five hundred, the number of racial clashes increased weekly.

In May after a particularly violent attack by whites on part of the Chinese camp and, two weeks later, the mysterious disappearance of two brothers, Leader Kwan called a meeting to calm emotions. Speculating that the brothers had left because the work was too hard, he reassured his men that the increasing number of conflicts with Europeans was not a serious problem and then asked whether there were any questions.

"You are kind to instruct us, Honorable Kwan-*Lingdouyan*," Sing-woo said with Confucian politesse. "I am unworthy to ask whether you think there will be more serious attacks like the one a couple of weeks ago that injured many men, destroyed tents and property, and jumped claims."

"The attack on the east camp by thirty to forty *kwai-lo* has been reported to the Buckland gold office. We have received word that a constable is being sent to help us. Only *one* claim was lost. And it was lost because only one man was left to guard it—against regulations."

No one had disagreed with Leader Kwan when he had earlier speculated that the two missing brothers had left of their own accord, but Ho-teng knew otherwise and decided to speak up:

"Honorable Kwan-*Lingdouyan*, I am a friend of one of the missing brothers. They are hard workers and had no reason to abandon their valuable claim to the *kwai-lo*. I fear they may have been *killed*.

It's been nearly two weeks since they disappeared with no word, Kwan-*Lingdouyan*."

Surprisingly, Kwan added credence to Ho-teng's concern. "Yes, it's possible, Fong-*Saang*"—Mr. Fong—"but they're not of our *tong* and were told not to dig a claim so close to the European's area."

Another man impolitely exclaimed, "If the *kwai-lo* killed and disposed of them to jump their claim—then *none of us is safe!*"

"Our safety is in numbers," Kwan said calmly. "We still outnumber the Europeans four to one. As long as we work within sight of one another and always leave at least two men at each claim at all times, the *kwai-lo* cannot say that we have abandoned a claim for them to take over. Remember our rules!"

A man rudely addressed the leader without his surname. "*Lingdouyan*, we men workin' on the edge of camp have had our tents slashed an' possessions stolen. We are pelted with stones as we work. If we go out alone, we're pushed around and robbed at knife point. The Europeans are carryin' on a terror campaign to drive us out. We *must* fight back!"

Kwan stood up abruptly, signaling the end the meeting, and said, "We are *guests* in the barbarian's land! It's true the *kwai-lo* do not want us here. But our troubles are few and manageable, as long as we follow our sacred *tong* oaths. To bring peace and harmony to our *tong*, each member must first discipline his mind *and his mouth*. Peace to you all."

On a cool July afternoon, the Fong brothers decided to treat themselves to a hot meal in one of the eateries in the Chinese camp center. Numerous shops and eateries, an infirmary, and a Chinese temple were nicely arranged along either side of the main dirt road that passed through the camp and dead-ended at the Buckland River. Around this commercial center were eight hundred huts and tents. The white camp was haphazard in comparison.

While the Fongs were eating, they were unaware that a raucous meeting of white diggers was underway in another part of the goldfield regarding the "Chinese question" and the effrontery of their "Chinatown." As the meeting came to an angry, inconclusive close, a group of ruffians announced that they were going to "visit"

Chinatown and asked others to join them. A mob of about 150 diggers armed itself with clubs and knives and headed for the Chinese camp.

The mob walked up the main dirt road and over a rise to enter the Chinese commercial center unannounced. They went into the first shops at the top of the street and began attacking the Chinese they found there, causing pandemonium. Those who resisted were beaten senseless and robbed.

From inside an eatery, the three Fong brothers heard the commotion and saw Chinese men running by the front door toward the river. They got up from the table, leaving their coats and Sing-woo's pack behind, and walked to the doorway to look up the road.

"What's h-happening, Yigo?" a frightened Min-chin asked Sing-woo.

Ho-teng replied for his elder brother:

"The shit-eating turds are attacking us!" He turned to run, but Sing-woo grabbed his arm.

"Saamgo, wait!" ordered Sing-woo. "Take Daidai."

Ho-teng grabbed Min-chin's hand, and they ran off together toward the river. Sing-woo ran back into the eatery to collect their coats and his pack.

Emerging, Sing-woo ran headlong into a tall, fat, white man. He bounced off him and fell back against the door jamb. The man swung his club at his head. Ducking, Sing-woo raised his pack. The club glanced off the pack and splintered the door jamb. Springing up, Sing-woo forced his shoulder into the man's protruding belly knocking him back. Losing his balance, the man tripped down two stairs and landed on his back in the dirt road. Sing-woo ran down the road and soon joined a throng of other Chinese backed up at a narrow ford across the Buckland River. Many of the Chinese could not swim. The white mob was less than thirty yards behind, running toward them yelling and waving their clubs, like sabers, above their heads.

Ho-teng and Min-chin had crossed the ford and were waiting on the other side of the river. They could not see Sing-woo until he appeared at the edge of the crowd. He entered the river and tried to swim across with his pack on his back and holding their coats.

"*Second Brother is being swept down the river!*" Min-chin exclaimed. "We must go downstream to try and help him, Third Brother!"

"We can't, Little Brother. The dirty, mangy dogs are just across the river. We must follow the others out of here. Yigo can swim. We can't fall behind. They'll kill us!"

They lost sight of Sing-woo as he was swept around the bend in the river.

Min-chin pointed at the village and cried out in dismay: "*Saamgo, look!—aiya!—they're burning the sacred temple!*"

Ho-teng grabbed Min-chin's hand and jerked him away. "Come on, Daidai, let's go. Don't look back, *we've got to get out of here!*"

Sing-woo let go of his brothers' coats and swam for his life through the torrent but could not make it to the opposite shore. Exhausted, he allowed himself to be swept back to the near rocky shore. As he pulled himself up over the rocks, gasping for breath, he was set on by two men wielding clubs, who beat him unconscious. They stole his pack containing the brothers' savings and cut off his queue. Sing-woo was left unconscious and bleeding on the rocks. Several other Chinese men were swept down the river and drowned.

No one helped Sing-woo. He regained consciousness twenty minutes later and hid in the rocks until the whites had left. The mob took its time stealing everything of value in the town and then destroyed most of it by setting fires.

Later that day, Leader Kwan regrouped his Sun Wei members at their goldfield site. Although badly bruised and cut, Sing-woo was overjoyed that his brothers had escaped the mob and were uninjured. They would have to start saving anew.

Twelve rioters were later arrested: one was convicted of rioting, and three others were found guilty of unlawful assemblage; the remaining eight were released. The four convicted ruffians were each sentenced to nine months' imprisonment.

Following the riot, a Chinese protectorate was established at Buckland. The Protector William Drummond ordered all Chinese, for their own safety, into two camps near the police station. The Chinese left in the morning to work their claims and returned at night. This led to encroachments and claim jumping that quickly overwhelmed the protectorate.

In November the Legislative Council of Victoria passed "An Act to Regulate the Residence of the Chinese Population." It charged every Chinese miner a residence fee of one pound sterling every other month, on grounds that the system of protectorates required the funds to protect the Chinese. The act also required the immediate payment of the ten-pound entry tax for each Chinese miner, if a payment receipt could not be produced. The Chinese communities in Melbourne and on the goldfields immediately organized a coordinated campaign to resist any payments while they petitioned the government for fairness.

An attempt was made to enforce the Chinese residence tax, but most either could not or would not pay it. This was interpreted by the authorities as a boycott that invalidated Chinese diggers' licenses and allowed white diggers to jump their claims at will. By February 1858 all of the best Chinese claims had been usurped, and Kwan's group was reduced to rewashing abandoned tailings for overlooked particles of gold. To escape the punishing residence tax, institutionalized violence, constant harassment, and the low return for their labor, Kwan led his group across the Victorian border to the Majors Creek goldfield in New South Wales.

◎

While walking down the corridor of Parliament House, Duncan could only guess what Owen Vernon, colonial secretary in Premier Cowper's ministry, wanted to discuss with him. When they had set the time for the meeting, Vernon had cryptically said, "I have some personal matters I'd like to discuss with you." A prominent liberal leader for many years, Vernon was the owner of *The Progressive* newspaper. Duncan and Vernon were two of the four members representing Sydney in the New South Wales Parliament and had worked closely on several bills, but they had never before met to discuss "personal matters."

"Congratulations, Duncan, I understand you just had a boy."

"I certainly did, three days ago—our first. We've named him Samuel."

"How's your wife; Grace isn't it?"

"Yes, both are doing well. Thank you for asking."

"That's wonderful. Makes this a great month for you, wouldn't you say, what with the passage of our Electoral Reform Bill?"

"I'm only a backbencher; you did all the real work, Owen."

"Don't be modest, Duncan, you worked hard to see it pass. The liberal-democratic coalition appreciates your contribution. Cowper mentioned to me how impressed he is with you."

"Thank you, Owen."

"You've got a bright future in politics, if that's what you want—in fact, that's what I'd like to talk to you about."

They were interrupted by a knock on the door and Vernon's secretary entered with papers for him to sign. "Excuse me, Duncan, I have to sign these and get 'em off. Won't take a minute."

"Please, go ahead." Duncan crossed his legs and settled comfortably into the luxurious leather sofa. So that's what this meeting is about, he thought, very pleased with himself. I've come a long way in only two years, from leadership of the Sydney Reform Association, where I honed my public-speaking skills, to an emerging leader of the liberal movement in New South Wales. My plan has worked well: lectures about the Eureka Stockade rebellion and articles in *The Progressive* led to meeting Owen Vernon, who then supported me for a Sydney seat in the first Legislative Assembly. At the age of only twenty-nine, I won the seat handily.

Finished signing the papers, Vernon said, "So Duncan . . . now that the Electoral Reform Bill has assured manhood suffrage and provided the secret ballot, what shall we do next?" He leaned back in his chair, clasped his hands behind his head, and waited for Duncan's answer.

"I reckon we work to obtain a majority vote of our assemblymen to change the constitution to require *election* of the upper house council instead of appointment for life. Once we achieve that we're done with the exclusives once and for all and can begin a glorious new era of the common man."

Vernon lowered his arms and placed them on his desk and looked intently at Duncan. "Would it be the right time then to push for a republic?"

"Hold on, Owen, I'm not a republican, and neither are you, unless you are going to surprise me. I have no desire to separate from the mother country. Britain's too important for our security and trade."

Owen's slight smile indicated agreement. Duncan continued. "However, Britain mustn't stand in the way of unlocking crown lands. This is one of the rights I fought for at Eureka Stockade. I intend to push hard for passage of the Crown Lands Bill so settlers can select and purchase small blocks of crown land on easy terms."

"The Crown Lands Bill is an easy populist issue," Owen said. "Once we achieve election of the upper house, its passage is assured. Although, I've heard that W. C. Wentworth will be returning from England soon. He's undoubtedly coming to promote his constitution's appointed upper house aristocracy—an aristocracy of *squatters,* illicitly occupying vast areas of prime crown land that they don't want to unlock, *or* pay for it. Well, their privileged days will soon be over."

Duncan smiled at Owen. "Now that we've removed the property requirement to be elected to the assembly, I believe Wentworth will be short votes to achieve his upper house of nobility. I don't see a House of Lords in Australia."

"Wentworth will also fight me on my Chinese Immigration Restriction Bill shelved in July by the large landholding interests," Owen said. "Since they've been denied free convict labor, they've been importing ever greater numbers of cheap Mongolians, coolie Indians, and Pacific Islander cannibals. The rich bastards aren't willing to pay a white man a decent living wage."

"The Chinese are overrunning us, and those foreign types will never fit into our white society," Duncan said. "By the way, have you ever heard Charles Thatcher's ballad about the Celestials that was sung around the goldfields?"

"No, but I'd like to. You want to give it a go?"

"I'll try, if you forgive my poor singing voice." With a smile, Duncan theatrically cleared his throat, "Ahem . . . here goes:

"Now some of you, perhaps may laugh,
But 'tis my firm *opinion;*
This colony some day will be
Under Chinese *dominion.*
They'll upset the Australian Government;
The place will be their *own;*
And an emperor with a long pigtail
Will sit upon the *throne.*"

Owen was grinning when Duncan finished the ballad, but turned serious again. "Too *damned* right, Duncan, we've got to stop the yellow invasion."

"I'll do everything I can to support your bill, Owen. The Chinese are draining us of our gold wealth and sending it to the emperor of China. They're pagans, smoke opium, live in stinking conditions, and are all gamblers. I saw enough of their kind in the goldfields. When the gold runs out, they'll be all over us, undercutting wages, and being a general nuisance."

Owen was enthused by what Duncan was saying. "Now I want to do something about the wild blacks too. It's an outrage in this day and age—stealing crops and killing livestock—it's got to stop. We need to control these natives. It's intolerable. They didn't stay on the church missions and protectorate's stations like they were suppose to for their own safety. We ought to take their children from them and bring them up properly to promote assimilation as the Select Committee on Aborigines recommended, and let the old ones just die off."

"It's been a difficult problem from the start," Duncan said. "My grandfather Nathaniel tried to solve it. There was no easy solution then, and there's none now. They don't seem to want or need much of anything. You can't teach them anything and the missionaries couldn't convert them. They'd rather sit around doing nothing. Just a lazy mob of dumb no-good-for-nothings. The sooner they die off the better. But I agree, we have a responsibility to stop their trespassing, stealing, and killing."

"It seems that you and I agree on most everything, Duncan."

Duncan beamed. "Like you, Owen, I'm for the politics of reform, liberalism, and majority rule. I want to see this colony reach its full democratic potential for the common man."

"So do I, Duncan, so do I. Cowper and I are forming a small, informal group of parliamentarians who share our vision and have an interest in policy. We want to generate political discourse during the recess. We'll meet in our homes and clubs and exchange energetic correspondence. I wonder whether you would like to join our little group."

"I would," Duncan said while nodding his head. "I'm honored, Owen." This was the entrée into the exclusive power circle he had been hoping for.

"**After a week** of hard work, one needs to relax, smoke a little, and enjoy *fan-tan* with friends," Ho-teng said. "Working all the time is not good for one's soul, *kwa?*"—right?

"I agree, *a*-Fong"—good friend Fong—"we work too hard," said Lau Mo-han. He took a drag on the pipe and held the smoke in his lungs for several seconds before exhaling.

"Pass me the pipe of many joys, *a*-Lau," Ho-teng asked. "Did you mix some opium in with the tobacco?"

"Yes."

"Good."

It was Saturday evening, and Ho-teng's best friend had invited him to meet his younger brother Lau Tai-kan and his friend, Kwok Yun-ming. They had arrived the day before from Sydney to join Lau Mo-han's gold-mining team at Lambing Flat. They sat cross-legged and reclined on a blanket spread out on the ground in Lau Mo-han's large tent. The three men watched intently as Lau Mo-han, the *fan-tan* game banker, poured a stream of small, smooth, river pebbles from a large jar into a bowl, which he then covered with a plate. The other three placed bets on numbers 1, 2, 3, or 4 that were inked into the blanket. When the betting was done, the banker overturned the bowl and counted the pebbles into groups of four.

"Three pebbles are left over in the last group," Lau Mo-han said. "*A*-Fong wins on number three. You're banker now, Daidai"—Little Brother.

Lau Tai-kan took the jar from his eldest brother. "Have you been digging for gold very long, Fong-*Saang*?"—Mr. Fong?

"For four and a half years, Lau-*Saang*." Ho-teng differentiated between the Lau brothers by using *a*-Lau for his close friend Lau Mo-han and Lau-*Saang* for Mr. Lau Tai-kan.

"Have you looked for gold in other places?" Kwok asked.

"My two brothers and I fulfilled our two-year indenture by working at Buckland River in Victoria and Majors Creek in New South Wales. We continued on at Majors Creek working for ourselves, but when gold was discovered at Pollock's Gully in the Snowy Mountains, we rushed there with ten other independent Sun Wei countrymen. We did very well until twenty, dirty, pig-faced bastards woke us up one morning with their guns and robbed us. They told us to pack up and get out and said they would kill us if we returned. So we came here in—"

"That's our problem," an agitated Lau Mo-han said. "Excuse me for interrupting, *a*-Fong, but the Europeans know that we will give up our diggings to a mob roll-up or to a murderous gang of claim-jumpers rather than fight! They have no respect for us, *kwa*?"

"We can't fight them and hope to win, *a*-Lau," Ho-teng said. "It's their country, and they do what they want."

"The *kwai-lo* think we're weak and pitiful," Lau Mo-han said.

"Don't think you can fight them because you are a big man, *a*-Lau," Ho-teng said. "My elder brother is nearly as big as you and was badly beaten up, had our money stolen, and his queue cut off at Buckland River. After that, we decided to avoid trouble . . . because they can jump our claims, beat us, even kill us, and there is no justice. They're *kwai-lo*, stinkin', motherless, barbarian devils, without honor or remorse."

"I imagine they think we are robbing them," Lau Tai-kan said.

The others looked at him disapprovingly, unsure of what he meant.

Lau Tai-kan thought for a second and tried an analogy: "It's as if we were back home, and a white man came into our rice paddy and stole some of our rice."

"No, that's not the same," Ho teng said. "That would be *my* rice, which I grew on *my* land, with *my* labor; that's different from finding gold hidden in the earth that no one owns."

"But it's *their* earth, not ours," Lau Tai-kan retorted.

"*Bai!*" For pity's sake! Lau Mo-han shook his head at his younger brother. "The *kwai-lo* allow other foreigners—Italians, Germans, Americans, Irish—to dig. I agree with *a*-Fong."

Lau Tai-kan was the persistent type and not ready to concede. He gave them a knowing smile. "Ah, but they're all Europeans and the same religion, that's the big difference, isn't it?"

"No, Little Brother," Lau Mo-han said. "The *big* difference is that we are too different from them—a different color, a different race, a different religion, and an ancient, higher culture. They have no culture and no manners. They're a crude, ignorant, mongrel people."

"They're all shitty *ngau-shee*"—cow turds, Ho-teng said matter-of-factly. Then, delighted with the graphic nature of his epithet, he hunched over laughing, "he-haw he-haw he-haw he-haw," hands covering his mouth. His silly, infectious laugh made the others laugh with him.

Lau Tai-kan finished counting the pebbles. "There's four pebbles left over. Fong-*Saang* wins again and splits it with *a*-Kwok also on number four." Lau Tai-kan pushed the winnings toward them. "Your turn, Fong-*Saang*."

Turning serious again, Ho-teng said, "They *use us* to find gold for them. That's what they do." He poured pebbles from the jar into the bowl. "Then they take it *away* from us. I've seen this happen at Buckland River, Pollock's Gully, and again here at Lambing Flat.

"We came here in June last year, after most of the Europeans had abandoned the goldfield. We dug hole after hole until we found a valuable seam of gold. There were about three hundred of us here then and less than fifty whites. We developed our mines working long hours, every day, almost without a break. The whites were lazy and jealous of us. Within three months, the news of our success had leaked out and the hairy, masturbating devils came rushing back. By November there were 1,500 of them, outnumbering us three to one. Then they posted notices around our camp to quit. A few days later a mob roll-up forced us off our valuable claim. We searched for a month before we found a poor claim at Ironbark. When that ran out in March, we moved to Back Creek, three miles from here."

"Still, there are no harsh, unfair taxes against us in this colony as there are in Victoria, although such laws are being considered," Lau Mo-han said.

"What brought you here, Lau-*Saang?*" Ho-teng asked Lau Tai-kan.

"I came because Yatgo"—Eldest Brother—"told me to come. He said that the commissioner had divided the goldfield into a Chinese zone and a European zone and guaranteed our safety."

"I wrote that letter to you many months ago, Daidai," Lau Mo-han said. "Things have changed, and you've come at a bad time. When I told you to come, Premier Cowper had been here with three hundred police and troops to make the *kwai-lo* sign an agreement with us. Now, only twenty police remain to enforce the agreement. The number of European diggers has grown to twelve thousand against our two thousand. The mangy, white devils do not respect their own agreements. I don't trust them. They will soon want our claims for themselves and will try to force us out."

"You don't expect a roll-up any time soon, do you?" Ho-teng asked with a concerned look. "It's been quiet for seven months. There's been no recent mass meeting against us, *kwa?*"

"I haven't heard of any," replied Lau Mo-han, "*yet!*"

Ho-teng had finished counting the pebbles. "*Ahh-sooo*, nobody picked number one so you *all lose*—this money goes to the next winner, *which will be me!*" he said jokingly. "The jar goes to you next, Mr. Banker Kwok." As he handed the jar to Kwok, he asked, "What is your honorable work in Sydney, Kwok-*Saang?*"

"I work in a laundry, and *a*-Lau is a cabinetmaker," Kwok replied.

"Really, I was a poor woodworker in Canton," Ho-teng said humbly in the Confucian tradition of self-effacement. "I apprenticed under Cheong-*Sifoo.*" By using the title *sifoo*, meaning "master,"

Ho-teng let them know that he had been trained by an expert woodworker.

Impressed, Lau Tai-kan said, "Ah, we could use your wondrous skills in our shop in The Rocks."

Ho-teng gave a questioning look. "The *Rocks*?"

"It's called 'The Rocks' because the houses are built on the steep, rocky hillside of Sydney Cove," Lau Tai-kan explained. "Most of the Chinese in Sydney live there. We have many shops, businesses, gambling houses, Chinese doctors, and pillow and opium houses of many delights. As a city man you would like it there, Fong-*Saang*."

"Sydney sounds very appealing. I'd very much enjoy the pleasures of a pillow house," Ho-teng said. "It's been too long since I've experienced the Clouds and the Rain, but my elder brother wants to return home soon."

"Are your brothers also city men from Canton?" asked Kwok.

"No, Elder Brother and Little Brother were farmers in my village, Yang-lu, fifty miles from Canton. Elder Brother doesn't like cities. He doesn't like gambling, and he doesn't like smoking opium. He's a good man ... but he has little enjoyment in life and only knows how to work, work, work."

"You must be very rich by now," Kwok said.

"I would praise the gods with many offerings for my good fortune if that were so. Sadly, times have been hard for us. To make matters worse, every time we get a little money, Elder Brother sends most of it with returning friends and *tong* officials to our poor family. We are making only enough to eat, clothe ourselves, and replace our equipment, and seldom have extra money for joys such as this evening—but even then, Elder Brother thinks I waste our money."

Ho-teng thought to himself, they'd piss themselves with envy if they knew I have eighty British pounds sewn into the clothes I'm wearing and ten more in my money belt, Sing-woo has a like amount, and even young Min-chin has thirty pounds. We're rich men worth more than two hundred pounds sterling, not counting our well-hidden gold dust.

"*Ho-wan!*" Good luck! Exclaimed Kwok because his friend Lau Tai-kan had bet on number three alone. "Three wins! The gods smile on *a*-Lau who wins the big pot." Kwok handed him the large winnings. The four men played *fan-tan* well into the night, until the effects of the opium made them somnolent, and they fell asleep.

Early in the morning, they were aroused by the sounds of loud cheering, shouting, and cries of "ROLL-UP! ROLL-UP!" and a band playing the tune "Rule, Britannia!" to which marchers were singing:

> "Rule, Britannia!
> Britannia rules the waves!
> No more Chinamen allowed
> In New South Wales!"

Ho-teng was first out of the tent. His eyes were met with a terrifying sight. A mob of over three thousand whites was coming up the road armed with pick handles, clubs, and muskets, most marching, but a few mounted on horseback. A marching band led them toward the Chinese camp. The marchers followed the green, white, and gold flag of Ireland, the American Stars and Stripes, and the Lambing Flat flag incorporating the Scottish cross of St. Andrew with the embroidered words "Roll-up, Roll-up, No Chinese."

Ho-teng stuck his head into the tent and cried:

"It's a ROLL-UP! *Grab your things and run!* I'm going to warn my brothers!"

Ho-teng quickly covered the three-mile distance to their Back Creek camp. Sing-woo and Min-chin were still asleep in their tent when Ho-teng ran down the track into their secluded valley yelling, "ROLL-UP! ROLL-UP!" While he roused his brothers, bleary-eyed men began to gather around the Fong's tent asking questions, trying to judge the seriousness of the situation.

"We've got to get out right away," Ho-teng said excitedly to Sing-woo, "this is a *serious roll-up!*" He grabbed his clothes and possessions from a corner of the tent and began to stuff them into his pack. Sing-woo and Min-chin stood dressing.

"Did you see any *kwai-lo* attack anyone?" Min-chin asked as he dressed.

"No, but it was a *huge mob!* I ran here as fast as I could to warn you."

"There's been no quit postings," the man in the next tent said. "They always give warnings."

"Maybe they won't come here," somebody said.

Ho-teng stuck his head out of the tent. "The dung-eaters are in the thousands. They *will* be coming here!"

Someone yelled, "*Quiet! I think I hear shots!*" The crowd hushed. Faint sounds of sporadic gunfire could be heard in the distance.

An argument started among the gathering crowd, and a large man angrily said, "I'm not leaving my claim, just *so it can be jumped!* We're in a hidden valley and should be safe."

"There's *no* safe area in a roll-up," Sing-woo said, and, at that moment, made the decision to leave their profitable claim. "Forget the tent. Pack only valuables and some food and water." To Ho-teng, he whispered, "I'll get our gold." He climbed down their mine shaft to retrieve the gold dust hidden in four leather pouches. Tying the pouches together, he hung them from his neck, concealed beneath his shirt. Rejoining his brothers, he helped them finish packing.

Groups of frantic Chinese, some of them injured, were coming into the valley saying they had barely escaped with their lives. The Fongs picked up their heavily laden bamboo poles and joined others escaping up the steep track out of the valley. They had walked only a short distance, when a large group of freightened Chinese came running down the track from Lambing Flat screaming:

"*Run—the roll-up horde is right behind us!*"

The vanguard of the roll-up mob caused panic in the camp. Some of the Chinese who had resolved to stay tried to protect their claims, while others grabbed their valuables and ran into the bush. The large number of whites streaming into Back Creek quickly overwhelmed anyone who opposed them and tore the camp apart looking for valuables. Realizing that the escaping Chinese must be carrying their valuables with them, the rapacious mob pursued them up the hill. Men on horseback rode past the line of Chinese laboring up the steep track and caught up with the main body at the crest of the hill. Using whips and pick handles, they rounded the Chinese as they would sheep in wild disorder, forcing them back down the track toward the mob coming up the hill.

Sing-woo shouted, *"Brothers, drop everything and follow me!"* Dropping his bamboo pole and attached baskets, Sing-woo jumped into the bush and headed for the thickest area of undergrowth where it would be difficult for horsemen to follow. Entering the dense underbrush, he stopped when he heard Min-chin scream:

"YIIIIGOOOO, hellllp!"

He saw a horseman between himself and Min-chin. Ho-teng was nowhere in sight. The horse was reared up, and its rider was whipping Min-chin, who had his arms over his head, protecting his face, as he tried to maneuver around the horse.

"Git down the hill, Chinky!" the rider was yelling. *"Downhill, damnya!"*

From higher ground, Sing-woo ran toward the horseman. Only at the last moment did the rider glimpse the Chinese man leaping from a rock ledge through the air at him. He turned his head and caught the full force of Sing-woo's head impacting his jaw. The rider fell from his horse while Sing-woo landed across the neck of the horse and slid down to his feet.

Sing-woo and Min-chin ran from the fallen rider as another horseman, who had caught sight of the clash, rode after them. The rider delivered a vicious pick-handle blow to the back of Min-chin's head and rode on after Sing-woo, who was sliding down a steep, dirt slope to the creek bed below. At the bottom of the thirty-foot slope, Sing-woo looked up and realized that Min-chin was not behind him. The horseman emerged from the bush further up the valley where the slope was more gradual and rode down the dry creek bed screaming and waving his pick handle at him. Sing-woo ran down the creek bed for a short distance, then climbed back up the slope into the bush, where he ran headlong into a group of whites coming uphill. He fought them off, but the horseman caught up and hit him with his pick handle. The group attacked him, clubbing and stabbing, until he passed out.

Ho-teng had followed Sing-woo and Min-chin for a few half-hearted bounds into the bush before fatalistically accepting his *karma* to be herded downhill along the track. A rider grabbed hold of his pigtail, pulled his head up against his jostling horse, and cut off his queue. Laughing scornfully, he shoved it under his belt with several others, some with bloody pieces of scalp attached. The frightened Chinese were attacked by the mob intent on subduing and robbing them of their valuables. Seeing the mob beating others, Ho-teng quickly undressed and gave up his clothes, money belt, and jade good-luck charm from around his neck. He sat meekly with a group of similarly disrobed and cowering Chinese watching their clothes being cut to shreds for the money and other valuables sewn inside. The smell of bonfires was thick in the air as their camp was put to the torch.

Ho-teng and Min-chin found their brother bleeding and near death later that day. They stopped his bleeding and spent the night hiding and keeping warm by huddling together. The next day, Sing-woo was delirious as they carried him to a temporary aid station set up by the goldfield commissioner to provide shelter and food and treat wounded Chinese, most of them had lost everything.

After two days of treatment, Sing-woo slowly came back to life. In a weak voice no stronger than a whisper, he said, "Daidai and Saamgo . . . praise the gods . . . you're both still alive. I thought . . . I thought, I was dead . . . but we're all alive . . ." His last few words before he fell back to sleep were "Our ancestors have watched over us."

He awoke later in the day much stronger.

Min-chin was at his bedside. "Yigo, you're awake again. I'm so happy!" He laid his hand on his elder brother's arm reassuringly. "Saamgo and I prayed for you before Kwun Yam, the Goddess of Mercy. A monk saved her from the mob."

"Thank you, Daidai. It must have helped. What does she look like?"

"She's more than two feet tall wearing a white flowing robe. She stands serenely on a lotus leaf and holds a vase of magical cures. We lit sandalwood sticks and made an offering and prayed for your full recovery."

Ho-teng walked up. "You look so much better, Yigo. We prayed for you."

"Yes, Daidai just told me. Thank you, Saamgo."

"Elder Brother, I want you to meet your cot mate." Ho-teng drew Sing-woo's attention to the man in the next cot. "This is Lau-*Saang*, the Little Brother of *a*-Lau, the friend I told you about. I had him moved next to you for company."

"Hello, Fong-*Saang*, please don't try to talk," Lau Tai-kan said consolingly. "I am very happy that you have returned to the land of the living."

In a weak voice, Sing-woo said, "I hope your elder brother was not injured."

Lau Tai-kan looked very concerned. "I fear Yatgo"—Eldest Brother—"may have been killed. He wouldn't leave his tent because he had money and gold buried under it. The mob didn't attack us immediately. We thought they'd give us time to collect our things. The three of us started to take down the tent, but the mob started pushing people around and then fights broke out.

"I also fear for my friend *a*-Kwok. In the commotion, I lost sight of him. I stayed beside Yatgo. We fought them with the hammers we were using to take down the tent. I saw a man hit my brother with a tomahawk and another knocked him to the ground with a club. It all happened in seconds. I was stabbed . . . once under my armpit and once in my back. I passed out. When I came to . . . women and children were picking through the clothes of those lying around me. I played dead. It was strangely quiet, except for the moaning of the wounded. After a while, I looked around and joined a group of injured countrymen. My brother was gone. Everything was destroyed and burning in several large bonfires. My clothes were ripped and torn—nearly off me—and my gold ring was taken along with all of my money. It was terrible."

"I see your queue was cut off, too," Ho-teng said to Lau Tai-kan, while turning his head to show his own missing queue. Turning to Sing-woo, he said, "Forgive me, Yigo, all my money was taken. The mob beat me. There was nothing I could do."

Sing-woo ran his eyes over Ho-teng's face, hands, and arms. He saw no visible signs of a beating and assumed that once again Ho-teng had found the easy path. Turning his head toward Min-chin, he asked, "Daidai, what happened . . . ? I'm sorry . . . we got separated."

"I was hit on the head from behind and stunned," Min-chin answered, "but I was able to crawl into dense underbrush." Leaning forward he whispered some good news into Sing-woo's ear: "We still have the thirty pounds sewn into my clothes."

Sing-woo could not keep his heavy eyelids from closing. He dozed off thinking: I don't care about the money, or the gold taken from us, or our injuries that will heal with time. All I care about is my brothers are alive, and we are together. Praise be to our benevolent ancestors, Lord Buddha, and Kwun Yam, who answered my brothers' prayers. He fell into a deep, peaceful sleep.

Lau Tai-kan's brother and friend did not show up at the temporary aid station during the three weeks that it was open. The Fong brothers tried to console Lau Tai-kan with the official report that no Chinese had been killed, although none of them believed it.

The police arrested three rioters for the mob violence against the Chinese. Several days later, a thousand men behind a marching band arrived in front of the police compound and shouted for the release of the three rioters. A captain led fifty-seven police out of the compound, lined them up to face the angry demonstrators, and announced that the prisoners would not be released. As the mob advanced, the police fired over their heads, and the mob fired into the police. The police returned fire as mounted troopers charged with sabers slashing. A demonstrator was shot dead and twenty others wounded. Several police were also wounded. Almost out of ammunition, the police withdrew and released their prisoners. Thirteen men were later arrested and tried for the mob violence. Two were sentenced to two-years' hard labor, and the remaining eleven were found innocent.

During Sing-woo's recuperation, Ho-teng decided that he wanted to return to China. "Elder Brother, I wish to leave this god-cursed, dung-eating, mongrel country and return home. If we watch our money, we have enough to purchase transport to Sydney, two hundred miles to the east, and pay our fare home."

Shocked at the foul mouth Ho-teng had developed, Sing-woo looked at him with disdain for a moment before answering. "No,

Younger Brother. We would arrive home with no money. It would be an unacceptable loss of face, and we would only be adding to our family's burden."

Ho-teng shook his head. "Nine times we've sent them money with trusted friends and Sun Wei officials. We've fulfilled our responsibilities."

"The money we've sent them has been spent. Our family is *starving*, Saamgo! There is no way for us to earn the money at home that we can make here. We must make more in the goldfields. It's the only way."

Ho-teng had anticipated his elder brother's reluctance to return home without money. "While you were recovering, we didn't want to tell you that New South Wales has passed the same residence fee as the one we escaped in Victoria. To get a mining license, we must each pay a ten-pound entry tax *plus* a residence fee of one pound sterling every other month. We don't have the money, Yigo."

"We will have to put ourselves under the protection of our ancestors and the gods. When I'm able to work again, we'll find a way."

Ho-teng raised his voice and spoke disrespectfully: "*Two times* we've almost been killed gold mining! You expect too much of our ancestors! We should not burden them further. There's another way, a safe way; we can work as cabinetmakers in Sydney with Lau-*Saang*. We can go with him. He says Sydney has a Chinese community that is very nice, and we'll be well paid."

After much discussion among the brothers, Sing-woo, as Eldest Brother, made the decision that they would go to Sydney. It was Min-chin's seventeenth birthday, August 12, 1861, when the Fong brothers and Lau Tai-kan arrived in The Rocks.

Lau Tai-kan introduced the Fongs to Wong Ching-tin the owner of Wong Cabinets located on George Street. Wong immediately took Ho-teng into his woodworking shop to see whether he was a trained craftsman or not. When he saw that Ho-teng was an accomplished woodworker, Wong agreed to start him at fifteen shillings a week, pay his brothers by the piece, and provide lodging. After talking it over with Lau Tai-kan, the Fongs accepted Wong's offer.

The Fongs and Lau Tai-kan shared the third floor above the workshop with seven other Wong employees. Each of two bedrooms was fitted with triple-decker bunk beds on opposite walls leaving a six-foot space between for daily living.

Lau Tai-kan was disappointed that there was no message from his eldest brother waiting for him in Sydney, but he did find his friend Kwok Yun-ming working at the laundry. Kwok said that he had run from the attacking mob and returned directly to Sydney. He hadn't seen or heard anything of Tai-kan's brother. Lau Tai-kan now felt certain that his brother had been killed. There were others missing from Lambing Flat, and rumors were circulating that Chinese killed by the mob had been thrown down abandoned mine shafts.

◎

Owen Vernon was meeting with Jeffrey Pickering, minister of public works, when Duncan joined them and announced:

"On good authority, I've just heard that Wentworth is preparing his resignation as president of the Legislative Council. He's returning to England!"

"Wentworth's going back to England!" Owen slapped his hands together jubilantly. "What wonderful news—for good, I hope." A grin spread across his face. "Why, the Bunyip Aristocrat has just returned from England—what, a year and a half ago?—April '61? Running away with his tail between his legs, is he?"

"I shouldn't gloat, Owen; he'll be remembered as the Thomas Jefferson of Australia, the writer of our constitution," Pickering said. "Though, I'll grant you that he's come to a sad end. I respected the man for years before he lost his way. He couldn't keep up with the times and made himself worse than irrelevant."

Duncan shared additional gossip. "He'll say that legal affairs require him in England. He's leaving his Vaucluse House in the hands of a caretaker. Over the past year, he's spent a small fortune refurbishing the house and grounds, so I'll take him at his word that he intends to return. I think he's leaving a most disillusioned and disappointed man who thinks the colony is lost to radicalism and mob rule—he sees you as the leader of the rabble, Owen."

"And you're my accomplice, I'm sure," Owen said, laughing.

"It's very sad that such a great statesman has to leave in this way," Pickering said. "I don't know why Wentworth returned at all after living in England for seven years."

"He returned with a mission that was singularly ineffective," Owen said. "It's no happenstance that he returned a month before the initial five-year appointments of the Legislative Council were about to expire. He wanted a hand in who would be appointed to the upper house council for life. Our Legislative Council Election Bill put an end to his hope for a hereditary House of Lords. And he lost on my Chinese Immigration Restriction Bill too."

"He didn't oppose your Chinese bill, Owen," Pickering said. "I don't recall that there was *any* substantial dissent."

"He was dead set against it until the blessed Lambing Flat riot. Goddamned Chinese caused a parliamentary emergency for Cowper. He had to personally go out there twice. Then the police had to go and arrest some rioters—bloody stupid thing to do with emotions running at a fever pitch. Rioters attacked the jail to release their mates—police shot, rioters shot—bloody civil unrest over *Celestials!* Wentworth was smart enough to realize that the Mongolians were a lost cause. Once our immigration restrictions take hold, the blood-sucking, greedy squattocracy will lose their main source of cheap coolie labor and have to start paying a white man's living wage."

"Wentworth really lost heart after the Crown Lands Bill was passed over his objections," Duncan said. "He was a giant of his time, but unfortunately for him, his time had passed."

Chapter 9

Boom Times

The morning sun shone brightly through the openings between the drapes. Eleanor was awakened by the movement of her husband's hands on her. "Oh you can't be serious . . . you naughty boy . . . get your hand out of there . . . this is our big day . . . ."

Alistair laughed. "Oooo . . . you're in big trouble."

". . . guests will be here in a few hours, silly." Giggling, she rolled over to face Alistair. "*Alie* . . . now don't get funny." She grabbed for his hands, and they playfully grappled. "Honestly . . . you've no sense of timing—you weren't interested last night."

"Well I am *now*. They won't be here until one; we've got plenty of time."

"*You've* got plenty of time; I have to organize lunch for eight men."

Despondent. "You can at least give a bloke a little kiss, can't ya?"

Kissing him quickly, she rolled away laughing. "That's all you get till tonight."

Eleanor had married for love. She had fallen for a tall, handsome, blond-haired, fun-loving Englishman with joyous blue eyes. They had met when he was building an addition onto her father's house. She was twenty-two; he twenty-eight, when they married in 1856. They had a girl, Priscilla, who was now five. A miscarriage in 1862 resulted in serious complications that nearly took Eleanor's life.

While they were dressing, Alistair expressed his concern. "I hope I don't muck this up."

"You'll do fine, dear. These men are your friends; they like and respect you as a reliable, hard-working builder. That's why they're considering investing in you—they trust you."

"But can I convince them that I'm up to owning and developing property with their money?"

"Well it's our money too. You've got to impress them with that. We'll have everything we own in this. You have the expertise and experience to make more money for them than any other investment they can make. That's the way to present it. You're doing them a favor. My brother Gilbert is going to invest for sure. I think my cousin Duncan will too."

"Felix Knox told me straightaway that he'll become a shareholder, and David Carver will too—probably."

Eleanor spent the morning directing the cook and maids in the preparations for the lunch. At twelve-thirty the guests started to arrive and were taken out onto the back veranda to enjoy the view of Port Jackson from the heights of Paddington. An aperitif was served. After all of the men arrived, Alistair led them into the front parlor to begin the meeting.

"Thank you all for coming to hear my proposal. You know from reading the incorporation document that this meeting is about investing in me, my company, and the continued spectacular growth of Sydney. Although Gilbert and Duncan are relatives, and I have built four of your homes, you may not know much about my background. My family emigrated from Bristol in 1841 when I was thirteen. Father was a master carpenter and immediately got a job managing a team of carpenters and convict laborers to build Victoria Barracks. He also supervised the construction of much of Paddington Village, across from the main entrance of the barracks, to provide workingmen's housing for the carpenters, quarrymen, stonemasons, and others working on the barracks. We moved into a little three-room cottage he built on Gipps Street in the village."

"I certainly hope you're going to provide wider streets than those little, narrow street in the village," Duncan said, "two carriages can hardly pass."

"I'll get into all that, Duncan."

"Oh, sorry, Alistair, I'll try not to interrupt."

"No worries . . . I worked for my father as an apprentice carpenter until 1848, when the barracks were completed. After that, I worked as an independent for a couple of years. At the tender age of twenty-two, in 1850, I set up Norman Builders with two employees to specialize in quality contract homes. We started doing mostly improvements to existing homes and gradually got into building new homes and villas. I've been doing that for ten years now and have eleven full-time employees and a long list of day workers.

"I've watched the value of properties I've built increase phenomenally as a result of the gold rush and population increase. The land value has increased faster than the cost of construction. The price of land in Sydney has become very dear, but not so in Paddington, and certainly not in Manly. I believe in William Gilbert Smith's holiday resort concept for Manly and would like to purchase an ideally located site on the Corso for a hotel—now—while the land is cheap. If I wait five or six years from now when the resort is more established and popular, the ideal site will have been purchased, or the land price will be too high. I also want to buy as much land as possible in Paddington, while it's reasonably priced. I've come to realize that long-term investment in residential and hotel properties, as the builder, developer, and owner, is a sure path to wealth." He stopped talking when the butler appeared at the doorway.

"Lunch can be served, sir, when you desire," the butler said.

Gilbert asked, "Alistair, why don't we break on your key word 'wealth' and partake of my sister's sumptuous lunch?"

"Good suggestion, Gilbert, this is a good place to break."

While dessert was being served, Alistair resumed his presentation.

"I want to build a better class of middle-income rental housing for families, like the better terrace houses being built in Woolloomooloo. I'd build rows of connected two-story houses of substantial brick and stone, instead of wood. The ground floor would consist of a front parlor, back parlor for dining, and a kitchen extension out back to reduce the fire risk. Upstairs, over the parlors, would be two or three bedrooms. They'd have deep backyards for a garden and a privy next to the back lane. Modern cast-iron, coal-burning fireplaces would be provided in the front and back parlors and in the main bedroom upstairs. The kitchen would have an indoor sink connected to a drain running underground to the backyard cesspit. Cast-iron lacework railings would be used on the front veranda and a decorative cast-iron fence and gate would enclose the small front yard. Previously these cast-iron adornments were expensive because they came from England, as ballast in the ships. Now they're manufactured here."

"They sound like charming little homes, Alistair, but what are the economics of the deal?" Peter Fletcher asked.

"Each terrace house will cost £220 or slightly more, depending on what I decide to put into them. What do you mean exactly by 'the economics of the deal?'"

"You know, the financial arrangements, return on capital, how long until profits go to the shareholders—those sort of things."

With a sly smile, Alistair turned and nodded toward his wife, who was quietly conversing with the butler. "Eleanor is the power behind the throne, gentlemen; she's handled the books for the seven years of our marriage and can answer those kinds of question better than me. Did you hear Peter's questions, Eleanor?"

"Yes, I did, though I don't wish to impose, Alistair," she said. The men around the table looked quizzically at her.

"She's not accustomed to discussing business with men, Alistair," Duncan said. "Eleanor, isn't rea—"

"That's not my experience," Felix Knox interjected. "Eleanor did an excellent job on the financing for my house, and the construction cost came in right as projected. Hearing no objections . . . I move we ask her to respond."

"I second that we hear from my sister," Gilbert said, chuckling.

Eleanor smiled to herself as she walked over next to Alistair. She would assure them that their money would be well invested.

"In June, gentlemen, the Winsley Estate will be selling 80-foot-wide allotments for approximately one pound per foot or £80 an allotment. We can subdivide these into 20-foot frontages to get four terrace houses where one large custom house would ordinarily be built. The standardized terrace house is the most profitable kind of housing that we can build for long-term investors. A series of identical units makes the most of investment capital with its narrow frontages, common walls, and standardized fittings. The £220 that Alistair mentioned includes only £20 for the land and the rest for construction of the house and appurtenances. The low cost of the land, as a proportion of"—

Alistair looked about to see how the men were regarding her. They're actually listening intently to what she's saying, he marveled. She really knows this financial stuff and presents herself well, stands proudly erect, shoulders back, composed, and with a self-assurance that's attractive. . . . a handsome woman but not the kind that men lust after . . . her figure's too slender right now, exaggerating her height . . . attractive hair style and soft brown eyes set in a pretty face. It's the total package I love, he concluded, as he returned to her presentation.

—"rent for such a house would be 15 shillings a week, meaning capital expended would return itself in less than six years, thereafter providing a yearly income of at least £40 for each terrace house. Taking construction interest payments into account, we estimate the shareholders should start to receive a return on investment in three to four years which will grow each succeeding year through rent increases . . ." Eleanor's words grew fainter as she self-consciously thought she was speaking too long and the men were losing interest. "Now I really must return to the kitchen, gentlemen . . ." She paused to answer any questions, but there were none. "I'm sure Alistair can answer any questions. Please excuse me, gentlemen."

As she walked away, Felix Knox spoke in a loud voice so Eleanor would hear. "*Very* impressive. What did I tell you, Duncan! Did she answer your question, Peter?"

Smirking, Peter nodded. "Most assuredly."

"Alistair, what makes you feel that middle-class, working people want to come out to the country to live in close-packed terrace houses?" asked David Carver. "Terraces seem more appropriate to me in the city."

"Industrialization of the city is driving the middle class in our direction. Fifty years ago Governor Macquarie inadvertently created a social divide between the west and east when he split the Botany Bay catchment roughly in half. He promoted commerce in the western half and used the eastern half to preserve Sydney's water supply at Lachlan Swamp and the Sydney Common pasturage. The mansions and villas built in Woollahra, Waverley, and Paddington have set the standard for clean, healthy, country living. The smoke-stacks of industry now darken the western sky and will continue to create undesirable living conditions there.

"Every Sunday we see the middle class driving out Old South Head Road to enjoy our beautiful community and picnic on the heights for the views of the harbor and ocean. Lately they've also been picnicking and hiking around Cascade Waterfall in Paddington valley, since the blacks left a few years back. Respectable middle-class famili—"

"Excuse me, Alistair, do you know why the Abos lived in the bush around Cascade Waterfall?" Peter asked.

Alistair thought it was an odd question and gave Peter a non-plus look. "I don't know ... for water, I fancy."

With a straight face, Peter said, "No, they lived in the bush because they had no *abo*-de."

Caught by surprise, the men suddenly erupted with loud laughter at Peter's unexpected witticism. After a minute of repartee, the men settled down.

Alistair wiped tears of laughter from his eyes with his serviette. "Well ... you certainly know how to loosen-up a bloke's boring presentation, Peter. Thanks for that—but now I can't remember what I was saying. Oh yes, 'terrace houses in the country' and middle-class families wanting to get away from the city, especially from slums like The Rocks and dirty industries. Old South Head Road to Paddington is the only reliable road to the eastern suburbs, bcause it passes over high ground. The road to Randwick crosses swamps that overflow, and New South Head Road transverses deep gullies and broad low-lying areas subject to frequent flooding. We now have two omnibus companies, with two- and four-horse teams, linking Paddington to the city. We have a public school, churches, shops, two hotels, and a new municipal government. At reasonable rents, I'm confident that our new, modern terrace houses will lease quickly to professionals, merchants, skilled tradesmen, and office workers who will travel to work in the city."

"Regarding government," Duncan said in an affected senatorial tone, "Paddington's recent incorporation should result in quicker developmental approvals and community improvements than depending on the Sydney Council. Paddington Council has already installed ten gas lamps along Old South Head Road and requested a direct water connection from the Lachlan Swamp supply. Within the next ten years or so, most Paddington houses should have water piped directly into them. Sanitation is becoming a popular issue, and Paddington Council will soon have to install sewers to eliminate cesspits and night soil disposal."

Henry Wharton expressed a concern. "There's been a shocking increase in the cost of land over the gold rush years, and I'm a little afraid that we may be buying land at a greatly inflated price."

Gilbert got Alistair's attention. "Allow me to give Henry my opinion on that." Alistair nodded. "I believe that good economic times will be with us for many more years, Henry. Gold continues to be discovered, our wool is in ever greater demand, and steam power is driving our growing industries. We're becoming a modern industrial state, by God. Immigration has nearly doubled Sydney's population in just twelve years, from fifty-four thousand people in 1851 to about one hundred thousand today, and a steady stream of new settlers keeps coming. I believe as long as we have population growth and economic expansion the price of land will continue to increase."

"I agree with you, Gilbert," said Peter. "And I like what I've been hearing. Now, Alistair, if I understand your proposal right, we'd be investing as shareholders in Norman Builders, which you will incorporate from a sole proprietor firm to a company run by a board of directors."

"That's right; the board will direct and approve, while I'll still run the day-to-day business as the president." Seeing Duncan yawning, Alistair brought the meeting to a close.

"Well, it appears that we've all grown a bit tired. I've gone beyond the two hours I told you this would take. I'll be talking to each of you over the next two weeks. I hope you'll all decide to participate. We will establish the company before June when Winsley Estate will be offering its allotments for sale. Thank you all for coming."

◉

Ho-teng had finished his six-day workweek, ten-hour workday, and sat in his room smoking a mixture of tobacco and opium while he waited for his friend Lau Tai-kan. He was looking forward to an evening of camaraderie with friends and a white prostitute— Emily—whom he had grown fond of. With an increasing sense of well-being, he contemplated the urbane life he had fashioned for himself over the past three years, in contrast to his brothers, who were locked in their backward peasant ways.

The Rocks isn't much different than Canton, he said to himself, they're both dangerous places, but I have an exciting life here that wouldn't be possible in our village or even in Canton. I'm respected for my artistry in wood, and I've developed many friendships in our community of nearly a thousand Chinese. Unlike my brothers, I get out for business and fun. I join friends in playing *fan-tan* and *mah-jong* and to discuss the meaning of life in opium parlors. I'm flexible and adaptable, have learned some English, adopted European dress, and pillowed several *kwai-lo* prostitutes, although none as young and beautiful as Emily.

Sydney's Chinese community was almost entirely men, sojourners who had left their wives and families in China. Their community was centered in a six-block area of The Rocks, most visibly on busy George Street, next to the Sydney Cove wharves, where seafarers had to pass by their shops and stalls offering fruits and vegetables, groceries, imported fancy goods, furniture, laundry and tailoring services, and gambling. Scattered through the back streets were Chinese boarding houses, cookshops, importers, shopkeepers, tradesman, cabinetmakers, herbalist doctors, gambling houses, brothels, and opium dens.

Ho-teng threw his arms wide as his friend Lau entered the room. "*Ho!*"—good!—"you're finally here, *a*-Lau. Are you ready for the forbidden fruits of life?"

"Yes... although, I think you've begun tasting life without me, *a*-Fong. That's opium I smell, *kwa?*"

"Yes, but I'm always ready to share my pipe with my best friend. Here, *a*-Lau." He handed his pipe to him.

Fong Ho-teng and Lau Tai-kan had become fast friends and indicated their close, informal friendship by preceding their surnames with the affectionate *a*- sound. They were the most accomplished woodworkers at Wong Cabinets and shared their enjoyment of the work, along with gambling, opium, and pillow houses.

"Did you bring any black stuff, *a*-Lau?" Ho-teng asked.

"No, I don't have any. We have to buy Two Dongs's opium anyway to smoke in his place. Which way do you want to walk there, *a*-Fong?"

Ho-teng's favorite opium house was run by a Cantonese man, Chow Tu-dong, who also provided three prostitutes for his customers' pleasure. When the brothel-keeper had married his white wife, he anglicized his name for her by placing his surname last, Tu-dong Chow. His white customers laughingly called him Two Dongs Chow—two-penises Chow—which he enthusiastically adopted to indicate his virility and easy way with the ladies.

It was seven o'clock and dusk; in another half an hour it would be dark. They had to plan their route through The Rocks to Cambridge Street, one of the streets arkwardly aligned across the rocky, steep slope stepping down to the harbor. The direct route, along George Street and up Argyle Street, at this time of day, would take them past rowdy groups of drunken ruffians and sailors lolling in the doorways of bawdy, public drinking houses. They agreed instead on the longer but safer route along gaslit residential streets, where they were likely to encounter only grimy children taunting with "Chingy-Changy-Chongy Chinaman" and other insults. Once at Two Dongs's house on Cambridge Street, they would stay the night and return in the early morning.

They walked up Essex Street, a grade so steep that horse-drawn vehicles could not ascend, north along Cumberland Street, down onto Gloucester Street, built on a rock terrace, and finally down Gloucester Steps to Cambridge Street, a dead-end lane. Along the route they passed many ramshackle, small cottages of one or two rooms haphazardly constructed in convict days from rubble stone, brick, and wood. Scattered among these were more recent, two-story, well-constructed brick houses.

The streets stank and oozed disgusting effluent; where it pooled, raised wood plank footways provided passage. The authorities had conceded years earlier that cesspits over rock did not percolate well; nevertheless, sewerage pipes and gutters were installed in only a few of the principal streets. Overflowing cesspits combined with horse droppings and the contents of chamber pots, often emptied at night into back lanes and streets, turned the streets into festering open sewers of excrement and filth. Household waste and rubbish thrown under floorboards or into yards added to the sickening, smelly mess that supported a burgeoning rat population. The Rocks relied on storms to produce torrents of water to flush sewerage and trash down its steep streets and lanes into the harbor.

Having safely arrived at their destination, Ho-teng knocked on the door of a single-story, plastered and white-washed stone cottage. Harriet Chow, the large, white wife of Two Dongs, opened the door with a smile of greeting. Ho-teng bowed his head and handed Mrs. Chow a small package, then spoke in his best pidgin English:

"Vely goo' eve'ing, Chow-*Taai*"—Mrs. Chow—"giftee to you . . . *oolong cha*, tea."

She took it from him with "Thanks, dearie."

He held up a second small, wrapped box. "Emily? Giftee to she?"

"She's busy right now, Ho-teng. Come in, Tu-dong's 'ere."

They walked through the door into a twenty-four-foot-wide room, twelve feet deep, that occupied the entire front of the house. At one end was a fireplace and kitchen with a long table where Two Dongs and Dottie, a heavyset white prostitute, sat eating.

An unusually large number of sofas, divans, and low tables filled the remainder of the room. The former two-bedroom house had been poorly remodeled to provide a center hallway connecting four small bedrooms in the back of the house. Chairs lined the hallway where a Chinese man sat waiting. The pungent fragrance of burning incense did not conceal the foul odor coming from beneath the loose-fitting, removable floorboards that covered an earthen floor, damp with fetid effluent trickling under the building on its way downhill.

Ho-teng used his English so the white women would appreciate his warm feelings toward Two Dongs. "Vely goo' eve'ing, Chow-*Saang*, goo' flien'."

"*Ho-yemaan*"—good evening—"Fong-*Saang*," a jovial Two Dongs greeted him. Tall, with a protruding stomach, Two Dongs considered Ho-teng a fellow clansman from Canton.

Taking Ho-teng aside by the arm, Two Dongs led him over to a large sofa. "I'm glad you're early, Fong-*Saang*, because I have something important to discuss with you before Emily comes out. She was arrested on Wednesday and held overnight."

"*Aiya!*—what for?" Ho-teng asked in Cantonese.

"For nothing! The copmen came in here and arrested her for idle and disorderly conduct under some vagrancy law. The magistrate said she was disturbing the peace. I paid the ten-pound fine, but they still kept her overnight in jail to teach her a lesson, they said. They told her they would be back for her if she didn't move out."

Harriet Chow set down a battered, mismatched tea service on a low table and joined them. Pouring a cup of tea for Ho-teng, she said slowly in English, "The cops don't like young, good-lookin', white women sleepin' an' smokin' opium wif no Chinamen, see, but there's nuffin' illegal abaht it, so they arrested 'er on some trumped-up charge." Unfolding her marriage license, she held it in front of Ho-teng's face. "This 'ere is *good!*—ho! Emily needs a marriage license, like me, ter wave under the noses of them coppers, then they can't do nuffin'. Yer savvy?—understand?"

Ho-teng shook his head. "No sabby, *taaitaai*"—madam.

Two Dongs translated what Harriet had said and continued in Cantonese. "You're Emily's favorite, and I know you like her too— so why don't you marry her? If you're married, you could visit her as often as you like. You wouldn't be responsible for her or have to pay anything, except for opium. If you go back home, you can leave her with us to take care of. I take good care of my three girls. It's a good deal for you, *kwa*?"

Ho-teng's head spun as Two Dongs's and Harriet's anxious eyes bored into him. "W'atee Emily say?" he asked Harriet.

Two Dongs answered for his wife in Cantonese. "Emily likes you and hopes that you will help her to stay out of jail and be her friend. She'd ask you herself if she wasn't too embarrassed."

Harriet, who understood a smattering of Cantonese, said, "She's afraid yer might say *m-hai*—no!"

Ho-teng did not know what to say. He needed time. Talking to Two Dongs in Cantonese, he said, "I have to think about it, Chow-*Saang*, and talk to my elder brother."

Disappointed or perturbed, Harriet got up and walked away.

Two Dongs agreed. "Yes, of course, your elder brother must be consulted. It's only right. You must decide quickly though, Fong-*Saang*, because we don't know how much time Emily has before the copmen return. Do not discuss it with her until you decide to marry her—before then will only upset her."

Ho-teng got up from the sofa and walked over to the table and sat down next to Lau Tai-kan, who was finishing a bowl of chicken noodle soup that Harriet had given him. Dottie placed a bowl of soup in front of Ho-teng, which he accepted with "T'ankee, Dottie."

"That's good soup, *a*-Fong," Lau Tai-kan said, rising from the table. "Now to find Rosie and have some good fucking." He laughed quietly to himself and walked toward the hallway and the four bedrooms.

Ho-teng was finishing the last spoonful of the soup when he heard Emily's voice. Turning, he saw her bid goodbye to another Chinese man.

She came bouncing toward him and threw her arms around his neck and hugged him. "I've bin lookin' forward to this evening, Hotee," her pet name for Ho-teng. She was a fine-looking, shapely, nineteen-year old with long, raven hair.

Ho-teng handed her the small, wrapped box with a big smile. "Giftee"

"A gift fer me? I love gifts." She tore away the paper, opened the box, and took out five brightly colored ribbons. "They're nice . . . pretty . . . I can wear this one with my red dress."

"In hail," Ho-teng said, pointing to her hair. "Hail plettee."

"You always bring me sumpin', Hotee. You're so nice. It don't hav'ta cost much. Jus' nice you're thinkin' abaht me."

"We're done fer today, Emily," Harriet said. "Yer c'n eat wif Ho-teng."

After eating, Emily whispered into Ho-teng's ear. "Let's do it now, before the opium, before we gits too tired. You do better before." Giggling like a school girl, she said, "We'll see you folks in a while; we got sumpin' to tike care of."

Taking Ho-teng by the hand, she led him to her room. As Emily lit a single candle, Ho-teng took the previously agreed amount of money out of his pocket and placed it on top of the chest of drawers. Standing in front of Ho-teng, Emily seductively pulled down her top gradually to slowly expose her small, nicely rounded, pink-nipple breasts and then laid down on the straw mattress. Ho-teng lustfully looked down at Emily as he undid his belt and took off his pants. Wearing no underwear, Emily pulled her skirt up to her waist, spread her legs, and reached out for him. "Come 'ere, Hotee."

After Ho-teng was done, they lay there for several minutes enjoying each other's embrace. Wiggling free from beneath Ho-teng, Emily slid to the side of the bed and cleaned herself over a bucket of water.

Emily sat on the edge of the bed next to Ho-teng and talked slowly in the hope that he would understand the essence of what she had to say.

"My 'usbind never give me presents, like you do, Hotee. Well, 'e worn't *really* my 'usbind, neither, 'cos we worn't never married, proper like. People say opium smokin' is bad, but it's better'n drinkin' the grog thet makes men mean an' violent, thet's wot I say. That's why I like opium an' Chinamen, 'oo are gentle an' nice. My man wos always on the grog an' took to beatin' me all the time, then throw'd me out into the street with only the clothes on me back. I wos in a terrible state when Harriet found me an' made me family—the best family I ever 'ad—with a roof over me 'ead, three meals a day, an' beautiful clothes." Taking his hand, she stroked it several times. "I want to smoke opium now, Hotee. Let's join the others."

Putting on his pants, Ho-teng said, "I *yen-yen* opium, too."

Two Dongs, Dottie, Lau Tai-kan, and Rosie had already started smoking their pipes in the main room, which had been rearranged into an opium parlor. They were joined by another Chinese man and a white sailor; others were expected as the evening proceeded. Harriet was in charge of taking the money and assisting the smokers, a responsibility she alternated with Two Dongs.

Ho-teng and Emily sat on divans opposite each other with a low table between. Two lamps sat on the table. Emily lit one lamp for herself and the other for Ho-teng while he bought ten pea-size balls of blackish opium paste for Emily and himself. Ho-teng attached an opium ball to the end of a long, blunt needle and cooked it over the lamp flame, twirling the needle to prevent the opium ball from catching fire. When the ball bubbled and swelled into a hot golden mass, he transferred it from the needle into his pipe's metal bowl about two-thirds of the way down his two-foot-long bamboo pipe. Lying down on the divan, he placed his head on the headrest and positioned the pipe bowl over the lamp flame to further heat the opium until it began to smoke. Deeply drawing on the pipe, he inhaled the smoke from the burning opium. It took several draws on the pipe before the opium ball burned-out.

There was little talk among the participants in the parlor, who shared the experience with looks of gratification. Ho-teng repeated this process five times, each time increasing the stupefying, sleep-inducing effects of the opium, until Harriet had to help him hold his pipe over the lamp just before he fell asleep.

The next day, Ho-teng tried to discuss the possibility of marrying Emily with Sing-woo.

"Elder Brother, I have a relationship with a woman that I want to discuss with you."

"You know I do not approve of you consorting with immoral *kwai-poh*"—white barbarian females—"but you do not respect me and do as you please. I do not wish to discuss these *kwai-poh*, if that is what you have on your mind."

"We aren't in our village, Yigo. White women are different from our women. Here they think sex is a natural act for men *and* women."

Sing-woo looked sadly at his younger brother. "These *kwai-poh* are degenerates, Saamgo. It's the duty of females to be chaste and uphold their virtue for the good of society. The society here is depraved. I'm greatly saddened that you do not see that."

"I'm a man, who wants to enjoy life. I don't want to be a celibate like you and Daidai. I don't know how you live without the pleasures of women. *It's not natural.*"

"We will return soon to our village and marry. I have asked you many times to join Daidai and me in our daily exercises, meditation, and prayers. We derive great strength and guidance in conversing with the gods and our ancestors. I have not seen you make a single offering at our altar for over a year. I'm very concerned that your constant opium smoking is leading you astray."

"Smoking opium relaxes me! There's nothing wrong with it. You do not appreciate that this is *my way* of communicating with the spirits. Opium relieves all pain, anger, and sorrow. What could be *wrong with that?*"

"Don't *raise* your voice to me, Saamgo," Sing-woo said sternly. "Opium is clouding your judgment; it's overtaking your life. You contribute to our savings only sporadically now, often you are too ill to work, and now money is missing from our savings."

"I didn't take it!" Ho-teng said without conviction.

"I believed Daidai when he said he didn't take it, but I regret that I do not believe you. Only we three know where we—"

"I didn't take—"

"—where we hide—"

"Why do you alwa—"

"Please do not deny it, Saamgo! I *found* the lottery tickets! I know that you recently lost fifteen pounds playing *pak-a-pu. Bai,* Brother, that money was for our destitute family!"

Ho-teng was stymied and had an unrepentant, belligerent look on his face.

Sing-woo said, "Your attitude forces me to take over

responsibility for all of our earnings."

Jumping up from his chair, Ho-teng said, "*Aiya*, I won't agree to that. It's a matter of face; *I make the most money!*"

Sing-woo said in a quiet, measured, compassionate voice: "Saamgo . . . please calm yourself. Sit down . . . please."

Ho-teng remained standing.

"Saamgo, please do as I ask . . . sit down."

Ho-teng reluctantly sat down.

"I am Elder Brother; I care deeply for you, Saamgo, and you are my responsibility. You must be careful not to insult the spirits of our ancestors. They can curse you in this life and the next. Your rebirth is at stake. Surely you must realize that you have departed from the Tao." Sing-woo believed devoutly that the Tao was the Natural Way of the Universe, guiding all life to peace and happiness; suffering lay in wait for all those who departed from it.

"Think of the serene face of Buddha. You must return to the Enlightened One's Eightfold Path. Certainly you recall some of the inspirational verses we were taught: 'When you have faults, do not fear to abandon them. If the will be set on virtue, there will be no practice of wickedness. A man who' " —

Ho-teng was not listening. When Sing-woo had evoked the wrath of their ancestors, he retreated into his own thoughts. I have a brother who is a monk and out of touch with reality. He's a good man but has become a pain in the arse with his constant moralizing. I can no longer rely on him for guidance. I'll placate him, and then do as I like.

—"can change, which will bring happiness to you and those around you."

"You're right, Elder Brother. I'll try to live a more righteous life. I'll join you and Daidai at dawn tomorrow to exercise and make an offering to our ancestors."

◎

Eleanor and Alistair were seated across from Gilbert and his wife Barbara at a wood picnic table in Steyne Park next to Double Bay beach. They were waiting for Duncan and his wife Grace to join them.

"Alistair, what are your latest thoughts on when you'll begin construction of the hotel in Manly?" Gilbert asked.

"That's one of the reasons for our outing today, Gilbert. I'd like to get your and Duncan's thoughts on a construction start date. As a director, you know that I've been avoiding this issue since we bought the site on the Corso two years ago. While we've got a great site at a bargain price, the resort is developing more slowly than I had anticipated. The three hotels there aren't doing that well and with the resort entrepreneur Smith gone back to England, I'm wondering whether we should delay construction until we are assured that the resort is a corker that won't let us down."

"I think the board will go along with whatever you propose, Alistair, as long as the terrace houses in Paddington keep renting as fast as Norman Builders can build them."

"Paddington's a beaut investment, all right," Alistair said with obvious satisfaction. "I'm pleased that Paddington Council was successful in getting a direct water connection from Lachlan Swamp's water reserve and has built its town hall. Oh, here comes Duncan and Grace now."

After a warm greeting, the three couples walked down to the beach.

Alistair said, "Now I know you've all been to Manly by ferry at one time or another; however, it's an entirely different experience on a sloop. I think you'll find it exhilarating. We're in luck, because there's a moderate wind out of the southeast, which means we can sail an easy beam reach by Shark Island directly to Manly." He pointed out the course. "To make it effortless, we'll sail with only the mainsail. It will take us well less than an hour to get there. I'll take Eleanor, Gilbert, and Barb out to the sloop and return for Duncan and Grace. You chaps can help me drag the dinghy down to the water. I'm taking off my coat in this heat."

The women at Eleanor's encouragement took off their shoes and lifted their dresses to walk in the shallows while the men dragged the dinghy to the shore and set the oars in place. Alistair and Gilbert took off their shoes and socks and rolled up their pants to hold the boat while Eleanor and Barbara got in. Together the two men pushed the dinghy into deeper water. Gilbert jumped in first, followed by Alistair.

Alistair rowed the dinghy out to his thirty-six-foot sloop, where it was moored to a buoy about one hundred yards offshore. While rowing back, he became overheated and started to sweat. Wanting to cool off and preserve his white shirt, he took off his tie and shirt, exposing his undershirt. Although president of his company, Alistair still thought of himself as an unpretentious construction worker who disdained false modesty. Coming into shore, he jumped out of the dinghy holding onto the boat rail, landed on a sharp shell, lost his balance, and fell sideways into the water. Thoroughly soaked, he rolled over in the shallow water and sat looking at a cut on the bottom of his foot.

"*Ha ha ha!* Are you all right, mate?" Duncan asked as he pulled the dinghy further onto shore.

"It's not funny, Duncan." Grace berated him for laughing. "He's drenched now. Did you cut your foot, Alistair? Are you hurt?"

"Only a little cut and my pride, Grace. I needed to cool off anyway . . . might as well take a little swim now."

Giving an "I'm okay" wave to Eleanor, Barbara, and Gilbert, who had been watching his mishap from the sloop, Alistair walked into deeper water and began to swim an awkward overhand stroke. Swimming out into eight or nine feet of water, he cautioned himself: Don't go any farther out over your head, you're not much of a swimmer. He tried an overhand stroke for twenty yards, swimming parallel to the beach, but his movements were unpracticed and clumsy.

Through the water, the fish smelled blood and sensed the irregular vibrations of a single, large, injured animal. It turned and with several, quick, powerful thrusts of its tail accelerated toward the source of the blood and erratic sounds of distress.

Thinking that he hadn't favorably impressed anyone with his pitiful overhand form, Alistair decided to try a backstroke to swim back to the dinghy. He rolled over on his back and started kicking his legs while trying to reach behind to swim with his arms. His antics attracted laughter and disparaging shouts from Gilbert, Barbara, and Eleanor who sat on the gunwale of the sloop. A large, dark shadow passed beneath the sloop heading toward Alistair. They all saw it. Disbelieving their eyes, shocked and speechless, they looked at each other for confirmation—a *shark?*

Approaching its quarry, the shark swam along the sandy bottom and focused ahead toward the struggling form on the surface. Just before impact, it thrust its tail one final time for maximum speed, rotated to position its large gaping jaws, and rolled its eyes back into their sockets for protection.

While making a dogged attempt at a backstroke, Alistair laughed at his lack of skill. I can't seem to synchronize the kicking of my legs with the movement of my arms. I'm hopeless. His assessment was confirmed when he glanced over at the sloop and saw Eleanor and the others pointing and yelling at him. I don't care if they're laughing at me, he thought, it's a beautiful day, the water's refreshing, and I'm enjoying myself. Even if I can't swi—!

WHAT THE HELL! Alistair felt a tremendous force explode beneath him, centered on his buttocks, launching him into the air. His arms flew out and the back of his head banged against something hard. His instantaneous first thought was relatively benign: two or three young fools are mucking with me! Then reality struck him—*JEEEZUS*, I'M IN THE MOUTH OF A *SHARK!* The two of them hit the water with a huge splash. *Fight! Gouge his eyes! He's thrashing meeee! HEELLLP!* Suddenly, miraculously, the shark let go.

Alistair surfaced gasping but amazed that he didn't feel any pain. He turned and located the beach and Duncan only a short distance away. A terrifying look was on Duncan's face—horror. Panicked, Alistair screamed, "*HELP ME!*" Reaching out to swim, he saw the shark rip into his upper right arm. "OH *NOOOO!*" The shark spun him around, dragging him into deeper water.

"OH NO, NO YOU DON'T, *YOU BASTARRD!*" Alistair pounded the shark's head with his left fist. "*LET GO OF MEEE!*" Struggling against the shark, he was pulled beneath the surface of the water. Again, the shark let go.

Swallowed a lot of water—*need air!*—which way to the sur-
face? . . . Can't seem to swim . . . in trouble!—*can't breathe!* . . . I . . .
I . . . caaan't *die!* . . . Eleanor . . .

When Alistair had decided to take a short swim, Duncan and
Grace sat down at a picnic table. Their conversation was interrupted
by a clamorous outcry from the sloop. Duncan stood up and looked
at the sloop and then at Alistair just as the shark struck him. Half
of the huge body of the shark cleared the surface with Alistair in its
jaws. The monster was twelve feet long or more. Terrified, Duncan
froze in place as Alistair and the shark disappeared beneath the water's surface. Grace's hysterical shrieks roused him to action.

Duncan ran toward the eight-foot dinghy. He was next to
it when Alistair came to the surface and screamed for his help.
Duncan pushed the boat into the water and paddled toward where
the shark and Alistair had gone under. He intended to beat the
shark with an oar if it resurfaced.

Alistair came to the surface eighty feet from Duncan. He was
floating face down surrounded by blood in the water. Alistair's right
arm was a grisly stump. Duncan anxiously looked around for the
shark as he tried to pull Alistair's limp body into the dinghy, nearly
capsizing the boat and throwing himself into the water. From the
crowd that had quickly formed, three young men swam out the
short distance to help and brought the body back to shore. Alistair's
left leg and part of his buttock had been ripped off, a mortal wound,
from which he had died from loss of blood within minutes of the
first attack.

Eleanor, Gilbert, and Barbara saw the gruesome attack on
Alistair. Unable to do anything but scream and hold each other in
horror, Eleanor fainted when Alistair was attacked the second time.
Mercifully, his body had been taken away when she, in shock, returned to shore.

Eleanor went into deep mourning that incapacitated her. She
collapsed at Alistair's closed-coffin funeral and was taken home
to her bed, unable to attend his burial. For six months, she secluded herself, having little contact with others, except Priscilla and
Gilbert's wife Barbara. She stopped eating and fell into a debilitating

depression. Her nurse complained to Barbara that if something was not done soon, she could die of a broken heart.

The board of directors of Norman Builders appointed Gilbert Armstrong interim president while they looked for someone to take Alistair's place. Gilbert didn't understand the business and could not give it the time it demanded.

It was Gilbert and Barbara who helped Eleanor out of her depression and restored her will to live. As a mother, Barbara appealed to Eleanor's motherly instinct to care for her eleven-year-old child, Priscilla, who was barely coping with the loss of her beloved father and feared losing her mother as well. With serious problems developing at Norman Builders, Gilbert asked Eleanor for help, so he and the other investors would not lose their money. The combination of her love for Priscilla and sense of responsibility to the shareholders brought Eleanor slowly back to purposeful activity.

From her bed, Eleanor listened to Gilbert explain the problems at Norman Builders. She suggested solutions, which he invariably pursued. While slowly recovering, she took walks with Priscilla and Barbara and began to work at her desk. After five months of helping her brother run the company, Gilbert asked her to meet with the board of directors.

When Eleanor clearly explained to the board what needed to be done to put the company back on a firm financial footing and grow in the future, they spontaneously created a new position, managing director, for Eleanor with pay equal to Gilbert's. She saw the opportunity for a new life and accepted immediately. Six months later, Gilbert was able to convince the board of directors that Eleanor did not need him. They appointed her president of Norman Builders.

Eleanor threw herself into the work. Due to continued good economic times and her natural abilities, she returned the company to its former dynamic condition. She obtained final development approval for a two-story, fifty-room hotel, named The Corso Hotel, at Manly and quickly began construction. The plans called for first-class facilities, including a restaurant, saloon, billiard room, sitting room, and library. The restaurant and sitting room were ideally

situated on Manly's main commercial concourse to have uninter-
rupted views of Manly Beach and the ocean.

On August 23, 1870, Eleanor and Priscilla were invited by
Duncan to attend a luncheon at Victoria Barracks to bid farewell to the Royal Irish 18th Regiment of the Line, the last British
troops to depart from Australia. The band of the Sydney Battalion
of Volunteer Rifles was playing when Eleanor and Priscilla arrived.
Thomas Armstrong, a member of the band, acknowledged them
with a nod of his head and a smile. The twenty-nine-year-old son of
Gilbert and Barbara had worked at Norman Builders for four years.

"Oh, Mother, doesn't Thomas look good in his uniform?"
Priscilla, now twelve, asked.

"Yes, he does, dear, very smart indeed." They walked toward
Duncan who was talking to several British officers. He turned toward them as they approached.

"Duncan . . . it was sweet of you to invite us."

"Hello, Eleanor, *and Priscilla*, my, you both look *soo lovely*." He
bent down to shake Priscilla's hand.

With a delightful curtsy, Priscilla said, "Thank you, Uncle
Duncan. We saw Thomas playing in the band!"

"You did? . . . so did I."

Eleanor said, "Thomas and the band will be leading the British
troops to Sydney Cove."

"Are *we* going?" Priscilla asked her mother.

"Yes, we'll all be going to see off the troops."

"It should be quite a procession." Duncan said.

"Are you sorry or glad to see the last of the British troops leaving?" Eleanor asked.

"It's time, I reckon," Duncan replied. "Though we need a military. The Sydney Battalion, being voluntary and receiving no pay,
cannot be expected to replace professional British troops. I'm supporting the Naval and Military Bill to give the government the
power to raise professional infantry and artillery companies and to
fund the fortification of Sydney Harbour. We're a rich country with
a small population that could be easily overrun by a foreign power,
if it had a mind to."

"Hasn't the British government pledged to protect our coast and shipping lanes?"

"Yes, but Britain's far away. Even by way of the new Suez Canal, it would take a fleet at least sixty days to get here. A lot of damage could be done before help arrives. We have to develop our own navy to patrol our coast and harbors. Victoria has a steamer warship and the start of a navy; New South Wales should have no less."

◎

By 1872 Ho-teng was an opium addict lamenting the mistakes of his life. He believed his greatest mistake was not marrying Emily, whom he had decided was the love of his life. Two weeks after Two Dongs had proposed her marriage to him, she had been arrested again and disappeared from The Rocks and his life.

Very concerned about Ho-teng's opium addiction, unhappiness, and deteriorating health, Sing-woo decided that the solution was for them to return to China. One evening, after dinner Sing-woo made his announcement.

"Saamgo and Daidai, we have stayed too long in this foreign land. I'm forty and Saamgo is thirty-eight, we are running out of time to marry and begin our own families. I have been saving our money, and we now have enough to return home and live comfortably."

Ho-teng slumped in his chair, dejected. "Now I *see why* we have had so little money to live on here. I'm not sure *I want* to return, Yigo. Unlike you, I have become used to life here."

Sing-woo ignored the slight. He asked Min-chin, "Do you wish to return or stay here, Daidai?"

"I was twelve when I came here, and I remember little of village life, except toiling in the fields. But I want to marry too; and my family is there, so I will go with you, Eldest Brother."

"I cannot force you to return, Saamgo, even though your life is not good here," Sing-woo said, while feeling sure that he would return with them when the time came to leave.

For several days after this exchange, Ho-teng was aloof and

despondent. Saturday night he did not return home to sleep, which was not unusual, but when he had not returned by Monday morning and missed a full day of work, his brothers became concerned. Lau Tai-kan told Sing-woo that Ho-teng had gone to Chow Tu-dong's opium parlor Saturday night. Although it was nearly dark, Sing-woo decided to go there. Since Chow Tu-dong's house was also a brothel, Sing-woo would not allow Min-chin to accompany him.

Sing-woo took the safe route up Essex Street and through the residential neighborhood. As he walked north on Gloucester Street he saw a group of four young men round a corner and walk toward him. To avoid them, he turned and nonchalantly walked back to Cumberland Place Steps. Out of their sight, he ran down the steps onto Cambridge Street and walked quickly north toward Chow Tu-dong's place. Walking past Gloucester Steps, he was startled to see the same youths reclining on the steps, hidden behind a stone wall. He thought to run, but before he could act, the four toughs jumped up and surrounded him.

The largest of the four, a whole head taller than Sing-woo, blocked his path and gruffly pushed him back. "This 'ere's our neighborhood, an' we don't like John Chinaman walkin' aroun' like 'e owns the damn place."

Frightened and avoiding eye contact, Sing-woo tried to think of something he could say in English to calm the situation. "Vely solly, no *sabby* En'lish plees."

"Wot'd yer say, Chow?" the brute said. "We ain't *no bloody English poms!* Yer fuckin' stupid *Chink!*"

In a quiet, singsong rhythm, a short youth standing behind Sing-woo said, "I'll give 'im a little bop, wi' me rock in a sock, t'see wot he got." He swung a rock inside of a sock in an arc and landed it squarely on the back of Sing-woo's head.

Stunned by the unseen blow from behind, but not knocked unconscious, Sing-woo reactively swung his right arm behind him hitting his attacker on the right side of his nose—breaking it.

The youth flew to one side and fell to his knees holding his face in his hands, blood spewing from his nose.

"*Gawddamn Chink! Broke me nose!*"

The other three ruffians attacked Sing-woo with a vengeance. Dazed, he fought back but was hit, punched, and knocked to the ground, where they set about kicking him with their pointed boots, especially worn for such a purpose. A kick to the head knocked Sing-woo unconscious and left him staring vacantly skyward.

The youth with a broken nose rose to his feet holding a brick that had been lying near him and smashed it into Sing-woo's face with all of his might.

Thwaack. A nauseating sound assaulted their ears and blood splattered their pants.

"Dammit mate, *yer killed the bugger!*" the brute exclaimed. Frightened, they ran from the scene.

After a few minutes of quiet, neighbors who had stayed in their houses during the brawl looked out from behind window coverings and partially-opened doors to see Sing-woo sprawled on the street. They could tell from his clothes that he was a Chinese man. Several came out to look. Repulsed by the appalling injury to his face, one women pronounced him close to death:

"Ain't 'e a sorry mess. 'Ardly breathin', 'e is."

A neighbor agreed. " 'E's as good as dead."

Shaking their heads and wondering what was becoming of their neighborhood, they retreated to the safety of their houses.

Sing-woo lay there for minutes more, until a man walking down Gloucester Steps noticed him lying in the street. He approached him slowly and, seeing his horrific facial injury, ran for a constable. By the time the constable arrived, more than a half an hour had passed since Sing-woo had been bludgeoned. The constable knelt down on one knee and picked up Sing-woo's wrist and felt for a pulse. When he could not feel a heartbeat, he tried the artery in Sing-woo's neck. He turned to the man who had ran to the police station.

"Sorry for yer trouble, mate, this Chinese bloke's dead."

Min-chin identified Sing-woo's body. The constable who handled the case was not available, so the desk sergeant read the constable's report to Min-chin: "The cause of death of the Chinaman was a blow to forehead and nose with a brick. The bloody brick was lying next to the victim's head. Murderer unknown due to no one in the neighborhood having seen or heard anything."

Ho-teng masked the pain of Sing-woo's murder with an opium-smoking binge at Two Dongs's place. Through neighborhood gossip, Harriet Chow found out who had killed Sing-woo and told Two Dongs, who then told Ho-teng. "Your brother was killed by The Rocks Push, a gang of larrikins. They're young hooligans who wear wide-brimmed straw hats, white shirts, jackets with upturned collars, bell-bottomed trousers, and high-heeled pointed boots. If you see a mob dressed like that, just run the other way."

After missing a week of work, Ho-teng returned to his living quarters above Wong's Cabinets late Sunday night. He listened to Min-chin describe the preliminary arrangements he had made for them to sail to China with Sing-woo's body.

"Can we afford the cost of traveling home as well as the cost of transporting our beloved brother's body in a coffin all the way to our village, Daidai?" Ho-teng asked.

"Yes, Saamgo."

"And still have enough to live on without burdening our family?"

"Yes, there will be enough for a while."

"How much is there in our savings?"

Min-chin expected this question and had thought about it, but could not think of a way to avoid telling Ho-teng. It would be inappropriate not to tell Elder Brother. He hesitated, and the indecision showed on his face.

"How *much,* Daidai?" Ho-teng asked again.

"I've spent part of it already to prepare Yigo's body."

"How *much* of it is left?" Ho-teng asked testily. Seeing Min-chin's hesitancy, he said, "I am Eldest Brother now, I expect you to follow the *teng-wa.*"

Min-chin had been well instructed by Sing-woo in Confucian *teng-wa,* the golden rule of obedience. He could not disobey his elder brother, even when he feared the likely consequences.

"The last time I counted, there was £184," Min-chin said.

"*Aiya,* is that all? After all our years of hard work? We *can't* afford the great expense of transporting Yigo's body home, Daidai."

"We *must* bury him next to our ancestors, Saamgo, or his soul will forever wander aimlessly in this hateful foreign land."

"It would be a waste of money. We'll have the Wing-on Funeral Home bury Yigo in the Chinese section of Rookwood Cemetery. We'll stay here for two more years and save most of what we earn, so when we return home we can live like emperors. When we're ready to go, we'll have Wing-on exhume Yigo's bones to take with us to bury in our family graveyard."

When Min-chin began to object, Ho-teng raised the palm of his hand toward him. "This is what I've decided. It will be best for you and our family, you'll see."

Over the following months, Min-chin watched with growing resentment as Ho-teng spent their savings on opium, gambling, and prostitutes. Within five months, it was all gone.

In March 1875 Ho-teng was fired from Wong Cabinets for absenteeism and poor work. Without a place to move to, he was permitted to stay above the shop as long as Min-chin paid his rent. Ho-teng became completely dependent on Min-chin, creating a desperate situation for them.

Min-chin realized he had to get his brother away from his debauched life in The Rocks. Moy Yue-kung, a green grocer on George Street, impressed with Min-chin's upright demeanor and knowledge of vegetable gardening, agreed to hire him and Ho-teng as gardeners at one of his market gardening plots in Alexandria. Min-chin agreed to live in a shed on the plot while they gardened and protected the crops from pilfering.

Ho-teng was outraged when he heard Min-chin's proposal. "You *can't* dictate to me! I'm Eldest Brother and demand respect. I'm *not going* to the country to garden and live in a *shed! Aiya*, have you lost your mind?"

Min-chin did not argue with Ho-teng. He gave notice to Wong Ching-tin and thanked him profusely for the years of steady employment. Wong said that there would always be a place for him at Wong Cabinets if he ever wished to return.

On the day Min-chin left Wong Cabinets for the garden plot, Ho-teng moved in with two male friends. His old friend Lau

Tai-kan, married with a baby, was not one of them. He had stopped smoking opium and gambling and now avoided Ho-teng.

Knowing Ho-teng's dissolute friends, Min-chin expected it would only be a matter of time before his brother would be forced to join him, because he had no other means of long-term support. A fortnight later, penniless and rejected by friends, Ho-teng suffered a terrible loss of face by joining his younger brother.

Min-chin took control of their money. He put his brother on an allowance, most of which he spent on opium to maintain his habit. Ho-teng hated the isolation of the market garden but liked hawking vegetables in the city to housewives who welcomed "John" with his baskets of fresh vegetables suspended from a bamboo pole across his shoulder. Ho-teng often remained in the city overnight with friends.

One evening in December 1878, when Ho-teng was visiting old friends at Wong Cabinets, he had a close brush with death. The Seamen's Union had been on strike for several weeks against the Australasian Steam Navigation Company for employing Chinese crews. A union demonstration in front of the company's Circular Quay headquarters suddenly turned into a riot. The unionists tried to set fire to nearby Wong Cabinets and other Chinese stores along George Street but were beaten back by the police. Stones were thrown through the windows of Wong Cabinets. A shattered piece of glass cut a deep gash across Ho-teng's neck, just missing his jugular vein.

◉

After nine years as Norman Builders's president, Eleanor was well established as a business and community leader. She was in her best form at the annual shareholders' meeting.

"The Corso Hotel is doing very well, thanks to Manly Council's ongoing improvements: the construction of the gentlemen's public baths, a separate bath for ladies, a tree-planting beautification program, and a new public wharf. Manly is now close to fulfilling the dream of its original builder, William Gilbert Smith, a true visionary who wrote that he envisioned 'a haven for tired city dwellers, who, robbed of vitality by city life, would come in large numbers to Manly's healthful resort by way of a short, refreshing ferry ride.'

"So in summation, the company has had a very good year of increased profit and growth. Due to Sydney's strong economy, we can increase residential rents as leases expire and continue our building plans in Paddington with confidence. Given The Corso Hotel's high occupancy rate, room rates may be reasonably increased next year. In all, we have every reason to believe that 1880 will be even more profitable than this year.

After the meeting, Duncan stayed to speak privately with Eleanor. When they were alone, he said:

"You're a prominent member of The Association for Protection of Aborigines, so I think you ought to know that your director, Daniel Griffith, is out of control and raising a lot of hackles. Someone in your organization has to impress on him that if he continues to be a pest he'll get less from Parliament, not more."

"What is Reverend Griffith doing that you have a problem with, Duncan?"

"He's *pushing* too hard. This black problem has been with us for a hundred years, and he and his fellow Anglicans aren't going to solve it in a year or two—what's the rush?"

"Frankly, Duncan, your attitude, just exhibited, is seen by the association as a big part of the problem. As colonial secretary, you recently removed the Aborigines from Circular Quay where they were making a living selling crafts and hiring out boats. You eliminated their livelihood by dumping them at La Pérouse and threatening to arrest them if they returned."

"Right! Arrest them for *trespassing* on government property and for public drunkenness! For goodness' sake, Eleanor, get the story right if you want to criticize me. For years they've been living illegally in the government boatshed at Circular Quay and taking sightseers out in a couple of old, leaky rowboats that put the government at risk. They sell worthless shell trinkets that fall apart as soon as money changes hands and, if all else fails, do a little begging."

"Be honest, Duncan, you had them removed to hide that side of Sydney life from the visitors to the Sydney International Exhibition. Now isn't that true?"

"I won't deny that was a *minor* factor in removing them, but they should have been removed years ago. It's my responsibility as colonial secretary, along with the police and Lands Department, to deal with the black problem. I don't appreciate Griffith's pushing to appoint a government protector of Aborigines and asking for crown land to establish more Aboriginal missions."

"I can't understand why you would object to the church's altruistic efforts to serve our less fortunate brethren," Eleanor said with disdain.

"Well, for your information, the government already tried that, and it didn't work. Missionary organizations—Anglicans, Wesleyans, and others—ran land grant missions at Blacktown, Wellington Valley, Lake Macquarie, Huntingdale, and other places subsidized by the government, and they all dwindled away by 1850. The missionaries also failed to convert the blacks to Christianity, I might add. Look, Eleanor, they're a dying race, for God's sake."

"So what do you propose to do—help them die?"

"We don't need to create another program. We already have programs that help indigents, including Aborigines, with food rations, blankets, and clothing to make their lives easier. We can provide these to Griffith's church-run missions. Parliament has neither the money nor the inclination to appoint a protector of Aborigines to administer government missions that will result in another round of ineffective, bureaucratic administration of the natives."

"There are abandoned and defenseless native children to be protected as well, Duncan."

"There are public and private orphanages for whites and blacks."

"There aren't any orphanages just for Aborigines that I know of. The Benevolent Foundation Orphanage in Bathurst, where I'm a benefactor, accepts only a few."

"There are others . . . regardless, how you spend your money is your business, Eleanor. I only object when you want crown land

and government funding to do it. So will you talk to Griffith about keeping his effort within the church and private funding, or not?"

"No, I won't talk to him, because I think he's right to expect that the government has a responsibility to improve the lives of our destitute and vulnerable Aboriginal people. We need to find a new solution and direction . . . and I'd like you to finds it, Cousin Duncan. I don't know the answer, but it's got to be something more than providing a comfortable bed for them to die in . . .

Duncan stood there with an aggravated look on his face, about to leave; she was no help to him.

But Eleanor was not done with him. "Now that we've discussed something on your mind, I'd like to talk about something on mine."

Eleanor composed herself. "Until recently, I've purposely avoided politics out of respect for your high office and because we women can't vote anyway. I've never talked to you about your lack of support for the bill that passed last year, finally giving women the right to retain personal savings earned themselves instead of it going automatically to their husbands. But I was hurt and dismayed by your public statements against the bill."

"Elea—"

"Let me finish!"

"You don't un—"

"Yes I do! You were instrumental in eliminating a provision of the bill that would have allowed women to retain real estate they brought into a marriage. Didn't you think how this *directly* affects me, your own cousin? How can I even consider remarriage when all of my real estate becomes the property of my new husband immediately upon my saying 'I do'?"

"Eleanor, I'm sorry if I hurt you, but there are larger issues than the individual that affect the kind of society we are trying to maintain."

"Yes—*maintain*—you're against change, Duncan. Men must share this world, and eventually will share this world, *equally*, with the opposite sex, whether you like it or not!"

Chapter 10

Who Are We?

Min-chin's employer, Moy Yue-kung, liked to make unexpected early morning visits to his garden plots in Alexandria to catch any irregularities and to keep his employees responsible. This morning he visited the shack where Min-chin and Ho-teng lived. Leaving the shack, Moy walked into the garden and spoke in a loud aggravated voice to Min-chin, who was directing the work of four gardeners.

"Your elder brother is *asleep* in the shack! I couldn't wake him!" Walking up to Min-chin, he whispered, "He has the look of death about him, Fong-*Saang*"—Mr. Fong.

Bowing, Min-chin humbly addressed him as Boss Moy. "Moy-*Loubaan*, I'm sorry; he's sick today. He'll be able to work tomorrow, sir."

"You know I pay him *only* when he works, *kwa*?"

"Yes, Moy-*Loubaan*. I did not pay him for the six days he was sick last month."

"Yes, I know. But I need workers I can depend on. I keep him only because he's your brother. The opium's killing him, and soon he'll be of no use to me—or anyone. He's taking a space that a better worker could fill. You must do something, Fong-*Saang*. I cannot allow this to continue much longer."

"Yes, Honorable Moy-*Loubaan*, I understand. You've been very patient and kind, sir. I'll think of something."

Moy Yue-kung had recognized that Min-chin was an intelligent and hard worker. He advanced him quickly from gardener, to assistant manager, and recently to manager of Moy's nineteen employees who included gardeners, fresh vegetable hawkers, green grocers, and cooks. Ho-teng resented his younger brother's success, another reason for his increasing use of opium to escape into a state of painless, stupefied euphoria.

Later that morning, Min-chin talked to Ho-teng, who was still lying in bed.

"Moy Yue-kung was here this morning, Saamgo, and caught you sleeping again."

"*Aiya!* Did you tell him I was sick?"

"Yes, but it's no good; he says you're always sick. He even tried to wake you but couldn't. His patience has worn thin."

"He relies on you, Daidai; he'll put up with me. I can work tomorrow." Ho-teng yawned and rolled over, away from Min-chin.

"You no longer have any will of your own, Elder Brother," Min-chin said to his brother's back. "You don't even bother to tell me anymore that you will try to quit the opium. Look at how thin you are. You spend all your money on opium. Your *friends* are all opium addicts who throw you out onto the street when your money runs out. Are you listening to me?"

There was no movement or answer from Ho-teng.

Exasperated, Min-chin indignantly said, "I have to go searching for you once a week now! Don't you have anything to say to me?"

"No," replied Ho-teng, who had heard little of what Min-chin said. "Now, let me sleep."

"I've tried everything over these many years since Yigo's death," Min-chin continued. "I know you blame yourself for his murder, but punishing yourself serves no purpose. We save very little because of your opium habit."

Still facing away from Min-chin, Ho-teng grumbled, "We save enough for you to send money home three or four times a year."

"Only twice a year! The spirit of our dead brother wants us to. You know I'm trying to save enough to rent our own garden and to go into business for ourselves. You've always wanted to make money—this is how to do it! Are you listening?—look at me, Saamgo. We can do this together if you have the will."

Three months later, for the second time that week, Min-chin went looking for Ho-teng after he had not returned from hawking vegetables in Sydney. He went from opium den to opium den asking for him.

"Yes, he's here," said the disreputable Yao proprietor, a man known simply as Sooi, who ran the most vile opium den in The Rocks. "He owes me a quid for the opium he smoked after he ran out of money. He said you'd pay."

Min-chin disdainfully eyed Sooi as he dug the money out of his pocket.

"Here's your pound," he said, slamming the money down on the counter to show his disrespect for Sooi.

"Bring him out," Min-chin ordered in a disgusted voice.

"*Diu neih.*" Fuck you. "Bring him out yourself!" the haggard proprietor said, turning his back to him.

Min-chin was reluctant to enter such an odious place, but after offending the proprietor he had no choice. As he entered the dark, sordid room, he smelled a sickening pungent odor, like the smell of burning fruit. The windows were closed and covered. A few small lamps provided meager illumination through a smoky haze. Unable to see, he waited for his eyes to adjust to the darkness.

Gradually he saw a wide platform that appeared to run continuously along the three walls of the single room with a walk space down the center. Several bodies were laying near him on filthy mattresses cushioning the platform. Min-chin bent down to look at the opium-yellowed face of the nearest sleeping man; he was not Ho-teng. Nauseated by the overpowering stench of unclean bodies, urine, and foul chamber pots, he covered his nose with a handkerchief as he walked down the aisle. His eyes met the unfocused gaze of a reclined man who was smoking his pipe over a glowing spirit lamp. Another man, propped up on one arm, was busy cooking an opium ball over his lamp. Three motionless bodies lay at the far end of the room. One was a woman. The man sleeping in the corner was Ho-teng. Min-chin put his hand on his shoulder, shook him gently and quietly said, "Saamgo." When he did not move, Min-chin shook him harder, but still he did not stir.

"Wake up, Saamgo. Wake *up!*" Min-chin said loudly in anger and frustration as he shook him. "*I can't carry you out of here!*" Still, Ho-teng did not respond.

Helpless, sallow, and emaciated, Ho-teng wore only pants, which were stained with fresh urine. Congealed sputum coated his lips and chin. He looked like a corpse: his skin hung down in bags and his bones showed as clearly as those of a skeleton. Min-chin shook him roughly again. For a moment, Ho-teng's eyelids flickered open; he looked vacantly at his brother with dull, senseless eyes and murmured something, before returning to a stupefied, drugged sleep. Min-chin thought he understood what he had mumbled:

"The pain of life is gone."

Heartsick, Min-chin sat down on the edge of the bench, covered his face with his hands, and wept softly.

He went back to the front counter.

"My elder brother wants to stay here and continue smoking. Give him as much as he wants for as long as he wants it. I'll pay his bill."

For several seconds, Sooi looked at Min-chin with a knowing, sardonic smile expressing a perverse humor. "Your brother's not well; he could smoke for several more days or a week before he's *done*. This could cost you as much as twenty pounds. Can you afford that?"

"Yes, I can pay you when he's done," Min-chin replied.

"*Ho!*"—Good! Sooi said with an air of finality, sealing the deal.

Min-chin left with a feeling of deep sadness. Four days later, Sooi sent word that Ho-teng had died in his opium parlor for reasons unknown.

◎

Duncan went to Norman Builders to meet his nephew Thomas Armstrong, who had recently been promoted to chief development officer of the company. Thomas wanted to show Duncan around their new office space before going out to lunch with him. They had not seen each other for two months, since the funeral for Thomas's father, Gilbert, who had died suddenly from a brain hemorrhage at the age of sixty-three.

As Thomas took Duncan on a tour of the company, he said, "Uncle Duncan, yesterday, I attended a meeting of the Association for Protection of Aborigines and was surprised to see how prominently the private association is led. Sir Robert Kensington, the association's president, said he is a colleague of yours. The vice-president is the Bishop of Sydney and seven members of Parliament serve on its council. I thought you would have been a member, considering your experience in dealing with Aboriginal issues when you were colonial secretary."

"Actually, Thomas, I opposed the efforts of the association to drag the government into its support. I was against providing financial assistance and setting aside crown land for missionary-run Aboriginal reserves. Now that the premier has appointed a protector of Aborigines and created an Aborigines Protection Board, ostensibly to oversee the expenditure of government funds at the Maloga and Warangesda Missions, we can expect ever more costly and fruitless efforts to rehabilitate, civilize, and train these degraded people. Of course, the real reason the premier set up the board was to encourage the natives to move to the missions from their fringe camps near towns."

"I don't know much about the politics of Aboriginal issues," Thomas confessed, "the meeting yesterday was about hiring teachers to teach the children how to read and write. Surely you'd agree that native children must receive a basic education, or the cycle of ignorance and poverty will be repeated generation after generation."

"No, I don't agree. You see—" Duncan stopped talking when Eleanor unexpectedly stepped out of an office and greeted them. She insisted they have tea in her office.

They sat down around Eleanor's meeting table. Thomas found himself irritated by Duncan's earlier surly remarks.

"Eleanor, we were just talking about the meeting I attended for you yesterday. I was telling Uncle Duncan how impressed I am with the politicians and others who lead the Association for Protection of Aborigines, and he was saying how he hadn't supported the association as colonial secretary."

Duncan did not shrink from the confrontational way Thomas had paraphrased their conversation. "The harsh reality is that most of the politicians who've joined the association see the missions as places to dump the blacks to get them out of the way. Towns like Cootamundra, Yass, Cowra, Gundagai, and Tumut are complaining about Aboriginal fringe camps and demanding that the Aborigines Protection Board remove them. My fellow politicians see the missions as a way to respond to the town councils' complaints."

This was the first time Eleanor had heard such an outrageous reason why some politicians supported the association. Thomas waited for Eleanor's response.

When neither Eleanor nor Thomas spoke up, Duncan continued. "The underlying problem is that there are more Aborigines than we thought. Parliament was surprised by the census of Aborigines, prepared by the protector of Aborigines, that came up with nine thousand natives in New South Wales compared with an estimate in 1876 of only one thousand. We wrongly assumed that they were going extinct because the Eora died out around Sydney."

Eleanor said, "All the more reason why you should support the Association for Protection of Aborigines, it seems to me."

"I would, if free food, clothing, and housing would keep them on the missions, but it doesn't. It attracts them for a while, then they just return to their fringe camps. They don't like any controls over them and are a real nuisance to the townspeople. The government may have to force them onto the missions and confine them there."

"You mean make them prisoners?" Eleanor asked. "That's hardly acceptable to the Christian missionaries, Duncan. They cannot force the Aborigines to stay on their missions. It has to be voluntary, just like the acceptance of religion, education, and giving up their primitive ways has to be voluntary. In time, the Aborigines will come to accept the benefits of European values and civilization."

Duncan looked at Eleanor with a condescending smile. "There may be a few politicians who are religious zealots and want to save heathen souls, but even they see the necessity of eliminating the fringe camps that steal from nearby farms and law-abiding townspeople."

"Haven't you become quite the cynical politician?" Eleanor said without rancor.

"I agree that I've become cynically *realistic*."

"Well, *realistically*, Duncan, I believe that most of the members of our association, politicians included, are responding to the human suffering of our indigenous natives. How can you be so cynical when these poor people are dying from hunger and disease, living in humpies, and cannot even afford clothing and shoes for their children? Half-caste girls—nearly as white as I am—are being ruined at an early age. Drunkenness is rampant, and they have no chance for a decent education. Unconscionable neglect by the government created these disadvantages."

"My word . . . well said, Eleanor, *you* should be a politician. However, just because our white, European sensitivities are offended by the way they live, you have to understand, this is the way they've *always* lived, as nomadic hunters, fishermen, and gatherers.

"And don't worry too much about affordable clothes and shoes; the blacks didn't wear *any* clothes, *or shoes*, until fairly recently. I'm *sorry*, but they don't want *our* religion, way of life, or values; mostly they just want us to *leave them alone*. That's been my policy for years; unfortunately, now that their numbers are so large, the government is being forced to address the issue."

Realizing to his chagrin that he had introduced a contentious issue, Thomas jumped in to present the common ground between Duncan and Eleanor.

"So in light of the current situation, Uncle Duncan, you feel there may be a role for the association to play between the townspeople and the missionaries?"

"Well, perhaps there is, Thomas," Duncan conceded. "At the moment, it appears that the objectives of the church and state coincide: the missionaries want to attract the blacks to their missions to save their souls and the government wants them out-of-the-way of the townspeople and farmers. Actually, I hope the missionaries are successful in attracting and enticing them to stay on the missions, otherwise, you'll see the government becoming authoritative and eventually force them to cooperate."

◎

Freed of the expense of his brother's upkeep and addiction, Min-chin was able to save enough in two and a half years to start his own market gardening business. A loan from the Sun Wei Tong was arranged to cover the land rent and workers' salaries for the first six months and to buy tools, supplies, plants, and seeds. He leased a two-acre plot on the east side of Shea's Creek halfway between Alexandria and Botany Bay. Within six months, he had turned out a saleable crop, and by the end of the first year he was profitable, thanks in part to a vigorous Australian economy and strong demand for fresh vegetables.

By mid-1883 Min-chin had accumulated sufficient wealth to think about marrying a woman from his family's Sun Wei District in China. As a businessman accustomed to buying goods, he wrote a list of his requirements:

1. Young woman, who has not known a man.
2. Strong for childbearing.
3. Five feet three inches or less in height. (Min-chin was nearly five feet seven inches tall.)
4. Peasant whose feet have not been bound, and who has worked in the fields.
5. Pleasant appearance but not beautiful. (He did not want a beautiful woman who could be a problem.)
6. Happy person.

He provided the list to the Sun Wei Tong along with money and gifts for a betrothal. Min-chin's family arranged a match with seventeen-year-old Lum-gum who accompanied a *tong* member to Sydney.

Min-chin first set eyes on his betrothed at the Sun Wei Tong headquarters in a formal premarital ceremony conducted by an elder and a monk. Lum-gum walked into the reception room in short, womanly steps that pleased Min-chin. Decorum dictated that they not speak to one another during the ceremony. The elder and monk asked them questions to confirm their willingness to marry the following day. The elder was Kwong Tang who would become a guiding light in Min-chin's life.

Lum-gum kept her eyes cast down, too embarrassed to look at Min-chin, and answered questions in a soft, polite, feminine way. Happily, Min-chin saw that she was petite, had a pretty face, and looked attractive in her embroidered, silk dress. He felt relieved, and a sense of pride swept over him. Praise Lord Buddha, the ancestors, and the gods; she will do very well as my wife.

Before Lum-gum had entered the reception room, the matrons assisting her had pointed out Min-chin through a crack in the door. She had prepared herself to marry a rich old man of thirty-nine; instead, she was elated to see a trim, square-shouldered, younger-looking man than she had expected.

When Min-chin spoke, Lum-gum felt a secret exultation: I can hear emotion and nervousness in his voice, although he's trying to hide it; he feels the importance of this moment as much as I do. He seems like a sensitive, kind man. A furtive glance at him confirmed her earlier distant assessment: I like his honest face, which isn't pockmarked or disfigured in any way. His clothes fit him well, and he carries himself proudly—not like a peasant. I thank the benevolent spirits of my ancestors for looking after me and providing me with a husband who appears to be a good man.

The next day they were married in the temple attached to the Sun Wei Tong headquarters. The facade of the three-story temple was flat fronted and nondescript, except for the glazed green roof tiles that were imported from China. The tiles' green color signified harmony. The interior of the temple was painted mostly in red and gold colors that bring good luck, prosperity, and happiness.

The ceremony was simple. The monk directed them in their marriage vows and in the making of offerings to secure their happiness and future good fortune.

On the ride to the four-room house Min-chin had rented in Surry Hills, he could think of little to say to his bride. Anything of a personal nature would have to wait until they knew each other better. He awkwardly pointed out a few places of interest along the way. She acknowledged the sights by smiling and nodding her head, stealing an occasional look at him.

Min-chin was exhausted, because he had been awake most of the previous night thinking through how a new wife should be handled. The same thoughts occupied his mind as they rode along.

I know I must take control to gain her respect, be self-assured but not arrogant, and impress her with my wealth and prospects. I want her to like me. I shouldn't treat her harshly like an employee. Although, if I'm too attentive, she'll think I'm weak and needy, especially because I have no family here. She could try to take advantage of me and become demanding. Perhaps I should express some dissatisfaction with her to start the relationship off on the right foot, so she won't feel too secure. On the other hand, she's probably already insecure in this *kwai-lo* land without the support of her family.

I'm not looking forward to tonight—our wedding night. I've been assured that she's a virgin, although I'm not sure how to tell. She acts like a virgin. I imagine that I know more about sex than she does. Hopefully, her mother told her what to expect and what to do. Thank you, Saamgo, for taking me twice to brothels, even though I didn't like the vulgar and unclean women. Perhaps Yigo was right when he said that sex is only satisfying when done with one's wife in the hope of having a son—I'll soon see.

When Min-chin showed her around her new home, she appeared surprised that only the two of them would share the entire house, which even had a separate bedroom with a door! She had lived in a three-room house with nine members of her extended family, a dog, pigs, and chickens.

Wishing to show humility and higher aspirations, Min-chin said, "This is a poor house, it's too small. We will move when the firstborn son arrives." Pointing to a wardrobe cupboard and a chest of drawers, he pompously said, "These are for your clothes alone."

She bowed her head in thanks. "These are for my humble clothes alone," she whispered disbelievingly in a voice just loud enough for him to hear, confirming to herself what she had just heard. She pleased him by opening and closing every door and drawer. "Noble Sir is too kind to his undeserving wife."

After she had unpacked, Min-chin showed her the beef and pork he had bought that morning for their dinner and a variety of vegetables. "These vegetables were grown in my garden," he said proudly. "I have nine employees who are gardeners and sellers of my vegetables. We will always have fresh vegetables in this house." Suddenly aware that he had neglected to list the requirement that she should be able to cook, he apprehensively asked, "Can you cook?"

Still not looking at Min-chin because it would appear unseemly, she answered, "Yes, Honorable Sir. I learned to cook from my mother and elder sister. I have cooked for my family for many years."

While she prepared dinner, Min-chin sat and read the Sun Wei Wa Po, the occasional newsletter of the Sun Wei Tong, to show her that he could read. Sing-woo had taught him to read and write hundreds of Chinese characters. Over the years, Min-chin had maintained a friendship with elder Wong Ching-tin, the owner of Wong Cabinets, in part, because he had a large personal collection of books. Wong graciously allowed Min-chin to borrow what he wanted to read. They would often discuss a book for hours after Min-chin had read it.

Lum-gum prepared a delicious meal that pleased Min-chin greatly. To show his appreciation, he slurped his soup loudly and belched throughout the meal. After the meal, affecting an air of seriousness, Min-chin said he had work to do and sat down at his desk. Lum-gum cleared the table and washed the dishes and pots and pans. When she had finished, she went into the bedroom.

By eight o'clock, Min-chin was feeling anxious. Soon he would have to perform his manly duty. He asked himself, Why is she staying in the bedroom? What is she doing in there? She should be out here where I can see her. I should feel aroused on my wedding night, though how can I when she's avoiding me?

He got up and walked around moving items noisily. When Lum-gum did not come out of the bedroom or respond in any way, he started to become agitated. The moment has arrived—am I to do everything to prepare for the Clouds and the Rains?

In a loud voice, he said, "Fong-*Taai*,"—Mrs. Fong—"you should get ready for bed."

When there was no answer from the bedroom, he became angry and marched down the short hall and stood at the partially opened door to the bedroom. Lum-gum was placidly seated on the edge of the bed intently sewing a garment.

Opening the door forcefully, he said, "Didn't you hear me tell you it's time for bed? Get ready for bed!" He was surprised by the shocked look on her young face. She dropped to her knees and kowtowed to him. He thought for a moment that she was going to cry. Quickly closing the door part way, he turned and walked back into the main room.

After fifteen minutes, he walked quietly down the hall to the partially opened bedroom door. The light was off in the room. Lum-gum was crying softly. Opening the door and sticking his head into the darkened room, Min-chin could make out that she was under the bed covers facing away from him.

"Are you crying?" he asked.

She abruptly stopped crying for a moment, then answered through sobs, "I-I'm sorry . . . my L-Lord. I do not mean t-to dishonor you. I'm a poor, dumb wife . . . wh-who acts like a child."

"Are you frightened?"

"Y-y-yes . . . I-I am a stupid p-person . . . who doesn't know . . . how t-to be a good wife."

He was pleased that she was afraid; she was obviously a virgin. Secretly, he was relieved that he didn't have to perform.

"This is a *bad* omen. We are not man and wife yet, not until we consummate our marriage. I cannot introduce you as my wife until then. Do you understand?"

Weeping, she stammered out, "Y-yes, sir."

Confused, he wondered what he should do to save face. Foremost in his mind was Yigo's saying: "A man needs face like a tree needs its bark." My manhood's being tested, he thought; I don't want to appear weak. Raising his voice and speaking forcefully, he said, "I can do what I want with you; we have been honorably married. I can demand my right as husband on this wedding night!"

Her sobbing increased.

Happily, it occurred to him that he could avoid the wedding night ordeal and still appear manly, wise, and magnanimous. He would use a religious precept learned from Yigo.

"I do not wish to force myself on you, for Buddha has taught me that Enlightenment is a state of mind where there is no lust or anger, only the light of wisdom and compassion. So you can go to sleep. I will control my desire this night, for your sake."

Feeling a satisfying aura of superiority, he climbed into the bed and purposely moved close to her. He was rewarded when she stopped sobbing and her rigid body relaxed. He fell slowly to sleep warmed by her body close to his and soothed by the sweet smell of her perfume.

◎

Samuel Armstrong did not want to be married in St. Andrew's Cathedral. He had wanted to oblige his bride's desire for a simple family wedding of twenty or thirty people, but his politician father Duncan insisted on a grander ceremony for his only child. Because the bride's family was not well-off, Duncan took it on himself to arrange a ceremony witnessed by three hundred people in the first cathedral built in Australia, with a reception in the ornate assembly hall in the new Sydney Town Hall.

During the interlude between the marriage ceremony and reception, a group of Armstrongs and friends conversed in the plaza between the cathedral and town hall. Eleanor asked the group:

"Do you think that the city council located the new town hall next to St. Andrew's for its symbolic attachment to the Anglican Church?" The group composed entirely of Anglicans nodded.

Curtis, Priscilla's husband who worked for the *Sydney Morning Herald*, said, "I don't doubt that there's some truth to that, though I think the city council also wanted to exhibit its independence from Parliament, which had offered several sites close to Parliament House."

"I think council also chose this site because it's more

centrally-located to serve the expanding city," a family friend said.

Peter Armstrong, the fifteen-year-old son of Thomas, asked, "Why doesn't St. Andrew's face George Street, Father? The front entrance is on the *back* of the building!"

Thomas placed his hand on his son's shoulder. "I have an observant son who's going to be an architect, I fancy. It's the result of a town planning fiasco, I'm afraid, Peter. Governor Macquarie and his convict architect Greenway had planned a great, European city piazza to cover the area now bounded by Liverpool, Kent, Druitt, and Pitt Streets—crowned by our Anglican cathedral."

"Why . . . that's six square blocks, a huge piazza," Priscilla said.

"Yes, it was intended for large public gatherings," Thomas said. "The cathedral's west side was made the most imposing facade, with its twin towers, large front doors, and stained-glass windows, because only from the west does the cathedral appear to be sitting on a hill. After Macquarie laid the cathedral's foundation stone, the piazza was eliminated from the city plans by Commissioner Bigge, who had been sent out by Britain to curtail Macquarie's extravagant spending. George Street was then extended south and the town hall faced onto it, so that our beautiful, neo-Gothic cathedral ended up with its back door facing the main street of the city. A great pity, I must say."

"And one doesn't just pick up a cathedral and turn it around," Curtis quipped.

"Indeed," Thomas said.

Looking at St. Andrew's and shaking his head, a family friend said, "I'm afraid the Catholics' St. Mary's Cathedral is going to be much larger and better positioned." (The first section of the Gothic Revival style cathedral had been opened for three years, since 1882.)

"Yes, I'm afraid you're right," Thomas said. "St. Andrew's will pale beside their cathedral when completed. The plans call for St. Mary's to be the largest Christian church in the empire outside of Britain."

Caroline, Thomas's wife, had been watching Kwong and Margaret Tang, who were talking to a couple nearby. (Kwong Tang was the elder who had conducted the premarital ceremony for

Min-chin and Lum-gum.) As the Tangs passed by her, Caroline touched Margaret on the arm and greeted them:

"Margaret, and Mr. Tang, how nice of you to come."

Caroline was a regular customer of Tang's two exclusive women's clothing stores specializing in fine, imported, Chinese silk dresses, nightgowns, blouses, chemises, undergarments, scarves, and other women's apparel, refashioned to fit European women. His stores were exquisitely decorated to resemble the most expensive women's stores along London's Piccadilly Circus and were staffed by refined white ladies. His wife Margaret had been one of his saleswomen.

Duncan had invited the Tangs because Kwong Tang was his main contact with the Chinese community and its Sun Wei Tong businessmen's association. Duncan had come to know him as a wealthy supporter of St. Andrews Cathedral, which he and his wife regularly attended. A member in good standing of the Freemasons and Oddfellows, the affable, irrepressible Chinese man was sought after for his humorous talks and repertoire that never failed to entertain.

"It was such a lovely wedding," Margaret said. "I couldn't keep myself from crying. They're such an attractive couple and seem so much in love."

Turning toward the men, Kwong Tang put his hands together as if praying for the young couple. "Lord Byron said it best:

> "Tis melancholy, and a fearful sign
> Of human frailty, folly, also crime,
> That love and marriage rarely can combine,
> Although they both are born in the same clime;
> Marriage from love, like vinegar from wine."

Margaret playfully nudged her husband. "You don't believe that!"

The men laughed, and Curtis said, "Too right . . . good on ya, Kwong."

Kwong Tang's life was a rags to riches story. He was born Ts'ing Kwong-tang. When he was thirteen, in 1846, he left his destitute village near Canton with an elder brother to seek work in Hong

Kong. They were recruited there to work for pastoralists in the colony of New South Wales. His brother died during the voyage. On arrival in Sydney, Kwong-tang was placed with a wealthy solicitor as a servant. Industrious, gregarious, and eager to please, he quickly learned English. His surname, Ts'ing, was dropped, and he become known by the two ideograms of his given name, Kwong Tang, written in the English style and order of the given name first followed by the surname. After two years, the childless solicitor and his wife liked him so much that they paid for his education. In 1853 he went off to the goldfields and made a fortune in two years.

Looking beyond the group, Thomas smiled and waved a salutation to a man in uniform. Others turned to see who he was waving at. "That's my old mate from the Sydney Battalion of Volunteer Rifles, Captain Joseph Ledsham. He was in the Sudan and told me earlier that we should all be proud of our troops' conduct in Africa. Although our relief forces were sent too late to save General Gordon besieged in Khartoum, the few skirmishes our boys were in sent the Dervishes running."

"It's a good thing we supported England and sent our troops to help," Peter said, supporting his father.

Duncan Armstrong had overheard the comments about the Sudan expedition as he circulated among his guests. Unable to restrain himself, he stepped into the group.

"I don't know that I agree with you, young Peter. We shouldn't be sending our troops off in support of the empire's adventures when they're needed here."

"Here?" queried Thomas.

"Yes, *here,* we're a vulnerable country with France and Germany moving into our area of influence and Britain providing inadequate protection. The French are threatening to annex the New Hebrides to add to their penal colony at New Caledonia. The Germans have annexed New Britain and would have taken eastern New Guinea if not for the British navy in Port Moresby."

Curtis agreed wholeheartedly. "Quite right, Duncan."

"So we need our troops *here*, not in the Sudan. And with that, I'd like to rudely excuse myself before I get drawn into a *political* conversation. Thank you all for coming, the reception in the town hall is going to be first-rate."

The group was silent for a moment after Duncan's political assault. Screwing up his mouth to speak out of one corner, Thomas quietly said, "Once a pollie always a pollie." The people near him smiled and chuckled.

"He's right though," Kwong Tang said, "we need a national army and navy to defend Australia, with a centralized command, instead of individual, uncoordinated forces from our six colonies."

"The British Parliament's recent approval of the Federal Council of Australasia is a step in that direction, Kwong," Thomas said. "The council will consider the military defense of Australia and New Zealand, Pacific island relations, immigration, quarantine, tariffs, and other such concerns. It could lead to a federal government before long. Like Duncan said, it's the only wa—"

Thomas was interrupted by his son tapping him on the shoulder. "Dad . . . they're calling everyone into the Town Hall now. I just got a peek at the assembly hall. You're all going to be surprised, if you haven't seen it yet. It's really beautiful!" He raised his hand as if pointing to something large above his head. "There's a huge chandelier in the center hanging down from a domed skylight with beautiful stained glass; the walls are bright colors, and there's a beautiful ceiling too."

◎

Min-chin requested a meeting with Kwong Tang, who had been his counselor at the Sun Wei Tong for several years.

"What would you like to discuss today, Fong-*Saang*?" Tang asked.

Min-chin respectfully used the esteemed title of elder, "Tang-*Jeungbui*, this humble gardener asks your learned advice regarding two matters. I seek the assistance of our *tong* to transport the bones of my two elder brothers back to our village for burial in our ancestral graveyard. The *yin* of this sad occasion will be balanced by the *yang* of the happy announcement of the birth of my first son. Also, I would like to obtain a loan from the Sun Wei Tong to purchase the land I lease for my gardens. A loan wou—" Min-chin stopped speaking abruptly when Kwong Tang grinned and raised his right hand slightly from the desk top.

"Before you go on, Fong-*Saang,* allow me to congratulate you on the birth of a son! I recall you have a girl; she must be about three now. Your *karma* has improved markedly with the birth of a son." Kwong Tang assumed that the birth of an Australia-born son and Min-chin's interest in buying land meant that he had finally decided to remain permanently in the colony.

"Thank you, Tang-*Jeungbui.*"

"What have you named the boy child?"

"Wing-yuen."

"Ah, 'forever,' which when joined with your family name means 'placed here forever.' An *excellent* choice for a first-born son of Australia. A son who will stay forever in his adopted land."

"Thank you," Min-chin said, although he was tempted to tell him that he preferred the tonal pronunciation meaning "long life."

Turning his head away from Min-chin, Tang covered his mouth and involuntarily yawned. "Please excuse me, Fong-*Saang,* I mean no disrespect. I'm a bit tired from the week-long centennial festivities and the state banquet last night. Did you see the fireworks yesterday in Lachlan Swamp?—I mean Centennial Park, its new name."

"No, but we could hear them." Min-chin was surprised that Kwong Tang would think he would attend a *kwai-lo* event.

"It was reported in the newspaper that fifty thousand people attended the festivities and enjoyed the bands, parades, and concerts. Governor Lord Carrington opened Centennial Park and said in his speech that the crown land was granted to the people of New South Wales forever. Did you attend any of the events? It's a short distance from Surry Hills."

"We couldn't attend because of the new born," Min-chin lied and wondered: Why is he going on about this *kwai-lo* celebration? It means nothing to me. This isn't like him, to try and impress me.

"Oh, yes, of course, how foolish of me." Kwong Tang could tell from Min-chin's attitude that he had no interest in the hundred-year celebration of New South Wales, but he felt an obligation to encourage him to take a greater interest in his adopted homeland.

"Well, you must take your family to the park for a picnic when you're able. Now that the city water comes from the Nepean River west of Parramatta, the former swamps and sand hills have been transformed. There's a grand circular drive at least two miles long, newly-planted trees and shrubberies, lakes, and gardens. Your family would find it quite enjoyable, I'm sure."

"Thank you, Esteemed Elder, for your gracious suggestion. We will visit as soon as we can."

Kwong Tang knew that Min-chin was the serious type, and that it was time to get back to business. "Now, about your elder brothers' remains, of course, the Sun Wei Tong can make all the arrangements to return your brothers' bones to your village. May I ask how your brothers died?"

"My honorable second eldest brother was killed by larrikins in The Rocks in '72 and my other brother died seven years ago from opium addiction."

"How very sad, on both accounts. The larrikin pushes and hoodlum gangs are terrorizing and assaulting law-abiding whites as well as our countrymen. Many poor neighborhoods are being victimized. These larrikins are cowards, no good sons of convicts. They are driving us out of The Rocks to Surry Hills and the Haymarket. Henry Lawson has even written a poem called 'The Captain of the Push' that condemns them:

> "As the night was falling slowly down on city, town,
>   and bush,
> From a slum in Jones's Alley sloped the Captain of the
>   Push;
> And he scowled towards the North, and he scowled to-
>   wards the South,
> As he hooked his little fingers in the corners of his mouth.
> Then his whistle, loud and piercing, woke the echoes of
>   'The Rocks,'
> And a dozen ghouls came sloping round the corners of the
>   blocks."

Kwong Tang stopped after the first stanza when he saw he wasn't entertaining Min-chin, who looked perplexed. His attempt to interest him in broader Australian topics was not going well.

"And your other brother died of opium . . . mm, mm. Opium is the scourge of our people. Our use of opium makes us look perverse to the whites. I chair a *tong* committee that is trying to get Parliament to pass a law banning the importation and sale of opium. Unfortunately, it doesn't look hopeful . . . Parliament is unwilling to lose the revenue and some politicians instill fear that beer, wine, spirits, and tobacco will also be abolished if opium is banned. Would you like to join my committee? You would meet city leaders and parliamentarians who support our anti-opium efforts."

"You pay me a great compliment, Tang-*Jeungbui*. I am vastly honored that you feel I could serve on your noble committee. Regrettably, I must humbly decline. I am not worthy—a poorly educated, common man. I speak little English and confess that I feel uncomfortable around the *kwai-lo*. They mistreated us terribly in the goldfields, killed my revered second eldest brother, and supplied the opium that poisoned my third eldest brother."

"You must put such negative thoughts aside, Fong-*Saang*, and work to improve our situation, if you intend to stay in Australia and raise your children."

"Oh, I have no intention of staying here for the rest of my life, Tang-*Jeungbui*. I will return to my village when I am ready to retire, hopefully at an age young enough to enjoy my declining years."

Kwong Tang realized that he had mistaken Min-chin's intentions. "Very well, Fong-*Saang*, each of us has a different path to follow. Now, considering your second request, what is the price of the land you want to buy?"

"The landowner wants £750, all cash, for the nine acres that I lease," answered Min-chin.

"*Waa!* . . . that's over £80 per acre! A preposterous price for swampy, bottom land along Shea's Creek!"

"There's a two-room hut on the property."

"Even so, that's at least double what it should cost. You know that, *kwa*?"

"Yes, I know the price is much too high, Tang-*Jeungbui,* but land prices continue to shoot up. I'm afraid if I don't purchase now, I'll be unable to afford it later."

"I cannot recommend that the *tong* finance such an inflated price, Fong-*Saang.* Did you go to the owner, or did he approach you?"

"I approached him."

"Does he want to sell?"

"Only if I meet his price."

"Then wait. I believe the colony's long boom may be over soon. We've had a rural recession for three years now, caused by the drought, and now unemployment is rising in the cities. I fear that Britain's economy is also cooling. If you buy now, you may be buying at the height of land speculation. When the economy cools, land prices should fall. I advise you to save your money, Fong-*Saang* and buy later when prices are lower. If you lose your lease, God forbid, you'll find other land to farm. Few people are interested in the low, swampy land used for market gardening."

◉

In May 1888 Sydney was at a fever pitch over Chinese immigration. The British government had advised the Australian colonial governments that its treaty with China, allowing Chinese immigration to Australia, would take some time to renegotiate. The mother country's prevarication and lack of urgency was intolerable to those Australians who believed that the Chinese were one of the main reasons for increasing unemployment and falling wages.

To make matters worse, the telegraph and newspapers sang with the news of the *Afghan* steaming toward Sydney to unload 268 Chinese passengers. The curiously named steamship had been prevented from landing its Chinese passengers in Melbourne on a technicality. The Anti-Chinese League arranged a public meeting for the third of May at Sydney Town Hall to hear speakers on the "Chinese Problem." Member of Parliament Duncan Armstrong, an advocate of prohibiting Chinese immigration and creating a white

Australia, was to be a principal speaker.

On the evening of the meeting, the town hall was crammed with over two thousand people who occupied every seat, sat in the aisles, and lined the walls. Duncan had scheduled himself to speak at the ideal time: after lesser orators warmed up the crowd but before the audience grew tired and lost interest. Identified by his trademark black eye patch, Duncan was a seasoned public speaker, who knew how to arouse and sway an audience and was not above using demagoguery when necessary.

An overflow crowd of three thousand thronged the entrance, sat on the monumental stairs, and flowed across the sidewalk out into the street. While the speakers spoke inside, their key points were passed along and then shouted from the top of the stairs to stir and excite the crowd outside.

Announced to wild applause, Duncan waved his arms and pointing at familiar faces in the crowd as he crossed the stage. At the podium, he steadied himself and paused to let the applause gradually die away and the hall to quiet and anticipation to build—then, at just the right moment, he began:

"The Chinaman says we treat him *unfairly*, because he has to pay an entry and residence tax to live in Australia. However, that hasn't stopped forty thousand Celestials from coming here according to the 1881census. And those were the ones the census takers cared to find!"—scattered laughter. "One in fifteen adult males is now a Chow in Australia, and the way they're flooding in here, the 1891 census is sure to show *one in ten of us is Chinese!*

"But still the Chinaman says we treat him *un-fairrr-ly*, even though we allow him to take our gold, buy our land with the money he hoards, travel freely, and reside in any city or town he likes. Does this wily, two-faced, yellow man give *us* the same freedoms in China— *No!* He forces the white man to live and trade in specially designated *concession areas* in his principal ports. Permission must be granted— by the *emperor!*—to travel outside of these concession areas. A white man cannot purchase land or live where he wants. *Is that fairrr?*"

Several shouts of "No!" came from the audience.

"Yet *we allow* the Mongolian to trade and work anywhere he

likes—freedoms the white man is not given in China. And what does he do? He takes our jobs by undercutting the fair wage. Will an Australian work for the cheap wages of a *Chinaman?*"

"No!" was the answer from many in the crowd.

"Does the capitalist care a lick about the white laborer if he can hire a *Celestial* for a pittance?"

Again, but louder, people in the audience yelled, "*No!*"

"The capitalist wants to tyrannize the white laborer and rule over him as he did in England for hundreds of years. The capitalist would like the white laborer to *beg* him, for *permission* to work—at wages so low he can't support his starving wife and young children. But the *Mon-ghoul-lian* has no wife or children to support. *Does he?*"

"NO!" shouted the audience.

"And he can live on the smell of a *cabbage leaf!*"

There was laughter and scattered comments of "*You got right, mate!*" and "*Sure can!*" and "*Skinny buggers!*" Duncan let the audience comments run their course.

"The Mongolian isn't your equal, not physically, mentally, or morally. *Is he?*"

"*NOO!*" echoed around the hall.

"That's *right!* He's inferior to the white man in every way and therefore willing to work for *nothing*—not so the Australian. Australians are from the British *white* race—a race that is, by its very nature, superior to all other races. The white man dominates, and will forever dominate, the yellow Asiatic, the black, the muddy Indian, and every other race with whom he comes in contact. Australia is in the business of nation building. *Do we need the yellow Chi-na-man?*"

A thunderous roar of "*NOOO!*"

"NO! We Australians say a thousand times NOO! We want a White Australia! The Chinese must GO! They don't look, think, or act like true Australians and can't assimilate. THEY MUST *GO!* THEY MUST *GO!*" He waved his arm up and down like a bandleader and led the chant: THEY MUST *GO!* THEY MUST *GO!*"

Loud applause, cheering, and "THEY MUST *GO!*" followed him to his seat.

A resolution was proposed and adopted by voice vote to totally prohibit Chinese immigration, regardless of British treaties with China. A deputation, including Lord Mayor John Harris, Duncan, labor leaders, and the head of the Anti-Chinese League, was empowered by the crowd to proceed immediately to Parliament House to present the resolution to the premier of New South Wales, Sir Henry Parkes. While the deputation and a mob of over five thousand marched toward Parliament House, Duncan in a loud booming voice led the chants: "THE CHINESE MUST *GO!*" and "THE CHINAMAN *OUT!*"

Hearing the approaching mob, the Parliament House guards locked the gate. Outraged, Duncan demanded entry.

"I'm a member of Parliament and *demand* my right of entry!"

When other parliamentarians demanded the same, the guards reluctantly opened the gate part way for them to enter. Seeing the gate being opened, the mob surged forward. Part of the mob was able to force its way inside Parliament House with Duncan and the deputation. A melee erupted inside. Outside, the mob rampaged up and down Macquarie Street shouting slogans, breaking windows, and roughing up constables and a unit of Water Police sent to restore order.

Premier Parkes locked himself in his office and refused to speak with Duncan and other members of the riotous deputation. Standing outside the premier's door, Duncan wrote a question for Parkes and gave it to Lord Mayor Harris to read. Members of the delegation suggested revisions and the mayor rewrote the question and slid it under the premier's door. The question said:

"In view of the probable arrival of the *Afghan* before daylight tomorrow . . . have precautions been taken to prevent the Chinese on board from landing?"

Parkes wrote a brief reply beneath the question and slid it under the door back to them. His reply was better than the delegation had expected. Lord Mayor Harris went out onto the veranda of Parliament House to read Parkes's reply to the mob.

"Premier Parkes is *with us!*" Harris said in a triumphant voice. "He's written a note, which says:

" 'Necessary steps will be taken to prevent the landing of the Chinese passengers from the ship.' "

Duncan wondered how Parkes intended to prevent the landing of those Chinese who were naturalized citizens or held proper papers to disembark. No such concern worried the mob, which cheered loudly. A large number of police arrived to end the tumultuous scene.

When the *Afghan* entered Sydney Harbour, Henry Parkes ordered the police to board her and place the ship under the smallpox yellow flag, a sham to quarantine the vessel so the Chinese could not be unloaded. Parkes telegraphed his fellow colonial premiers to ask for an immediate intercolonial conference on Chinese immigration and cabled Britain's colonial secretary explaining the crisis and implying that he was being forced to act independently. With the help of Duncan and Owen Vernon, Parkes pushed a Chinese exclusion bill through the lower house Legislative Assembly that essentially provided for the elimination of Chinese immigration and naturalization. The upper house Legislative Council, however, would not be rushed and took its time to fully consider the bill.

While Premier Parkes was attempting to persuade the Legislative Council to approve his bill, several Chinese on the *Afghan*, who were former residents of Sydney, hired a lawyer to appeal to the Supreme Court. In short order, the Supreme Court ruled that forty-eight Chinese holding exemption certificates, which permitted them to return to Australia, were free to land. Parkes allowed them to disembark at three o'clock in the morning, and the *Afghan* returned to Hong Kong with the remaining Chinese.

The intercolonial conference on Chinese immigration was convened in Sydney in mid-June with premiers and delegates arriving from all of the colonies in Australia. Duncan spoke regarding the United State's Chinese Exclusion Acts of 1882 and 1888.

"We should follow America's example. Although their '82 Chinese Exclusion Act suspended entry of some categories of Chinese for ten years, the Chinese government earlier this year agreed to even more restrictive immigration measures. This only came about because of American violence toward the Chinese, calls to expel all Chinese, and threats to discontinue Chinese trade.

The new treaty suspends Chinese immigration to United States for an additional *twenty years* in exchange for America's agreement to continue trade and allow the Chinese residing in the United States to stay and reenter if a spouse, child, parent, or assets worth one thousand dollars was left behind. Copies of the American acts are in your package of information." In conclusion, Duncan said, "We must be firm with Britain that we will not accept a treaty that allows more Chinese in, under any circumstances."

The intercolonial conferees resolved there should be uniform immigration laws among the Australian colonies and drafted the Chinese Immigration Restriction Bill designed to eliminate Chinese immigration and naturalization. The bill was dispatched to Britain for ratification with a request that it renegotiate a new treaty with China, similar to that of the United States, to virtually prohibit Chinese immigration to the Australian colonies.

◉

Eleanor ran down the list of sales prices that Norman Builders had received for land sold during the past six months. "These sales far exceeded what I had expected, Thomas. You're putting the company in fine financial shape."

"Thanks," Thomas said. "There's still plenty of capital out there, Eleanor, and well-located land like ours commands a premium. The problem is that our cash cache is reinvested at interest rates far below the annual percentage increase in the value of land."

"The increasing land values are speculative and not likely to continue. You're converting it into cash, which I'd much rather have now than land. Good work, Thomas."

"I can't say I enjoy doing this, Eleanor. I don't like curtailing our development plans, reducing staff, and incurring the resentment of confused employees. I must say . . . I liked it much better when we were *forward* thinking and *growing*. If your expected recession doesn't materialize, we're going to look pretty silly buying back our land at higher prices."

"Please, let's not get into another are-we-doing-the-right-thing discussion. I know you have grave reservations about the wisdom of my strategy. It's a *defensive* strategy to protect the company, its investors, and you and me."

Thomas took a long drag on his pipe and blew the smoke toward the floor. "I understand your strategy, Eleanor. And I agree that the economy is going to slow in the next year, but I think it will bounce back after that, as it has in the past. I think we've sold enough of our land inventory now."

"I think we have to prepare for a recession, perhaps even an economic depression, Thomas. This company has been my life since Alistair died, nearly twenty-five years ago, and I don't want to put it in jeopardy. This boom started with the gold rush in the fifties—*forty* years ago—that's a long time. Just look at the unrealistic land prices, the rural recession, Britain's economic downturn, low wool prices, increasing unemployment, and now these strikes that are wreaking havoc on the economy. These selfish unions, which have joined together to stop all intercolonial and coastal shipping, don't stop to think what they're doing to the country's economy. In fact, the recession may have already begun."

"There are dark clouds, certainly, though it's not all bad." Thomas wanted Eleanor to look on the bright side. "Sydney's population continues to grow, four hundred thousand now, along with the country reaching three million people, and the manufacturing sector seems to be doing well. Plus, I think that federation of the colonies is going to happen, which should reduce the costs of doing business in many areas, promote free trade between the colonies, and eliminate some duplication—like creating one military force to replace six."

"Federation is a bright spot, I grant you. Sir Henry Parkes will push through federation if anyone can."

"He'll chair the Australasian convention here in March," Thomas said. "New Zealand agreed to participate in the convention, which will try to draft a national constitution."

Eleanor rose from behind her desk and walked over to the window and stood there looking out at the city. "But it's going to be years before we see any economic benefits from federation, if it happens at all." Turning, she looked seriously at him. "Thomas...I'd like you to start paying down our debt with some of that cash cache."

Thomas's face dropped.

"*My God,* Eleanor, we'll need that to buy land in the future! Our lenders are pushing to *lend* us money, not take it back. They already think we've gone mad!"

"Then explain to them what we're doing—or tell them nothing at all if you like! Or tell them I've gone mad, if that's what you *believe!*"

Thomas was surprised, Eleanor hardly ever raised her voice. "You may be right, Eleanor; I just don't know, although I think you don't know for sure either."

"Of course I don't know—no one knows—although I *am sure* it's the right time to be conservative. We can take on new construction contracts, Thomas, but *we're out* of the development business for the time being. We should be satisfied with the success of Paddington and our resort projects in Manly, especially The Corso Hotel. It's time now to manage these assets rather than put them at risk."

Chapter 11

A New British Nation

Kwong Tang and Min-chin had become close friends over the years. Their offices were only three city blocks apart, and they regularly ate lunch together. On Kwong Tang's recommendation, Min-chin had been appointed an elder of the Sun Wei Tong in recognition of his many years of membership and success in business. To show their friendship, the two men added affectionate prefixes to their surnames: Min-chin called his former councilor *lou*-Tang, meaning "revered, wise elder" Tang, and in return, Kwong Tang used the prefix *a*- before Fong to show his affection for Fong Min-chin.

"The Sun Wei Tong is being strained to its limits to support our needy members during this recession, *lou*-Tang," Min-chin complained during lunch. "At the same time, we have less revenue because the Chinese exclusion laws are keeping our tong membership from growing."

"The recession may also be a deterrent to coming to Australia," Kwong Tang said.

"Life is still better here than in China, *lou*-Tang. I think many would come if the harsh *kwai-lo* immigration laws weren't keeping them out."

"Life doesn't seem too bad for you, *a*-Fong. Yee Kam Sun mentioned to me that you wanted to borrow money from him to lease more land."

"*Bai!* I can't discuss business without everyone knowing my business!"

"We are a small community, *a*-Fong; there are no secrets. You already lease more than ten acres, don't you? How many more do you want to lease?"

"I lease eleven now, and have the chance to lease another four acres."

"I thought you wanted to *buy* your market garden land."

"I do, but the landowner is very rich, and even with the recession, he keeps raising his selling price. Although he will lease me more land, it takes money to hire workers to drain the land, make it fertile, plant, harvest, and market. The *tong* has no money to lend, and since so many banks have failed, the remaining banks aren't lending either, especially to us. The landlord is offering a low rent, but I can't risk it without a loan. No one knows how much longer this recession will last."

He's certainly doing well if he can afford to expand, Kwong Tang thought to himself. I've had to change lenders twice this year to borrow adequate operating funds. "You are very fortunate to be in the market-gardening business; people always have to eat."

"I think the recession is bringing more customers to the Belmore Park Market. My stall does nearly as much business there on a weekend as all week hawking door-to-door."

Kwong Tang dejectedly placed an elbow on the table and rested his cheek on his fist. He envied Min-chin's recession-proof business. "Luxury women's clothing is not a good business to be in during a recession, *a*-Fong. Your labor costs have probably fallen because so many of our brothers are out of work."

"My labor costs may have fallen a little."

"*My* costs continue to go up. My sales are down, but my operating costs are up. I have to do something soon. My long-time, white women employees will not accept layoffs or less pay. I'm going to have to close one of my stores. It's the only way that I can justify laying off employees and reducing my overhead costs."

Min-chin felt sorry for his friend. "That's a good idea, *lou*-Tang. Your best customers will stay with you and shop at your remaining store."

"I've let it go on too long. I didn't want to sack loyal, well-trained employees. At least I'll be able to keep the best ones at my remaining store."

"You are fortunate to have such loyal employees who you can depend on," Min-chin said while thinking of his own situation. "I should have brought my family members here to work for me before the *kwai-lo* immigration restriction laws were passed. My kin can't get passage now. Few ship captains will accept Chinese passengers bound for Australia for fear that they will be rejected and become their responsibility. We are a peaceful, hard working people who provide many needed services here. I don't understand why the *kwai-lo* are such racists."

Kwong Tang had always overlooked Min-chin's animosity against whites, but on this day, at this time, it was too much. "It's because we Chinese do not respect the Australians and do not try to fit in."

Min-chin was taken aback by Kwong Tang's obvious criticism of his dislike for whites and was unsure of how to respond. "What do you mean?"

Kwong Tang decided to be uncharacteristically blunt. "Look at yourself, *a*-Fong. You have done very well in this country; still, you have no regard for the whites. After living here most of your life, you continue to call them *kwai-lo*, white barbarian devils, not worthy of our respect. You have bothered to learn little English and deal with them only when you must. You are always going home *next year*, but you don't, because life is better here."

Min-chin was staggered by Kwong Tang's bad manners in attacking him personally. Yes, he admitted to himself that he hated the whites, but rightly so; they hated him, had killed Sing-woo, and mistreated all Chinese.

"What does my disregard for whites have to do with their racism?"

"Don't you see, *a*-Fong? The whites want racial and social harmony in their country. We have to do everything we can to fit in: learn English, dress in their clothes, respect their values, accept intermarriage . . . even participate in their religion. As long as we feel superior and keep apart from them, we can only blame ourselves for their discrimination of us."

"I can't believe you blame their discrimination *on us*. They will *never* accept us because of the color of our skin and our different ways. We shouldn't have to change our religion to theirs. Their values *are* terrible. They have no manners, no respect for elders, a violent nature, and their women are whores!"

Kwong Tang's head jerked back in astonishment, and his face took on a severe, offended countenance.

"My wife is *not a whore!*"

"*Oh* ... oh, of course not, so sorry, *lou*-Tang." Min-chin had forgotten Kwong Tang was married to a *kwai-poh*. "Please accept my most sincere apology." He bent his head low, nearly touching the table in penitence. "This foolish man talked *laapsaap!*"—rubbish!— "and meant no disrespect."

At the same time, though, Min-chin was thinking: Kwong Tang shouldn't have attacked me. He's forgotten his Confucian manners and become a rude *kwai-lo* himself. I should have expected this. He's married to a white and converted to her religion and has departed from the Tao Way of the Universe and forsaken Lord Buddha's Eightfold Path.

◉

Late Friday afternoon, Eleanor's secretary asked Thomas and his son Peter to join Eleanor in her office at the end of the day. They entered together and were surprised to see drinks and a plate of hors d'oeuvre on Eleanor's meeting table.

Rising from behind her desk, Eleanor said, "I thought it would be nice to finish the week off with a toast to Peter for successfully completing his first six months at Norman Builders. Has it gone well for you, Peter?"

"Yes, wonderfully, Aunt Eleanor." Peter preferred Aunt to the correct title of Great Aunt. "I like the bookkeeping department, and I like the people here. When The Sydney Deposit Bank failed, because of this depression, I didn't know what I was going to do."

"Your four years of banking experience will serve you well here, Peter," Eleanor said. "We're happy you've chosen to join us.

You represent the third generation of Armstrongs in the company, you know."

"I'm happy to be here, Aunt Eleanor," he said, sitting down next to his father.

"You've had a valuable, firsthand lesson of the potent, negative effects of excessive debt during a depression," Thomas said. "My entire work life has been through a growth period when debt was good business. I have to tip my hat to Eleanor who was concerned about the evils of too much debt. We'd be in a sorry state now if Eleanor hadn't seen this depression coming."

"Thank you, Thomas, but you were the one who sold the properties, paid down the debt, and placed us on a strong financial footing."

"Dragging my feet all the way, I'm sorry to say."

"Well, we aren't through this yet, although I think we'll be all right. Let's not talk about business. What are your interests outside of the office, Peter, if I may ask?"

"I play rugby, cricket, and sail with Dad on the weekends. And I'm still seeing Anne, my girlfriend—you met her at Christmas."

"She's a lovely girl. Is it serious?" Eleanor asked with a smile.

"Could be. We'll have to see. We've been friends for nearly a year now."

"Are you interested in community service, church programs for the needy, or anything like that?" Eleanor asked.

"I've never had time with school and work, but I'd like to."

"At Norman Builders, we encourage our employees to take an interest in community affairs. We give time off during work hours, within reason. It's not an obligation, mind you. If you have an interest of this sort, Peter, you should feel free to pursue it. Your father and I have been active in many community organizations over the years, some business oriented and others purely altruistic."

"For instance," Thomas said, "Eleanor and I have been involved in the Association for the Protection of Aborigines. It runs missions for Aborigines using private and church funding. Oh, by the way, Eleanor, have you heard that the Methodists are turning over their La Pérouse mission to the government's Aborigines Protection Board?"

"No, I haven't," Eleanor answered. "I'm sorry to hear that."

"Seems the church and its contributors are content to let the government run the mission."

"Well . . . I'm concerned that the government APB missions are being run on a much less benevolent basis than the missionaries run the church missions. Close to two-thirds of the colony's Aborigines are now resettled onto government missions and reserves." Shaking her head, she said, "I hope it's not true, but I've heard that the APB and police are forcing them into the missions and restricting their comings and goings, like Duncan predicted would happen."

"I hope that's not government APB policy," Thomas said. "Talking about benevolence, what is the status of the Benevolent Foundation Orphanage in Bathurst?"

"It too is suffering from a lack of funding. The government may have to take responsibility for its orphans."

"Would the APB take it over because it serves Aboriginal orphans?"

"I doubt it. The percentage of Aboriginal orphans there is very small. No, I'm more worried about what will happen to the orphans if the foundation has to close." She paused and then smiled. "I'm *worried* about too many issues—that's my problem—I can't do justice to any one of them." Quietly, almost to herself, she said, " . . . and I'd like to put more time into women's suffrage."

"That's the right for women to vote," Thomas said to Peter. "I support her efforts, of course."

"I think women should be allowed to vote, too," Peter agreed artlessly.

The men waited for a response from Eleanor, but she was looking out the window, her expression pensive. Seeing her distracted, Thomas and Peter concentrated on their drinks and the appetizers.

Still preoccupied, Eleanor turned and said, "You know, Thomas . . . I turned sixty this year."

"Yes . . . I attended your sixtieth birthday party—so did Peter, for that matter."

"Yes, of course you did. My goodness, senility is already setting in. Well, I've been meaning to talk to you for a couple of months about something that's been on my mind. Somehow, having your son here seems like a good time to ask it. I'd like you to take over my position as president at Norman Builders, subject to the board's approval, while I'll remain chairman."

Thomas raised himself up in his chair and then sat back down again. "I'm shocked; I don't know what to say—I mean—of course—I accept, Eleanor. I'd like to become president with you as chairman."

"Congratulations, Father."

"Good. I thought you'd be pleased, Thomas. You've earned it. It will be a gradual transition; I'll still come here every day, of course. This will give me more time to pursue my other interests. Since women recently achieved the right to vote in the colony of New Zealand, I'm more hopeful than ever that we can achieve it in Australia. I've been elected to the council of the Womanhood Suffrage League of New South Wales and with federation coming on, I want to work for a federal constitution that will include the right for women to vote."

◎

Following an evening lecture by Mark Twain at Sydney's Protestant Hall, Duncan and Grace, Eleanor, and Priscilla and her husband Curtis went to a fashionable restaurant for supper. They were in high spirits and discussed the American's lecture while waiting for their food.

"What a wonderful way to tour the world," Curtis said, "giving lectures billed as . . ."—he paused and dramatically swept his hand across in front of him as if reading a marquee—"the 'world-renowned laughmaker.'"

"Actually, he didn't give a *lecture* at all, did he?" Eleanor said. "He just told funny anecdotes, reminiscences, read from his novels . . . did this, then a bit of that . . . made an observation or two, rambled on—somehow making it all a delightful evening."

"I found his presentation style immensely entertaining," Duncan said. "He's really a social commentator. The interesting thing is that he can be both serious and funny at the same time."

"But many of the things he said weren't *really* funny, were they?" Grace said with a questioning look. "It's just the *way* he says things that make people laugh, don't you think?"

Duncan cringed at his wife's assessment and mockingly said, "He's a *humorist*, Grace."

Feeling sorry for Grace, Priscilla spoke quickly to mitigate Duncan's ridicule. "I liked his dry, satirical humor. I remember having greatly enjoyed *The Adventures of Tom Sawyer*. From the passages he read of *The Adventures of Huckleberry Finn*, I'm looking forward to reading it as well."

"I'm going to tell some of my fellow parliamentarians that they are like Mark Twain," Duncan said, "who 'tried the art of lying and became an instantaneous success.' " Everyone laughed heartily. Duncan often told self-effacing jokes about politicians, thinking it made him appear unpretentious.

"Being in the newspaper business," Curtis said, "I liked the one about his early life when 'he shared the disaster that sooner or later seems to befall the *average* American—he became a newspaper editor.' "

The laughter of the group was infectious, and now Eleanor joined in with a story. "Remember when he drew us all forward to the edge of our seats to hear him whispering confidences, and then said he had a secret to tell that 'he didn't wish to go beyond this room *and the newspapers!*' "

"Ha ha ha ha." Curtis repeated the punch line, under his breath: " 'This room and the newspapers.' "

Priscilla said, "Twain drew *me* in when he got serious and said that he was preparing a book about Australia's fauna—'the emus, kookaburras, kangaroos, boomerangs, jackeroos, larrikins'—I couldn't hear the rest for all the laughter."

Chuckling, Duncan said, "He surprised me when he said United States, like here, is 'suffering women for women's suffrage.' "

Priscilla immediately took offense. "I don't recall that."

"Yeh," Curtis agreed with Duncan, not reading Priscilla's umbrage. "He said something about women's suffrage and then joked about 'women suffering all the way homing.' "

"*What?*" Priscilla said, tilting her head and looking quizzically at her husband. "*What*, pray tell, is that supposed to mean?"

"Well ... I'm not sure, actually, what *way homing* means. I guess it—"

Eleanor interrupted. "*Wyoming*, Curtis, you misunderstood his accent; he said Wyoming, a state in the United States that gave women the right to vote years ago. I didn't understand, though, whether he was speaking for or against the issue."

"*Clearly*, he was poking fun at it," Duncan said in a voice of authority.

Priscilla's face flushed. "*How* can you say that so *assuredly?*"

"Because he's an *intelligent* man," Duncan flippantly retorted and then laughed.

"Ha h—" Curtis quickly suppressed his spontaneous laugh when he saw his wife's angry look.

"Is that funny to you?" Priscilla indignantly asked Curtis.

"Come now, let's not disagree over something we can't even recall clearly," Eleanor admonished.

Fortunately, the waiter arrived with their food. Nevertheless, the lightness of the evening was gone.

Well into their meal, Curtis said, "I read in the *Australasian Banking Record* that the worst of the depression may be over. It reported that there's increased demand and better prices for our mutton and beef in England, commodity prices have risen substantially, wheat production and sales are up, and British capital and investors are evidently returning."

"I think the worst may be over," Eleanor agreed. "It's taken five years, but Norman Builders is finally getting back to the level of construction we had in 1890."

Duncan was sullen over the earlier exchange with Priscilla. He sat brooding about the impudence of women suffragettes who had had the temerity to attack him and other parliamentarians over the years. He thought how Priscilla had become one of *those* women. Impulsively, he said, "I'd like to conduct a poll of all the women in the colony to determine how many *want* the vote. Most of the women I know don't support women's suffrage and are, in fact, concerned that it'll have a negative effect on the family." Looking at Eleanor, he asked, "Do you feel that your crusade is fair to those women who are afraid their lives will be negatively affected?"

Eleanor sighed. She had hoped Duncan was done with the argument he had earlier provoked. She didn't wish to spoil the evening.

"I expect that there are many women who are fearful of change, Duncan. Each woman will have to come to her own conclusion, just as each parliamentarian must. Although, I feel certain that women will in time win the right to vote."

Duncan turned to his wife. "Do *you* want the vote, Grace?"

"Dear, don't embarrass me; you know I'm not a political person. I'm happy with my place in the home."

"*There*," Duncan said triumphantly. "And as for Wyoming, it was a *territory* of the United States when it gave the vote to women in 1869. Since then, no other state in America has seen fit to give women the vote."

"Well, women *won the vote* two years ago in New Zealand and last year in South Australia," Priscilla said.

"Those *colonial* approvals will be overturned by Australia's federation," Duncan said. "The federal governments of Britain, United States, and Canada haven't approved women's suffrage so why in God's name should Australia?"

Without a moment's hesitation, Priscilla said, "Why do you feel it's necessary for Australia to *follow* rather than *lead*, by doing what it knows is right, fair, and equitable?"

Flummoxed by her retort, Duncan faltered.

"Well—now—in fact—the approval of the Married Woman's Property Act in 1893 was supposed to satisfy women's desire for equality, but now I see we were bamboozled. It's only encouraged women to push harder to be given the vote."

"Women aren't asking to be *given the vote*," Priscilla said. "We expect to *win the vote!*"

"You remind me so much of your mother at your age," Duncan said in his most patronizing tone.

Exasperation showed in Priscilla's red cheeks. She expelled a long, frustrated breath—"*Pshaw!*"—while looking to the heavens for divine guidance.

Eleanor stood. "I'm going to the ladies' to freshen up. Priscilla, would you join me?"

"*Yes!*" Priscilla plopped her napkin on the table while looking angrily at Duncan.

Would you like to join us, Grace?" Eleanor asked.

"No, I'm fine, thank you."

Walking into the ladies room, Priscilla said, "He's *insufferable!*—so patronizing!"

"I was offended too, dear. But that's just Duncan."

"We were having such a nice evening, then he had to pick a fight. He was trying to bait you, Mum, because he doesn't agree with your suffrage work."

"Yes, I know, dear."

"He's so mean-spirited. I'm going to tell him what I think!"

"We shouldn't offend him, Priscilla; we're his guests."

"Well, this is the *last* time I'll ever accept an invitation from him! I don't like being invited to be insulted or to see you insulted. How can you *stand* his patronizing attitude?"

"I'm used to Duncan, dear. He and I have been disagreeing on most everything for years. He only respects people who can stand up to him, but then has a problem with strong-willed women."

"Oh, he should be *very* happy with little, meek Grace then."

"Come on now, buck up, Priscilla, he's one of your closest relatives. Don't be too hard on him. In spite of himself, he respects you, and I'm sure loves you."

◉

Duncan provided Eleanor with a copy of the draft of the Australian Constitution Bill. After reviewing the draft, Eleanor talked to Priscilla about her disappointment.

"Colonial states' rights have squashed our attempts to include women's suffrage. Only those Australian colonies where women already have the vote, and that's South Australia alone, will be able to vote in federal elections."

"It's only a draft, Mum; the issue hasn't been decided yet," Priscilla said optimistically.

"I'm afraid it has on the federal level, dear. States' rights have become sacrosanct."

"Then we'll have to win the vote in New South Wales first."

"Yes," Eleanor agreed. ". . . Aborigines have also been treated shabbily in the constitution. I feel that my work with The Association for the Protection of Aborigines has come to naught. States' rights have disallowed the federal Parliament from making any laws with respect to, and I quote: 'the Aboriginal race in any state' and have even demanded that 'Aboriginal natives shall not be counted' in the national census. Evidently, the states want total freedom in how they treat their indigenous people."

Priscilla shook her head in shared despair. "The poor native people . . . I feel sorry for them; they have no one to defend them in this process."

On the first of January 1901, the sun shone brilliantly through a cloudless, crystal-blue sky as a new nation—the Commonwealth of Australia—was about to emerge joining six colonies: New South Wales, Victoria, South Australia (which included the Northern Territory), Queensland, Western Australia, and Tasmania. It had taken numerous federation conventions spanning nearly a decade, countless draft constitutions, one failed referendum, and lengthy discussions with the British government until, finally in 1899, a Constitution Bill was approved by majority referenda votes in each of the colonies, and Queen Victoria issued her royal proclamation approving federation.

Throughout the difficult federation process, in numerous speeches, Duncan had said, "We will become *independent* Australian Britons upon passage of the constitution. Although independent, our love for our British mother will remain undiminished. We will remain under her flag as a proud member of the British Empire, use her currency, follow her traditions, and rely on her navy for security."

The Australian Constitution was a monumental accomplishment of practical legislation, of which Duncan felt justifiably proud. But there was no Declaration of Independence, no stirring nationalistic prose put to song, no Bill of Rights, and no new and inventive form of government. Instead, its framers found pragmatic words to unite six colonies that shared a growing sense of Australian "oneness" while maintaining their separate state constitutions and British attachments. A federal government was established with legislative powers over national matters such as military defense, foreign affairs, trade and commerce, currency, taxation, immigration, and naturalization. The queen, however, continued as the absolute head of state, who through her appointed governor-general, could veto any bill passed by the Australian Parliament. And the Privy Council in London remained the ultimate judicial authority, above the Australian High Court.

As the birthplace of the nation and its oldest city, Sydney was chosen to host the inauguration of the commonwealth. Her streets and buildings were decorated with flags, banners, garlands, pictures of the queen, and displays of Australia's new coat of arms, which incorporated an emu and a kangaroo and a depiction of the southern cross constellation. Ornate commemorative arches were erected along many of the principal thoroughfares.

Thanks to Duncan, the Armstrongs were seated in some of the best seats to observe the inauguration ceremony in Centennial Park. They searched for Duncan among the dignitaries standing in the white, eight-arched pavilion where Governor-General Lord Hopetoun would swear in the first prime minister, Edmund Barton, and his federal cabinet.

Christopher climbed up onto his seat, pointed, and shouted, "THERE'S GRANDPAPA!"

"Mustn't shout, dear," Grace quietly admonished her rambunctious grandson while his father, Samuel, made him sit in his chair.

They saw Duncan standing among New South Wales delegates and agreed that he looked distinguished in his black formal suit, top hat, and black eye patch contrasting with his full, snowy white beard.

Quite the elder statesman, Grace marveled. She looked over at Christopher and was appalled that he was sucking on a shilling coin his father had given him, in advance, for being a good boy during the day. She scolded him:

"For goodness' sake, Christopher, take that filthy coin out of your mouth—a Chinaman might have touched it!"

As the governor-general arrived in an open carriage drawn by four horses, Christopher stood up on his seat again and yelled, "*Look at the horseees!*"

Duncan took his seat and sat ramrod straight observing the ceremony along with seven thousand other invited guests and over sixty thousand spectators standing, sitting, and lying on blankets on the nearby grass slopes. The end of the ceremony was marked by a twenty-one-gun salute, cheering, hats flying, and cannon blasting. As Duncan enthusiastically pumped every hand within reach, neither he nor anyone else in the fervent crowd could imagine that within the month the new nation would be in mourning.

The British Empire's beloved Queen Victoria, who had reigned for sixty-three years, longer than any other monarch in British history, died on January 22, 1901. Her affable son Edward VII would succeed her, replacing the staid Victorian era with a period of enlivened cultural and intellectual life, that would come to be called the Edwardian age.

The first major piece of legislation proposed by the new federal government was an exclusionary immigration bill that would support its White Australia Policy ideals of racial purity, cultural homogeneity, social unity, egalitarianism, and mateship. Britain opposed the bill's explicit racial ban fearing it would offend non-whites in its vast empire and the proud Japanese with whom it had a strategic alliance. The Immigration Restriction Bill was passed after a deceitful dictation test was approved permitted customs officers to give the test in "any European language" to selectively reject unwanted immigrants, especially English-speaking Chinese. The Prime Minister, Edmund Barton, told Parliament:

"The doctrine of the equality of men was never intended to apply to the equality of the Englishman and the Chinaman." Alfred Deakin, the attorney-general and minister of justice, who introduced the bill, indicated that one of the strongest motives for federation was ". . . the desire that we should be one people, and remain one people, without the admixture of other races."

◉

Following her sixty-eighth birthday, Eleanor felt the need to reconsider her will and list of charitable commitments. She was considering greatly increasing her contribution to the Benevolent Foundation Orphanage in Bathurst that was in danger of being closed if a major benefactor or two could not be found. She had supported the orphanage financially from its inception. Because of the need it filled, it had grown into a large facility.

Before she committed herself, however, she decided to inspect the orphanage, which she had not visited for eight years. To break up the two-day carriage ride to Bathurst, she stopped for two days in the resort town of Katoomba in the Blue Mountains to visit friends. She and her coachman left Katoomba at eight in the morning and approached the orphanage at a little after four in the afternoon.

Rather than go directly on to her hotel, she decided to stop briefly at the orphanage to announce her arrival and arrange a time for her visit the next day. Little did she know a drama was unfolding inside that would soon involve her. As her coachman reached for the front door handle, he was knocked back by a young white man rushing out.

"*Sorry, sir!*" the young man yelled over his shoulder as he ran toward his horse tied to a hitching post. He jumped up into its saddle and rode off hastily.

"My word, *he was* in a hurry," the coachman said to Eleanor as he held the door open for her. "Hope he didn't *rob* the place!"

The drama had started a half an hour earlier when the young man had brought in an emaciated, young Aboriginal girl. The seriously ill child had been taken directly to the nurse's station and the matron notified. When the matron entered the nurse's station, she was repelled by the grave condition of the skeletal child with its distended stomach, sunken cheeks and eyes, and festering skin.

It's impossible to estimate her age, the matron thought, perhaps as young as three or as old as five. She's not over twenty-five pounds for goodness' sake!

"Who brought her here?" she asked the nurse.

"A young man, I didn't get his full name—John something. He said he found her on his property. He's waiting outside."

"Is he black or white?"

"White."

The matron gave a look of puzzlement. "Bring him in here. I want to see how she reacts to him."

Entering the room, the young man took off his hat and smiled at the little girl, but she showed no sign of recognition. The matron estimated that he was fifteen or sixteen.

"I'm told you found this little girl on your property. Where is that?"

"About forty miles from here on the Capertee River, missus, in our bush paddock. I was lookin' fer strays an' jus' come up on her. She was layin' on a rock like she was dead. When I rode up close t'see if she was, she woke up and tried to run but couldn't—too weak—she just laid where she fell, lookin' up at me. I gave her water an' tucker. Poor little piccaninny threw up most of it later."

"Why did you bring her here?"

"Ye're a hospital fer Abo kids, ain'tya?"

"No, this is an orphanage for young children, including Aborigines."

"I didn't know what else t'do. My dad said I was a fool to git messed up in this an' told me to take 'er back where I found her. Said it wasn't none of my business, an' that her people would be back fer her; an' if they weren't, still weren't none of our business. My mum agreed with him. So I brought 'er here. It's most a whole day's ride."

"Were her people living on your property?"

He shrugged. "I dunno, missus. Never seen no young 'uns. Saw some blackfellers an' their gins once an' awhile. We knew they were about or passin' through. Though never saw her, before I come up on 'er on the rock."

"Her people were probably nearby. You shouldn't have taken her."

"*No*, they weren't! I made a sling fer 'er from my swag an' rode all around yellin' fer 'em and lookin' fer signs of their camp, but I didn't see none. No . . . she didn't act like her people were aroun'; she was alone—got lost or somethin.'"

"Her people would have found her."

"*What!* You sound like my parents! *Look* at her, lady! She's 'bout dead. One day more without food an' water, an' she'd be dead, or a dingo would've got her. I couldn't 'ave that on my mind."

Folding her arms in front of her, the matron looked sternly at the young man. "I don't know that we can take her."

"Well, *I can't* take 'er back! My Dad's goin' t'be right mad if he hears about this. Yer said you have other little Abo kids in 'ere."

"Yes, although you have to understand that each one of them came to us in a proper way, mostly through the Aborigines Protection Board or police. Your walking in with one is most unusual. She's a full-blood. I'll have to check whether we can take her."

"Well I've *got*ta leave now! I can't stay here; I gotta git back. I can't wait fer yer to do no checkin'. I did what I thought was right. It's *not my fault* I found her."

"I know that, but you're trying to make her *our* problem now. You'll have to wait here while I check whether I can take her or not."

"She don't have no other place to go, lady. Now I *hav'ta* leave, an' I can't take 'er with me, so yer'll just hav'ta keep her. I'm sorry, I *gotta* leave." He turned and ran down the hall and out the door into Eleanor's coachman.

Eleanor went into the office and was informed by a secretary that the administrator had left for the day; the matron, however, was down the hall in the nurse's station. While the secretary went to fetch her, Eleanor stood in the doorway of the office. Before the secretary reached the nurse's station, the door opened and the matron and the nurse stepped into the hall. Eleanor was shocked to see that the nurse was carrying an emaciated Aboriginal child.

Wanting to know why the child was starving, Eleanor walked toward the women and child while the secretary told the matron that she had a visitor. Walking up to them, Eleanor said:

"The poor, little thing—she's just skin and bones!"

The matron looked harshly at Eleanor, resenting her interference.

"I'm sorry, allow me to introduce myself. I'm Eleanor Armstrong, a benefactor of the orphanage. I wrote that I would be visiting."

"Oh, yes—*yes, Mrs. Armstrong.*" The matron's attitude changed immediately; she showed a welcoming smile. "We were expecting you tomorrow."

The matron told the nurse to go about her business and explained to Eleanor the circumstances of the sickly child's arrival, illustrating a clear need for the orphanage. She had intended to obtain the administrator's approval before accepting the child, but the young man had rushed away.

"Yes, we saw the lad rushing from the building as we entered. I'm sure he thought he was doing the right thing," Eleanor said.

They agreed on a time for Eleanor to visit the next day.

Eleanor visited the facility for three hours the following day. She was shown throughout the three-story building. She was relieved to see that all of the children looked healthy and well cared for. In the infirmary, a doctor told her that the emaciated Aboriginal girl was mute, unresponsive, and may not survive. By the end of the tour and after a substantive meeting with the administrator, Eleanor decided that the orphanage had to stay open, and she would become a major benefactor.

For the next few days, the little Aboriginal girl clung to life. She hardly made a sound, except for weakly crying when she was given injections. Listless, she did not react when spoken to. When it appeared that the child was responding to treatment and would live, the matron decided to try to determine what had happened to her. She asked Molly, a sixteen-year-old Aboriginal kitchen helper, to talk to her.

"We aren't sure she can hear well or even speak, Molly. She hasn't said anything that sounds like words. I'd like you to talk to her in your language. You came from the area where she was found and perhaps she'll understand you. I want you to ask what happened to her."

Molly had no schooling and spoke only pidgin English. "Mi sabi; mi go yabber to tat pikinini, ma'am." I understand; I'll talk to the little girl, madam.

The child was lying in bed. Molly got down on her knees and looked into the child's face . "*Barrdarrgindo . . . ?*" Do you understand me . . . ? "*Wawu nayini nura?*" Where's your country?

The little girl stared at her blankly.

"*Ngaya Kanggilgurlu.*" I'm Kanggilgurlu. "*Nayina narrinyeri callemondah nura.*" My people are from the foothills country.

Appearing disinterested, the child looked away. Molly turned the girl's head back toward her and held it there. "*Yare wungawudana?*" What happened to you?

Still no response.

"*Hiingyini djiadi?*" Can you speak?

The girl squirmed and started to whimper. She raised her little hand and tried to push Molly's hand away from her face.

"*Yare matye gaiyara?*" What's your name?

Agitated, the little girl said, "*Baraga ngaya*"—you're hurting me.

Contact! She can hear and speak! Molly beamed up at the matron.

"What did she say?" the matron asked.

"Mi tink pikinini i bin sayim name Baranga." I think the child said her name is Baranga.

Elated, Molly decided to try individual words: "*Yuru?*"— hungry? "*Nggununy?*"—food? "*Bado?*"—water? "*Waruwi*"—girl. "*Wiyanga*"—mother.

"Wiyangee!" Mummy! the girl said. "*Wiyangee, diamo Wiyangee?*" Mummy, where's Mummy?

Molly asked, " '*Wiyangee,' illi gawudaminji wiyanga?*" '*Wiyangee,*' does that mean mother? "*Yare waugawugian wiyanga?*" What happened to your mother?

"*Wiyangee?*" The girl asked for her mother again and began to cry. "*Wiyangee, diamo Wiyangee?*" Mummy, where's Mummy? "*Arrungwa jalga.*" I couldn't find her. She pulled at her hair. "*Minyagan Wiyangee.*" I want Mummy.

Molly could not understand her. Frustrated, she looked up at the matron. "Pikinini i krai." The child is crying.

"Did you understand what she said, Molly?" the matron asked.

Molly sadly shook her head. Standing, she said, "Mi no sabi lingo." I don't understand her language. "Mi bin sabi '*wiyangee*.' " I understood "*wiyangee*." "Tat pikinini no blang tribe mi." That child doesn't belong to my tribe.

"That's enough for today, Molly," the matron said. "At least we now know that she can hear and speak. It looks like Baranga will be with us for a time."

◉

In early 1902, at the age of seventy-five, Duncan was diagnosed as having an inoperable brain disorder that affected his manual dexterity but not his ability to think and speak. Unable to walk well or write, he began to dictate his memoir to Curtis, in the hope that he could complete it before his death; however, within months, he was confined to bed.

On April 26, 1902, the Armstrong clan was called to Duncan's house. As he slipped into and out of consciousness, he rallied enough to whisper, "I'm not afraid to die . . . I've had a good life. I *was* afraid . . . fifty years ago . . . at Eureka Stockade . . . but not now." He drifted off while Grace, seated next to Samuel, sobbed quietly at his bedside.

Duncan stirred and suddenly asked, "Is the war over?"

"They're still negotiating the peace treaty, Dad," Samuel answered. "It's been six weeks now, so they must be close to signing."

Duncan fell off to sleep again, the memory of a day in October 1899 playing vividly in his febrile mind. The Armstrong clan were standing on the veranda of Parliament House cheering the New South Wales volunteers as they marched by heading for the Boer War. Having been roundly criticized for opposing the Sudan expedition, Duncan had been a leading proponent of sending Australian colonial soldiers to join forces with those from New Zealand and Canada to help Britain fight the Dutch Boers in southern Africa.

He was talking to Samuel. "The integrity of the British Empire is at stake. Make no mistake about that, Samuel. If the Boers are permitted to defy British authority, then other parts of the empire will do the same."

Little Christopher was waving excitedly with both hands at the passing troops. "I'm going to be a soldier when I grow up, Grandpapa!" The specter of young, dead Australians haunted him as did the dead at Eureka Stockade. He awoke with a start.

"Duncan, darling," Grace said taking his hand. "I'm here."

"Grace . . . how many died?"

"How many?—who?" she asked, confused.

"Not many, Dad," Samuel said, assuming he was back to the Boer War. "Less than three hundred . . . out of sixteen thousand volunteers."

"That's not *too* bad. I'd . . . I'd like to stay around . . . till peace."

But Duncan was not to live until the peace treaty was signed in Pretoria on May 31, 1902, when the Boer leaders agreed to British annexation of their two republics leading to the Union of South Africa in 1910.

"Eleanor . . . she here?" Duncan asked.

"She's right here, Dad," Samuel said as he gave up his seat to Eleanor.

Taking hold of her cousin's limp hand, Eleanor said, "Hello, Duncan, it's Eleanor."

"Eleanor, I hope you'll forgive me . . . for fighting you on your women's vote."

"Don't think about that now, Duncan . . . you have a right to your opinion. I didn't take our disagreement personal."

"I was one of those who opposed you . . . kept it from happening."

"I know, Duncan."

"If all women . . . if they were all like you . . . I wouldn't have fought it."

"I forgive you, Duncan, if that's what you'd like to hear. I'm sure you did what you thought was best for the country."

Eleanor did not tell Duncan that women's suffrage had been granted by the Australian Parliament three days earlier. All of the family members, except Priscilla, had agreed with Eleanor that it would serve no purpose to tell Duncan. The Parliament was lauded by women suffragettes for its Commonwealth Franchise Bill that placed Australia in the proud position of being the first self-governing federal nation to give women the right to vote and to stand for office in federal elections. Female activists felt that all of the state parliaments would soon be forced to follow the lead of the federal government and grant women's suffrage at the state level.

"Thank you, Eleanor . . . wouldn't want . . . to pass . . . with you thinking I didn't appreciate you. I've tried to work for the good of our country. I'll die a happy man . . . majority rule, secret ballot . . . land reform, federation . . . no race problems like America . . . a white Australia guaranteed. . . . got everything I ever hoped for. . . . the envy of Britain itself . . ."

Later that evening, Duncan died in his sleep.

P.S.—As poet and as Yankee I will greet you, Texas Jack,
For it isn't no ill-feelin' that is gettin' up my back;
But I won't see this land crowded by each Yank and British cuss
Who takes it in his head to come a-civilizin' us.
Though on your great continent there's misery in the towns,
An' not a few untitled lords and kings without their crowns,
I will admit your countrymen is busted big, an' free,
An' great ekal rites of men and great on liberty;
I will admit your fathers punched the gory tyrant's head—
But then we've got our heroes, too, the diggers that is dead,
The plucky men of Ballarat, who toed the scratch so well,
And broke the nose of Tyranny and made his peepers swell,
For yankin' Lib's gold tresses in the roarin' days gone by,
An' doublin' up his dirty fist to black her bonny eye;
So when it comes to ridin' mokes, or hoistin' out the Chow,
Or stickin' up for labour's rights, we don't want showin' how.
They come to learn us cricket in the days of long ago,
An' Hanlan come from Canada to learn us how to row,
An' "doctors" come from Frisco just to learn us how to skite,
An' pugs from all the lands on earth to learn us how to fight;
An' when they go, as like as not, we find we're taken in,
They've left behind no learnin'—but they've carried off our tin.

—Henry Lawson
Australian writer and poet
"A Word to Texas Jack"

EPILOGUE

The epic, multigenerational, family saga of the fictional Armstrongs and Fongs living through the history of Sydney, Australia, continues in a sequel novel *A Gift of Sydney,* which takes the reader from 1903 through the 2000 Summer Olympic Games held in Sydney.

The coastal Eora Aboriginal people, represented by the historical natives Bennelong and Pemulwuy, had largely died out by 1850. The emaciated Aboriginal girl, Baranga, whom Eleanor Armstrong saw in the Benevolent Foundation Orphanage near the end of *Destiny in Sydney,* lives on to start the Hudson family, the third fictional family featured in the sequel. Their family story involves difficult lives where hope of escaping the oppressive missions lies in excelling at sports and fighting in war. The sixties bring civil rights and better opportunities for Aborigines that help a female offspring achieve greatness in the 2000 Summer Olympics.

Fong Min-chin and his son Wing-yuen continue the Chinese story. Theirs is one of success in business, improvement of their Chinatown community, fighting in Vietnam, intermarriage with whites, and election to one of the highest political offices in Sydney government.

The negative consequences of the Armstrong's convict heritage lessen with each generation. Christopher, a child in *Destiny in Sydney,* grows up to fight at Gallipoli and in the Middle East as a light horseman during the Great War, while his cousin Nigel pilots a fighter plane over France. Nigel's son, Archibald, continues the Armstrong's warrior tradition by fighting the "Desert Fox" Rommel at Tobruk and the Japanese in Papua New Guinea during World War II. Throughout the story, the family stays involved in the building of Sydney, including the Sydney Opera House, contributing greatly to the development of a city renowned as one of the most beautiful and livable in the world.

HISTORICAL NOTE

The chronological story of *Destiny in Sydney* is generally true to the flow of history concerning the important issues of the day, timing of events, and involvement of historical people. The interpretations of real incidents and portrayal of personages, however, are mine alone, recognizing that historians often differ in opinions, sometimes strongly, on such matters. There are large and small controversies over such wide-ranging historical matters as Britain's reasons for colonizing New South Wales, rationales for violence against the Aborigines and Chinese, explanations for the White Australia Policy, effectiveness of governors, conduct of Governor Bligh on the day of the coup that overthrew him, and greatness of John Macarthur beyond his contribution to the wool industry. From my reading of personal diaries, letters, journals, memoirs, and historians' accounts, the story of Sydney evolved as a matter of informed choices.

The First Fleet was fortunate to have a number of outstanding leaders, foremost among them Arthur Phillip, his adjutant Philip Gidley King, and Captain John Hunter. These three left their accounts, as did Judge Advocate David Collins, Lieutenants Watkin Tench and William Bradley, and Surgeons John White and George Worgan. Jacob Nagle, an adventurous American able seaman, who signed onto the HMS *Sirius,* wrote his memoirs from Canton, Ohio, USA. These nine men are all included in the novel.

Major Robert Ross, lieutenant governor and commander of the marines, was also a real person. The novel portrays two of the many recorded confrontations between Ross and Governor Phillip that led to their dislike for each other. Ross's adjutant, Captain George Evans, who became Nathaniel Armstrong's friend, is a fictional character as is Nathaniel's closest mate, Lieutenant Thomas Nichol.

An extraordinary personality in Australia's early history was John Macarthur, the acknowledged Father of Australian Wool. I have tried to be true to both his genius and faults in telling the defining events of his life as they actually occurred. His wife Elizabeth was a remarkably capable woman, who deserves to be called the Mother of Australian Wool, as the imaginary Moira O'Keeffe Armstrong says in the novel.

Although women were largely excluded from the upper levels of the male-dominated business community until well into the twentieth century, there were a few exceptional women who overcame the barriers to their participation. One such woman was Mary Reibey (1777-1855), who served as the inspiration for the fictitious character Eleanor Armstrong Norman. Reibey was transported to Sydney in 1792 for horse stealing. Two years later, she married a free settler, who acquired property and carried on a shipping and trading business. While he was away trading, up to a year at a time, she managed their businesses, including Hawkesbury farms and a trading store and timber yard in Sydney Cove. When he died in 1811, she was thirty-three and had seven children. She bought additional ships and expanded her trading business while buying more real estate. Reibey developed residential and commercial buildings in and around Sydney, as the fictitious Eleanor does. In 1817 Reibey helped establish the first bank in Australia, the Bank of New South Wales, by being its landlady and later a shareholder. She contributed money and her time to church, educational, and charitable organizations, again as Eleanor does. Mary Reibey's real estate development activities preceded those of Eleanor Armstrong Norman by more than fifty years.

The principal Aboriginal characters Bennelong, Pemulwuy, Colebee, and Arabanoo were all real people as were the other Native Australians mentioned: Nanbaree, Booroong, Yemmerawannie, Gooroobaroobool00, Tedbury, and Bungaree. The phonetic spellings of their names are inconsistent among historians. I have tried to use the most accepted spellings. Nearly all of the events in the novel involving these notable Aboriginal Australians are based on incidents described in the writings of the time. All of the journals of the First Fleeters refer to them as Indians, natives, blacks, and, occasionally, as indigenes. It was not until Macquarie's governorship that the terms

Aborigine and Aboriginal were widely used. For years, the lowercase word "aboriginal" was used both as a noun and an adjective; I have consistently used Aborigine as a noun and Aboriginal as an adjective. The emaciated Aboriginal girl, Baranga, and her story are invented.

All of the Chinese, including the three Fong brothers, are fictional characters. The events in the Fong's lives were typical for Cantonese men who came in large numbers for the Australian gold rush. They were assisted by secret brotherhood associations called *tongs*; although, the Sun Wei Tong is a made-up name. The whites in the goldfields were threatened by the foreignness of the Chinese. As sojourners, the Chinese did not try to fit in. Bigotry on both sides led to violence against the Chinese at many goldfields, including that accurately described at Bendigo, Buckland, Pollock's Gully, Lambing Flat, and Back Creek.

The imaginary Chinese elder Ts'ing Kwong-tang, who becomes known in the novel as Kwong Tang, borrows from the remarkable life of the popular Sydney leader Mei Quong Tart (1850-1903) known as Quong Tart. Tart arrived from Canton at the age of nine and was rich from gold mining by age twenty. Adopting the dress and manners of an English gentleman, he opened a chain of exquisite tearooms and restaurants across Sydney that attracted the social elite, which helped him to become a socialite himself. An Anglican, Tart married the Englishwoman Margaret Scarlett and had six children with her. Well liked for his entertaining personality, he was in constant demand as a speaker at social and charitable functions where he would sing Scottish songs, play the bagpipes, and recite poetry, especially that of Robert Burns. Well connected to local politicians through the Oddfellows, Freemasons, and his philanthropy, he served as a spokesman for the Chinese community and pushed for the banning of opium. He was brutally beaten by a white robber and died of his injuries months later.

In the novel, Evans refers to the "nigger slaves" in Rio, Tom deplores "Disgusting papist zealots!" David Collin says the natives are "children of ignorance," the young white boy who saves the emaciated Aboriginal girl says "You have other little Abo kids in 'ere," children in The Rocks taunt with "Chingy-Changy-Chongy Chinaman," and

Eleanor says "I'll remain chairman." These offensive terms, among others, are used not to be sensational but to be historically accurate. It would have been misleading not to have used racist, religiously biased, and sexist terms, in moderation, that were common at the time.

Because *Destiny in Sydney* is a fictional story based on history, the reader may want to know whether some specific part is fact or fiction. By chapter below, I have tried to anticipate readers' questions in this regard:

Chapter 1- NEW HORIZONS
Johnie Armstrong of Gilnockie and his ballad written before he was hanged by the English is recorded history.

One of the well-accepted reasons the British government decided to send convicts to New South Wales was because they could no longer send them to the United States as "indentured servants" following the American Revolution.

The descriptions of the First Fleet (a capitalized proper noun now but not so in 1787) are accurate, including the fact that women convicts and marine wives took their children on the voyage; although, there is no agreement on the exact numbers.

Chapter 2 - ARDUOUS VOYAGE
George Worgan, the surgeon of the *Sirius*, did have his pianoforte on board. He and Captain Hunter often played for the enjoyment of the other officers. Worgan left his pianoforte with his student Mrs. Elizabeth Macarthur when he returned to England in 1791.

The two attempted escapes by the imaginary John Prescott are similar to those of the actual convict John Power, who received the punishments described. Two hundred lashes were not an unusually high number. In fact, Judge Advocate David Collins wrote in his journal of another man: " . . . sentenced to receive seven hundred lashes; which sentence was put in execution upon him at two periods, with an interval of three weeks." I changed Power to Prescott because I ended his life fictionally.

Gulliver's Travels, first published in 1726, does include the passage about New Holland described by Nathaniel Armstrong.

Six of the First Fleeter's journals indicate the name of the celestial display they observed as *aurora australis*, in Latin, southern goddess of dawn. Maps for five hundred years had made the assumption that an "unknown southern land," in Latin *Terra Australis Incognita*, had to exist to balance the weight of the land masses in the northern hemisphere. Little wonder that Australia came to be chosen as the name for the great southern continent.

Chapter 3 - STARVATION

The unexpected arrival of two large warships just days after the First Fleet arrived at Botany Bay caused the excitement and speculations described. Some historians believe La Pérouse was gathering military intelligence and that the history of New South Wales would have been different had not Louis XVI been dethroned and guillotined in 1793 during the French Revolution. There is no doubt that Arthur Phillip was suspicious of La Pérouse, but it is a matter of conjecture whether Phillip rushed to Sydney Cove to claim it for the Crown and quickly sent Philip Gidley King to settle Norfolk Island because of the Frenchman's unexpected arrival.

To take advantage of the prevailing westerly winds and sea currents in the Roaring Forties, between the 40° and 50° southern latitudes, Captain Hunter did, in fact, choose to circumnavigate the world to buy supplies in Cape Town for the starving Sydney colony.

It is also fact that epidemics, including smallpox, caused a catastrophic decline in the Aboriginal population in the Sydney region a year after the arrival of the First Fleet. Having read stories that American Indians were given blankets used by smallpox patients to cause a smallpox epidemic, I wondered if the same thing might have happened in Sydney, especially after reading Tench's journal: "It is true, that our surgeons had brought out variolous matter in bottles; but to infer that it [smallpox epidemic] was produced from this cause were a supposition so wild as to be unworthy of consideration." I am convinced from my research that Tench's conclusion is correct.

Convict Robert Fox is fictitious, but his convict friend James Ruse is a notable figure in Australian history. Ruse's story is essentially true: He was the first convict emancipated, the first to receive crown land, which Phillip called Experiment Farm, and, later, one of the pioneer farmers along the Hawkesbury River. Experiment Farm Cottage is a historic site on Ruse Street in Parramatta that can be visited.

Chapter 4 - RUM CORPS GENTRY

Elizabeth Farm, located in Parramatta, was built in 1793 by John and Elizabeth Macarthur and is Australia's oldest surviving homestead. It is part of the Historic Houses Trust of New South Wales. The house and gardens are open to visitors.

The Green Hills settlement on the Hawkesbury River was re-named Windsor in 1810 by Governor Macquarie.

Pemulwuy's head was cut off by the men who shot him to enable the authorities to identify the formidable resistance leader's face before paying the reward. Governor King sent the head, preserved in spirits, to naturalist Sir Joseph Banks in London and lauded the warrior's bravery in an accompanying letter.

The story of the uprising in 1804 of mostly Irish convicts that culminated in the Battle of Vinegar Hill, as it became popularly known, is largely accurate. There were two rebel leaders, Philip Cunningham and William Johnston, who came down the hill to parley with Major George Johnston. To eliminate the confusion of two Johnston names, I omitted reference to rebel Johnston's name and had Major Johnston arrest Cunningham instead of William Johnston, whom he actually arrested. The leaders of the rebellion were hanged and their bodies left to rot in suspended iron cages as described. There is a memorial monument to the battle in Castlebrook Cemetery, Old Windsor Road, at Rouse Hill north of Parramatta.

Robert Campbell's story is true. He is best remembered for breaking the trade monopoly of the East India Company.

Chapter 5 - MUTINY AGAINST BLIGH (OF THE *BOUNTY*)

Governor Bligh admitted at the trial of mutineer Major Johnston that he had hidden in his servant's room for a considerable time. Others testified that he hid for up to two hours. It is clear from personal accounts, letters, reports, and court testimonies that Bligh hid himself behind or under the bed in some manner. There are those writers who have colored him a coward for this act. I have written it as

Bligh's spiteful attempt to avoid capture, resulting in his humiliation.

Chapter 6 - MOCKERY OF MACQUARIE

Doctor D'Arcy Wentworth and his son William C. Wentworth are historical figures. In 1813, after many unsuccessful attempts by others, young W. C. Wentworth, Gregory Blaxland, and William Lawson did discover a way over the barrier of the Blue Mountains essentially as told.

Bennelong's death was moved forward one year to 1814. His obituary in the *Sydney Gazette*, as read by Nathaniel Armstrong, is accurate.

The story of Commissioner Bigge and his mockery of Governor Macquarie's enlightened administration, from which Macquarie never fully recovered, is recorded history.

Chapter 7 - EMANCIPIST PREVAIL

The history of the Native Institution is factual. It was relocated from Parramatta to a land grant known as Black's Town (Blacktown in 1862), which I have changed to a more grammatical Blacks' Town.

On his around-the-world voyage on the *Beagle*, Charles Darwin did visit Sydney in 1836 and then rode a horse over the Blue Mountains to visit a sheep station where his companion shot a platypus to provide Darwin with a specimen. Darwin wrote, "We passed through large tracts of country in flames; volumes of Smoke sweeping across the road," but his life was never in danger as dramatized in the novel.

Chapter 8 - ANTIPODEAN EL DORADO

To make the three Chinese brothers' kinship names as simple and uniform as possible, I have taken the liberty of having both Sing-woo and Min-chin refer to Ho-teng as Saamgo, meaning Third Eldest Brother. However, this is grammatically correct only for Min-chin because the suffix "go" means "older" brother.

The Taiping Tienkuo—the Heavenly Kingdom of Great Peace—religious crusade and the chaos and deaths of tens of millions it caused in China is well documented.

There was a Eureka Stockade. The lead up to the battle, the essential issues, the battle itself, and the aftermath are accurately reported.

The California Rangers, as the organized rebellious American miners called themselves, did fight the British redcoats there. A black American, John Joseph, was the first defendant chosen to be prosecuted and the first acquitted.

Owen Vernon is a fictitious politician. W. C. Wentworth, the principal writer of the New South Wales Constitution, did leave the colony a disappointed man for the reasons given.

Chapter 9 - BOOM TIMES

Port Jackson is the proper name of the body of water beginning as an inlet of the Tasman Sea between the North and South Heads and running west past Sydney Cove to meet the Parramatta River; however, after Sydney grew into a large town, Port Jackson gradually became better known as Sydney Harbour.

There have been many recorded fatal shark attacks in Sydney Harbour, including two in Double Bay, where the fictional Alistair Norman was killed by a shark.

The first Chinatown in Sydney was near the docks in The Rocks. Hoodlum gangs, known as larrikin pushes, terrorized the residents there. Opium dens were legal until the early 1900s when laws prohibited the sale of opium and later banned its importation, except for medical purposes.

The Benevolent Foundation Orphanage (in Bathurst) is a name created for the purposes of the story, but many charities ran orphanages at the time, including at least one in Bathurst, St. Joseph's Orphanage.

Chapter 10 - WHO ARE WE?

Henry Lawson's poem "The Captain of the Push" was quoted by the imaginary Kwong Tang in 1888, four years before it was published.

The *Afghan* incident is factual, including the rabble-rousing meeting at the Sydney Town Hall and the march and attack on Parliament House. The indefatigable Premier Henry Parkes resolved the riotous situation as described and later went on to be the architect of Australian federation.

Chapter 11 - A NEW BRITISH NATION

Mark Twain, the American humorist and writer, gave several lectures in Sydney in September 1895. He was on a worldwide lecture tour to pay off his debts.

It is historical that the White Australia Policy was enacted to keep out the Chinese and other "colored" people from nearby Asia and Oceania, while encouraging the creation of a white British country fifteen thousand miles from Britain. It is a fact that under the White Australian Policy customs officials could give a dictation test in "any European language" of their choosing and used this ploy to exclude unwanted English-speaking immigrants who were deemed undesirable to settle in Australia.

The emaciated Aboriginal girl, Baranga, and her story are fictional. Aboriginal orphans were usually institutionalized separately from white children, although Governor Brisbane mixed black and white girls in Parramatta's Female Orphan School.

In 1902, the Commonwealth of Australia could rightly claim the honor of being the first self-governing federal nation to extend the right to vote to women. Prior to 1902 only political subdivisions had granted women's suffrage: the Wyoming Territory in 1869 and the U.S. State of Wyoming in 1890 and the British colonies of New Zealand in 1893 and South Australia in 1894.

ACKNOWLEDGMENTS
AND SOURCES

When I decided to write a historical novel, the dramatization of the history of Sydney was my obvious first choice. But the story of Sydney would never have been written without the hospitality and goodwill of Sydneysiders, a major factor in attracting my wife and me back to this eminently livable city after an absence of twenty-five years. The story is first and foremost written for the multicultural citizens of this truly international city who helped me in too many ways to list: Max McKeough, Anne Parbury, Christine and Stafford Watts, Karen Samociuk, Jane Reeves, David Callaghan, Jan Murrell, and Tomoko and Masao Igarashi.

The novel is dedicated to my wife, a published author (Judith W. Richards), who researched with me, wrote early drafts, and edited the manuscript. Her collaboration was invaluable to me and made the process so much more enjoyable.

Americans who read parts or all of the manuscript and provided comments are Sharon Soemann, Jim and Judy Laughrey, Bob and Carol Carper, John Ryan, Gary Rubens, Judy and Stu Searles, Tom and Pat Baubonis, Lori Cucuzzella, and David Simonson. I thank them all for their thoughts and encouragement.

I am indebted to Nigel Parbury, formerly with the New South Wales Ministry of Aboriginal Affairs and author of *Survival: A History of Aboriginal Life in New South Wales*, who kindly reviewed the entire manuscript and provided insightful comments and corrections; and to Professor Sik Lee Cheung, Stanford University, who advised me regarding the Cantonese language and culture.

I am grateful to all of the above family members, friends, and experts who provided written revisions and verbally advised me.

However, I must confess that I did not always follow their advice or make the revisions they suggested, and, therefore, assure them that any shortcomings in the story or outright errors that may exist are entirely my responsibility.

When designing the front cover of *Destiny in Sydney*, I gained inspiration from several sources that should be acknowledged. The three Aborigines opposing the arrival of the HMS *Supply* in Botany Bay drew concept images from W. Macleop's drawing of two Aborigines opposing the landing of Captain Cook's longboat, an illustration in Andrew Garran's *Australia: The First Hundred Years*, 1886. The long, winding, single-file line of Chinese men heading for the gold fields was prompted by two similar drawings: a pencil sketch by Charles Lyall, circa 1854, and an engraving from the *Australasian Sketcher*, 1875, in the National Library of Australia.

AuthorSupport took my rough cover design, Family Tree chart, and four maps and turned them into professional quality illustrations. They did the interior layout formatting and placed the entire book into print-ready form. I enjoyed working with them and thank them for their artistry and technical expertise.

Finally, I want to thank the librarians at North Sydney Stanton Library where I did most of the initial research. After they had seen me there day after day, they took an interest in my research and suggested many books and references that I would have missed otherwise. And, I should mention the excellent State Library of New South Wales, Mitchell Library, with particular praise for its original documents section and copies of Sydney newspapers from 1842 to the present.

PRIMARY SOURCES:

The Australian National University. *Australian Dictionary of Biography*. See: www.adb. online.anu.edu.au.

Baker, Hugh and P. K. Ho. *Cantonese: A Complete Course for Beginners, Teach Yourself.* 2nd ed. Sydney: Hodder & Stoughton, 1996.

Baker, Sidney J. *The Australian Language*. Melbourne: Sun Books, 1976.

Barnard, Loretta, et al., eds. *Australia Through Time*. 10th ed. Sydney: Random House Australia, 2002.

Bateson, Charles. *The Convict Ships 1787-1868*. Glasgow: Brown, Son & Ferguson, 1985.

Bickel, Lennard. *Australia's First Lady: The Story of Elizabeth Macarthur.* Sydney: Allen & Unwin, 1991.

Blake, Barry J. *Australian Aboriginal Languages.* Sydney: Angus & Robertson, 1981.

Bradley, William, *A Voyage to New South Wales, December 1786 - May 1792.* Sydney: Facsimilie copy at Mitchell Library, Library of New South Wales (includes 29 watercolored pictorial renderings of places visited), 1969.

Brodsky, Isadore. *Heart of the Rocks of Old Sydney.* Sydney: Old Sydney Free Press, 1965.

——. *The Streets of Sydney.* Sydney: Old Sydney Free Press, 1972.

Brooks, J. and J. L. Kohen. *The Parramatta Native Institution and the Black Town: A History.* Sydney: University of New South Wales Press, 1991.

Butler, Richard. *Eureka Stockade.* Sydney: Angus & Robertson, 1983.

Chambers, John H. *A Traveller's History of Australia.* Gloucestershire, UK: The Windrush Press, 1999.

Choi, C. Y. *Chinese Migration and Settlement in Australia.* Sydney: Sydney University Press, 1975.

Clark, Manning. *A Short History of Australia.* 4th ed. Ringwood, Australia: Penguin Books Australia, 1995.

Clark, Ralph. *The Journal and Letters of Lt. Ralph Clark, 1787 - 1792.* Paul G. Fidlon and R. J. Ryan, eds. Sydney: Australian Documents Library, 1981.

Cobley, John. *Sydney Cove 1788.* London: Hodder & Stoughton, 1962.

Cohen, Lysbeth. *Elizabeth Macquarie: Her Life and Times.* Sydney: Wentworth Books, 1979.

Collins, David. *An Account of the English Colony in New South Wales.* 2 vols. London: T. Cadell Jun. & W. Davies, 1798 and 1802.

Cronin, Kathryn. *Colonial Casualties: Chinese in Early Victoria.* Melbourne, Australia: Melbourne University Press, 1982.

Day, David. *Claiming A Continent: A History of Australia.* Sydney: Angus & Robertson, 1996.

Diamond, Jared. *Guns, Germs, and Steel, The Fates of Human Societies.* New York City: W. W. Norton & Company, Inc., 1999.

Duffy, Michael. *Man Of Honour: John Macarthur: Duellist, Rebel, Founding Father.* Sydney: Macmillan, 2003.

Eldershaw, Barnard M. *Phillip of Australia: An Account of the Settlement at Sydney Cove 1788-92.* Sydney: Angus & Robertson, 1972.

Ellis, M. H. *John Macarthur.* Sydney: Angus & Robertson, 1955.

——. *Lachlan Macquarie: His Life, Adventures, and Times.* Sydney: Angus & Robertson, 1978.

Evatt, Herbert Vere. *Rum Rebellion: A Study of the Overthrow of Governor Bligh by John Macarthur and the New South Wales Corps.* Sydney: Angus and Robertson, 1938.

Fitzgerald, Ross and Mark Hearn. *Bligh, Macarthur and the Rum Rebellion.* Sydney: Kangaroo Press, 1988.

Fitzgerald, Shirley. *Red Tape, Gold Scissors: The Story of Sydney's Chinese.* Sydney: State Library of New South Wales Press in association with the City Of Sydney, 1997.

——. *Rising Damp: Sydney 1870-90.* Melbourne, Australia: Oxford University Press, 1987.

————. *Sydney 1842-1992*. Sydney: Hale & Iremonger, 1992.

Fitzgerald, Shirley and Garry Wotherspoon, eds. *Minorities: Cultural Diversity in Sydney*. Sydney: State Library of New South Wales Press, 1995.

Flannery, Tim, ed. *The Birth of Sydney*. New York: Grove Press, 1999.

Gandevia, Bryan. *Life in the First Settlement at Sydney Cove*. Sydney: Kangaroo Press, 1885.

Gittins, Jean. *The Diggers From China, The Story of the Chinese on the Goldfields*. Melbourne, Australia: Quartet Books, 1981.

Hughes, Robert. *The Fatal Shore*. New York: Vintage Books, 1988.

Hunter, John. *An Historical Journal of the Transactions at Port Jackson and Norfolk Island*. London: John Stockdale, 1793.

Irvine, Nance. *Mary Reibey - Molly Incognita: A Biography of Mary Reibey, 1777 to 1855, and Her World*. Sydney: Library of Aust. History, 1982.

Joy, William. *The Exiles*. Sydney: Library of Australian Classics, 1987.

Karskens, Grace. *The Rocks: Life in Early Sydney*. Melbourne, Australia: Melbourne University Press, 1997.

Keneally, Thomas. *A Commonwealth of Thieves: The Improbable Birth of Australia*. Sydney: Random House Australia, 2005.

King, Hazel. *Elizabeth Macarthur and Her World*. Sydney: Sydney University Press, 1980.

King, Philip Gidley. *The Journal of Philip Gidley King, Lieutenant, R.N. 1787-1790*. Paul G. Fidlon and R. J. Ryan, eds. Sydney: Australian Documents Library, 1980.

Laidlaw, Ronald. *Australian History*. Sydney: MacMillan Educ. Aust., 1991.

Lydon, Jane. *Many Inventions: The Chinese in the Rocks 1890 -1930*. Melbourne, Australia: Monash Publications in History, 1999.

Mackaness, George. *The Life of Vice-Admiral William Bligh*. New York: Farrar & Rinehart, 1931.

Markus, Andrew. *Fear & Hatred: Purifying Australia & California 1850-1901*. Sydney: Hale & Iremonger, 1979.

Martin, A. W. *Henry Parkes, A Biography*. Melbourne, Australia: Melbourne University. Press, 1980.

Matthews, Stephen and Virginia Yip. *Cantonese: A Comprehensive Grammar*. London: Routledge, 1994.

McCullough, Colleen. *Morgan's Run*. New York: Simon & Schuster, 2000.

Miller, James. *Koori: A Will to Win*. Sydney: Angus & Robertson, 1985.

Molony, John. *Eureka*. Australia: Viking, 1984.

Moorhouse, Geoffrey. *Sydney*. Sydney: Allen & Unwin, 2000.

Morris, Jan. *Sydney*. London: Penquin Book, 1993.

Nicholas, F. W. and J. M. *Charles Darwin in Australia*. Cambridge: Cambridge University Press, 1989.

Norman, Lilith. *Historical Notes on Paddington*. Sydney, 1961.

Nunn, Judy. *Beneath the Southern Cross*. Sydney: Random Hse Aust., 2000.

Oldfield, Audrey. *Woman Suffrage in Australia (Studies in Australian History)* Cambridge: Cambridge University Press, 1993

O'Neill, Richard. *Patrick O'Brian's Navy*. Philadelphia: Running Press, 2003.

Parbury, Nigel. *Survival: A History of Aboriginal Life in New South Wales.* Sydney: New South Wales Dept. of Aboriginal Affairs, 1986 and 2005.

Phillip, Arthur. *The Voyage of Governor Phillip to Botany Bay, with an Account of the Establishment of the Colonies of Port Jackson and Norfolk Island.* London: John Stockdale, 1789.

Price, Charles A. *The Great White Walls Are Built: Restrictive Immigration to North America and Australasia 1836-1888.* Canberra: Aust.Institute of Intern. Affairs in assoc. with Aust. National University Press, 1974.

Project Gutenberg Australia. *Dictionary of Australian Biography.* See: www. gutenberg.net.au.

Raffaello, Carboni. *The Eureka Stockade.* Melbourne, Australia: Melbourne University Press, 1963.

Read, Peter. *A Hundred Years War: The Wiradjuri People and the State.* Canberra, Australia: Australian National University Press, 1988.

Reed, A. H. and A. W. *Aboriginal Words of Australia.* Australia: New Holland Publishers, 1994.

Rees, Sian. *The Floating Brothel.* Sydney: Hodder Headline Australia, 2001.

Reynolds, Henry. *The Other Side of the Frontier.* Melbourne, Australia: Penguin Books, 1981.

Ritchie, John. *Lachlan Macquarie, A Biography.* Melbourne, Aust.: University Press, 1986.

Rolls, Eric. *Sojourners: The Epic story of China's Centuries-old Relationship with Australia.* Australia: University of Queensland Press, 1992.

Shaw, A.G. L. and H. D. Nicolson. *An Introduction to Australian History.* Sydney: Angus & Robertson, 1959.

Sommers, Cedric Emanuel and Tess Van. *Early Sydney Sketchbook.* London: Rigby Ltd., 1978.

Sonder, Richard W. *Paddington 1860-1910: Its History, Trade, And Industries.* Woollahra, Aust.: Salux, 1980.

State Library of New South Wales. "Historical Records of Australia" series in the Mitchell Library, Sydney.

Steven, Margaret. *John Macarthur.* Melbourne, Australia, 1968.

Tench, Watkin. *A Narrative of the Expedition to Botany Bay.* London: J. Debrett, 1789.
———. *A Complete Account of the Settlement at Port Jackson.* London: G. Nicol & J. Sewell, 1793.

Travers, Robert. *Australian Mandarin: The Life and Times of Quong Tart.* Sydney: Kangaroo Press, 1981.
———. *The Grand Old Man of Australian Politics: The Life and Times of Sir Henry Parkes.* Sydney: Kangaroo Press, 1992.

Turnbull, Lucy Hughes. *Sydney, Biography of a City.* Sydney: Random House Australia, 1999.

Ward, John Manning. *James Macarthur, Colonial Conservative 1798-1867.* Sydney: Sydney University Press, 1981.

White, John. *Journal of a Voyage to New South Wales.* London, 1790 and Sydney: Angus & Robertson, 1962.

Willard, Myra. *History of the White Australia Policy to 1920.* Melbourne, Australia: Melbourne University Press, 1974.

Willmot, Eric P.. *Pemulwuy: The Rainbow Warrior*. Sydney: Bantam, 1988.

Woolmington, Jean, ed. *Aborigines in Colonial Society: 1788-1850*. 2nd ed. Armidale, Australia: The University of New England, 1988.

Worgan, George B. *Journal of a First Fleet Surgeon (1788)*. Sydney: The William Dixon Foundation, 1978.

Id Photography

About the Author

D. MANNING RICHARDS has twice lived and worked in Sydney, Australia, for a total of five years. He has received Bachelor of Science and Master of City Planning degrees and is an avid amateur historian. His writing of short stories led to this first novel *Destiny in Sydney*. A sequel, *A Gift of Sydney*, will be published in autumn 2012. He lives in Virginia with his wife. His most recent information may be found at www.DManningRichards.com.

(Reserved page)
Reading Group Guide
Destiny in Sydney

(Reserved page)
Reading Group Guide
Destiny in Sydney

Breinigsville, PA USA
27 December 2010
252164BV00001B/1/P